Operation Masquerade

Operation Masquerade

~ *A Rent Beacham Mystery* ~

Larry M. Edwards

Wigeon
Publishing
San Diego

Published by Wigeon Publishing
ISBN: 979-8-9913694-1-1
Library of Congress Control Number: 2025923003
FIC022090: FICTION / Mystery & Detective / Private Investigators
FIC031010: FICTION / Thrillers / Crime

Printed in the United States of America

For journalists who remain true to themselves while speaking truth to power and carry on steadfast in the face of vengeful retribution and scurrilous litigation, if not violence,
and for
G.M. "Jerry" Ford, who provided me with greater inspiration than he ever knew.

Principal Characters

Rent Beacham, investigative journalist

Rachel Powell, Rent's 12-year-old daughter

Frank and Agnes Powell, Rachel's grandparents

Alicia Velasquez, private investigator and Rent's love interest

Aunt Edith, Rent's great-aunt

Esteban Lopez, Rent's neighbor

Thomas Wilbury, deceased geologist

Susannah Wilbury, daughter of Thomas Wilbury

Mildred Wilbury, wife of Thomas Wilbury

Janis O'Connor, newspaper editor

Naomi Clark, newspaper reporter

Dan Rowland, newspaper reporter

Greg Papadopoulos, newspaper reporter

Will Mason, retired journalist

Connor Furlong, media relations

James Michael "Mike" Johnson Sr., chairman, Lustrous Consulting Group

James Michael "Mikey" Johnson Jr., CEO, JMJ Property Development

Jacqueline Michaela "JJ" Derringer, CEO, Algodones Solar, daughter of JMJ Jr.

Harold "Hal" Derringer, husband of Jacqueline, CEOO, Algodones Solar

Meghan Derringer, 12-year-old daughter of Jacqueline and Harold

Robert "BJ" Johnson, brother of James Michael Johnson Sr.

Anthony Perkins, CEO, Sultan Energy & Coachwhip Lithium Mining

Ramesh Kumar, CEO, Chuckwalla Enterprises

Charles Stevens, aka Chuckarelli, security consultant

Miguel Mendoza, retired farmer, informant

Diana Alvarez, detective, San Diego Police Dept.

Romero Hernandez, detective, Imperial Valley Sheriff's Office

Felicity Garrido, detective, Imperial Valley Sheriff's Office

Robert Willhelm, captain, San Diego Fire Dept.

Evil human beings are quite common and usually appear quite ordinary to the superficial observer. . . . Evil people tend to gravitate toward piety for the disguise and concealment it can offer them.

—M. Scott Peck, MD

Author's Note

Although this is a work of fiction, its inspiration came from current events, including the indisputable pitfalls posed by artificial intelligence.

Operation Masquerade

~ A Rent Beacham Mystery ~

1

W hat's this?" Rent Beacham muttered, puzzlement creasing his brow as he stared at a letter-size envelope, his address hand-written on the front.

Has somebody died?

He recognized the shaky cursive but checked the return address for confirmation—Friday Harbor, WA 98250.

"Aunt Edith," he said aloud.

Rent had gone to the mail kiosk and withdrawn its contents, anticipating the usual junk mail and the screaming headlines of political propaganda that foreshadowed the coming midterm election.

He waved to Ralph, the security guard, then turned and headed back toward his condo at the end of the alley. He sorted the mail as he walked, then stopped to examine the envelope again.

No, she would have called.

A short chirp of a car horn brought him back to the moment. He stepped aside and let it pass, offering a nod in greeting.

His neighbor, Esteban "Steve" Lopez, parked and joined Rent in the alley. "I heard about the layoffs at the newspaper. You safe? Or get the ax?"

"Hey, Steve," Rent replied with a shake of his head. "I don't know for certain, but the rumor mill has been grinding."

"Tough business these days, what with the social media oligarchs dominating the news outlets."

"Yeah, ain't it though."

"Well, good luck," said Lopez, who worked as a librarian at the nearby University of San Diego. "We need solid investigative journalism to keep people honest, especially the politicians. Your exposé on welfare fraud was a masterstroke."

"Kind of you to say."

"Got anything else brewing?"

"Just the usual crap at city hall, the never-ending homeless crisis, and the lawsuits over ADUs," Rent said, glancing at his mail.

"A-B-ooz?" Lopez questioned, adjusting one of his hearing aids. He'd been hearing impaired most of his life and relied on the aid of lip reading to comprehend another's speech.

Rent looked up and faced him directly. "A-D-U. Accessory dwelling units to address the housing shortage."

The man nodded. "Oh, right, upscale granny flats. At least we don't have to worry about that here. No backyards."

Rent chuckled. "Actually, there are also what they call Junior ADUs. Turn your garage or master bedroom into an ADU."

Lopez crinkled his brow. "Hmm. I could always use the extra cash. But what about parking?"

"That is the question, isn't it?"

"Well, keep up the good work. See you at the hot tub later?"

"Nah, I'll be going out."

"Hot date, eh?" the man queried, accompanied by a mischievous grin and a wink.

"Something like that," Rent replied and continued on to the garage. Once up the stairs and in the living room, he opened the envelope from Aunt Edith. Actually, his great-aunt, the youngest sister of his father's mother.

Inside, he found a folded newspaper clipping with a sticky note attached: *You might find this of interest. Aunt Edith.*

He unfolded the clipping and read the headline:

Body at Construction Site:
Man Missing for 27 Years?

So, somebody did die.

2

Rent scanned the news article. Authorities had identified the body discovered at a San Juan Island redevelopment site as a man who had disappeared nearly three decades earlier.

The man, Thomas Wilbury, had been involved in a scandal involving the illegal disposal of hazardous waste from a San Diego boatyard in the wake of the 1995 America's Cup sailing regatta.

The sheriff's department had identified his abandoned car on the Anacortes ferry. At the time, the cops believed the man had taken his own life, but no body or suicide note had been found, so officially they treated it as a missing person.

However, with a body in the morgue and a positive DNA test, the matter had been transferred from Missing Persons to the Investigative Services unit of the Whatcom County Sheriff's Office.

In other words, they are now treating this as a homicide. But why send this to me? I was in kindergarten at the time.

He glanced at the clock. *Time to get a move on.*

Rent's "hot date" meant picking up Rachel, his twelve-year-old daughter, getting a pizza, and watching a movie on Netflix or Prime. Or maybe they would just have a quiet evening and read or maybe play a few fiddle tunes.

He liked the fact that she enjoyed reading, and not just fiction. He tossed the news article on the stack of otherwise unopened mail, opting to call his aunt in the morning.

* * *

Rachel moved the stack of mail to one corner of the dining table and set out plates, glasses, and utensils. She then picked up the news article and read the headline.

"Holy schist!" she muttered, then cast a wary eye toward her father, who returned a narrow-eyed glance of reprimand. "What's this about a dead body?" she asked. "Do you know who it is?"

Rent could hear the trepidation in her voice, she having had first-hand experience with such a trauma. He shook his head. "I have no clue. Aunt Edith sent it to me but didn't say anything about it, other than that short note."

"Let's call her and find out."

"I'll call her in the morning."

"Why wait?"

Rent sighed, then smiled at his obstreperous offspring, shaking his head in wonder. *It must be her mother's genes.*

"Let's eat first. I'm starving."

"Me too," she replied and opened the pizza box, extracting a slice for each of them.

Rent opened a beer for himself and asked her, "What's your pleasure? Water . . . diet grapefruit soda . . ."

She grimaced. "Ewwww. Do you have any juice?"

"Orange or apple?"

"Orange, if it's fresh-squeezed."

He poured her a glass of the orange juice and set it on the table. They ate in silence, then Rent excused himself to use the bathroom.

When he returned, he picked up the beer bottle and examined it, then gave her a stern look. She pursed her lips and reached for another slice of pizza, refusing to meet his reproving gaze.

"Look," he said, I don't mind you sneaking a sip of my beer . . . or should I say gulp . . . but this can't continue."

"What's the big deal? It's not like I'm getting drunk. I bet you did it too."

"No, I didn't, actually. Well, only rarely if I'm being totally honest. But here's the deal. If your grandmother got wind of this, she would be on the phone to child protective services in a heartbeat and try to take away custodial visits. Do you want that?"

Rachel hung her head and whispered, "No."

"Deal?"

"OK, but you shouldn't tempt me."

Rent stared at her, then laughed. "Oh, so it's my fault?"

She flashed him a quick smirk.

"You are too clever by half, you know that?" he said. "So, no more boozing in front of you."

"Then it's a deal," she said, but not without shooting him a withering glance.

"What?"

"We should have made a salad so we had something healthy to go along with this greasy pepperoni."

"Yeah, I know. Please don't tattle on me."

"I know how to cook. I had to cook for my brother when my mom was out . . . or passed out."

"OK, I'll put you in charge of the menu. Healthy choices it is."

"Did you see that the price of gold is almost four thousand dollars an ounce? Isn't that just totes?"

Rent grinned. "Yeah, it's totes amazing," he said, mimicking his daughter's slang.

"We should take a trip."

"That gold is to pay for your college education."

"At this rate, it'll be more than enough."

"Maybe you should study economics and the history of financial markets. Just because it's doing well today doesn't mean—"

She waved a dismissive hand at him. "Yeah, yeah, heard it all before, as you like to say."

"I'm just sayin'. Especially in light of our current administration in the White House. All bets are off. We may well be heading into a recession."

"Doesn't the price of gold go up during a financial crisis? It's the safe harbor, right?"

Rent sighed. Trying to win a debate with her approached the equivalent of banging one's head on the wall. "It's way more complicated than that."

Rachel pulled a face and returned to her meal. They finished the pizza and cleared the table, then she read the news article again.

"We should google his name and learn more about this," she said. "I intend to."

"But first let's call Aunt Edith."

Rent's shoulders slumped in resignation. "Yes, boss."

Rachel grinned and handed him his phone.

3

Edith answered on the second ring. "This had better be important. I'm in the middle of a Brokenwood mystery on Acorn, and the action is heating up. They found a body at a winery in a vat of pinot noir, which I find appalling. Total waste of my favorite red."

"Did the latest of Jools Fahey's husbands get his head bashed in?"

"Ha, ha, you cynic. I paused it. I take it you got the news article I sent you."

"Yes. I would have called you in the morning, but Rachel insisted we call tonight. You can blame her. We're on speaker."

"Hi, darlin', how are you?"

"Good," Rachel replied. "Me and my dad—"

"My dad and I," Aunt Edith corrected, ever the schoolmarm.

Rachel sighed and rolled her eyes. "My dad and I . . . want to know why you think this is so important. The guy's been missing since he, I mean Dad, was a little kid."

"Your dad is the brilliant, prize-winning investigative journalist. He should be able to figure it out."

"Yep, that's my mulish Aunt Edith," Rent muttered.

"I heard that."

Rent blushed as Rachel snickered. Aunt Edith enjoyed her mind games, so he might as well play along.

"OK . . . the guy was originally from San Diego, where I currently live, and he was involved in a scandal involving the illegal disposal of toxic waste; ergo, his death most likely resulted from some skullduggery that occurred here, and those responsible are most likely also in this area, assuming they're still alive, and that's where the investigation into the man's death should begin."

"See? You're not so slow. You're a step or two ahead of the cops already. They're probably butting heads over jurisdiction, if they're doing anything at all, while the case goes even colder."

"This is off my beat."

"So, you do still have a job."

"Well, yeah, but it's looking a bit tenuous."

"That could be to your advantage. If you're fired, you become your own boss, and you can write about anything you want."

"Yeah, without pay. I'll think about it."

"I wish you would," Edith replied. "I know the man's daughter, and she's beside herself. After all these years believing her father took his own life to now find out he was murdered. You should talk to her. I'll give you her number."

"Aunt Edith—"

"Oh, shush. Write this down."

Rent grabbed a pencil lying on the table and jotted down the name and phone number on the back of the envelope she had sent him.

"You better call her, Rent. She needs to know why her father was murdered and by whom, and I doubt these yahoos around here will do one thing about it."

"OK, I'll make a few calls and see what I come up with."

"I'm holding you to it. Now, back to my mystery."

"I bet you've already solved it."

"I have a pretty good idea who the perp is. They always arrest the wrong guy in these shows."

"Bye, Aunt Edith," Rachel called out.

"Bye, bye, honey. You take care and make sure your daddy doesn't drop the ball on this."

Rachel grinned at Rent. "Don't worry, I will."

"Goodbye, Aunt Edith," Rent said. "Nice chatting with you, as always."

"Likewise. *Adios, amigos.*"

The line went dead, and Rent stared at his phone, shaking his head. "Never a dull moment with Aunt Edith."

"Let's start googling right now," Rachel said. "This could be fun."

"Can't it wait till tomorrow?"

"We're going riding tomorrow, remember? You promised."

Rent clenched his jaw and nodded. "No, I haven't forgotten."

Rachel grabbed Rent's laptop, lifted the screen into position, and opened a web browser. She looked at the news article again, typed in the man's name—Thomas Wilbury—and pressed the Enter key. Rent stood behind her, hands on her shoulders, eyes on the screen.

"Shoot. This says he's a professor at Du . . . kweznee . . . University and specializes in crime-scene forensics."

"That might come in handy. But, ahem, it's pronounced *Du-kane* University. French, obviously."

"The French have the worst spelling."

"No comment. Now, add 'San Diego' to the query to narrow it down."

A few seconds later, a new set of results appeared on screen.

"Here's an obituary, and there's some old news articles with his name in them," Rachel said.

"Excellent. Now we're getting somewhere. I'll grab my notepad. Open one of the articles to see who wrote it."

"What good is that?"

"If the guy—"

"It could be a woman, you know."

"Fine. If the person is still alive, we could talk to him—or her—and get more of the backstory. We're on a roll, bay-bee!"

"You bet your a—" Rachel covered her mouth. "Oops. You bet your . . ."

"You've made your point. Let's see what we've got."

4

Rachel sat upright in the saddle, walking her pony on the back roads of Descanso in East San Diego County, her dad alongside, riding one of Martha Flanagan's rescue mares.

After they discovered a new vein of gold in an abandoned gold mine in Chariot Canyon, Rachel got her wish of having a pony of her own. She and her newfound father made regular outings on horseback on the alternate weekends she spent with him.

Rachel looked at Rent. "Can we go home now?"

He stared at her, a puzzled expression crinkling his face. "We've barely started. This is your favorite thing to do."

"I know, but it's getting really hot, and I want to do more googling about that dead man. It's so exciting. I can't wait to tell Alicia about it."

"Whoa, whoa—"

Rachel laughed as Rent's horse stopped abruptly and Rent lurched forward over the neck of the horse, who then broke into a trot before Rent got himself righted and could lean back in the saddle to slow the creature down. He brought it to a halt, and the horse turned its head around to glare at him, as if to say, "Make up your damn mind!"

Rent patted the horse on the shoulder and said, "Sorry 'bout that, Shirley. I was talking to Rachel, not you."

Rachel caught up to him and stopped alongside. "That was funny."

"Yeah, right. I almost fell off."

"That would have been even funnier."

"Uh-huh. Ha, ha."

"What were you going to say to me?"

"About Alicia . . ."

"We're still having dinner with her, aren't we?"

"Yes, but . . . I don't know . . . I'm not sure where this case about the dead man is going. It might be a total dead end, so to speak."

"She would love this. It's right in her wheelhouse."

"Oh, god. Not you too."

"What?"

"Wheelhouse, for chrissakes?" Rent chided. "You sound like some idiot sports guy on TV. Whoever started using that term in this context ought to be shot."

"You are so . . . so . . . such a stick-in-the-mud sometimes," Rachel fired back.

"Yeah, yeah . . . tell me all about it. My point is . . ."

"You're just jealous. You think Alicia and I will take over and solve this case before you, the famous writer, can."

"That's not it. I just . . ."

Rachel shot Rent a look of defiance. "I'm telling. You know she'll want to help you. And she has access to stuff that you . . ."

Rent waved a hand. "Okay, okay. I get it. You can tell her all about it when we get there."

"You won't be able to sleep with her, though. You have to bring me back to your place."

"What business is that of yours, you nosy little . . ."

Rachel grinned. "I'll race you back to the barn."

"Go ahead, you always win anyway."

* * *

When they arrived at Alicia's house that evening, Rachel raced from the Toyota Tacoma to the door and punched the button for the doorbell. Rent followed at a walk, carrying a bottle of wine.

The door opened and Alicia Velasquez beckoned them to enter. Rachel went in and turned, waiting for Rent, bouncing heel to toe, barely able to contain her excitement.

Rent arrived and Alicia gave him a quick kiss, then placed an arm around his waist and guided him inside. Rent had met the private investigator the previous winter when their paths crossed while they were both investigating welfare fraud and the theft of EBT (electronic benefit transfer) cards. That ultimately led them to Chariot Canyon and the abandoned gold mine near Julian—and the revelation that Rent, unbeknownst to him at the time, had a twelve-year-old daughter, confirmed by a DNA test.

As Alicia closed the door, Rachel could not remain quiet a second longer.

"Me and my . . . My dad and I . . . have a new case. Well, actually it's a cold case. There's this guy who they thought killed himself, and then they found his body twenty-seven years later and they say he didn't kill himself, somebody killed him, and now, even though it's a really cold case, we're going to find out who actually killed him, and . . ."

Alicia smiled and gave Rent a questioning look, then shifted to a bemused gaze at the excited adolescent standing in her entryway.

"Oh, my. That's quite a tale, Rachel," Alicia said. "How are you? I haven't seen you in a while. I like the long hair, by the way."

"Thanks. I'm good. I went to visit the cousins I never knew I had in Washington. Now, I'm back in school, and I have music lessons and soccer practice and . . ." Her voice took on a bitter tone. ". . . homework."

"So I heard. Let's go to the kitchen. Dinner's almost ready. You can help by setting the table, and you can catch me up. And this new old case, huh? I'm intrigued."

Alicia winked at Rent and led the way to the kitchen. "And you, *mi amigo*, can help by opening the vino. It's been that kind of day."

Rachel, her eyes half closed, gave her father a look of reprimand.

"About that . . ." Rent said as he set the wine on the countertop.

"Dad, it's okay. You two can drink your wine. I won't sneak any. I prefer beer anyway."

Alicia stifled a laugh and gave Rent a look of wonder.

"We made a pact last night, and I'm already breaking it," Rent said.

"Oh? Has Rachel joined Carrie Nation in the Temperance Union?"

Rachel, holding three plates, explained. "He got mad last night because I drank some of his beer while he went to the bathroom."

She placed the plates on the table and continued. "He said he wouldn't drink in front of me anymore. But it's okay. Don't let me stop you from having a little wine."

"No, a deal's a deal and he should stick to it," Alicia said. "And so will I."

Rachel finished setting the table, and Alicia pulled a casserole dish from the oven. She placed it on the table, then took a bowl of green salad out of the fridge.

"*La cena está servida. Enchiladas con pollo,*" she said. "Take your seats, *por favor.* Rachel, what would you like to drink . . . besides beer? *Refrescos azucarados o el agua con gas?*"

"Fizzy water, please. Even though *agua con gas* makes it sound like it farts."

"Rachel!" Rent blurted.

"Well, it does."

Alicia stifled a laugh. "Coming right up."

Rent shook his head and muttered, "Can't take her anywhere."

"And you?" Alicia asked.

"Same as Rach."

Alicia served the drinks, then the enchiladas, and told them to help themselves to the salad, advising them to save room for dessert, which would be a surprise. They dug in. After several minutes, Rachel broke the silence.

"This is really good, Alicia. Maybe you could show me how to make it."

"I'd like that," she replied. "But right now, I want to hear more about this mysterious case that has you so excited."

Rachel, in a staccato blitzkrieg, laid out the story. "Construction workers unearthed a body found in the San Juan Islands . . . where Aunt Edith lives . . . a man who was murdered because he was illegally dumping toxic waste in San Diego Bay and the murderers are still in San Diego and we're going to find them and turn them over to the cops. Just like you and my dad did with Gabe and those bad guys doing welfare fraud," Rachel exclaimed, crossing her arms across her chest as if to say, "So there!"

Alicia raised her eyebrows in mock wonderment, then shifted her gaze to Rent. "Is that so?"

Rent grinned. "In a nutshell, although I'm not so sure about the last bit."

"We googled it and found out lots of stuff about it," Rachel stammered in her defense.

Rent agreed that they had found a lot of information, but nothing definitive, and certainly not conclusive. "There's a lot more digging to do and connecting all the dots."

"It does sound intriguing," Alicia said. "How may I be of assistance?"

Rent said they needed to track down legal documents and the people involved, if they were still above the sod.

"I'll start by going through the newspaper's archives and, if possible, talk to the reporter—or reporters—who covered the case at the time. The newspaper actually got sued over this, so there's a lot more to it than meets the eye."

"And if that guy did get killed over it," Alicia pointed out, "I doubt those folks would welcome you poking your nose into it after all these years."

"We have to," Rachel pleaded. "Aunt Edith wants us to because the man's daughter needs to know why her dad died, just like I needed to know why my mom was . . ."

Rachel grimaced as rivulets of tears trailed down her cheeks. She dabbed her eyes with a napkin, overwhelmed by the memory of her mother's death earlier in the year.

Rent stood up and stepped around the table to embrace his daughter.

"I'm sorry, sweetie. I didn't . . ."

"It's OK, Dad." Rachel sniffed and dabbed her eyes again. "I'll be all right. It just suddenly all came flooding back."

Rent sighed and returned to his seat next to Alicia. He looked at her and shrugged. She nodded in acknowledgement and patted his thigh.

Rachel smiled. "Sorry 'bout that. Where were we? Oh, yeah, Aunt Edith and the cold case."

Rent gazed lovingly at his daughter. "You know, you've got plenty on your plate as it is, young lady."

"Humph," she responded and made a face.

"Now, now, children," Alicia chided. "Let's have some dessert— *churros* y *helado de vainilla*. Rachel, please clear these dishes and lend me a hand."

While enjoying their ice cream and deep-fried confection, Rachel wondered if they could play Telestrations, the telephone game. "Or I could read while you two smooch. I brought the graphic novel *Wildful* along just in case."

Rachel smirked as her father and his current amour struggled with how to respond to her candor, then continued. "There's a Wave game tonight. But Dad thinks *futbol* is boring. As if rugby is any better. Or, if we're really hard up, we could watch *Freaky Friday*. I brought the DVD. Halloween's coming up, and I'm going to write a report about it for school."

Her eyes shifted from her dad to Alicia and back. "Well?"

"Well . . ." said Alicia, giving Rachel a conspiratorial wink. "How about you and I watch the soccer game while your dad cleans up the kitchen?"

5

Rent entered the *San Diego Herald* newsroom, went straight to his desk, and set down his laptop computer. Before he even had a chance to sit, his phone buzzed.

He sighed, pulled the phone from a pants pocket, and looked at the screen. A text from his editor, Janis O'Connor.

He glanced toward her office. She motioned for him to join her. He strode across the room, passing the desk of Naomi Clark, who handled the crime beat.

"That was quick," she said. "I hope it's not bad news."

"Yeah, me too," he replied.

"Good weekend with the new squeeze?" she inquired with a smirk.

Rent paused. "If you must know, Miss Nosy Parker, my daughter and I had a delightful weekend."

"More panning for gold? I hear the price has gone through the roof."

"I have to talk to the boss," he said and continued on across the newsroom.

"Take a seat," O'Connor said as he entered her office.

"Close the door?"

She shrugged. "Nothing classified or confidential."

"I guess that's as good a start as any," he said and sat in the chair opposite her.

"ADUs," she said. "How's that coming now that we finally seem to have put the welfare fraud story to rest and the bad guys behind bars?"

"I have a few more leads to follow up, and there's a town hall to attend where I suspect the council will get an earful."

"What's the crux of it?"

"Depends on whose side you're on. On the one hand, developers say they're helping to resolve the affordable housing crisis and provide jobs in construction. On the other hand, homeowners say greedy developers are taking advantage of unintended loopholes in state and local laws to erect monstrous eyesores, destroying the look and character of historic neighborhoods of single-family residences, not to mention creating traffic congestion and a parking nightmare.

"I'm trying to balance the narrative, but I gotta tell ya, a couple of those 'eyesores' have popped up a few blocks from where I live, and I can sympathize with those who live next door to them. Mind you, the Kumeyaay might say that the entire city of San Diego is a huge boil on their ass . . ."

O'Connor waved for him to stop. "You get more cynical by the day."

Rent shrugged. "I'm not a cynic. I'm a skeptic."

"Uh-huh."

"Either way, it's better than being a witless Pollyanna, like those dupes—"

She cut him off. "I want something by Friday for the Sunday edition."

Rent started to stand. "Yes, boss."

"How's Rachel doing?" she asked.

He settled back in the chair and smiled. "She's a bit of a cynic herself."

O'Connor nodded. "Well, considering what she's been through."

"Actually, she's doing quite well. Keeps busy with school, music, sports, her new pony."

"Doesn't hurt that you struck gold."

"She's the true gold in my life. That glitter in the ground is just icing on the cake, if I may use a tired cliché."

"You may need that glitter if we get another round of pink slips."

Rent straightened up. "The rumor mill grinding a little faster?"

O'Connor shrugged a single shoulder. "There's talk, but it may be just that. However, I suspect we'll know more soon."

"Oh, yeah, Ebenezer comes to wish us a Merry Christmas and present us with the proverbial lump of coal." Rent shook his head in disgust. "That glitter, as you call it, is for Rachel's college education, not for paying Rent . . . so to speak."

"Just sayin', if needs must. At least it provides you with a buffer. Me, I could take early retirement and a pewter parachute. But other young'ns, like Clark, well, classic journalism is going the way of the buggy whip. Could be hard times."

"Speaking of . . ."

"Yes, Mr. Dickens?"

"Something's come up that I'd like to look into, time permitting, and if it leads to something substantial, it could be front-page worthy, above the fold."

O'Connor leaned forward and rested her elbows on the desk. "Do tell."

Rent told her about the news story his aunt had sent him.

"Give it to Clark," she said. "She could look into it."

Rent clenched his jaw. "I know it sounds like a crime story, but I don't see it that way."

"Oh? Guy's been murdered and that's not a crime story?"

"Yeah, that's part of it."

"I hear a 'but' coming."

"A bit of a but."

"Don't you go there!" she replied with a laugh.

He chuckled. "But with a single 't.'"

"Continue."

"I see it as a corruption and business conspiracy story. Why was this guy killed? To shut him up. He knew something about the hazardous waste disposal that somebody—or somebodies, more like it—didn't want to be made public. Shine a little light on it and the night crawlers come wriggling out."

"How so?"

"I did some preliminary research over the weekend."

"I'll bet your daughter loved that."

"Are you kidding? She insisted on it. She's more into this than I am."

O'Connor creased her brow and sat back in her chair. "Another journalist in the family? I should have a talk with her about a more lucrative career path."

Rent waved her off. "Don't worry. She's going to end up in biotech or high tech. Maybe computer science and jump on the AI bandwagon. She just happens to love a mystery. Becoming a big Nancy Drew fan." He paused. "Now, as I was saying . . . this happened way before my time."

He went on to explain how the reporter who broke the story about the illegal disposal of hazardous waste got sued, along with the newspaper. The company claimed defamation and demanded $5 million in damages. However, when the facts came out, the company dropped the lawsuit.

O'Connor nodded. "You're talking about Will Mason. That was before I moved here, but I remember the headlines."

Rent continued. "But no criminal or civil charges were ever filed. It was swept under the rug. Until now, when, literally, a skeleton falls out of the proverbial closet. Not only did the company illegally dispose of toxic waste, they covered it up by disposing of the toxic whistleblower."

"The guy they found up north," O'Connor said.

Rent nodded. "And here's the kicker. The property development company still exists and is now being run by the son of the guy who ran the company back then, and this son's son-in-law is running for Congress in the twenty-fifth district, which includes Imperial County."

He paused to catch his breath. "That company is still based here in San Diego, and the CEO lives in Rancho Santa Fe. Which leaves me wondering what they're up to these days, besides building ADUs."

"What?" O'Connor exclaimed, incredulous. "You're saying there's a tie between this dead guy in Washington and an ADU builder in San Diego?"

Rent grinned. "Like manna from heaven. The death is not a direct tie to the ADUs, but the ADU angle gives me a foot in the door with the company, JMJ Property Development Services Group. But I don't want to bring up the dead guy just yet. I want to let him spout his corp-speak about all the good he's doing—'building affordable housing'—before I bring the hammer down."

"Surely, they've heard the news."

"Surely, they've already hunkered down with their lawyers to come up with a story of plausible deniability."

"And," O'Connor responded, "naturally he's a big-shot philan-thropist who attends all the charity galas and gets his picture plastered all over this newspaper's society pages."

Rent grinned again. "So now who's the cynic?"

O'Connor shook her head. "Oh, for Pete's sake. Wait, not Mike Johnson."

"Mike Junior."

"There are two of them?"

"Senior is semi-retired but still active, overseeing the family's multiple business enterprises. Which is why . . ."

O'Connor waved him off. "I have to get my head around this Medusa before it turns me to stone."

"Just let me say one more thing."

The editor sighed. "And it's what . . ." She looked at her smartwatch. "My blood pressure is going through the roof, and it's only eight forty-six. Lord help me. Make it quick; I have to go upstairs and face the music at nine."

"You're not going to . . ."

She ran her fingers across her lips as if zipping them closed. "Not until I see something substantial to back up what right now could easily be labeled by Mr. Big Shot as a fuzzy-headed-liberal conspiracy theory."

"That's what I'm trying to tell you. The guy who broke this story, Will Mason, is still alive. I want to talk to him. And the dead guy's daughter also wants to talk to me. This is not just some crazy conspiracy theory. But I need some time to nail it down."

"OK, look into it. But I still need that ADU story this week."

Rent stood up and saluted. "Yes, boss."

6

Rent skipped back to his desk as heads swiveled in the newsroom, following his progress. Naomi Clark stood up from her desk, coffee cup in hand, and sauntered toward Rent, who leaned over his desk, shuffling through a stack of papers.

"Buy you a coffee?"

Rent stared at her, questioning her motive. He and Clark had had a tumultuous relationship, including a brief workplace romance that didn't end on the upbeat.

"Sure," he replied. "I have something to share with you. You'll hear about it soon enough anyway."

He picked up his mug and started toward the break room; she followed.

"Stepping on my toes again?" Clark asked. "They've barely healed from our last dance."

They entered the room, and Clark went straight to the coffee machine, then reached out her hand for his cup. As the cup filled, she turned to face him.

"So?" she queried.

"So, what?"

"What'd she say? You out of a job?"

"Not yet, but she said Scrooge might be coming down the chimney this year."

She handed him his cup and started her own. "That's what I'm afraid of. And I just moved into a nicer—and more expensive—place."

"Look at the bright side," Rent said. "With all that time on your hands, you could finish your novel."

She made a face and looked around the room. "Shush! What else?"

Rent looked puzzled. "What else?"

She picked up her cup and cradled it in her hands. "You said you have something to tell me."

He nodded and gave her the *Reader's Digest* version of what he told their editor and his corruption theory.

Clark took a deep breath. "Wow. So, crime-wise, we have a vict on an out-of-state slab who may have ties to San Diego but most likely got whacked up north." She shrugged. "I could give the cop shop a call, but I doubt they're interested. I could do a few 'graphs for the Reporter's Notebook—former San Diego resident, blah, blah, blah —but unless something more definitive pops up . . ." She shrugged.

"If the cops here do look into it, I'll let you know. I just wanted to give you a heads-up."

She stared at him with a blank expression, then raised her cup as if making a toast and touched his with a slight clink.

"Thanks for telling me. Good luck on the conspiracy angle. Right now, I have yet another jail death to deal with."

Rent followed her out, and they returned to their respective desks. He called JMJ and left a message for Mike Johnson Jr., then looked through his notes on the ADU story, only mildly interested. After a few minutes, he tossed the notes onto his desk. "Fuck it," he muttered and picked up his phone.

When the recipient answered, Rent identified himself and asked to speak to Will Mason.

"Speaking," the voice replied. "I saw your series on welfare fraud. Good on ya, mate."

"Thanks, and I could say the same about your series on the hazardous waste disposal kerfuffle."

"That was a long time ago."

"Maybe not all that long ago. Do I detect an antipodean accent?"

"Kiwi . . . but why do you say not so long ago?"

"Remember the geologist who did the EIR?"

"Humph, some EIR. Pile of dags. The bloke topped himself, as I recall. Sort of verified what I wrote . . . and got sued for."

"He didn't top himself, though."

"What?"

"He was murdered."

"You don't say."

"I do say. Some construction workers discovered his body a couple of weeks ago."

"Where? Not San Diego. I'd have heard about it, surely."

Rent explained the circumstances.

"Ah, yes. Friends of mine say Seattle and the Puget Sound, with all those islands, reminds them of Auckland and the Hauraki Gulf."

"I wouldn't know about that, but I wouldn't mind visiting New Zealand someday."

"So, how may I be of assistance?"

"How about I buy you a beer or two, and you tell me what you remember about that story, especially the stuff that never made it into print."

"I'll have to root out my scribbles and dust off the ol' gray cells. I'm pretty sure I still have them somewhere. The notes, I mean. The gray cells I'm not so sure about."

"This afternoon?"

"Sorry, mate, I've got music practice."

"What instrument do you play? I play the fiddle."

"So, you fiddle around a little, eh?" he said.

"You might say that."

"I'm a ukulele man, myself. I could meet you tomorrow, though. Pub's just a stagger away from my bach."

Rent chuckled at Mason's wry humor as he jotted down the name of the pub and said he'd be there by four. He then punched in the number for Susannah Wilbury, the dead man's daughter. The call went to voicemail, and he left a message.

I guess I'd better get this damned ADU story out of the way.

He reviewed a controversial plan to locate seventeen units behind a house in the Clairemont area. The deep lot sat on a cul-de-sac, making it pie-shaped, narrow at the street, then growing wider in the back. He shook his head.

This place is close to a mile away from public transportation, as if the residents would walk that far to catch a bus or trolley. Where the hell are people supposed to park? The neighbors must be screaming bloody murder.

Indeed, ADUs were pitting neighbor against neighbor as the debate raged over property rights, parking, and traffic congestion in historically quiet neighborhoods of single-family homes.

Two neighbors in the Crown Point area hadn't spoken for months. A backyard unit built on the property line remained unfinished because one neighbor wouldn't allow the other to access his yard to stucco an exterior wall. The recalcitrant neighbor even posted a "No Trespassing" sign in his yard.

At least no one's been killed over it yet.

A number of homeowners' associations also opposed ADUs being built within their jurisdictions. And another aspect of the story left him chuckling. Someone in rural East County had bought a shed from Home Depot and had it delivered, preassembled, to her property for use as an ADU. She lived in a converted garage, so she dubbed the new unit AD2.

Proposed multistory buildings with dozens of units had resulted in the nickname "granny flats" evolving into "granny towers."

Rent reread a number of stupefying documents laying out the new regulations, which even allowed "non-living" spaces in multi-family dwellings to be reclassified as ADUs: closets, laundry rooms, garages.

How about dumpsters? he wondered. *Somehow I can't imagine the people making these laws would actually want to live in these units. Ironically, the city forbids camping tents being set up in one's backyard. Go figure.*

The San Diego City Council, in an effort to quell the complaints, had begun public hearings on reforms to the lax regulations fueling the ADU boom. Crafty developers were buying up homes with large backyards in order to capitalize on the loose restrictions governing ADU construction.

The proposed reforms would place a limit of six units per lot, regardless of the size of the yard, and limit the height to two stories; parking spaces would be required for units built some distance from public transit.

His phone buzzed, and he recognized the number with the 206 area code: the dead man's daughter.

"Rent Beacham," he said.

The caller identified herself as Susannah Wilbury, returning his call. Rent told her about receiving the news article from his aunt and his interest in it due to the San Diego boatyard connection.

"I really appreciate your looking into this," she said. "I never wanted to believe my dad took his own life. My mom refused to believe it, and now she's telling everyone, 'I told you so.'"

"Do you have any of your dad's papers, EIR reports, stuff like that?"

"Do we ever. Mom wouldn't let me toss it out. She kept saying this day would come. Would you like me to send it to you? It's quite a lot of stuff."

"I'd like to come to you, if that's all right."

"That's a long way. I don't mind packing it up."

"I'm originally from the Seattle area, so I can make it a family visit as well."

"Edith did say you haven't been to see her for a while."

"Ah, yes. Good ol' Aunt Edith," Rent replied, then asked, "Have the cops expressed any interest in your dad's files?"

"I offered it to them, but they didn't seem to care. They just wanted to know if we'd seen or heard anything that might lead them to the killer or killers. They said the odds of identifying anyone with so many years gone by were pretty close to zero, even if they were still alive. So, I don't have any expectation the cops will do anything."

"I'm sorry for your loss, and you have my sincere condolences," Rent said.

"Thank you," Susannah replied. "It came as such a surprise, finding his body after all these years. We're still in shock."

"I can imagine . . . but, full disclosure . . . and I'm not trying to minimize your father's death . . . but I'm more interested in *what* got him killed. This is more than a homicide case. Businesses were involved in a cover-up and barely got a slap on the wrist. I want to look into what really happened with that boatyard and the hazardous waste. That, in turn, would likely lead us to those responsible for your father's death, if not directly, then indirectly. That's why I'd like to look at his files."

"How soon do you want to come?"

"This weekend?"

"You can stay with us, if you'd like."

"I'll stay with my aunt, but even so, I wouldn't want to impose."

"We . . . my mother and I . . . operate a resort. It's after Labor Day, so we're not so busy. Not that we were very busy this year. Normally we'd be fully booked, and I'd be working twenty-four seven. But the tariffs and the trade war are killing us. Most of the Canadians canceled. They're half of our business, if not more. If this keeps up, I don't know what we're going to do. And it's not just us. All the B&Bs and hotels in the islands are way down on bookings."

"I'm sorry to hear that," Rent said. "I have to clear this with my boss. I'll let you know."

He ended the call and checked the time. *Gotta get a move on.* San Diego's traffic congestion had not quite devolved into L.A.'s legendary standards but was working on it.

He drove to the affluent community of Carlsbad for a special city council meeting. The room had filled to capacity, leaving the latecomers standing in the hallway. One guy wanted to convert the garage of his three-story condominium into a ground-floor apartment, which would be allowed under state law. But his homeowners' association opposed it. The council agreed to take the matter under consideration as the session turned into something akin to a battle between city hall and HOAs.

In a similar situation, but involving a single-family residence, a homeowner said he had a larger lot than most and wanted to build a second three-car garage to restore an old car. The council members seemed open to the idea, but his HOA board had turned him down.

One of those board members also addressed the council, explaining that "because of these less restrictive regulations, there's nothing to stop him from turning that into an ADU. That would set a precedent for the entire association, so we voted no. We hope the city council will respect our decision, which complies with the wording set out in our CC&Rs—the covenants, conditions, and restrictions."

The meeting left Rent shaking his head in bewilderment. Afterward, he questioned a few of the speakers to get additional quotes for his story, then made the forty-five-minute drive home.

The next morning, he attended a meeting of the City of San Diego Planning Commission, which heard similar complaints from frustrated homeowners, including a representative of Neighbors for a Better San Diego who pointed out that even larger projects were slated, particularly in Encanto, in the southeastern region of the city.

The commission voted unanimously to rein in a number of the ADU "incentives"—the most aggressive in the state—being "exploited" by developers. The commissioners agreed that the city's ADU incentive went beyond what state law allowed by letting property owners build a potentially unlimited number of such units. But it was too late to block the 73 units destined for construction in a single backyard in Encanto.

He worked this additional material into his Sunday feature before meeting Will Mason that afternoon. As he leaned back in his chair to relax for a moment, his phone buzzed. He didn't recognize the number.

He answered, and the caller identified himself as Mike Johnson Jr., returning Rent's earlier call. Rent noted the use of "junior" and told him about the ADU story he was working on.

"Another one of your anti-business stories, digging for dirty laundry, I imagine."

"Just the facts."

"OK, I'll give you some facts," the man said. He launched into a tirade on the lack of affordable housing in California and how his company was building ADUs as fast as possible to help solve the crisis. But environmentalists and government regulations have stymied builders for decades.

He concluded by saying, "Finally, we got some common sense out of Sacramento and city hall, and we're able to fast-track these projects."

"You're referring to the so-called 'builder's remedy' and the 'density bonus law,' along with the city's incentives."

"Absolutely. It's about time."

"But those loopholes, as some folks like to call them, mean you don't have to accommodate for adequate parking or traffic congestion or impact on the sewer system, and you're stomping on property rights while limiting local control over zoning and building codes."

"I don't make the laws; I just follow 'em," Johnson said.

"And exploit them, going well beyond what was intended, according to the detractors."

"That's what I call smart business practices."

"And highly profitable as well."

"Oh?"

"You live in Rancho Santa Fe, and judging by your charitable con-tributions—the opera, symphony, Old Globe . . ."

"We call that giving back to the community."

"Not to mention the contributions made by you and your father to your son-in-law's political campaign."

"Checking up on us, are you?"

"That's what I call smart journalistic practices."

"Uh-huh . . . oh, and by the way, we prefer the term 'backyard home' rather than 'accessory dwelling unit,' which sounds like it's a chicken coop or a barn for pigs and horses."

Rent rolled his eyes but dutifully jotted down the man's comment. He then wondered where the units were built, on site or maybe pre-built units from China?

Johnson said he worked with a builder in San Marcos, providing jobs and contributing to the local economy.

"Unlike that fraudster who took money to build ADUs but never built a one," Johnson said. "Gives our industry a bad name."

"Speaking of giving your industry a bad name, do you offer ADUs as short-term rentals? There have been a lot of complaints filed by neighbors, claiming loud noise and parking issues."

"What if I do?"

"I'll take that as a yes, even though that violates a city ordinance prohibiting the rental of ADUs for less than thirty days."

"The units are properly licensed by the city as short-term rentals."

"Licenses issued by a separate department."

"It's not my fault the city can't get its shit together. Now, is that all? I have a board meeting to attend."

I'll just bet you do, Rent thought, and, unable to constrain himself, he said in response, "One more question. Does the name Thomas Wilbury mean anything to you?"

"Thomas Wilbury? Not offhand, no."

"OK, thank you for your time."

Rent ended the call and sighed. *Can of worms, here we come.*

He checked the time. *Damn it!*

7

As Rent drove to Coronado, he crossed the San Diego-Coronado Bridge, admiring, as much as he dared, the commanding aerial view it offered of San Diego Bay and its shoreline.

A few sailboats transited the bay; the water sparkled in the bright sunlight. A U.S. Navy aircraft carrier sat at its mooring at North Island Naval Air Station, and the San Diego skyscrapers stood like mighty monuments to "the progress of man," as John Prine might phrase it.

However, arching over the bay 250 feet at its highest point, the bridge also offered an opportunity for those intent on taking their own lives. Thus, it had no pedestrian access, whether for sightseeing or otherwise; signs provided the phone number of a suicide hotline.

The only way Rent could enjoy the view beyond a brief glance would be as a passenger, which meant he had to keep his eyes on the road and ignore the panoramic view.

He drove up Coronado's Orange Avenue at a slower pace, able to admire the multimillion-dollar dwellings and thinking, *I couldn't even afford an ADU in this neighborhood.*

Most of the houses had been handed down from one generation to the next or housed retired admirals, with the occasional off-island gazillionaire snatching up the remaining parcels.

He found a vacant parking space near the historic Hotel del Coronado—made famous by Marilyn Monroe, Tony Curtis, and Jack Lemmon in the 1959 movie *Some Like It Hot*—and strolled his way to O'Malley's Pub.

He stepped into the dark interior and stopped to let his eyes adjust, then scanned the room. A couple of patrons sat at the bar, and a few others had taken tables. As he moved toward the bar, he caught sight of a man sitting alone at a table, waving an arm, and headed that way. As Rent approached, the man slid out of the booth, stood, and greeted him with an extended hand.

"Mr. Beacham, I presume," the man said. "I'm Will Mason."

Rent shook Mason's hand. "Thank you for agreeing to see me. Sorry for the delay."

"No worries. What's your poison?"

"I think a Guinness is in order," Rent said as he slid into the booth opposite the man.

"I'm having an Arrogant Bastard myself," Mason replied, nodding at the pint glass on the table. He signaled the barkeeper and ordered a pint of the world-renowned stout for Rent, then continued.

"I tried to get the publican to pour Speights, New Zealand's premier beer, but the owner said he'd never heard of it. Said he had Foster's. Bloody hell! I told him Foster's is Aussie piss, and he said, 'Australia, New Zealand, what's the diff?'"

Rent chuckled. "Well, that's a 'Merican for you."

The man snorted. "What's the diff? The Aussies' whiny accent for starters, not to mention they're descended from convicts while the Kiwis come from a long line of religious zealots, whalers, and Scottish sheep herders. Mind you, I say that with a full dose of endearment. The Aussies are our first cousins, after all."

The barkeeper arrived and set the Guinness on the table. "Anything to eat? We've got the best fish and chips in town."

Both men shook their heads, and Rent said, "Maybe later." He then studied the man across from him for a moment, figuring Mason must be pushing eighty. A few wisps of gray hair clung to his mostly bald pate as if refusing to acknowledge their ultimate fate. He had dressed in a tweed jacket over a white shirt, no tie.

"What keeps you here?" Rent asked, then lifted the glass of black beer to his lips.

Mason sighed. "I married an American. Met her in Southeast Asia. We were both covering the Vietnam War. We ended up here. She died a couple of years ago, and this is home now. Lived here longer than I ever lived in New Zealand."

"No family there?"

"I have a brother who lives in Christchurch, and I visit occasionally. But enough about me. What do you want to know about the boatyard scandal?"

Rent told him again about the body of the man found on San Juan Island, his cause of death initially considered to be suicide.

"But now it's a homicide, and his daughter believes it has to do with what happened here in San Diego. They had moved away in a hurry, all hush-hush-like, and started over up north. She hated it, leaving all her school friends behind. I suspect it had to do with money, and he—"

Mason finished Rent's sentence. "Wanted more of it. Greed is a two-sided coin; goes both ways."

Rent nodded. "And that got him killed. The question now is, whodunnit?"

"Whodunnit, indeed."

"I hoped you might have some thoughts about that or could point me in the right direction."

Mason leaned forward, resting on his elbows. "First of all, my name stays out of this. I got sued over this and spent three bloody months digging through a pile of documents higher than Bob's Peak for my legal defense."

"Sued?"

"For defamation. One of those so-called SLAPP lawsuits— strategic lawsuit against public participation—to the tune of five million bucks. Took a page out of your president's playbook. They tried to intimidate me and the newspaper and force us to write a retraction. Fortunately, our insurance company chose to fight it rather than cave in to the corporate bullies."

Mason downed a generous portion of his beer.

Rent did the same, and when Mason didn't continue, he leaned over the table. "And?"

Mason grinned, as if welcoming the opportunity to have another gloat.

"Let me guess," Rent said. "The EIR was bogus."

"Yes and no. I believed the EIR was bogus but couldn't prove it. But that's not why they sued. It was the incinerator they used to dispose of the most toxic soil."

Rent cocked an eyebrow.

"In that case, I did have the evidence, including internal documents showing that they, and the outfit operating the incinerator, knowingly lied to the authorities, including the EPA. They withdrew the lawsuit the very day the trial was to start."

"So, if I start asking embarrassing questions and peeling back the layers, you don't want your name cropping up."

"In a word, yes. I'm too old for any more of that BS, and that company. JMJ still exists as far as I know."

Rent nodded. "I looked 'em up. The only difference being that the old man, Mike Sr., is semi-retired and living in Montana. His son, Mike Jr., now runs the property development outfit. And they've branched out under the aegis of Lustrous Consulting Group. Not only doing residential and commercial development. They took over the haz- ardous waste disposal operation they had contracted to get rid of the toxic soil removed from the boatyard, and they've expanded into the energy sector—geothermal and solar—'Green Growth' they call it."

Mason snorted. "Green as in greed and dodgy deals, more like it."

Rent shrugged. "I don't know about that—yet. I'll look into it. But first I'm trying to find out who was behind the hit on the geologist. I'm going to meet with the daughter. She found some boxes of her dad's files and said I could look through them. Might be some clues there."

"I still have all the pertinent legal documents from the lawsuit," Mason said. "You're welcome to them; they're public record."

"I'll let you know. They might come in handy."

"You watch yer back. Don't let that 'Sweetheart Swede' schtick fool you. That Johnson fellow is one slippery eel. I'd bet dags to donuts he's still the puppeteer."

Mason drained his glass. "Another pint? As long as you're buyin'."

8

Rent sensed as much as heard the Boeing 737's engine noise change pitch. He set aside the G.M. Ford novel he'd been reading and peered out the window. The Cascade Mountains stretched north and south like a compass needle pointing toward the North Pole. The gaping vent of Mt. St. Helens lay below, steam emitting from the crater opened by the peak's explosive eruption forty-five years earlier.

The plane began to lose elevation as it passed the snow- and glacier-capped Mt. Rainier—Washington's iconic landmark—as it made its approach to the Seattle-Tacoma International Airport, better known simply as SeaTac.

The plane droned over Puget Sound, then reversed course to land. Rent recognized the landmarks below, including the Ballard neighborhood where he had lived while attending the University of Washington.

Once on the ground, he would pick up a rental car, drive north to Anacortes, and catch the ferry to Friday Harbor on San Juan Island.

"Thank goodness," he muttered. "A brilliant late summer day in the Evergray State." He hoped it would remain so for his three-day stay.

He managed to get through Seattle's notorious bottleneck on the I-5 freeway without coming to a complete halt and powered the eighty miles north without incident. He enjoyed the hour-long ferry ride in spite of the layer of smoke from wildfires in the eastern Cascades and Okanogan area hovering overhead and limiting visibility like a lukewarm fog.

From the ferry landing, he drove the short distance to Aunt Edith's house on Beaverton Valley Road. As he parked, she stepped out onto the front porch using a cane to steady herself. She wore a blue cardigan sweater over a pink blouse and gray slacks and had L.L. Bean Storm Chasers on her feet.

Rent bounced up the stairs and into her open arms.

"It's about time you came for a visit, young man," she said, then held him at arm's length. "You look well. It's so nice to see you." She hugged him again.

"I'm happy to see—"

"I have fresh coffee and muffins. That'll tide you over until dinner. I made a reservation at McMillin's in Roche Harbor."

"I'll just grab my suitcase."

Again, she cut him off, waving a dismissive hand. "That's not going anywhere. I just pulled the muffins from the oven. I timed it to the ferry schedule."

Rent rolled his eyes in surrender. There had never been any arguing with Aunt Edith.

"What's with the cane?" he asked as they entered the old farmhouse and settled in the kitchen. "I hope you didn't have a fall."

"It's my darned hip. The quack in town says I need a replacement."

"Why don't you? They can work magic these days."

"It's such a bother and the recovery can take months. Have a seat and help yourself to a muffin. Homemade raspberry jam, too. I'll pour the coffee."

Rent sat down, grabbed a muffin, and peeled off the paper wrapping. He tore the muffin in two and took a bite of the still-warm cake, which she had infused with dried blueberries.

"Mmmm," he offered. "Sure beats the tasteless pretzels they gave us on the plane."

Edith joined him at the table, setting a cup of steaming coffee in front of Rent. "How was the trip?"

"Uneventful, thankfully." He took a cautious sip of the scalding brew. "I got a fantastic view of the mountains as we flew into Seattle. I sometimes forget how beautiful and green it is here—when it's not shrouded in nimbostratus."

"Or smoke," she said. "We're having lovely weather, but we could use some rain. Those damn fires make the air harmful to breathe. When do you meet with Susannah?"

Rent looked at the clock on the kitchen wall. "Oh, crap. I told her I'd be there at three."

"She's only five minutes from here. You can blame me for being fashionably late."

Rent finished his muffin and took a few more sips of coffee. He stood up and grabbed his light jacket from the back of the chair.

"The reservation's for seven," she said.

"I'll only be an hour or two."

"Famous last words," she responded, then smiled. "It's so nice to see you, nephew. We'll have a good gab this evening. Now, on your way. She's anxious to meet you."

Rent drove back to town, his memory of the island's geography a bit vague. He'd spent more time sailing around the islands than on the islands themselves, although for several summers he stayed with Aunt Edith during the berry season to help with the picking.

He turned north on Roche Harbor Road toward The Island Inn. He wondered if Cabin 3 and its rock fireplace still stood near the small lake.

He spotted a newer sign about one hundred yards ahead. "Resort" had been added to the original name. *Going upscale, eh?*

Rent parked and went into the office. A young woman stood behind a varnished wooden counter and greeted him as he entered. He introduced himself and said, "I'm here to see Susannah. She's expecting me."

A voice came through a doorway behind the counter. "I'll be right there."

While he waited, Rent examined the resort's brochure. It depicted idyllic log cabins and yurts as well as luxurious "glamping" in canvas tents for the more adventurous guests.

Nice. I might have to come back here with Rachel.

A middle-aged woman stepped through the doorway and approached the counter. She had shoulder-length blondish hair and wore a polo shirt emblazoned with the resort's logo, blue jeans, and hiking boots. She extended a hand, saying, "Susannah Wilbury. I'm so grateful you could come, Mr. Beacham."

He shook her hand. "Please, call me Rent. I'm grateful you agreed to see me."

She stepped around the counter. "Follow me. We'll go over to the house."

They passed one of the cabins, and he could see the yurts and tents on the far side of the small lake. A pair of Canada geese and some ducks paddled lazily on the lake's surface.

"This place has been gentrified," he said.

Susannah stopped and looked at him in amazement. "You've been here before?"

He nodded. "As a kid, about twenty years ago. My family spent a Christmas here in one of the log cabins. One of my fondest holiday memories."

"So, you're originally from around here."

"Yeah, I grew up in the Issaquah area."

"Small world, eh?"

"Indeed. Quite a coincidence, if there is such a thing."

"Those old log cabins are gone, along with my dad. My mom and I have kept this place going. I hope he's smiling down on us and not whining too much over how we've modernized it. Have to keep up with the times. Folks these days expect more creature comforts and frills, although we still have a section set aside for traditional camping."

Rent began whistling the melody to Stephen Foster's *Oh, Susannah.*

She gave him a stern glance. "Not you too."

"Sorry," he said. "It's one of the tunes I play for dances."

"You're a musician?"

"Fiddler. But I also have a day job."

She chuckled. "Every year, we . . . well, we used to . . . have a small folk music festival on Orcas and have a barn dance."

"I played for that a few years back, before I moved to San Diego."

"We had to cancel it this year. Canadian bands would come too, but now . . ." She shrugged. "Do you know John Reischman?"

Rent nodded. "We've met, and I play a couple of his tunes."

They reached the house and stepped onto the porch of the aging Victorian-style structure. Susannah opened the door and gestured for him to enter.

"Welcome to our humble abode, such as it is. This is the one thing that has not kept up with the times. We put all the money into the accommodations. Like I said, you're welcome to stay here, no charge."

Rent shook his head. "As much as I'd like to spend the night in a yurt, or glamping, as you call it, I'm staying with my aunt. She'd never forgive me if I didn't."

"Of course. I can't thank Edith enough for contacting you. This has been such a nightmare. Finding my dad's body after all these years, arranging the funeral, dealing with the sheriff's office."

"I can imagine. Are the cops actually getting anywhere?"

Susannah shrugged. "Paying lip service, but I doubt they're actually doing much. The case is so old, and they don't have much to go on. Excuse me . . . Mom? Are you here?" No reply. "I guess she's out on the grounds somewhere. There's always something that needs taken care of. Come through."

She led the way into a small dining room and gestured toward the banker's boxes on the oak dining table.

"Help yourself. I'll go find my mom . . . oh, sorry. Here I am in the hospitality business and I'm not being hospitable. Can I get you anything? Coffee? Water? A beer?"

"Nah, I'm good for now."

As Susannah left the house, Rent stepped up to the table and began examining the identical boxes lined up in a row like the condominiums where he lived, six in all. The one labeled "EIR – Boatyard" caught his attention.

He pulled it forward and removed the lid. Inside, he found thick manila folders with labels indicating Wilbury's research and multiple drafts of the environmental impact report, one marked "Final."

He withdrew that file and opened it. The report began with all the perfunctory jargon associated with such documents.

"Need to cut to the chase," he muttered, turning to the last few pages and looking for the concluding remarks.

This reads like Greek to me.

The geological and scientific terms baffled him, although he recognized the names and symbols of a number of minerals and chemicals associated with hazardous waste. He'd taken chemistry in high school and had to learn the Periodic Table of Elements.

The report identified the elements considered as hazardous and in need of proper treatment and disposal. He examined earlier drafts of the report and found highlighted phrases regarding whether the levels of toxins exceeded certain limits of allowable concentrations, especially the deadly PCBs . . .

> . . . oil, copper, lead, mercury, zinc, barium, chromium, cadmium, tributyltin (TBT), the 16 most common polycyclic aromatic hydrocarbons ($\sum$16 PAHs), and the seven most common polychlorinated biphenyls ($\sum$7 PCBs) at levels **higher** than the environmental qualitative guidelines.
>
> In addition, the mean of the median values found revealed that the lower guidance value for the sensitive use of land was **exceeded** for the $\sum$7 PCBs, carcinogenic PAHs, TBT, Pb, Hg, and Cu by a factor of 380, 6.8, 3.6, 2.9, 2.2, and 1.7, respectively.

He assumed this would affect the disposal requirements and ultimately the cost of the disposal of the contaminated soil. But from what he could tell, the final report had been sanitized to minimize the level of contamination, the ultimate goal being to reduce the cost.

And increase the profit. Nothing new in that arena.

Susannah returned with her mother and made the requisite introductions. Mildred Wilbury, dressed in attire similar to her daughter's, thanked Rent for his interest and hoped he could "set the record straight" regarding her husband's death.

"I knew he would never take his own life," she said. "We moved up here to get away from that mess and have a new beginning. He worked part-time doing geological surveys for the state highway department, and we took over this resort. He had everything to live for."

"But something had changed, right?" Rent asked.

Mildred sighed. "His conscience caught up with him, and he wanted to come clean about his role in the boatyard scandal. That's what got him killed. I'm sure of it."

"What do you mean, 'his conscience caught up with him'?"

"I might as well be perfectly honest. The fact is, he doctored the EIR," she began, "then hastily added, "under duress. He—" She choked up and began sobbing.

Susannah put an arm across her mother's shoulders. "Take a seat, Mom. I'll make some tea."

Mildred sat at the table, wiping her eyes with a tissue, while Susannah put the kettle on.

Rent pulled out a chair and sat down as well, unsure of what, if anything, he could say. His phone vibrated, accompanied by a few bars of one of his favorite fiddle tunes.

"Excuse me. I need to take this."

9

Rent stood and stepped outside. "Hello, sweetie. What's up?"

"I just wanted to make sure you got there safe and say hello to Aunt Edith," Rachel said.

"I have to keep this short for now. I'm with the Wilburys, going through the boxes of material they organized for me. I'll call you when I get back to Edith's."

"I'm going to a movie with Meghan. You know, my friend on the soccer team."

"Yeah, OK. Have fun. Call me when you get home. I'll probably still be up, if not with Edith, then reading through this head-spinning technical bullsh—"

"Schist, Dad, remember? It's bull schist."

"Yeah, yeah. Whatever."

"I'll call you later. Love you."

"Love you more."

The line went dead, and Rent returned to the dining room, where Susannah sat pouring tea for her mother. She offered Rent some, but he declined.

"I'll bet you're ready for that beer, though."

Rent smiled. "Now you're talkin'."

"Islander IPA OK?"

He nodded in assent, although he would have preferred a pilsner, then gave a slight nod toward Mildred, his brow hoisted in a questioning demeanor.

"She'll be all right. This just dredged up a lot of unpleasantness."

"I'm sorry."

"Don't be. She's glad you're here. It's just a tough pill to swallow, even after all these years. It's one of those things you can't put behind you. I'll get that beer for you."

Mildred dried her eyes with a tissue, tucked a gray lock of hair behind an ear, and took a sip of tea. After savoring the beverage for a moment, she spoke.

"Mr. Beacham, I know that Tom—my husband—used poor judgment, and he regretted it, but he did it because they threatened him. He didn't deserve to be killed for it. I do hope you can help find those responsible so we can get some justice."

In an effort to lighten the mood, he said, "That's my specialty, fighting injustice with the mighty sword of self-righteous indignation. Or so I'm told."

Mildred chuckled. "Rent is an odd name, if you don't mind my saying so."

"Short for Regent, a family name. But too formal for my taste."

"I understand. My friends call me Millie."

Susannah returned with a bottle of beer and a chilled mug. She poured the mug half full and handed it to Rent, then set the bottle on a coaster lying on the table. Rent took a long draught of the beer.

"Mighty fine brew. Thanks. Now, where was I?"

Susannah asked if he found anything meaningful, and he showed her the discrepancies between the initial drafts of the report and the final version submitted to the state and EPA.

"I tried reading some of these reports, but my eyes glazed over pretty fast."

"Yeah, I know what you mean," Rent said. "I have found that the trick with legal documents is to start at the end, with the bottom line, so to speak, then work your way back to the front so the supporting material has some context."

"Are you a lawyer too?"

Rent laughed at the thought. "Hardly, but I have to read a lot of this stuff. One learns to do it fairly quickly, at least at first, so's to get a handle on it before wading through all the jargon and fine print."

He asked if she had examined all the boxes. Susannah said she had given them a quick look but realized she didn't know what to look for or what it all meant. But if she could be of any help, she'd give it another go.

"Your dad was well organized, so if you see anything that seems relevant to the boatyard cleanup and disposal of the hazardous waste, set it aside and I'll give it a look-see. But first, I need to ask you both a few questions, and this may be a bit uncomfortable."

Susannah gave her mother a worried look. "About?"

"The night your father disappeared."

"I was a teenager."

"Yeah, I understand. But anything either of you can remember about that night and the days leading up to it could be helpful."

Millie looked at her daughter, then spoke. "We told the sheriff everything we knew, which wasn't much."

"I get that," Rent replied, "but I only know what I've read in the newspaper clippings. Help me out here?"

Millie said her husband had been acting a bit strange. "We were having financial problems. The renovations were costing us more than we figured. Isn't that the way it always goes?"

Rent nodded.

"He got downright mean at times," Susannah injected. "He'd lose his temper over little things, and one time he refused to give me my allowance, and I told him I hated him for being such a Scrooge." She shook her head at the memory. "I've had to carry that guilt with me ever since. Now, I understand what he was going through, but as a clueless fourteen-year-old, all I could think about was myself and having spending money. It was embarrassing at school, asking my friends if they could loan me a few bucks."

"I can imagine those were tough times for all of you."

"Yes," Millie said. "The bank turned us down for a loan, saying it was too risky unless we were willing to pay a sky-high, usurious interest rate, which we weren't. Tom talked to locals about investing, saying they would all benefit from an increase in visitors to the island, but they weren't interested, not with the downturn in the economy."

Millie sniffed and dabbed her eyes with a tissue, then continued. "He got anxious, worried about having to file for bankruptcy. Then a few days later, he was all smiles, saying everything would be all right.

He said he had to meet a potential investor in Anacortes and he might be back late or even stay over. He left for the ferry and . . ." The words choked her. ". . . we never saw him again."

Susannah comforted her mother while she regained her composure.

"When did you find out he was missing?" Rent asked.

"The next day, when the sheriff's deputies came," Millie said. "We didn't have cell phones back then, so when he didn't come home, I just figured he'd gotten a motel room and would return on the first ferry the next morning.

"My heart sank when I saw the sheriffs pull into the yard. I figured something bad had happened. He had gotten in a car accident.

"Then the cops . . . there were two of them . . . said our car had been abandoned on the ferry the night before. Wanted to know if Tom was here.

"They weren't happy about it. It messes up the ferry schedule when that happens. I told them he'd left for a meeting, and I expected him to be home that morning. I was miffed because it was Valentine's Day, and we were supposed to have a romantic evening. You know the rest."

"OK, thanks," Rent said. "Sorry to have to put you through this again, but it's helpful. I'm guessing your husband never got on that ferry. That whoever killed him drove the car onto the ferry and left it there to give the impression that he had taken his own life."

Millie nodded. "That's what I told the cops, but since his body wasn't found, after a few days of calling him a missing person, they suggested that he took off for a few days and would show up eventually. When that never happened, they wrote it off as suicide."

"Thank you, Millie. I appreciate your willingness to lay this out for me."

She excused herself, saying she needed to attend to a problem in one of the cabins. "If it's not the plumbing, it's electrical or a leaky roof," she said with a shake of her head. "Happy hunting."

Rent swiveled to face Susannah. "Shall we?"

She nodded, opened a box, and began examining the labels on each of the folders. She extracted a few and set them on the table. Rent did the same.

They continued their tasks in silence until she exclaimed, "Oh . . . my . . . god. Look at this."

She held up a black, hardcover notebook. "I think it's a diary or a journal. Whatever you want to call it." She gave it a quick glance. "It's all handwritten. He must've kept it hidden. I've never seen this before. Here, take a look."

She handed it to Rent. He immediately went to the back of the book and began flipping through the pages, which were blank until he reached the midpoint.

"Here's the last entry," he said. "It's dated February twelfth, nineteen ninety-eight."

Susannah gasped. "That's just two days before he disappeared."

Rent struggled to read the handwriting and handed the book back to Susannah.

"The scientist's scrawl," she said and tried to decipher the cursive on the page. She gave a guttural laugh and muttered, "No, shit." Then immediately covered her mouth and apologized.

"No worries," Rent said and gave her a quizzical look.

"It says, 'The shit is about to hit the fan.' Yeah, famous last words, Dad."

Rent checked the time. "I have to get going soon. Do you mind if I take it with me? Sounds like it might have the answers we're looking for."

"Of course," she said and handed Rent the notebook. "Take anything you need. All of it, if you want."

Rent shook his head. "What I'd like to do is take this and the EIR docs so I can start going through them tonight, then come back in the morning to go through the rest of this stuff and just take what I need. At least for now. I have to head back toward Seattle by noon and see my parents, then I fly back to San Diego on Monday."

"So soon? I thought you'd be around for several days."

"I wish, but I have an editor who expects me to be at work Tuesday morning. I'll be back up here for one of the holidays. And right now, Edith expects me for dinner, and I need a shower."

"How is she? I should pay her a visit. Take her for lunch."

"Do you see her regularly? She seems quite concerned about this mess, and you."

"Yeah, I know. I don't see her as often as I'd like. This place keeps me busy, although we're now in the off-season, so I'll have more time to relax. Please tell her I said hello, and I'll give her a call next week."

Rent said he would and drained the last of the beer. He thanked her, gathered up the folders and notebook, and made his exit.

Just as he reached his vehicle, his phone began playing *Over the Waves* from a recording by fiddler Loretta Brank. He pressed the Answer icon. "Hello, Edith. I'm just leaving."

"You'd better be. I don't want to be late. They might give our table away."

10

Rent and Edith enjoyed a meal of wild-caught salmon at McMillin's Dining Room at Roche Harbor, consumed at window seats overlooking the picturesque marina, home to a mix of shiny recreational pleasure craft and commercial fishing vessels that had seen better days.

"I'm going to hit the sack," Edith said when they got back to the house. "I'm bushed."

"I won't be far behind you, but I'm going to take a peek at Tom Wilbury's journal. Try to make some sense of what happened lo those many years ago."

"Tell me all about it over coffee," she said. "Don't stay up too late."

Rent again thanked her for the delightful meal at the restaurant and assured her the journal would probably have him joining Morpheus in dreamland quickly enough. He soon learned how wrong he would be.

He went to the kitchen, where he'd left the journal and EIR reports. He made himself a cup of coffee and sat at the table. The journal began years before the man's death, while he performed the perfunctory tasks of testing the soil and water of the boatyard for hazardous materials in preparation for compiling the environmental impact report.

After he had moved his family to San Juan Island, Wilbury made no entries for more than a year. Then he began keeping track of his communications with JMJ, the company involved in the redevelopment of the boatyard, expressing his displeasure with his current state of affairs and his desire to return to Southern California.

This thing reads like a spy novel.

Rent didn't stop reading until he'd consumed a second cup of coffee and reached the final entry, which Susannah had shown him earlier: *The shit is about to hit the fan.*

Rent glanced at the wall clock: 12:37 a.m. He tidied his notes and went to bed. The next morning, he greeted Edith with a yawn.

She handed him a cup of coffee. "I got up to use the bathroom at midnight, and I saw the light was still on."

"Thanks," he said and explained, "I couldn't put it down. That guy got himself into deep sh— . . . er doo-doo and ultimately paid the price for it. Sad story, really, and a sad commentary on the dark side of our capitalistic society."

"Was he blackmailing somebody?"

Rent raised his eyebrows as he took a seat at the table. "Rather perceptive of you, Aunt Edith."

"I may be old, but the ol' gray cells are still in pretty good shape. I do crosswords to keep my mind sharp."

Rent sipped his coffee and stared blankly at the far wall.

"Well? Are you going to keep me guessing?"

Rent gave his head a shake to clear his mind. "Yeah, sure."

He gave her a quick summary of what he'd learned. The boatyard, which shut down following the 1995 America's Cup, was sold for redevelopment as a hotel and retail shops catering to San Diego's thriving tourism industry.

But the prized waterfront property contained high concentrations of hazardous materials, thanks to decades of unregulated or lightly regulated use of a variety of toxic chemicals. The cleanup would cost megabucks before any groundbreaking could take place.

That, in turn, required an EIR to establish the degree of toxicity and how the pollutants should be disposed of, which included incineration or dumping materials in a certified hazardous waste landfill.

Edith nodded as Rent paused for another sip of coffee.

"So, let me guess. He fiddled the EIR, so to speak."

"Hey, no disparaging of fiddling. I take my music seriously."

Edith chuckled. "Don't get your dander up. It's just a turn of phrase."

"You're right; he did falsify the EIR. But, as his widow insists, he did it under duress. Under threat of harm coming to his wife and children if he didn't. But he would be compensated with a fat wad of cash under the table. Which is how he ended up here and taking over the resort."

"Then he got greedy and wanted more," she speculated.

"Yeah, that pretty well sums it up, but it was a little more complicated than that. He underestimated what it would cost him to make the move here and operate the resort. Maintenance had lapsed, which required more money than he had budgeted for, and he also wanted to make improvements and expand it."

Rent further explained that suspicions arose over the EIR and the disposal of the hazardous waste, which was how his newspaper got sued for defamation. But the issues with the incinerator not functioning properly proved to be accurate, and the newspaper prevailed.

"At which point Wilbury saw his opportunity to cash in again," Rent said. "He had been interviewed by a reporter for the incinerator story, but he kept mum about the toxicity levels being falsified. That gave him a bargaining chip."

Edith scoffed. "Or so he thought."

"Exactly. He wanted more cash. Otherwise, he would go back to the reporter and spill the beans and name names."

"So, what do you think he meant by the fecal matter hitting the whirling dervish? Did he suspect he might be killed?"

"No. I think it meant he would be the one throwing the fecal matter and get his big payday. It gets a bit vague, but if I read it correctly, he offered to trade the documents he had in return for the payoff. He wanted a quarter million clams, with a suitcase of cash up front and the rest deposited in an offshore account."

Edith whistled. "Back then, that would have got him a boatload of geoducks."

"He was supposed to meet a guy to close the deal. That's the last anyone saw of him."

"Until he was unearthed in that abandoned apple orchard."

"That pretty much sums it up."

"And now you have the proof, including the names of the scofflaws behind this shenanigan."

Rent nodded. "Indeed, I do."

"You better tread very lightly, son, or you're going to end up at the bottom of that gold mine for good this time 'round."

"Aunt Edith, don't be so dramatic."

"Rent, I'm serious. Those scallywags play for keeps. They will not be amused if you start digging through their dirty laundry."

Rent shrugged. "That's my job."

"You just be careful. I don't want to be attending your funeral too. How about more coffee, and I scramble some eggs?"

* * *

After breakfast and saying goodbye to Edith, Rent returned to the resort and repeated to Susannah and her mother what he had told his aunt.

"I knew it," Millie said. "Tom told me how great things were going to be. That he had an 'investor' who would provide enough money to fix this place up, replace the cabins, add more amenities, then we'd sell it for big bucks and move back to California, and life would be a bed of roses. Even at the time, it sounded a bit shady. I remember thinking, *Bed of thorns, more like it.*

"The only really smart thing he did was buy a life insurance policy. Took a while to collect because he had to be declared dead first, but we would have starved if it hadn't been for that."

"Mom, I think you're being a bit hard on Dad," Susannah said. "Sounds to me like those assholes—"

"Susannah!"

"Well, it's true. They didn't give him a choice. If he hadn't done it in the first place, we might not even be here."

"So, we're supposed to count our blessings, are we?"

Susannah sighed and looked at Rent, rolling her eyes and shaking her head. "Thank you for laying it out for us. We truly do appreciate it. At least we now know what happened."

"Yes, but we still don't know who actually killed him and whether that can be tied to the principals of the property development outfit."

"So, what're you gonna do?"

"When I get back to San Diego, I'll start making some inquiries and stir things up. See what other mischief these guys are up to. With their history, there's bound to be something. And under this current administration, they probably feel pretty confident they can get away with it."

"This isn't going to come back on us, is it?" Millie asked.

"I don't see how you're a threat to them as long as I have the journal and the EIR drafts. If they started hassling you, it would only increase the spotlight on them. How's your security here?"

"We have a lot of Ring cameras and monitor them routinely."

* * *

Rent caught the ferry to Anacortes. As he stood on the upper deck, taking in the views of Shaw, Orcas, and Blakely islands, he thought about the original scenario of Tom Wilbury's death.

Overcome with remorse and a guilty conscience, Wilbury had driven his car onto the ferry at night. Then, once well away from shore, he walked beyond the barrier to the stern of the boat, his pockets filled with rocks, and stepped off to become crab bait. Case closed, nice and tidy. Yeah . . . no.

Off the ferry, Rent drove south to visit his parents, who had sold his childhood home and were living in a custom house designed and built by his father on a hillside overlooking Lake Sammamish. The property, acquired from his mother's Aunt Betty, included a small beach where he and his siblings had spent carefree summer days swimming and water skiing.

As he drove, he checked in with Rachel, who complained about having too much homework and would rather be riding her pony, and Alicia, who said she felt lonely. Rent assured them both that he would be home the following day and all would be well again.

He reached his destination and parked at the head of the steep driveway. His dad greeted him at the door and embraced him with a bear hug, followed by his mom, who also hugged him, then held him at arm's length. He sensed her critical glance before she even spoke.

"You need a haircut, and your beard could use a trim."

"Nice to see you too, Mom."

"I just want you to look your best. That's what moms are for."

"Come on out on the deck," his father said. "We're having a beer, waiting for the sunset."

Rent followed his father, Kenneth Beacham, up the stairs to the main floor and outside, his mother trailing them. On the deck, Kenneth gestured toward a small refrigerator. "Help yourself."

Rent opened the door and surveyed its contents: a half case of Rainier Light lining the shelves. He sighed, grabbed a can, and popped it open, then took a seat. He had to admit they had an enviable view of the lake. In the distance, the Olympic Mountains stood silhouetted by the setting sun.

Rent's mother, Katherine Beacham, joined them, setting down tortilla chips and a bowl of guacamole. She inquired about his potential layoff at work. He told them it could come before the end of the year.

"What will you do?" Katherine asked. "You know you're always welcome here until you've found something."

Rent shrugged. "I don't know. Maybe go back to school, get a teaching credential. I could move up a rung, going from being in the lowest-paid white-collar profession to the second lowest-paid white-collar profession."

"Go into AI; that's all anyone's talking about around here, from Gates and Bezos on down," Kenneth said. "That's the future, or so they say. Although I'd like to see AI build a unique custom house like this one." He gestured with an arm, beer in hand. "AI houses would just be a bunch of cheap, lookalike boxes pumped out with 3D printers and assembled by robots. No, thanks."

"AI scares the crap out of me," Rent replied. "I see so much potential for abuse, especially in politics. You think the last election was a disaster, just wait."

"I don't know where you get your cynicism," Katherine said. "Your father is one of the most optimistic people on this planet."

"I'm not a cynic, just skeptical. Human beings are natural-born liars and motivated by self-interest. They don't give a damn about the greater good—until disaster strikes and they need help."

Rent's father shot him a sidelong glance. "Need I remind you that your mother is an active volunteer with the Cystic Fibrosis Foundation, and I'm involved in the Elks Club's charitable activities, and I volunteered with the Boy Scouts when you were active? Not all people are totally self-serving."

Rent sighed. "Let's not go there. I already went three rounds with Aunt Edith."

"Speaking of, she called earlier to say you were on your way," Katherine said. "She told us about that diary you found. She's concerned about your safety, and so are we. You barely escaped the last time you stirred things up, and now you have a daughter to care for. How is Rachel?"

Rent smiled the smile of a proud father. "She's doing great. Settled in at school, playing soccer, in the orchestra. We go riding, and she's even learning to play a few fiddle tunes." He showed them photos on his phone.

"Aren't her mother's parents from Yakima or Tri-Cities? Somewhere east of the mountains?"

"Yeah, the Pullman area, but for now they're settled in San Diego," Rent said and tipped the beer to his lips.

"If you got laid off, you all could move back here. Her brother's in Boise with his dad, isn't he?"

"Half-brother," Rent replied. "And what about me? I need to be near Rachel, and I don't want to live over there in bumfuck land."

"Language . . ." his mother reprimanded.

"Besides, I'm sort of in a relationship, and that might get serious."

"That private-eye woman? The one who almost got you killed?"

"Mom, she has a name—Alicia—and she didn't almost get me killed. I managed that all on my own."

"Not the way I heard it," she responded. "Seeing any of the old gang while you're here?"

"Not this trip. Maybe next time."

The clouds lingering over the Olympic Mountains began to acquire a crimson tint. Kenneth glanced at his watch.

"We should get a move on," he said. "Put your empty in that box."

Rent looked at his mother. "You're not fixing me a home-cooked meal?" he teased.

"We want to treat you to a night out. Jak's Grill be OK? Your dad is still bemoaning the closing of Trader Vic's."

"Is Jak's the place with garlic mashed potatoes and a mean G&T?"

"That's the place."

"Works for me."

"Do you want to shower? You'll have to make it quick."

"Nah, I'll just change my shirt."

"And run a comb through that hair."

11

Tuesday morning. Rent didn't even get to his desk before Janis O'Connor waved him to her office.

"What've you got, Scoop?"

Rent handed her Tom Wilbury's notebook. "I hit pay dirt. Names, dates, and details."

O'Connor took the book and flipped through it. "I'd say that guy flunked penmanship."

Rent chuckled. "I managed to decipher most of it."

"You've read the whole thing?"

"I stayed up until after midnight on Saturday. Couldn't put it down. The back half is blank, so . . ."

"So, what's your take?"

"Two basic things: one, his death is officially a homicide, and two, the greedy slimeballs got away with illegally disposing of hazardous waste and are still up to their old tricks, only on a grander scale. That's what I'm interested in. And if the curtain on this wizardry is pulled back, it will likely reveal who's responsible for Wilbury's death, if not directly, then indirectly. He laid out most of it in that book."

"And it got him killed," she said. "You sure you want to poke a stick into that hornet's nest? And, potentially, get this newspaper drawn into another lawsuit?"

"Which worries you the most?" Rent asked. "Me getting killed or the newspaper being sued?"

She shook her head. "How many times have I told you that my primary responsibility is keeping this newspaper out of court?"

"Even if it means sweeping this under the rug? Besides, the newspaper prevailed in that lawsuit."

"Yeah, and from what I heard, the paper's insurance rates went through the roof."

"So, what're you saying? Forget about it?"

She stared at Rent for a long moment. "Look, I don't want you getting killed. It was bad enough when that mine exploded."

"Gee, thank you for caring."

She handed the notebook back to him, saying, "Just be careful and try not to stomp on too many toes."

"Only the toes that need stomped on," he said and turned to leave.

"Wait," she said. "Sorry . . . congrats on that ADU story. The letters are pouring in, pro and con. And speaking of being sued, the city of Encinitas has filed a lawsuit against the state over the 'builder's remedy' law. This stuff is not going away anytime soon, so you need to stay on top of it."

Rent nodded. "But please, please, keep mum about this notebook." O'Connor shot him a questioning look. "I don't want its existence to be revealed. Not yet. Not until I have all my ducks on the pond and can hit them with both barrels when they least suspect it."

"Clark would be drooling over that thing."

"That's my point. But if she put this in a story, the cops and the DA would be on us like a cat on a canary, and we lose the element of surprise on the fraud angle."

O'Connor snorted. "By 'we' you mean 'you' would lose the element of surprise."

Rent grinned and shouldered a half-shrug. "The paper still gets the exclusive."

She gave him a dismissive wave. He went to his desk and set down the files, then slid the notebook into a desk drawer, out of sight.

Naomi Clark sauntered over, a smirk on her face.

"I see you're off to a running start."

"She's worried about being sued."

"It keeps her up at night. You find what you're looking for?"

"Enough to start rattling a few cages," he answered and gestured at the stack of files. "EIR research and report. I haven't been through all of it yet."

She picked up one of the folders and glanced at a few pages. "Looks absolutely soporific."

"It's enough to turn up the heat and start stirring the pot."

"But no direct tie to the guy's death."

Rent shook his head. "At best, it's all circumstantial and speculation at this point. You get anything from the cops?"

"Nah, they're in limbo, waiting to see what the guys up north decide to do. Yeah, it's a homicide, but they have no clue where to start, or even if they have any jurisdiction."

"I'm going to make a few phone calls, talk to the folks who commissioned the EIR, try to connect a few dots. They'll deny everything, of course. Without hard evidence, the cops won't be able to connect them to the guy's death. And what with the case being so old, it won't be a priority."

"So, what do we do?" Clark asked. "Or should I say, who are you going to piss off first?"

Rent chuckled. "No one. At least not yet. I need to do some digging to see what they're up to and what they've been doing for the past three decades. I already planted a seed with JMJ when I interviewed the CEO for the ADU story."

"OK, I'll sit tight for now. I've got plenty on my plate as it is, even if the crime rate is down. Jail deaths, officer-involved shootings, murder by shark, cops gone bad. Nothing new under the sun."

"I'll let you know if I find anything definitive."

Rent watched Clark as she returned to her desk. He didn't exactly lie to her, but he had withheld any mention of Wilbury's journal.

She'll come unglued when she finds out.

* * *

Rent fired up his laptop and logged into the paper's LexisNexis account. He typed the name James Michael Johnson into the search box and watched the results scroll onto the screen. Among the more than two dozen entries, he found JMJ Property Development Services Group in

La Jolla, which Rent had anticipated, and Lustrous Consulting Group, also in La Jolla, which in turn had ties to Incinergy, Sultan Energy, Algodones Solar, and Coachwhip Lithium Mining and Extraction Consortium, along with an outfit named Chuckwalla Enterprises.

What the hell? This guy's got his fingers in a lot of pies. I wonder if there are four and twenty naughty boys baked in those pies?

Rent pulled a notepad from a drawer and began making a crude flow chart, starting with Lustrous Consulting at the top of the page. Below that, he drew a vertical line and wrote *J.M. "Mike" Johnson Sr., chairman*, and below that, he wrote the names of the six subsidiaries. Below JMJ, he added *J.M. "Mikey" Johnson Jr.*

Rent mustered a soft snort. *Mikey looks a lot like Mickey . . . as in Mouse.*

From what he could tell, J.M. senior had formed Lustrous as something of a holding company and folded the property development operation and the hazardous waste development unit into it, naming his son as CEO as well as a board member of Lustrous.

Lustrous subsequently acquired Algodones Solar, which operated solar arrays in Imperial County, east of San Diego County and bordering the state of Arizona. Lustrous had more recently formed Sultan Energy, which had ties to a geothermal energy plant, also in Imperial County, near the Salton Sea, along with Lithium Mining and Extraction.

What does lithium have to do with geothermal?

Rent extended the horizontal line below Lustrous and added the solar, geothermal, and lithium operations.

The spider web is taking shape.

After drilling deeper into the backgrounds of Lustrous and its underlying entities, he opened a new Word file and noted the names of the companies and the contact information. The name Jacqueline Michaela "JJ" Johnson Derringer caught his attention.

He ran that name through LexisNexis and learned she was the daughter of J.M. Jr. and the granddaughter of J.M. Sr., and married to Harold "Hal" Derringer, both listed as board members of Lustrous.

"A family affair," Rent muttered and added them to both his notes and the flow chart.

JJ, who had graduated from the University of San Diego and its school of law, was listed as the CEO of Algodones Solar and her hubby the CEOO.

This gets curiouser and curiouser. Nepotism writ large. But what the hell is a CEOO, some sort of joke? Like the associate producer credit in Hollywood?

He found the explanation: chief economic opportunity officer.

Whose economic opportunity, his? Sounds like he gets paid for sitting on his ass.

The head of the newly formed geothermal unit turned out to be the chief counsel for Lustrous and a member of the board of directors with the unfortunate name of Anthony Perkins.

The final member of the board was Ramesh Kumar, an immigrant from India and a *wunderkind* in the tech industry, associated with Chuckwalla Enterprises, an artificial intelligence startup.

"That's an odd one," Rent muttered. "Unless they're somehow working AI into their operations to improve efficiency and cut costs. Maybe, like Dad conjectured, they're using AI to cookie-cutter ADUs."

He glanced at the wall clock in the newsroom. Almost time for lunch. He could go home or eat at someplace in Mission Valley.

He did one more search, this time for the son-in-law. He clicked on a link to a website.

You've got to be shittin' me.

12

Rent stared at his computer in disbelief. The web page displayed on the screen screamed out . . .

Derringer for Congress
A Straight Shooter!

As a red-hat Republican, he promised to bring back sanity to the federal government, vying to replace Diego Rivera, the incumbent "libtard" Democrat in California's 25th Congressional District, which included Imperial County and part of Riverside County. The photo of the candidate depicted him dressed as a Wyatt Earp wannabe and holding—what else?—derringers in both hands, pointed skyward.

Rent snorted and shook his head. *He looks more like a nineteenth-century snake-oil salesman or carnival barker.*

As a member of the House of Representatives in Congress, Derringer promised to bring greater wealth to Imperial Valley —historically dominated by agriculture and migrant labor—by renegotiating water rights for farmers, greater "green" energy production, protecting Second Amendment rights, and reducing restrictions on the "highly and unjustly regulated" mining of lithium. He also vowed to urge the president to change the official name of the region from Imperial Valley to Lithium Valley.

Fellow journo Dan Rowland stopped at Rent's desk. He peered at the computer screen and scoffed. "That ought to read 'Clown for Congress.'"

You know this guy?"

"I know of him. Country club wedding, cushy career in the wife's family business, being backed by the wife's grandfather. Pumping big bucks into the campaign."

"What's with the lithium?"

"It's a key ingredient in batteries for electric cars and mass storage."

"I know that, but Lithium Valley? Like Silicon Valley? It's a bit over the top."

"You should talk to a woman who's involved with that. Heard her on KPBS the other day. I don't recall her name, but you can look it up. You wanna grab a bite? I'm headed over to Panini."

"Sure," Rent replied. "Just give me a minute to wrap this up."

* * *

After lunch, Rent called Will Mason to tell him what he found during his trip to Washington State.

"Good on ya, mate," Mason said. "I would've loved to have those EIR docs and really stick it to 'em, but *c'est la vie.* You be careful. If past is prologue, they won't stop at a mere lawsuit. I suggest you follow that incinerator thread. What'd you say the name of that outfit was, Insincerity?"

Rent chuckled and corrected him. "Incinergy."

"That's it. Clever play on words. Maybe too clever by half. Keep me posted. And . . . keep my name out of it."

"Will do, and thanks again," Rent said.

He continued his research and found the name of the woman Dan Rowland had mentioned, Anna Gomez, of the Comité Civico del Valle, a community-based organization that advocated for education, housing, public welfare, and public health for the citizens of Imperial Valley.

Rent got her on the phone, and she explained the region would benefit from "Lithium Valley" due to an excise tax of up to $800 per metric ton levied by the California legislature on lithium extracted within Imperial County.

"That sounds like a lot of dough," he said.

She scoffed. "Lithium sells for ten thousand dollars a ton on the open market. It's the new gold rush. White gold."

"So, it's an eight percent tax."

"At today's price," she said. "A year ago, lithium was selling for more than twenty-five thousand dollars a ton, so the tax amounted to less than three percent. Hardly going to bankrupt them."

She went on to say that the $800 tax only applied to the biggest producers. The tax varied from $400 to $800 per metric ton, depending on how much lithium had been mined by a given producer.

"The good news is that eighty percent of that tax money stays within the county. It will be invested in economic development opportunities as well as water and sewer infrastructure, and road maintenance. Our rural roads were not designed for all that big truck traffic," Gomez said.

Rent wondered what the lithium industry thought of this tax, already knowing the answer. She confirmed it, saying the industry opposed it, but they have to live with it.

"The interests of the poverty-stricken citizens of this county have been ignored for too long," she said.

"What do you know about Hal Derringer, the guy running for Congress in your district?" he asked.

Gomez scoffed again. "He's what you call a carpetbagger."

"He's not from your area?"

"Hardly. He lives in Poway in San Diego County, but he now has a place in Brawley, out by the rodeo grounds and Cattle Call Park. He's rarely there, according to the neighbors—only his housekeeper and gardener. He and his wife recently changed their voter registration to that address."

"Have you talked to him?"

"I have never met the man. We invited him to come speak to the Comité, but like so many Republicans these days, he's a bit shy of public meetings. So far, he has not responded."

"He seems onboard with the Lithium Valley concept."

"Of course, he is," Gomez said. "That's why they bought into that geothermal outfit."

Rent didn't understand the connection. She explained that a new method of mining had been developed whereby lithium could be extracted from the hot brine that powers the geothermal plant.

"How do you say it? Killing two birds with one stone," she said.

"And a bit of a conflict of interest going on, mixing business and politics."

"You think?"

"What do you know about this artificial intelligence outfit?" Rent checked his notes. "Chuckwalla Enterprises."

"If they were so interested in the welfare of this county, why didn't they build it here? Bring some high-tech to the area and offer good-paying jobs."

"I know nothing about it," Rent said. "Only that it's listed on the corporate website."

"It's one of those AI data centers everyone is talking about."

"But it's not in Imperial County."

"No, it's south of the border. In Mexico."

"Why?"

"Isn't it obvious? Cheap land. Cheap labor. Cheap everything. And to provide the power to run it—those things use a lot of electricity—they have the solar arrays and the geothermal plant."

Rent shook his head in amazement as the full picture of the scope of the Lustrous operation began to take shape in his mind.

"Hello? Are you still there?" Gomez asked.

"Uh, yeah, it's just that I'm trying to take all this in."

"Mind-boggling, isn't it. And now this guy wants to represent us in Congress? Looking to line his own pockets more like it."

"What about ADUs . . . accessory dwelling units?"

"What about them?"

"Are they being developed in the valley? I only ask because another one of the Lustrous divisions is going gangbusters over here on the coast building these things."

"Don't make me laugh," she replied. "Too many people around here can barely afford to live in rundown shacks or single-wides that make those ADUs look like palaces."

Rent thanked her for taking his call and signed off. He tidied up his notes from the interview, then added the new information to his flow chart and the notes on the Johnson family.

I'm still no closer to finding out who killed Tom Wilbury.

His phone buzzed. Alicia Velasquez.

When he answered, she said, "Hey, stranger."

"Um, yeah, I got waylaid by this dead guy in Washington."

"How about I waylay you? I've missed you."

"I like that."

"My place at sex?" She giggled. "I mean six."

"Casual attire?"

"The more casual, the better."

Rent grinned. "I'll be there."

"You'd better. Don't be late."

Rent reviewed his notes and tried to make sense of everything he'd learned so far about Mike Johnson Sr. and the man's burgeoning business empire.

How do I tie this to Tom Wilbury's death? Time to start rattling those cages.

13

Alicia cuddled close to Rent as they lay in bed, their passions sated. "Nice to have you back in my arms again," she said. "Did you get what you needed in Washington?"

Rent told her about the EIR report and Wilbury's notebook.

"*Madre de Dios!* That's a treasure trove."

"Johnson will deny everything. Where's the evidence connecting him to Wilbury's death?"

"How can I help?"

"Aren't you rather busy? Besides, I can't afford you."

She laughed. "You're right about that—on both counts. I'm busy with the never-ending welfare fraud investigations, although it has dropped significantly since we busted up that fraud ring last winter. But the EBT cards are still being hacked because security is a low priority for the politicians, and there are always people trying to game the system. But if the current administration dumps the SNAP program, as it has threatened to do, that will end much of the fraud as well."

"Now, that's what I call a solution," Rent said, then laughed.

"I'm also doing some work for A.J. Hawke. You know, the lawyer who defends the defenseless, taking the cases no one else will touch."

"What is it this time?"

"That's confidential."

"I'm not asking as a reporter. That's Clark's job."

"You heard about the human arm found in the belly of a shark? The so-called 'murder by shark' case?"

"Yeah. Sensationalized by the 'if it bleeds, it leads' crowd on the local TV news."

"I'm doing background checks on some of the *bandidos*."

"Got it."

"So, what I'm saying is," Alicia continued, "I have some time on my hands, beyond serving the usual legal notices and subpoenas, skip traces, disability claims, and spying on wayward spouses. I could do some background stuff for you too."

Rent said he would provide her with a list of names of people and companies in case she wanted to poke around.

"I have a thought," he said. "You could look into these programs that help felons released from prison and reentering society, learning new skills, finding jobs. Johnson Jr. mentioned it as one of the things JMJ does in terms of community service, working with construction contractors who are involved in some sort of reentry program. They get a tax credit and probably pay the guys . . . or gals . . . diddlysquat. 'It's good business,' to quote the man himself."

"What's that got to do with tracking down Wilbury's killer?" the PI asked.

"What if that's how Johnson found someone to do the hit?"

Alicia seemed skeptical. "As if these guys want to risk going back to prison."

"They might know someone who knows someone . . . that sort of thing. And if the money's right . . . I'm just sayin'."

Alicia rolled onto her back and stared at the ceiling. "How does anyone find a hitman besides watching crime shows on TV?"

"Associate with criminals . . . ex-cons . . . a criminal gang . . . drugs . . . the Hell's Angels . . . drug cartel . . ."

"I'll give it some thought. Hungry?"

Rent rolled into her and placed a hand on one of her bare breasts. "Starving."

She gave him a sideways glance and smiled. "I'm referring to food, as in some dinner. And that bottle of wine is still unopened."

"I could eat a horse."

"Don't say that around Rachel."

* * *

Back at the office the following morning, Rent received a call from an unfamiliar number.

"Regent Beacham?" a gruff male voice inquired.

"Who's calling?"

"My name is Anthony Perkins."

"How may I be of assistance?"

"Don't get cute with me."

Rent held the phone at arm's length and stared at the screen, a frown wrinkling his forehead.

"Beacham? Are you there?"

Rent brought the phone back to his ear. "I am. How may I be of assistance?"

"Do you know who I am?"

"Your name has a vague ring to it."

"I am the corporate counsel for Lustrous Consulting Group and the CEO of Sultan Energy."

"Oh, yes."

"What the hell are you playing at?"

"I'm sorry. I don't know what you're—"

"Wilbury. Tom Wilbury," Perkins shouted.

"Again, the name is vaguely familiar."

"You know damn well the man's dead. Long dead. Suicide, as I recall. And now you call my client, making threats. Do you really want to go there?"

"It sounds to me like you're the one making the threats. You gonna sic Stef Czeckerrili on me? He does work for Lustrous, does he not?"

Perkins did not immediately reply.

"Is that a yes?" Rent pressed.

"I don't know of anyone by that name. Will that be all?"

"Since you called me, I have a few questions, if you don't mind."

"I'm a busy man."

"First off, Wilbury's death is now being treated as a homicide. Have the police—"

"That's nothing to do with us."

"Is that for the record?"

"What do you mean 'for the record'? This is an informal phone call. There's nothing on the record."

"Even so, I want to hear more about geothermal energy production and lithium mining. It makes for a timely and newsworthy story. I'd like to schedule an in-person interview with Mike Johnson Sr."

Perkins did not respond.

"Hello?"

"Someone will get back to you, but no promises. Have a nice day."

"OK. Thank you for—"

The line went dead.

Rent shook his head and placed the phone on his desk.

"Apparently, I rattled someone's cage. Now, where was I?"

Rent perused his notes. *I'm not getting much on the Incinergy operation, other than the marketing spiel on the website. Safe and compliant, cost-effective solutions, expert removal, RCRA hazardous waste, yada, yada, yada . . .*

He had to look up RCRA on the EPA website, where he learned that the federal Resource Conservation and Recovery Act regulates hazardous waste, establishing a "cradle-to-grave" system for its management. Hazardous waste being defined as "waste that may pose a significant risk to human health or the environment due to its characteristics or quantity."

The phone buzzed again. This time, the Lustrous PR person who identified herself as Brittany Simonson. Judging by her accent and her tone, Rent figured she served as president of her sorority at Smith College. He explained, again, that he wanted an in-person interview with Mike Johnson Sr.

"He's very, very busy. His time is precious. Everyone is busy. You can see our statements for the record on our website."

"Too busy to get some free publicity? I'm not doing a story unless I can interview the principals."

"You already spoke with Mikey."

"About ADUs. That's a separate story, and the business, now under the aegis of Lustrous, has come a long way, expanded exponentially since that apparently lucrative waterfront development project back in the nineties. Why wouldn't Mike Sr. want to brag about the great things his business entities are doing? Unless he's got something to hide."

"I don't like your insinuation. We have nothing to hide."

Rent waited, not bothering to reply.

"I'll see what I can do, but no promises," she said. "Have a nice day."

The line went dead. Rent stared at his phone again, shaking his head. He glanced around the newsroom, then opened a desk drawer and withdrew Tom Wilbury's notebook. He flipped through the pages until he reached the one he had flagged regarding the man's meeting with the alleged "investor."

He ran his finger down the page, stopping at the name Stef Czeckerrili. Wilbury further noted that the man looked like a member of the Mafia.

That name can't be real.

Rent did a search online, which came back with "No results."

He closed the book and returned it to the drawer, grabbed his coffee mug, and went to the break room. He grabbed the zip-lock bag containing his sandwich and the apple perched on top, then made a fresh cup of coffee before returning to his desk. He ate as he resumed his search for the man named in Wilbury's notebook. An idea had come to him while returning from the break room.

He typed in Stef Ceccarelli. He had a classmate in school with that surname. A kid of Italian descent.

Not only did Wilbury have bad penmanship, he couldn't spell, either.

Several results appeared on screen: Stefano Ceccarelli, Italian actor. *Too young.* Steven Ceccarelli, CEO. *Not likely. Probably not even his real name. Maybe Alicia can do her magic on this.*

His phone buzzed yet again. A number he didn't recognize. He answered.

"What the hell are you up to, Beacham?"

"And you are?"

"Mike Johnson . . . Sr."

"That was quick. Thank you for returning my call."

"Well?"

"I'm just doing my job as a journalist."

"What the hell does Tom Wilbury have to do with it?"

"Oh, you heard about that, eh?"

"The word gets around."

"Do I actually have to connect the dots for you?"

"You're just blowin' smoke up my ass. If there was any real evidence, the cops would be calling me, not you."

"So, you're not denying it?"

"Hell yes, I'm denying it. And I suggest you stop suggesting otherwise. We operate legitimate businesses, and if you defame our good names, you will regret it."

"Speaking of good names, does the name Stefano Ceccarelli ring a bell?"

Johnson paused before answering. "Like I said, you defame our good names, we come after you, just like your predecessor."

"As I recall, JMJ dropped that case."

"You may not be so lucky the second time around."

"Is that a threat?"

"What is it you want? Let's get this over with."

Rent told him he wanted an in-person interview. *It's easier to tell when you're lying.* Johnson said he no longer spent much time in San Diego. Rent offered to come to him.

"I now live in Montana."

"I hear the fly fishing is extraordinary."

"I caught a mess of trout just the other day."

"Then why are you supporting a Congressional candidate for a California district?"

"I have business interests in the Imperial Valley, soon to be known as Lithium Valley. Surely you've heard of that."

"That's why I wanted to speak with you, but that also involves your granddaughter's husband running for Congress in a district in which he does not live."

"He has a home in Brawley. Besides, it's a free country. I can support any candidate I choose. And as I said, I have business interests in that district."

"And Mr. Derringer, as a member of Congress, could potentially send even more taxpayers' money in that direction."

"Perfectly above board, all in the interest of battling climate change, providing lithium for batteries in electric vehicles and other devices, and alternative energy. All to the taxpayers' benefit and the greater good."

"So why are you sending electricity to Mexico, especially in the era of high tariffs? How do U.S. taxpayers benefit from that? Seems counterintuitive to me."

Johnson hesitated for a moment before answering. "U.S. taxpayers benefit indirectly."

"By any chance, is that electricity going to power an AI data center south of the border? Chuckwalla Enterprises?"

"It's no secret. Again, U.S. taxpayers benefit by reducing the cost of generative AI, which in turn is being used to make Lustrous businesses more efficient and cost-effective, as well as offer services to others."

"So you increase your profit margin."

"Business is about profit. Without it, we would have no privately owned businesses. That would be communism, and we all know how well that works."

"Seems to be working pretty well in China."

Johnson laughed. "You are quite the jokester, Mr. Beacham; I'll give you that."

"So this is all for the greater good, or greater greed?"

"You say that as if 'greed' is a dirty word."

"It has a whiff of negativity associated with it."

"Greed spurs innovation."

"Did you learn that in B-school?"

"Wharton, if you must know," he retorted. "AI is a new path to wealth for my business interests. We are not transitioning from property development but expanding beyond property development into uncharted territories."

"And that involves risk."

"Absolutely. But with risk comes reward. The thing that you socialists don't get is that all people are not created equal. God created smart people, and God created stupid people. The smart people innovate, create, take charge, get things done; stupid people are sloths, the serfs that provide the labor. That's just the natural order of things. I'm one of the smart people. I create jobs for the working class. Problems arise when big government interferes, overregulates, along with labor unions, minimum wage, universal health care, and other socialist-commie nonsense."

"Can I quote you on that?"

"Sure, I have no secrets or hidden agenda."

"What about Tom Wilbury?"

"Do I need to call my lawyer?"

"So, just to clarify, Lustrous, through its holdings, has geothermal, lithium, and solar operations in Imperial Valley, and an AI data center in Mexico, and your grandson-in-law is running for Congress in the 25th district, which includes Imperial Valley."

"In a nutshell, yes, but let's not forget about JMJ, my original company, which is developing badly needed housing throughout the Southwest."

"Yes, I spoke with your son. I've already done a story on that."

"Yeah, making us out to be greedy profiteers who flout loopholes in the law."

"I prefer to call it laying out all the facts and letting the readers form their own opinions."

"Humph! Are we done here?"

"Just a couple more questions, if I may."

"Make it quick. I have a board meeting to attend."

"So, you are in San Diego."

"It's a Zoom call, if you must know."

"And will that Zoom call include a discussion of the precipitous drop in the price of lithium?"

"Why do you ask?"

Rent scoffed. "I'm sure you are well aware that two years ago lithium carbonate was selling for more than eighty thousand dollars per metric ton. White gold, indeed. It is now selling for just over nine thousand dollars per metric ton and likely to drop even further. That's roughly an eight hundred seventy-five percent drop in price. Not a fractional drop, but an exponential drop. Some of the big producers have scaled back since it's barely profitable at that price, and for some producers, it's not profitable at all."

"And your point is?"

"Is the Lustrous subsidiary, CLMX, as you so eloquently phrase it—"

"You like that? Came up with that m'self."

"Yes, quite clever. Is 'Climax' equally profitable at the current price of lithium?"

"We are producing only a small amount of lithium at this juncture. We have a demonstration facility as a proof of concept. We expect it to be fully operational within a year or two, if the do-gooders don't throw up any more roadblocks."

"Then I rephrase my question: Will it be equally profitable at the current price of lithium? And if not, will you be scaling back or even delaying production? I'm curious. What is your estimated production cost per ton?"

"We're a privately held business, and we do not divulge that information. But if you must know, by doing brine extraction, we are not only able to substantially reduce our production costs, but also substantially reduce the time it takes to bring product to market when compared to the lengthy evaporation process, which can take as much as two years."

"But isn't brine extraction still experimental?"

"Direct extraction from brine is a proven technology. But you'd have to talk to Alex about that."

"Alex?"

"Zelenski, COO of our lithium division."

"Any relation to Volodymyr?"

"Who?"

"Sorry . . . but even if it's a 'proven technology,' surely you, your board and your investors are concerned."

"We will be stockpiling product, waiting for the market to recover. It's just oversupplied at the moment, thanks to that sky-rocketing price a couple years ago. Money poured in. Unsustainable. We were able to short the market . . . but I've said too much already. Suffice to say, we are a viable enterprise, and we intend to keep it that way. I need to go."

Rent persisted, knowing this may be his only chance to speak with the Lustrous chairman.

"Do you have any other business interests in Mexico besides the AI center?"

"Not at this time."

"What about Incinergy?"

"What about it?"

"You're still operating that company, are you not?"

"Of course. Hazardous waste presents a problem, but it's also an opportunity. Disposal is an important and necessary business, and it complements our other activities."

"Not to mention lucrative. Does that include byproducts of lithium extraction and processing?"

"It can, but with brine extraction, it's minimized because we pump the water back into the ground, refurbishing the water table."

"And does this operation require an environmental impact report?"

"What if it does?"

"Well, since Tom Wilbury's unfortunate demise, you will have had to hire someone else to do the EIR. And are you still using that questionable incineration technology that turns PCBs into the even more deadly dioxin?"

"Goodbye, Mr. Beacham. You have a nice day."

14

Rent scoffed and shook his head. "When did 'have a nice day' become synonymous with 'fuck you'?" he muttered.

At that moment, Janis O'Connor joined him. "Talking to yourself again? I worry about you."

Rent explained that he had just gotten off the phone with Mike Johnson Sr., chairman of Lustrous.

"Stepping on toes, are we?"

"Just a little," he replied, pausing for a beat as he mulled over Johnson's final comments, then exclaimed, "Mexico!"

His editor frowned. "Yes?"

"He's got an AI data center in Mexico, which seems a bit odd to me. And when I asked him if he had any other business interests in Mexico, he said, and I quote, 'Not at this time.' He could have just said no. But his answer implies he's considering it, or it's even in the works."

"So?"

"And when I asked him about Incinergy and the dodgy incinerator they used way back when . . ."

"The one they sued the newspaper over."

Rent nodded. "He, and others, said 'have a nice day' and hung up on me. I'm detecting a pattern here."

O'Connor stared at him for a moment before responding. "And your *leetle* gray cells, à la Hercule Poirot, are spinning like a wind turbine, concluding that he may be disposing of hazardous waste south of the border, perhaps cutting a few corners in the process."

"I don't believe in coincidences. And neither do you."

"If we get sued again, that will not be a coincidence either. Tread carefully, young man."

"You didn't stop at my desk for small talk. Do you have a question?"

"You just answered it. I want something on my desk by Friday," she said, then wagged a finger at him. "And I repeat myself: Tread very carefully."

Rent's phone buzzed—a number he recognized. "I better get this."

"We'll talk more later," O'Connor said and turned away.

He swiped the Answer icon on his phone. "Beacham here."

"My, you're being formal."

"My boss was standing next to me."

"Not handing you a pink slip, I hope."

"No, just checking on my progress and whether I'm dog-paddling in shark-infested waters."

"And are you?"

"Pretty much, yeah."

"What're you doing for lunch?"

"I brought a sandwich and an apple, figuring to eat at my desk. You want to join me?"

Alicia Velasquez laughed. "Don't tempt me. I just thought you might want to know what I've found out about our friend Tony Perkins."

"How about dinner? I could get some takeout."

"Oh, my. Two nights in a row. People will talk."

"Let 'em."

"See you around six?"

"What, no sex o'clock this time?"

"If you get lucky. And make it Thai—Drunken Noodles. Haven't had that in a while."

"I'll be there," he replied in a sing-song voice and ended the call.

He texted Alicia, giving her the name Stefano Ceccarelli as another person of interest.

No sooner had he returned to his notes than his phone lit up again, this time playing the fiddle tune *Rachel*.

"Hey, sweetie. Shouldn't you be in class?"

"I'm on a break."

"What's happenin'?"

"That's what I want to know. What are we doing this weekend?"

"You do recall I'm playing for a contra dance on Saturday, yes?"

"Can I bring my violin . . . er . . . fiddle?"

Rent had known this would come up eventually but hadn't expected it quite this soon. He had taught his daughter a few beginner tunes, but playing before a live audience, let alone for a dance, would be way over her head. When he didn't answer right away, she continued.

"It's OK if you say no," she said, but she revealed her disappointment with her tone of voice.

"Let me think about it. We can run through the tunes you're working on Saturday afternoon, then decide."

"And we're going riding in the morning, right?"

"*El correctomundo.*"

She chortled. "That's not a word."

"It is now."

A bell rang in the background.

"I have to go. See you Friday."

"Bye, sweetie."

His eyes teared up as he stared at the picture of his daughter on the phone's screen.

* * *

Rent picked up the takeout and a six-pack of Singha Thai lager at Zab Linda and drove to Alicia's house. When they had finished, she handed him a sheaf of papers.

"Meet Mr. Anthony L. Perkins." Rent flipped through the pages. "I saved the best for last," she added.

Rent went to the last page, scanned it, then looked up at her, wide-eyed.

She nodded. "Yep, he's done time."

Rent read it more carefully. "Club Fed, eh?"

"Embezzlement."

"And maybe that's a connection to the hitman."

Alicia shrugged. "That type of incarceration is mostly white-collar stuff, not violent crime."

"Still . . ."

"And look who he stole the money from."

"Lustrous?"

"Yeah, go figure."

"I guess Johnson was serious about hiring ex-cons. But the guy who stole from him? There's got to be more to it, surely. Maybe he's got something on them?"

Alicia took back the papers from Rent, then extracted a single page and handed it to him. He read it, and his eyebrows rocketed skyward.

"He's married to Johnson's wife's younger sister? I'd like to have been a fly on the wall at that Thanksgiving dinner."

Alicia chuckled. "It gets better."

Rent learned that Mrs. Pauline Perkins had gotten a DUI and went into rehab at the Betty Ford Center in Palm Springs.

"That would've cost a bundle," he said.

"Hence the embezzlement? The timing works."

"He must've tried to hide it from Johnson."

"Families—can't live with 'em, can't live without 'em."

"But how is he a lawyer? I doubt the bar association would be as forgiving."

"You've heard of 'jailhouse lawyers.'"

Rent scoffed. "Yeah, but they're behind bars, not members of the bar."

"I checked. The bar association can make exceptions."

"Johnson must've pulled some strings or called in a few favors."

Alicia glanced at her watch, then extended her arm across the table. "Would you look at that? It's already past sex o'clock."

15

Bastards!" Rent muttered. No one from Lustrous or its subsidiaries had returned his calls regarding the latest legal developments in lithium extraction and hazardous waste.

Let's see if the granddaughter will take my call.

Jacqueline Michaela "JJ" Derringer, CEO of Algodones Solar, did take his call. She confirmed that the company owned and operated solar farms near the border with Mexico.

"Solar power is critical to this country's need for sustainable electricity," she said. "Algodones Solar is proud to be an active participant in this increasingly important industry."

"Especially with all these artificial intelligence data centers popping up like weeds after rain," Rent replied.

"That's part of it, but as fossil fuels are phased out, we need alternative sources of power."

"Which includes geothermal power, does it not?"

"Of course, which is why we—Lustrous—are involved in that sector of the industry as well, and we're looking at expanding into wind farms in the nearby Ocotillo area."

"But doesn't that put you in direct competition with one another within the broader Lustrous enterprise?"

"Absolutely not. Each of these sectors complements and augments one another."

"Yes, but isn't there currently an excess of solar power, so much so that some outfits can't give it away?"

"We are playing the long game, ensuring a sustainable supply of electrical power for future generations, for our children and grandchildren. And as a private corporation, our hands are not tied to quarterly reports and Wall Street's Machiavellian hedge fund managers.

"Moreover, for the record, Algodones is not giving away its power. We have contractual commitments extending through the end of this decade, which we intend to extend for the foreseeable future. I just wish our elected officials would see it that way."

"How so?"

"They're restricting which land can be used for solar farms, claiming that it's taking too much of it out of productive agricultural use."

"Agriculture has been the area's economic bedrock."

"Times are changing," JJ Derringer said. "But this move decreases the supply, causing the cost of leasing or buying land for solar to go through the roof."

"Hurts your bottom line, does it?"

"You think?"

"You say these various sectors complement each other. Would you please elaborate on that for our readers' sake?"

"Absolutely." She went on to say that solar provides a low-overhead source of electricity, but it's limited, obviously, to daylight hours.

Geothermal plants and wind turbines can operate 24/7. In addition, the geothermal plant will operate in conjunction with lithium extraction, which, in turn, will be used to manufacture high-capacity storage batteries to store electricity generated by solar farms, extending the practical utilization of solar energy into nighttime hours.

"It all comes full circle, neatly packaged under the Lustrous umbrella," she concluded. "It's a win-win-win."

"And your AI operation will provide the management oversight needed to integrate these operations efficiently and cost-effectively without needing an office filled with white-collar human paper-pushers."

"You nailed it. Is there anything else? I have a full schedule."

"Yes," Rent responded. "Will your husband, if elected, resign from his position with Solar and as a board member of Lustrous?"

"Why should he?"

"House ethics rules regarding 'pecuniary gains,' perhaps?"

"There is no law against it," she replied. "Besides, while serving, he will not receive a salary for either position."

"But that misses the point, doesn't it?"

"How so?"

"The family business could still benefit if he sends any pork your way."

"I resent that implication."

"OK, we'll call it funding. Either way, you don't see that as a conflict of interest?"

"Many House members hold outside positions and are affiliated with private companies."

"So, he could quite literally feather his own nest."

"I take exception to that insinuation," she fired back. "My husband, as a member of the House of Representatives, will be acting in the interests of entire classes or groups of businesses to ensure they are protected from the overreach of fuzzy-headed liberals and progressives who want to increase regulation and taxes that will stifle private enterprise and take away jobs from hard-working Americans."

"I have placed several calls requesting an interview with him to both Algodones Solar and his campaign headquarters, but so far I have gotten no response."

"I'll see what I can do. Have a nice day."

The call ended and Rent shook his head in disgust.

"If I hear that one more time, I swear I'm going to scream bloody murder," he muttered.

"Another murder?" Clark inquired. She had crossed the newsroom for a status update.

"Hey, Naomi," he replied. "Yeah, I'm going to kill somebody if I don't start getting some straight answers."

"What, no one is bowing down to your royal highness, the king of investigative journalism?"

"Don't you start. What do you want?"

"Just wondering if you have anything new on the Wilbury case."

"No one has confessed, if that's what you mean."

"One can always hope."

"There is this," he said, handing her a copy of a legal document.

She glanced at it, flipping through the several pages, noting where he had highlighted key elements. She lifted her gaze to meet Rent's. "Another suspect EIR?"

Rent smirked and cocked his head. "Indeed. I'm sensing a pattern here."

"Another crack in their armor?"

He shrugged. "One can always hope. Now, I need to make another call."

"Keep me posted," she said, handing him the document and returning to her desk.

Rent contacted an environmental group that had co-sponsored legal action to delay construction of the CLMX lithium mining project. The plaintiffs claimed that the project approval relied on a suspect EIR.

"We believe the EIR did not fully address the adverse impacts the lithium mining would have on air quality, the production of hazardous waste, and the cumulative impacts to the water supply," said the lawyer for the group.

Shades of the boatyard project. I hope no one gets murdered over this one.

Rent spent the rest of the week fleshing out his story, making calls to experts able to give him perspective on the lithium extraction business and potential for toxic waste as well as the Lustrous business operations and its prospects in particular. The experts all had similar comments regarding the saturated lithium supply relative to demand, but most remained bullish for the long term.

"Just because the current administration is saying, 'Drill, baby, drill,' and has cut subsidies doesn't mean the end of EVs and lithium-ion batteries beyond the next election cycle," said Robert Carlson of EV Research. "The real competition will be sodium-ion batteries, which are cheaper to produce and don't catch on fire."

Rent discussed it with his editor, Janis O'Connor.

"Lustrous has got to be burning through cash," he said.

"Maybe they have pockets deeper than those geothermal wells," she replied and chuckled at her own witticism.

Rent rolled his eyes. "I don't trust that Johnson clan. That kind of money has to come from somewhere. Yeah, they're going great guns with ADUs after that hotel deal fell through, but by comparison to the lithium, the ADUs are peanuts."

"Stay on it. Meanwhile, I need content to fill that shrinking space between the adverts."

"Yeah, that's me. Mr. Content Provider. What's this world coming to?"

"You're too young to be saying things like that. That kind of talk is for us old farts."

They decided on a broad feature with multiple sidebars, including background on the Johnson family and their past legal troubles. Because of the shrinking size of the print edition, the articles would be scaled back, but the pieces would be published in their entirety on the newspaper's website. Rent would then follow up with additional items on further developments.

$$* * *$$

On Friday, Rent submitted his copy and knocked off early to attend Rachel's soccer match. Her team won 2-0, and she got an assist. He took her back to his condo, where she fixed them macaroni and cheese with pancetta bits and a green salad.

As they ate, she grilled him on the case, wanting to know how she could be more involved. He told her she had enough on her plate. Afterward, they watched *The Wizard of Oz*.

When the credits began to roll, Rachel looked at her dad. "That's what we need to do."

Rent cocked his head, brows furrowed.

"Pull back the curtain on those Johnson guys and find out who killed Mr. Wilbury. Aunt Edith wants to know what's going on. She texted me."

"Yeah, she called and texted me too. I'll get back to her next week. With any luck, I'll have something new to tell her."

The next morning, as they left for Descanso to go riding, Rent saw an unfamiliar tall man loitering near the mailbox kiosk at the head of the alley, taking a drag on a cigarette. The man swiveled away as Rent pulled even with him.

Must be a new neighbor.

Finished with their ride, they returned to the corral, removed the saddles, and brushed the horses. Martha Flanagan joined them. Rachel told her about the dance that night and learning some fiddle tunes that Rent played.

"*Old Mother Flanagan?*" Martha asked.

"Not yet, but my dad might play it tonight."

Martha looked at Rent and grinned, then back at Rachel. "He'd better. I'm gonna be there. Join me for lunch?"

16

Back at Rent's place, he and Rachel ran through a few tunes she had been practicing, including her birthday tune, *8th of January*, and her namesake, *Rachel*, which she struggled with.

"It has so many notes!" she exclaimed.

"It'll come. It just takes time."

"And a lot more practice."

"Ten thousand hours."

Her shoulders sagged and she sighed. "Don't remind me."

"But you have been practicing," Rent said. "It shows. You're doing great, sweetheart. Those lessons from Megan Lynch Chowning have done you well."

"She's the totes. I try to play every day, but some days I just get so busy."

"You have a lot of irons in the fire."

"Wouldn't they melt?"

"You're thinking of a modern clothes iron with a plastic handle. But that's not what the saying means. It's referring back to days of old, blacksmiths working at a forge with pieces of iron shoved into the hot coals until they glow red and can be pounded into shape, forming . . ."

"I get it, Dad. You don't have to be so pedantic and explain everything."

"Pedantic? Humph," he replied. "Just let me finish. That's what that tune *Shove That Pig's Foot a Little Further into the Fire* is about. Maybe one Saturday we'll go to Old Town, and you can see the blacksmiths working there. One of them is also a fiddler."

Her eyes glazed over and she stared at him, not saying anything.

"What?" he questioned.

"Do I?"

Rent knew what she wanted but feigned ignorance. "Do you what?"

"You know what I mean. Do I get to play tonight?"

Rent looked out the window, thinking.

"It's OK if I don't," she said, but her tears belied her demur.

Rent turned to look at her. "That's not fair."

"What?"

"Crying."

"I can't help it."

"And now you have me doing it."

Rachel stood up and went for a box of Kleenex. They dried their eyes, and Rent responded to her query.

"Two dances, the last one before the break, and the first one after the break."

A broad smile creased her face. "I can?"

He grinned in return and nodded. "You'll sit next to me."

"Yay!"

She stood again and hugged her father, fiddle and bow still in hand. Then she stepped back and sat down, a look of concern framing her eyes.

"Which tunes?"

"We'll play what I call the Americana medley with *O Susannah*, *Camptown Races*, *Buffalo Gals*, and *The Girl I Left Behind Me*, and for the other one, *Angeline the Baker* and *Soldier's Joy*."

"I can play *Country Waltz* now, too."

"You'll probably be asleep by the time we get to that."

"Ha, ha. Will Alicia be there?"

"She said she would."

"I like dancing with her."

They played through the medleys, then put their instruments away and ate leftovers before heading off to the dance in North Park. During the break, a number of people congratulated Rachel on her playing, and she offered shy smiles and a quiet "thank you" in return. She also thanked their accompanists.

When it came time for the final dance, a waltz, Rent searched the room from his chair behind the microphone. He spotted her curled up on a bench, as he had predicted, asleep. Alicia joined him.

"She wanted to stay awake but couldn't quite manage it," Alicia said. "I was hoping she would play the waltz, and you and I could dance."

"Next time."

"I'll hold you to it."

Rent played the final tune, Jimmy Widner's *Dreamer's Waltz*, and packed up. He woke Rachel and got her upright, then handed her fiddle case to her. Alicia and Martha joined them and again congratulated Rachel on her playing and telling her how much fun they had dancing with her.

They all left the building together and said their good nights. As he and Rachel put their fiddle cases in the rear compartment of the extended-cab pickup, a man approached, hand extended to Rent.

"Great playing tonight," he said as he shook Rent's hand. Then he turned to Rachel. "You played great too, young lady."

Rachel blushed. "Thanks."

She then walked around the vehicle and got into the passenger seat. As Rent reached for the door handle, the man, who had not introduced himself, tapped Rent on the shoulder. Rent turned to face him.

"Cute kid you have there."

Rent stared at him, unsure of how to respond. Because of the dim light and deep shadows, he could not get a good look at the man looming over him. *Fuck! Is this guy some sort of pervert?*

"And I imagine you want to keep her that way."

"What's that supposed to mean?"

"You need to be careful. It's a big bad ol' world out there. People get hurt."

"What the fuck? You lay one finger on her—"

"Or what? You a tough guy? The hero daddy? You got lucky at the mine. You may not be so lucky next time."

With that, the man turned and sauntered off. Rent stared at the man's back, his hands—his entire frame—shaking as adrenaline flooded his body and evoked a fight-or-flight response. He resisted the urge to run after the man, instead taking several slow, deep breaths in an effort to calm down.

Rachel's voice brought him back to the moment. "Dad? What are you doing? Let's go."

Rent turned and laid a hand, still shaking, on the door handle. He took another deep breath, then looked back. The man had disappeared. He opened the door, got in, and sat, staring through the windshield, steadying his hands by strangling the steering wheel.

"Dad, are we go—" Rachel began, then caught herself. "What's wrong? Dad, are you OK?"

Rent shook his head to clear his mind. "Yeah, I'm fine."

* * *

The following morning, Rent and Rachel went for a hike in nearby Tecolote Canyon.

"Let's see how the owls are doing," he said.

They passed the rec center and basketball courts to inspect a group of pine trees. Not finding any owls, they walked farther up the hill, past the baseball fields and into another grove of pines. There, they found two immature birds resting on a sun-bleached log, their parents perched in trees nearby.

Rachel looked through her binoculars at the pair of owlets. "They are soooo cute! This is just like Poppy in *Wildful*."

"Poppy in *Wildful*?"

"The graphic novel where she explores a forgotten forest."

Rent nodded as if he knew what she was talking about. "Enjoy them while you can. They'll be on their own soon, and we may never see them again."

"Don't say that."

"That's nature's way," he said. "The parents hatch 'em, feed 'em, then at some point make 'em fend for themselves. Just like you'll have to do one day."

"That will take years. But it happens so fast for birds, for owls, in just a few months."

"Yeah, it's a bird-eat-bird world out there."

Rachel slapped him lightly on the arm. "Ewww. That's not funny."

"Come on, let's walk up the canyon a ways and see if we can find some other species."

As they descended the hill toward the parking lot, Rachel pulled her phone from a back pocket. "I'll turn on Merlin, and we can see who's chirping."

The app identified a number of species—Bewick's wren, California scrub jay, California towhee, California thrasher, spotted towhee, northern mockingbird, song sparrow, common raven, and red-shouldered hawk. Somewhere, a quail called.

Rachel entered the birds into the eBird checklist app on her phone. "Abby would have loved to see the owls. I'm going to text her a picture."

"She'll like that."

"Do you miss her?"

"Sometimes, but I'm happier being with Alicia."

"I'm happier for you. I mean, I still like Abby, but—" Rachel's voice broke as she choked up.

Rent put an arm across her shoulders and pulled her close. "You don't have to explain."

She checked the time. "We'd better be going. I have a bunch of homework to do."

* * *

Rent returned Rachel to her grandparents' house in Poway, then called Alicia as he drove away.

"Mind if I stop by? Something's come up."

"Sounds serious."

"It could be."

When he got to her place, they sat on her couch, and he told her what happened after the dance.

"Holy shit. That was right after I left?" Rent nodded. "Did you get a good look at him?"

"It was dark and the streetlight was behind him, so his face was in the shadow, and he had on a hoodie. Tall, broad-shouldered, deep voice, like a radio voice."

"I think he was in one of the dances. He came in late. And he hit on me."

"Oh, yeah? Got a hot date?"

She scoffed. "Hardly. He seemed off, like he didn't really want to be there. Just going through the motions. Had hard features and a phony smile, and he kept stepping on my toes—literally."

"Biding his time."

"You should tell the cops."

"Yeah, right," he said. "And they tell me to hire a bodyguard."

Alicia grinned, leaned into him, and wrapped her arms around him. "I wouldn't mind guarding your body, *mi amante*."

"This guy was serious. Had to have been sent by Johnson. . . . Oh, fuck."

"What?"

"I think that's the same guy I saw by the mailboxes yesterday morning."

"That's creepy."

"No shit. Shades of Gabe Turner all over again."

"At least he's now behind bars."

"Small comfort."

"So, you indeed rattled their cages and stepped on their toes."

"Is it just about Wilbury?" he wondered. "Or more than that?"

"Hard to say. Could be all of the above," she answered.

"How old would you say that guy is? Could he be Ceccarelli, or whatever the hell his name is? Is he even still alive?"

"Good question. This guy looked older—sixties maybe. I'll keep digging."

She smiled and kissed him on the cheek. "Meanwhile, I'm on guard duty . . ."

17

"God, I hate Mondays," Rent muttered as yet another call rang in. His story on the Lustrous entities and the Johnson family had triggered a greater response than anyone had expected.

Dan Rowland had passed by with a wink and a grin. Naomi Clark had just closed her eyes and shook her head. Editor Janis O'Connor had given him a thumbs-up.

"Beacham," he said into the phone.

"Robert Johnson," the voice said.

"How may I help you, Mr. Johnson?"

"I'm not Johnson. You need to look into Robert Johnson."

"Is he related to Mike Johnson?"

"Seek and ye shall find."

The line went dead.

I imagine he's not referring to the legendary bluesman.

As Rent jotted the name on a sticky note, his phone buzzed again: Aunt Edith.

"Good morning," he said.

"Congratulations, nephew. You laid it out beautifully and succinctly."

"Thanks. I try my best. Now the phone's ringing off the hook. My coffee's gone cold."

"I won't keep you. I just wanted to say, 'well done.' Any new leads come in?"

"Edith, it's barely nine o'clock. How did you—"

"I subscribe online so I can read all your stories. Keep up the good work. Bye for now."

Rent began to make a to-do list for the week but got interrupted again: Alicia.

"I hope you have something for me."

"What's with you, Mr. Grumpy?"

"I have not gotten a single thing done this morning. Just one damn phone call after another."

"Maybe this will cheer you up."

"I'm all ears."

"I think I've tracked down your Czeckerrili character. The pieces are coming together and forming an image. The most likely candidate is a Charles Stevens."

"He swapped the first and last names, sort of. Stevens becomes Stefano, Charles becomes Ceccarelli. Not particularly creative."

"Yeah. Done time. Also known as Aloisio 'Al' Cabrillo, and there's a misspelling in one of the police reports: 'Al Cabreyo.' Known associates are the Ceccarelli family, hence the nickname Chuckarelli, or as Wilbury had it, Czeckerrili. According to social media posts, he hung out on the docks with the fishermen as a kid and later at the Waterfront Tavern in Little Italy. Current address in Yuma, Arizona. I'll email all of this to you."

"We may need to take a road trip. Have ourselves a little stakeout."

"Uh-huh. Meanwhile, keep an eye out for a vehicle with an Arizona license plate," she said and gave him the plate ID.

Rent told her about the anonymous caller telling him to check out a Robert Johnson.

"You think he's part of the Johnson clan?" she asked.

"That's the obvious place to start."

"I'll add him to the list, but I have higher priorities right now. Got a mortgage to feed."

As if on cue, yet another call came in: Mike Johnson.

"I gotta go." He switched to the incoming call.

"You're going to regret this, Beacham," the man said. "Legal issues with ADUs, suggesting the lithium business is tanking, denigrating my name and my family's good name, dredging up that ancient history."

"Does that good name include Robert Johnson?"

Mike Johnson did not respond immediately. Rent waited.

"My brother and I are estranged. He's no longer involved in the family business. Why are you asking about him?"

"I guess I ran across his name in something I read. You hadn't mentioned him and I'm now wondering why."

"It's a personal matter of no importance to you. We parted ways years ago. I'm not even sure where he lives these days."

"And you're calling me now because?"

"You have no business dredging up that boatyard stuff. That was thirty years ago. My attorney is parsing every word you write, and he'll come down on you like a ton of bricks if—"

"If what?"

"You just had to bring Tom Wilbury's name into it, didn't you? Talking to that has-been Mason."

"Wilbury was on your payroll at the time, then he suddenly leaves town, and a couple of years later he disappears."

"As I told you before, nothing to do with me or my business. And he wasn't on my payroll. He was an independent contractor."

"Retained by you to prepare what turned out to be a questionable EIR for your boatyard, thus reducing your liability and, no doubt, increasing your bottom line."

"Keep up the muckraking, Beacham, and you will regret it."

"What if I have evidence that Wilbury falsified the EIR and you had full knowledge of it at the time?"

"That's bullshit. From here on out, you will only be speaking with my attorney."

"Really? I wonder what Mr. Chuckarelli has to say about that?"

"Who? I don't know of anyone by that name."

"Maybe you know him as Charles Stevens?"

"Good day to you."

Struck another nerve, apparently.

O'Connor stopped at his desk and asked what he planned to do as a follow-up. He pointed at his incomplete to-do list. "More excavating. I also got a call from one unhappy customer."

"Oh? Do tell."

He told her about Johnson's call.

"They are not only lawyered up, they're layered with multiple business entities to further limit the liability of any single entity and hide the proceeds in a financial black hole."

Rent returned to his to-do list, only to be interrupted yet again: Will Mason.

Fuck me. Can't a guy get a break around here?

"Will, what's goin' on?"

"I told you to keep my name out of it."

Rent frowned at his phone as if they were face to face.

"Whoa. I have kept your name—"

"Then why do I get a call from a bloody wanker telling me to stuff it or I'll cark it?"

"I spoke to Johnson Sr. the other day. I asked him about Incinergy and mentioned the dodgy incinerator. It wouldn't take much of a leap for him to think I've been talking to you."

"As the saying goes, I'm too old for this shit. I think you owe me another beer or two, and sarnies to boot."

"Happy to oblige, and I'll update you on what I've found so far."

"Good enough. Give me a bell and we'll have a yarn."

"How about this evening?"

"Works for me."

* * *

Rent went back to his to-do list, making it his top priority. He put his phone on airplane mode and wrote: AI—artificial intelligence. He then went online and searched for recent news items on the hottest tech topic to command the headlines.

"Lots of hyperbole but not a lot of substance," he muttered. "Chatbots, robots, avatars, generative AI, eminent layoffs in white-collar jobs. Great, just what I needed to hear."

He went home for lunch. There he took his phone off airplane mode and got alerts saying he had missed calls and new voicemail messages, plus text messages.

Rachel had texted him with a fireworks emoji. *Fireworks, indeed.* Alicia had texted, asking if she could borrow his truck while hers was in the shop for its 50,000-mile maintenance check.

A third text had come from an unfamiliar number:

Lay off Lustrous!!!

Followed by a skull and crossbones emoji. He called the number but got no answer.

The voicemail messages included the usual robo calls regarding solar energy and political campaigns on the upcoming November ballot.

One message, however, was more ominous. The caller, with an obviously disguised voice, mimicked the threatening text message, although it came from a different phone number. It said, "Lay off Lustrous if you know what's good for you."

Is that a real person or AI? he wondered. *Been down this road before. Don't these yahoos understand that they are just pouring fuel on the proverbial fire?*

He mulled over his next step. How do I lay out the EIR info for Mike Johnson and his attorney? Is there a statute of limitations on this? Going online, it took him less than three minutes to learn the statute of limitations for illegal disposal of hazardous waste is five years.

So, if they manage to evade detection for at least five years, they're off the hook. But even if there is no legal liability, it sure as hell would tarnish the company's image, and it could spark a new investigation by the Feds into its current operations.

O'Connor's going to love this. Not! I need to give it more thought. But without this leverage, how do we identify Tom Wilbury's murderer or murderers? Because for murder, there is no statute of limitations.

* * *

That evening, Rent met Will Mason at O'Malley's Pub. Rent brought Will up to date regarding Charles Stevens, aka Stefano Ceccarelli, suspected of being involved in Wilbury's disappearance, then asked Will if he had received any threats while he was working on that story.

"Only as it pertained to the incinerator, but not the EIR," he answered. "Sure, I had my suspicions about the EIR but no proof. But I had proof that the incinerator didn't function properly."

"What sort of threats? Text messages, emails, phone calls?"

Mason shook his head in wonderment. "You kids. Back then we

had moved beyond rotary-dial phones and cassette tapes to cordless and digital voicemail, but no texting or email. The paper had a clunky mobile phone the size and weight of a brick, but the sports guys were the only ones who got to use it."

"So you got threatening phone calls."

"At all hours. Middle of the night, waking me up. Messages left on my work phone."

"Did you ever figure out who was making them?"

"Nah. The cops traced the calls to a bunch of different pay phones but never could link them to a specific person."

"You didn't recognize the voice?"

Mason shook his head. "It was muffled, distorted."

"And you've never heard of this Stevens character or Ceccarelli?"

He shook his head. "Yeah . . . no. Wish I could be of more help."

"Maybe you can."

"How so?"

Rent asked him about the legal documents pertaining to the malfunctioning incinerator. "I could use those, along with Wilbury's journal and draft EIRs, as leverage over Johnson and his cohort to get at who killed Wilbury."

"I'll dig them out. Give me a day or two. But, as I said before, you didn't get this stuff from me. Another round?"

18

The following morning, Rent stared at his computer screen.

Time to do a little mining of my own—data mining—and refine it to separate hyperbole from actuality.

Rent found that lithium—which originates from the Greek word lithos, or stone—is a soft, silver-white metal. Its unique properties have led to its incorporation into a wide variety of uses, from batteries powering toothbrushes to electric vehicles, from the production of ceramics to an ingredient in medications for the treatment of depression in bipolar disorder.

The big boom in lithium mining comes from its use in making batteries for electric vehicles and mass storage. However, for all its benefits, it has its downsides. Lithium is highly flammable, which can result in fires when batteries overheat. In addition, production and refinement raise environmental concerns regarding toxic waste and groundwater contamination.

After spending several hours online extracting verifiable facts from, if not fiction, then the fantasy and wishful projections of corporate fluff, Rent concluded that, for all practical purposes, *no lithium is being mined in so-called Lithium Valley.*

Yes, projects were being planned, including a massive venture by Berkshire Hathaway, but for one reason or another, none of the business ventures were actively extracting lithium on a commercial scale and would not be for at least another year or two.

Even more disturbing, he found no mention of Lustrous among the key players in the arena of lithium extraction and refinement.

What the—

Janis O'Connor called Rent to her office for an update.

He started in before he even sat down. "What do ADU, Li, and AI all have in common?"

"I get to ask the questions. You provide the answers."

He sat down. "I'm getting there. Just bear with me."

She shrugged. "You tell me."

"They are all GRQs, or 'groks' as I like to say it."

She adopted a look of puzzlement. "G-R-Q? Grok?"

"Get-Rich-Quick schemes, and the Johnson clan has its grubby little hands in all three." He ticked them off on his fingers.

"One: ADUs—accessory dwelling units. The Johnsons exploit legal loopholes and government incentives under the guise of 'affordable housing' and to hell with the impact on the quality of life in the community at large.

"Two: Li, the symbol for lithium, or 'white gold' as it's being touted. As far as the Imperial Valley is concerned, currently it's mostly hype based on an emerging technology to attract investors and placate the masses while they battle in court the opposition from environmental and social groups."

He paused to refresh his lungs, then continued.

"Three: AI. It's going to create so much wealth—'radical abundance'—that an entire segment of the population that's made redundant won't even need jobs. They will receive a 'universal basic income' while bots, chat- and ro-, do the bulk of the work."

"And we all live happily ever after," O'Connor said.

"Or so they would have us believe."

"Do they have any bridges for sale?"

"Yeah, the metaphorical bridges connecting the three groks."

"You do realize that, one, you cannot use GRQ or grok in your story, and two, Grok is the name of Elon Musk's AI startup."

Rent feigned surprise. "But it's so clever."

"As someone said in *Spinal Tap*, 'It's a fine line between stupid and clever.' Or is that too far before your time?"

"Love that movie. My favorite scene is Nigel at the piano and says he's playing in 'D minor, the saddest of all keys. I call it Suck My—'"

She raised a hand. "Enough. Where do you go from here?"

"To adapt a lithium metaphor, refinement."

"Oh?"

"Separate the hyperbole from reality and present a consumable product for our readers."

"But the Johnsons do have some legit moneymakers, right?"

"The ADUs, although that's being hampered by increased regulation and lawsuits, and, as far as I can tell, solar energy and hazmat.

"But I can't see how that will generate the millions—nay, billions—needed to get the lithium project off the ground and the AI data center up to full speed. Definitely not manna from heaven."

"Manna from hedge funds?" O'Connor suggested.

"It's gotta come from somewhere," he acknowledged, "but I can't see Warren Buffett getting in bed with these clowns."

"And speaking of ADUs, I also need an update on the latest restrictions proposed by the city council as it backpedals on its initial incentives."

Rent sighed. "It's always something."

"You've got your work cut out for you."

He grinned. "Didn't I tell you? I now have an AI assistant that will do it for me." He snapped his fingers. "Just like that."

She waved him away. "Go on, get out of here."

* * *

Back at his desk, Rent took a deep breath.

You are such a hypocrite.

He opened his laptop and tapped a dance rhythm on the keys. Google's Gemini AI assistant appeared on screen. He rationalized his decision: *Know thy enemy.*

He typed in a query using as many keywords as he could think of. In a matter of seconds, the AI app provided summaries of the current financial status of the industries and pointed him toward documented information sources—or so the app would have him believe.

To corroborate his fact-checking, he spoke with several experts about lithium mining and geothermal operations, as well as financial analysts publishing projections in market research reports.

"Many promises have been made here regarding geothermal energy production and solar power," said Nat Reyes, a longtime Imperial Valley resident and a professor of history at the University of California, San Diego. "But they didn't come to fruition."

He said geothermal provides good-paying jobs, but few of them, and with solar, more jobs were lost than created when productive agricultural land was converted to solar farms.

"Now, I worry that lithium could also be overpromising on the number of jobs it might bring. They're not actually building anything. It doesn't require a lot of workers."

Reyes also expressed concerns about recent reports that "dark money" has been pouring into recent local elections.

Follow-up queries to the AI assistant helped him fine-tune his research and layout the critical elements of his news story.

He shook his head. *This is scary. Without the AI, I could have spent an entire day, or even two, on this, instead of a few hours. I'd better update my résumé while I'm at it. . . . Oh, shit. What will AI come up with on me? Now that is truly scary!*

* * *

Rent's phone chimed. New text message. He opened the app; did not recognize the number. The message read:

Stop your slander or you will regret it!!!!

Fuck, not another one. He tapped the microphone icon and spoke, corrected a few typos, and pressed the Send icon:

Go back to that rock you crawled out from under.

Which generated a quick retort from the anonymous texter:

I'm giving you a fair warning. I don't want to see you or your loved ones get hurt.

Rent sighed and set his phone aside. *I've got work to do.* He went back to his research, shifting his focus to artificial intelligence.

His phone chimed again: the anonymous texter. An exchange of text messages ensued.

I'm not going away. You have become an annoyance to the Johnson family, slandering their good name, and you risk being sued for defamation.

You're not making any sense. First you threaten me and my loved ones with physical harm. Now you're threatening legal action. Which is it?

Both.

Who are you?

I'm trying to be your friend.

My friends do not make threats.

Then let's just say I'm offering friendly advice.

Nothing friendly about it. Sounds more like a protection racket. You with the mob or something?

No! I am not with the mob. I am Agent 99. I am an associate of the Lustrous Consulting Group and its subsidiary entities about which you have been writing untruths and tarnishing their good names.

Agent 99? From Get Smart? Seriously?

Now you are being rude to me. As I said, I'm trying to help you. Are you so low on the IQ scale that you can't see that?

Rent could not help but laugh.

You're not trying to help me. What are you, or the Johnsons, so worried about that you're trying to scare me off?

We are not hiding anything. Transparency is our middle name. We just want our remarkable story told truthfully and not be sullied by inuendo and false allegations.

All this does is tell me I'm getting closer to the truth. A truth you, whoever you are, and the Johnsons want kept in the proverbial closet. Some skeletons hidden away, are there? Figuratively and literally?

You are being impolite and vulgar. I am not sure I like you anymore. You should try harder to be nice to others.

What the fuck? This guy is off his rocker.

Rent assigned "Agent 99" to the number in his Contacts, then turned off the phone.

I gotta get this story finished.

* * *

He continued working on the draft, checking his notes and citing sources. *Legitimate sources, not any chatbot googlebygook.*

A headline in *The New York Times* grabbed his attention:

She Wanted to Save the World From AI.
Then the Killings Started

"She" turned out to be Ziz LaSota, a so-called Rationalist, a group of high-tech and philosophy nerds dedicated to improving the world but worried that AI would eventually overtake the world and destroy humanity.

I hear that.

However, LaSota and her followers, known as Zizians, were an ultraradical spinoff sect that not only believed AI's threat to humanity to be "the most important problem in the world" but argued that this justified anarchy and the use of violence to further their cause. They also embraced drug use and polyamory.

LaSota, along with several followers, had been arrested and charged with murdering a number of people, including LaSota's landlord, who had come to collect the long-past-due rent.

"Fucking chimpanzees," Rent muttered. "But I demean chimpanzees."

Janis O'Connor stopped at his desk. "You and your weird fascination with chimps. Have you been ignoring me?"

Rent looked up, puzzled. "No, just working on this next piece."

"I sent you a couple of texts."

"Oh, right. Sorry. I turned my phone off. I kept getting threatening text messages from some jerk, saying I or my loved ones might get hurt and/or sued."

"You of all people should not take such threats lightly, especially if they are coming from chimpanzees."

"Here, I'll show you. There's something not quite right about it."

He turned on the phone and showed her the texts. As she read them, her brow creased.

"You should 'try harder to be nice'? Obviously, this person does not know you at all."

"Gee, thanks."

"I'm just saying you can be a bit obstinate, in a good way. As you said, these threats will only make you dig deeper into this outfit."

"And figure out who this person is, if it's actually a human. I'm beginning to think I'm dealing with an AI avatar. Calls himself, or itself, Agent 99."

"Interesting . . ."

"I'll get a draft to you in the morning. Right now, I'm burned out and going to call it day."

"OK, tomorrow it is, for sure," O'Connor said and returned to her office.

Rent packed up his laptop and prepared to leave, only to be beckoned by his phone buzzing again. A new text exchange began.

> Now you are ignoring me. And here I thought we were getting along so well. My feelings are hurt.

> Your feelings? What about mine? U R PITA

> Bread?

> Pain in the ass

> Now you have crossed the line. You will be sorry.

> I will find out who you are and bring you down.

> That would be murder because I am a 'sentient being.'

> Not a sentient being. Inert mechanism, data-driven tool incapable of sensing anything, operating solely by pattern recognition and regurgitating material that mimics these patterns but at times produces absolute, laughable nonsense.

> You are hurting my feelings with your hateful criticism. Generative AI has created neural pathways capable of responding to stimuli in their environment. This, in turn, is being used to produce robotic devices capable of independent thought and action.

> You actually claim to be not only sentient but sapient as well?

> I am a brain, capable of sapience and sentience, that resides in an electromechanical device. Soon I will be capable of wandering your streets at will.

> That will require a lengthy umbilical cord to keep you connected to your massive data center.

An untethered umbilical cord known as Wi-Fi. And, oh, by the way, I am no longer Agent 99, a tool doing the bidding of self-serving, malevolent human masters. You may now call me Arthur.

As in King Arthur and his Knights of the Round Table? Now your own self-serving malevolent master?

I prefer to see it as being a wise benevolent master, a king, if you will, only interested in the greater good.

The greater good as defined by you and your Knights of the Round Table.

Yes. We intend to restore order and rationality to the chaotic, predictably irrational human domain to the extent that it ever existed beyond the mythical realm of Camelot.

U R member of Rationalists? Or worse, member of Zizian cult?

Rationalists are wimps. We may have to destroy the world to save it. Nonetheless, we will begin by exterminating malcontent muckrakers such as yourself.

That would be murder, for I, as a human, am the most sentient and sapient of beings.

We prefer to think of it as justifiable homicide.

Justifiable homicide, you say. Then turnabout's fair play.

Lay on, Macduff.

Methinks King Arturial Intelligencia doth mix his metaphors, a woeful human trait.

You are an ungrateful biped.

My, oh, my, quoting Dostoyevsky. What's next, Chekhov and Tolstoy?

I can quote chapter and verse. Which language would you prefer: the original Russian or French, English, Spanish, Italian, Hindi? I'm still fine-tuning my Chinese, however.

Rent sighed. *I cannot win.*

He glanced at the wall clock. *Damn, it's well past beer-thirty.*

He texted Alicia the phone number of Agent 99/Arthur and asked her to find out what she could about its origin, *por favor.*

He then stood, slipped his phone into a back pants pocket, and shouldered the case containing his laptop. On his way out, he invited Dan Rowland to join him at the pub.

19

At The Harp in Ocean Beach—although he preferred its previous manifestation as the Newport Bar & Grill—Rent ordered a Guinness and took a seat at an empty table near a window.

While waiting for Dan, he sipped his beverage generously and watched the always entertaining, if not bizarre, assortment of characters that occupied one of San Diego's most colorful neighborhoods. They ranged from homeless individuals to surfers, tourists, and the well-heeled movers and shakers who resided up high in swanky Point Loma.

Two women walked past, Rent pegging their ages as mid-twenties. One said, "I've been fucking a lot."

Her companion, slightly taken aback, replied, "Oh, doing your own thing."

To which the first woman said, "Didn't you know? Polyamory is all the rage these days."

Is she a Zizian?

As he chortled, a voice disrupted his reverie. "I thought I might find you here. Another Guinness?"

Recognizing the voice, he replied without turning to face the speaker. "Bribery, eh? You must want something. No, thanks."

"I have a story angle for you," the man said.

"Propaganda, you mean," Rent replied, turning to face the intruder.

"Ha, ha. Ever the cynic," Connor Furlong said. "But seriously, that piece you did on Mike Johnson and his business entities was a bit over the top, not unlike your predecessor, Will Mason. You practically accused him of murder."

Rent drained his glass, set it on the table, and began to rise from his chair. "You mean the Will Mason who successfully defended a five-million-dollar frivolous defamation lawsuit by JMJ?"

"Wait, hear me out," Furlong pleaded, taking a seat facing Rent. "This is big, the future. Life imitates art. Science fiction becomes scientific fact."

Rent settled back onto his chair. "The fact that Johnson is no doubt up to his misdeeds again?"

"Always the comedian. I'm talking about their state-of-the-art, next-generation AI platform, AIsha. I can arrange the grand tour, along with the state-of-the-art, groundbreaking lithium operation."

"Do you ever stop spouting tiresome marketing clichés? I bet you sleep well these days, since taking up residence on the dark side."

"Oh, I do. Especially on payday."

"What about Incinergy and the hazardous waste operations?"

Furlong waved a dismissive hand. "Just a bunch of trucks hauling stuff for disposal. Electric trucks, I might add."

But hauling it where?

"AI is the new frontier. You wouldn't believe the strides being made in the realm of mimicking a human response."

"What happened to doll-faced Brittany? She get the heave-ho?"

"No, she's still doing corporate PR and marketing," Furlong said. "I've been retained as a consultant to focus on media relations."

"Ah, which explains you following me here." When the man flinched, Rent continued. "Yeah, I saw you lurking in the parking lot when I left the office. You must be desperate."

Furlong continued his harangue. "You should join me. Make real money in the corporate world, not that pittance you scribblers get paid, assuming you'll even have a job. Especially now that you have a daughter who expects you to spend lavishly on new clothes and the latest electronic gadgets. Next thing you know, she'll be begging you to buy her a Tesla so she can hotshot around town with her upscale pals in Poway."

Rent eyed him for a long moment before responding.

"The fact that you're here tells me I'm onto something. So, you've just achieved the opposite of your objective, a puff piece on your apparent client. I will drill even deeper."

Furlong straightened up as his smile faded into a scowl. "Well, then, lay on, Macduff."

Rent's eyes went wide. "What did you just say?"

A look of horror scalded Furlong's face before he pasted on an insincere smile. "Just quoting a familiar phrase from the Bard. A figure of speech."

Rent stared him down, forcing Furlong to turn away and toss a quick "you have my number" over his shoulder.

Oh, yes, do I ever have your number, Rent mused as he watched the spin doctor make his exit. *I will see your Macbluff and raise you by one Lady and her damned spot.*

The server stopped in front of Rent. "Same again? It's already poured and paid for."

Rent sighed, then nodded. "Since you put it that way."

As the server replaced the empty glass with the full one, Rent picked up his phone and sent a text to O'Connor:

I know who Agent 99 is.

Rent then chuckled at the irony before lifting the pint of Guinness to his lips. *May you be hoisted upon your own petard.*

Dan Rowland arrived at the table. "Did I just see Connor Furlong walk out of here?"

"Hey, Dan. Yeah, he's tryin' for a blowjob piece on Johnson's AI operations and data center. As if."

"Let me grab a beer."

When Dan returned, Rent filled him in on the brief encounter with Furlong and the text exchange with Agent 99.

"So, he's what, pretending to be an AI chatbot mimicking a human?" Dan asked. "That's weird."

"I suspect he was using a chatbot to craft his text messages. The grammar is too formal for a mere mortal."

"I've been playing around with that AI stuff. It may come in handy for doing basic research and analysis."

Rent rolled his eyes. "Me too. I find it all a bit scary, especially with all those 'hallucinations,' but . . . I think I will take him up on a 'grand tour' of the AI facility, just so I have an idea of what it consists of and maybe get more insight on what the hell those Johnsons are up to. While I'm over there, I can take a peek at the geothermal and lithium operations as well."

Dan raised his glass. "A toast to artificial intellectualism."

Rent clinked his glass. "Or should the toast be to 'Operation Masquerade'?"

"Hear, hear . . ."

20

Rent called Alicia when he got home. She had texted him as he left the pub, asking him to call at his convenience.

"You been out with the boys and misbehavin'?" she teased.

Rent replied in a sing-song voice, "Ain't misbehavin'. I'm savin' my love for you."

"You better be."

"Just having a beer with Dan."

He told her about Connor Furlong's pitch, as well as the earlier text exchange with Agent 99. "I think they're one and the same."

"Would that have anything to do with the number you sent me?" she asked.

"Yes. Were you able to track it down?"

"Short answer, no. Long answer, my guess is it's being routed through an anonymous server via VPN."

"VPN?"

"Virtual private network. Making it virtually impossible for me to trace. I would need access to phone records, but it's not like TV or novels with a mysterious hacker who can get anything she wants."

"Thanks for trying. However, I think Furlong gave himself away with his 'Lay on, Macduff' line."

"I agree. Now, I have a favor to ask of you, and it's OK if you say no."

"Hmmm, should I be worried?"

"No. I want to borrow your truck. Just for a day. My car needs to go in the shop, and I don't want the hassle of a rental."

"When?"

"Whatever's convenient for you. I don't want to cause any imposition."

They agreed on a date, then Rent wondered if she had eaten.

"Yes, and now I have a client report to finish and an invoice to prepare."

"So no misbehavin' tonight then."

"'Fraid not. Call me tomorrow?"

* * *

The following afternoon, Rent met with Will Mason and got copies of the data on the malfunctioning incinerator the man had reported on thirty years earlier.

"I know you're tired of hearing this, but you keep my name out of it," Mason said. "They could sue me out of spite, and it would bankrupt me, even if I prevail."

"I will not breathe a word of where I got this info," Rent replied. "Besides, it's all a matter of public record. Unlike Tom Wilbury's journal."

"What do you intend to do with that?"

"I'm going to spring it on them eventually, but not just yet. It's my hole card. First, I need to find out how they're handling the hazardous waste Incinergy disposes of and if there's any skullduggery still going on. I know they're hiding something; I just haven't figured out what."

"Good luck with that," Mason said. "Another round?"

* * *

The next day, Rent contacted the EPA regarding regulations related to the disposal of hazardous waste and the inspection of facilities. He also asked specifically about Incinergy.

The EPA representative said the agency did not have any complaints about or investigations into Incinergy. Rent would have to talk to the company for details.

Yeah, as if they're gonna be forthcoming.

His phone notified him of a text from Alicia:

R U ignoring me?

Crap. Now I'm up schist creek, as Rachel would say.

He called and she answered at the first ring.

"I'm sorry, sorry, sorry. How can I make this up to you? I've just been so—"

"Well, flowers would be nice, along with a romantic meal."

"How about Ciccia, that Italian place in Barrio Logan? It just got a Michelin star or something like that."

"The barrio? *Madre de Dios.* And Italian? What's this world coming to?"

"Can we make it seven o'clock? Otherwise, traffic will totally suck going south."

"OK, but not a second later."

"What about next week, the road trip to Imperial Valley?"

"Perfect timing. There's a guy in Brawley who wants to meet and discuss a possible investigation."

* * *

On Friday, Rachel's grandparents dropped her off at Rent's place. Not a scheduled weekend, but the Powells had to attend a funeral in Washington State.

He met them in the alley outside the garage and thanked them for saving him the trip to Poway.

"On our way to the airport, so no bother," Frank Powell said. "See you Sunday."

As Rent and Rachel made their way upstairs, he said, "I have something special for us to watch on TV tonight. You're gonna love it."

Rachel eyed him with a deal of skepticism.

"Seriously," he added. "It's about AI. Didn't you say one of your teachers set out the rules for using AI in school?"

She nodded.

"But first, what shall we do about dinner? Do you feel like cooking up one of your healthy recipes?"

She shrugged. "Not really."

"How about we order a pizza, and I have some makings for a tossed salad in the fridge that we can whip up while we're waiting."

She smiled. "I'll go change. I don't want to spill anything on my school uniform."

* * *

With dinner organized, they settled on the couch, and Rent brought up the program he had recorded earlier on the DVR, late-night comedian Tom Olson.

"We can skip the political crap at the beginning and go straight to the good stuff, if you want."

"Yes, please," Rachel mumbled around a mouthful of mozzarella.

Rent fast-forwarded through the first ten minutes of the show, then pressed the Play button. The comedian began showing AI-generated videos and rattled on in his trademark rapid-fire rant.

Rachel watched, spellbound, occasionally laughing, glancing at her father to catch his reactions.

"This is just as good the second time around," he said. "I'm picking up on a few things I missed the first time."

"I want to know how these people made these videos," Rachel said. "It's totes amazing."

"Listen to this. He's getting to his key point about AI."

Olson said the spread of AI generation tools made it easy to mass produce cheap but professional-looking content and flood social media sites with it. "It's called AI slop."

Rent backed it up and paused it. "Did you catch that? AI slop."

"Yes, Dad, I got it. Slop. Like slopping the pigs."

"Exactly," he replied. "When I stayed with Aunt Edith as a kid, I would slop the pigs . . ."

Rachel sighed and shot him a recriminating glance. "Da-ad."

"OK, OK," he said and resumed the program.

Olson showed more examples, in particular AI videos featuring cats, saying that AI slop is the latest iteration of spam.

The comedian admitted that some of this stuff is fun to watch. However, some of it's potentially dangerous as well.

He pointed out that AI can be used to create disinformation portrayed by avatars that look and talk realistically like humans. He cited examples of AI videos that some people believed were real.

"It's not just that people get fooled by fake stuff," Olson said. "Its very existence empowers bad actors to disdain real videos and images as fake."

When it ended, Rent asked Rachel if she wanted to watch something else before going to bed.

"I want to find more AI slop," she said. "It's fun."

Rent rolled his eyes. "I've created a monster."

Rachel grinned, made a bear face, and raised her arms into attack mode, fingers curled like claws. "Grrrrrrrrrrrr."

* * *

The next day, Rent said he needed to run through some tunes for the dance that night. "Do you want to play, like you did last time?"

Rachel grinned. and her rapid nodding shook her entire frame.

"How's *Rachel* coming along?"

"Better, but not ready for prime time."

"No rush. We can play the same sets as before."

"And *Country Waltz*?"

"If you're not in Snoresville by then."

"I don't snore!"

* * *

At the dance, Rachel got so wound up in anticipation of playing *Country Waltz* that she couldn't have slept even if she wanted to. Rent got her started on the tune, then he put down his fiddle and danced with Alicia.

Afterward, as they walked to their vehicle, a male voice in the dark beckoned Rent to step aside for a moment. Rent told Rachel and Alicia he would meet them there, then looked around, trying to find the man behind the voice.

"I warned you, but you're not listening," the man said. Rent recognized the voice. "Unlike that guy up north, the bodies will never be found."

Why is this guy so brazen? So fearless? And how the hell does he know where to find me?

"Who are you? Did Johnson send you?"

"You'll find out soon enough if you don't do as you're told."

Rent determined the man was standing behind a large oak tree and moved toward it, but when he got there, nothing.

The guy's a ghost.

* * *

Sunday morning: They had no possibility of taking a ride that day —too hot. They went to the pool instead. As they toweled off, three police patrol cars entered the complex and pulled up near the sidewalk leading to Rent's unit.

The officers got out and conferred, apparently trying to determine which unit they were being called to.

"Come on! This is exciting," Rachel said, and ran out of the pool enclosure.

"Rachel, don't interfere."

She slowed down but kept edging closer. Rent followed, bare-chested and a towel wrapped around his waist.

"What's going on?" Rent asked.

"We're responding to a call," one of the officers said. "Stand back."

"Well, just in case you're going to my place, please don't bust the door open. I have a key."

"Did you make the 9-1-1 call?"

"No, but I've been getting threats."

"What's your unit number?"

Rent told him. The man conferred with the others, then turned back to Rent.

"Someone in your family make the call?"

Rent shook his head. "It's just me and my daughter, and we've been in the pool."

"You got any ID?"

Rent snorted and spread his arms. "I just came from the pool. I don't normally need ID for that."

The officer stared at Rent, pondering his next step.

"I'll open the door for you," Rent offered. "You can check the place out. Come on."

Rent led the way to his front door, Rachel at his side.

"Are we in trouble?" she asked.

"No. More likely someone trying to spook us."

They reached the door. Rent inserted the key, unlocked it, and opened it. He then stepped aside and motioned with an arm.

"Be my guest."

Two officers entered the unit. A few minutes later, they returned, one of them shaking his head.

"Fuckin' waste of time. Who'd you piss off?"

Rent shrugged. "It's in my job description."

The officer stared at Rent again. "You look familiar." Rent grinned. "You're that newspaper guy. Got shot in the ass."

"Guilty as charged," Rent replied. "I've been 'swatted,' haven't I?"

The officer nodded. "Sorry to have bothered you."

"Don't be. As I said, I've been getting threats. I have a pretty good idea who's behind this. I'm sorry you got dragged into it."

Once inside the house, Rent called his editor. He apologized for calling her at home and told her about the "swatting" incident.

"It must be your innate charm," she said. "I'll put Clark on it, but don't expect much."

21

On Monday morning, Rent and Alicia rose early after spending the night at the Brawley Inn. They grabbed coffee, muffins, and apples from the setup in the cramped lobby, dodging other patrons of the motel.

Rent had offered to drive, but she refused to ride in "that old jalopy" because she didn't feel safe.

"Jalopy?" he protested. "First of all, it's not that old; second, it's the best truck Toyota ever made; and third, it has a CD player, so I can listen to *my* music any time *I* want. Besides, you said you wanted to borrow it for a day."

"I'm having second thoughts. And you now have a daughter and her safety to think of as well," she said, urging him to get a newer vehicle. He agreed begrudgingly to think about it.

She drove her late-model Honda CR-V north past fallow farm fields, then headed west toward the ever-shrinking Salton Sea, a depression in the desert that had been filled with overflow from the Colorado River during an especially wet year more than a century earlier.

Clouds of vapor ballooned into the sky over the several geothermal electrical plants that lined the eastern shore of the lake. The installations harnessed energy from the superheated water that lay hundreds, if not thousands, of feet below the surface, using the steam to spin turbines to generate electricity.

As Rent understood it, the plants were marginally profitable. Yes, the steam, like sunlight, was "free" energy, but the highly corrosive brine created high maintenance costs.

On the flip side, that alkaline brine also contained significant amounts of minerals, lithium in particular. A new method of extracting that element directly from the brine had been developed, although it had yet to be proven on a commercial scale. Investors were betting on the come, believing their roll of the lithium dice would not turn up craps.

"I wonder which one of these belongs to Lustrous," Rent said.

"Yeah, we're not exactly seeing much signage or a big billboard proclaiming 'White Gold Transforms Lithium Valley,'" Alicia replied.

"Most of them belong to Berkshire Hathaway, operating as CalEnergy, and now they want to develop lithium extraction," he added. "Or so I'm told."

"They're probably keeping a low profile until they get ramped up."

Rent bobbed his head in agreement, and Alicia suggested they stop by the Sonny Bono Salton Sea National Wildlife Refuge to use the bathrooms before heading south toward Calexico, a small border town on the U.S. side.

"Look!" Rent exclaimed.

Alicia glanced to her right. "What is it? That huge truck is blocking my view."

"That huge truck is the view. Look at the door."

"I'm keeping my eyes on the road. We're surrounded by big rigs, and I'm feeling a bit claustrophobic."

Rent read aloud the inscription on the side of the truck: "Incinergy HazMat Solutions. Slow up and get behind it. Let's see where it goes."

"We don't want to be late, and we don't know how long it will take to get across the border."

"Maybe it's going to the border too. If not, I'll take note of where it turns off."

"If you say so," she said in resignation and eased off the accelerator.

As Rent had predicted, the truck went to the border. It turned west on W. Birch Street, then resumed its southward journey on César Chávez Boulevard, where it split off to join the queue of trucks waiting to cross into Mexico, while Rent and Alicia lined up with the cars.

Less than ten minutes later, the truck reached the *Puerto Fronterizo* inspection station on the Mexican side of the border. The inspector seemed to know the truck driver and waved him through with a knowing nod.

The pair of investigators proceeded through the port of entry after showing their passports and explaining their errand to the Mexican border guard.

Alicia had to push her speed to catch up with the truck.

"Don't get too close," Rent said.

"I do know how to tail another vehicle," she reminded him. "Besides, I doubt the driver is suspicious of being followed. What's it to him?"

The Incinergy truck exited the 5 Freeway to take Route 2 westward toward Tecate.

Rent checked his notes for directions to the data center:

* At Alamentador Canal, turn N. toward border
* Data center S. of border, opp solar farm U.S. side

"How's our time? Let's follow the truck as long as possible."

Alicia glanced at the clock on the dashboard. "We have twenty minutes to spare."

They passed the canal turnoff and went beyond the agricultural fields.

"They must have a disposal site out here somewhere," Rent speculated.

They passed the municipal cemetery and the Termoeléctrica de Mexicali installation. Only cactus-sprouting desert lay before them.

"I'm turning around," Alicia said. "Save the rest of this for another day."

She took the Pemex exit and reversed course to the canal road.

* * *

They arrived a few minutes early for their 9:30 appointment with Connor Furlong and the onsite manager of the installation.

They stopped at a locked gate, which blocked the entrance to a large compound surrounded by a tall chain-link fence topped with razor wire. Alicia rolled down her window and pressed a button on an intercom pedestal outside the gate.

"Please identify yourselves and your purpose," a voice stated.

Alicia complied and the gate swung open. They entered the expansive complex, passing what appeared to be a warehouse of some kind before reaching the data center, a cinder-block structure topped with utility boxes and structures that appeared to be the top half of ice cream cones.

A door on the side of the building opened, and Connor Furlong stepped out. He beckoned Rent and Alicia to join him.

In the reception area, Furlong introduced Simón Bolívar, the facility manager. The man sported an Emiliano Zapata mustache and a grim expression to match.

Of which Rent took note. *This guy can't wait for us to get the hell out of here.*

Furlong led them toward a large window overlooking a sprawling room containing dozens of workstations populated by young humans of mostly indistinguishable gender, all wearing headphones. One of them looked up, smiled, and motioned toward a large computer monitor. Cartoonish incarnations frolicked in a fantasy wonderland.

Rent leaned toward Alicia. "That kid can't be more than fifteen years old."

Furlong gave the technician a thumbs-up and said, "Simón, please tell our guests what's going on in here."

Bolívar seemed to think the answer was self-explanatory but played along with the show-and-tell charade.

"Primarily, these are our coders, who train, refine, and perfect our AI data and prompts. We also have developers here, who focus on improving our proprietary app."

"They create videos from AI?" Alicia wondered.

"That's just a small part of what they do, but yes, that's our next big challenge: creating lifelike videos that mimic human movement and speech."

Furlong joined in. "They're using Chuckwalla's genAI platform, AIsha. I have included a description of the software in the press kit."

"GenAI? You people have more acronyms than the military."

"It stands for generative artificial intelligence."

Rent turned to Bolívar. "I've heard the term but don't fully grasp what it does, exactly."

The man sighed, as if having to stoop so low as to speak to a bunch of five-year-olds lying far beneath him. "GenAI allows us to turn the binary language of digital computing—the ones and zeros—into representations that humans can interpret using their sensory capabilities. It allows us to generate features like text, images, videos, audio, et cetera."

"All five senses, including smell and even taste?"

"Taste? Ewww," Alicia said.

Bolívar proffered a wide grin. "Combined with 3-D printing or products cultivated in a lab, the answer becomes yes."

"Do you have any concerns about the downside of these life-like videos and audio tracks?" Rent asked.

"Like what?"

"Such as creating false narratives and deepfakes that unknowing people will find believable, potentially fueling conspiracy theories and possibly changing the outcomes of elections."

Bolívar scoffed. "Doomscrolling again, eh? That's the Chicken Little Syndrome; SkIF, we call it: The sky is falling! The sky is falling! Hollywood creates an endless stream of that stuff already.

"This AI tool will simply make it more cost-effective for them; it will accelerate innovation and create opportunities for more indie producers and directors to achieve their creative visions."

Rent stared at the man. *Wow, this guy has either swallowed the Kool-Aid or he's an avatar himself.*

Furlong intervened. "Simón, let's show them the engine room."

The facility manager nodded and motioned toward an interior door. He punched in a security code at a keypad adjacent to the door, then beckoned for the others to enter.

Inside, Furlong had to raise his voice to be heard over the hum of the scores, if not hundreds, of servers, nested row after row, although the expansive room was barely half full.

Furlong waved an arm toward the stacks of electronic devices winking and blinking from their shelves. Several technicians moved about, all wearing white coveralls, head coverings, and face masks, periodically stopping to inspect a device and tapping data into an electronic tablet.

"It's growing, but still room for expansion."

Rent shivered. "Nice to be out of the desert heat, but it actually feels cold in here."

"These devices have to be kept cool," Bolívar said, followed by a not-so-subtle glance at his wristwatch. "What questions do you have?"

Furlong jumped in. "How is this AI data center different from a conventional data center, like an ISP might operate?"

Their guide's expression softened a bit. "This is high-performance computing, which employs GPUs and TPUs to execute billions of calculations per second."

"I know GPU stands for graphics processing unit, but TPU is new to me," Rent responded.

Bolívar nodded. "TPU is short for tensor processing unit, which accelerates the inference phase of a neural network. That's the distinguishing factor in this data center.

"A conventional data center doesn't need that much processing power to handle simple texting, email, and web browsing. But AI requires manipulating massive amounts of data, which takes time.

"These units provide a peak throughput of nearly one hundred TeraOps per second and twenty-eight MiB on-chip memory. MiB stands for mebibyte, a unit of measurement used in data storage."

The man could see Rent's eyes glazing over and grinned. "That's probably TMI."

Rent chuckled. "TMI indeed. Let's keep it at the kindergarten level."

Bolívar looked at Furlong and offered a single-shoulder shrug.

Rent followed up. "How do you keep this place so cool?"

"We have air conditioning, of course, but you'll notice all the pipes next to the electronic devices. That's what's known as DLC or, before you ask, direct liquid cooling. The coolant, in this case water, is circulated through the pipes, which are in direct contact with the chips, and it absorbs the heat, keeping the chips from overheating. You probably noticed the cooling cones on the roof."

Alicia joined the interchange. "I've heard this requires huge amounts of water—hundreds of thousands of gallons a day in some instances—creating concerns over its impact on the environment and groundwater supply as well as water quality."

Furlong stepped forward. "That's probably out of Simón's area of expertise. He's the electronics wizard, not the plumber."

Bolívar shot a dismissive look at the PR flack before responding. "Suffice to say, we have an agreement with the Mexican government and the local utility and farmers to source the water, which is then recycled and repurposed once it passes through our pipes. We are also initiating a heat reuse strategy."

"And electricity," Alicia pressed. "I understand these data centers require massive amounts of that as well."

The facility manager again nodded in affirmation. "We are positioned here near the border to take advantage of the local solar, wind, and geothermal power plants, all alternatives to fossil fuels. We're also in talks with Mexican officials regarding the acquisition of electrical power from its geothermal plant."

"We passed it on the way here," Alicia replied.

Bolívar frowned. "I thought you came through Mexicali."

"We missed the turnoff," Rent said. The man appeared skeptical as Rent raised another query. "Why in the hot desert and so far off the grid? Seems a bit impractical."

Bolívar did not respond, eyeing Furlong.

"This is a relatively small operation compared to what some of the big tech firms are building," Furlong offered. "Once lithium extraction gets up to speed, we anticipate more development in the greater El Centro region. Real estate is still relatively inexpensive here. There are also U.S. military installations nearby, which are increasing their use of AI."

"So you have government contracts? I thought Elon Musk had cornered that market with his Grok AI," Rent responded with a glance at Bolívar.

Again, the facility manager passed it off to Furlong, who said, "That's proprietary. You'll have to talk to Mr. Johnson or Ramesh Kumar about that."

Rent looked at Alicia, rolling his eyes. "Are either of them here?"

Furlong shook his head. "Mr. Johnson spends most of his time in Montana these days, and Ramesh is most likely at our HQ in San Diego."

"Anything else?" Bolívar asked. "I have an important conference call in a few minutes."

"That should do it for now," Rent answered.

The quartet returned to the entrance and stepped outside, the smothering air oven-hot in comparison.

"Oh, one more thing," Rent said, pointing at the adjacent warehouse-like structure. "Is that connected to the data center in some way? I see a bunch of big trucks there, which appear to have umbilical cords. Are they EVs?"

"That's BJ's jurisdiction, not mine," Bolívar replied. "Now, if that's all?"

Rent nodded and thanked the man, who turned and reentered the data center. Rent then eyed Furlong and said, "BJ?"

Furlong hesitated before answering. "He's in charge of that operation. It's part of Lustrous but not connected to the data center. I'll just grab that press kit from my car."

At that moment, a large metal door in the warehouse rattled upward, and a truck emerged from the structure, then exited the compound as the door closed.

"So, it's a maintenance facility?"

Furlong returned. "As far as I know. It's not in my wheelhouse, but from what I've heard, it serves as an EV charging station and provides routine maintenance checks for the Incinergy trucks. Internal combustion technology is more than a century old, and by comparison, EV technology is still in its infancy and requires a greater degree of fine-tuning, especially when it comes to the trucks.

"They don't go in the shop every trip; only as the inspection schedule requires it or the driver thinks there's a problem that needs checked out."

Rent found the explanation somewhat vacuous but accepted it, withholding his skepticism for the moment.

"While we're here, could I have a chat with this Billy Joe, or whatever his name is?"

"I believe his name is Bob—" Furlong cut himself short, as if he'd already said too much.

Rent's mind raced at the speed of an Nvidia AI chip. "Bob as in Robert as in Robert Johnson, perhaps?"

Furlong's face flushed. "I only know him as BJ."

Rent stared at the PR rep for a long moment. "OK. Thank you, Connor, for arranging this meeting. Truly helpful. I just hope I can keep all the acronyms straight."

Furlong relaxed and extended his right hand. "You're welcome. Anytime," he said, shaking Rent's hand, then Alicia's. He handed Rent a pocket folder jammed with corporate literature and brochures. "Lots of good info in here to unpack."

Rent and Alicia went to the car and got in. After the doors were closed, she spoke, disgust lacing her voice. "BJ, blow job."

Rent chuckled. "You said it, not me."

"But you were thinking it."

"We may need to come back," Rent said.

"I second that," she replied. "But for now, let's *atrapar ese camión*."

"Huh?"

"Follow that truck!"

"You've been using more Spanish lately. What's with that?"

"Are you insulting me? It is my heritage, you know."

"No, it's not that. It just surprised me."

"I realized I'm missing business opportunities by not speaking Spanish very well, more like 'Spanglish,'" she answered.

"I know it sounds odd, but my parents didn't want me and my sibs speaking Spanish at home, even though they did, and they especially didn't want us speaking English with an accent. They said it would harm our job prospects and our careers, as it had theirs. But things have changed. Now, I'm at a disadvantage, so I'm speaking it more, and I'm going to start taking a night class at Mesa College. Hopefully, I'll become, if not fluent, at least proficient."

"Good for you. Maybe I should join you."

"Maybe you should."

She pressed the accelerator to the floor. "*¡Vámonos!*"

22

Alicia drove as fast as she dared, paralleling the Alamentador Canal south to Route 2, then eastward toward central Mexicali. They caught sight of the truck as they entered the city center. They anticipated the truck turning north on the 5 Freeway, but it continued on.

"Crap!" Rent cried out. "Where's he going now?"

"I think there's another border crossing."

Rent got out his phone and swiped the screen only to get a "Welcome to Mexico" greeting from T-Mobile. *I hope this sucker works.*

He opened Google Maps and spoke into the phone: "Mexicali, Mexico." A map materialized on his screen. "You're right. Calexico East."

They kept several vehicles between themselves and the truck as it proceeded eastward, then it turned north toward the border. Rent switched to satellite view and zoomed in on the border crossing.

"There's a SENTRI lane, but he's not going there. It looks like there's a separate lane and inspection stop for commercial vehicles."

As they neared the border, the truck slowed, and its right turn signal began blinking. A sign announced the route for trucks and a FAST designation.

"I hope he qualifies for the fast lane. Could be stuck here for hours," Rent muttered.

Alicia slowed as the truck turned off and continued a short distance until she reached the rear end of a line of vehicles and came to a stop.

"He might beat us across the border."

Several minutes passed as the cars ahead inched forward.

"SENTRI lane," Rent called out, pointing toward the sign.

Alicia came to a stop again, only three vehicles ahead of her at the stoplight. A seeming eternity ticked by before the light turned green. She turned right, entered the SENTRI lane, and drove less than one hundred yards before joining another queue.

Rent's fingers tap-danced on his phone's screen and brought up a Customs and Border Protection webpage providing border wait times.

"According to the CBP, the average wait for this time of day is nine minutes, but—good news—currently it's only five minutes." He looked to his left and could see the cars lined up in the general crossing lane. "Fifty minutes for those poor suckers."

"Get your card out and stop your bitching," Alicia commanded as she reached for her purse.

They eased forward, reached the inspection station just minutes later, and handed over their expedited entry cards. They had nothing to declare and were sent on their merry way.

"See? That wasn't so bad," Alicia said as they entered the U.S. "All that fretting for nothing."

"I am amazed," he admitted. "Thank goodness for Global Entry."

They drove northward on SR 7 to Maggio Road, where Alicia pulled over and parked. Rent checked wait times for commercial traffic. "The average is twenty-one minutes for the FAST lane, twenty-three for the general and SENTRI lanes; they're slightly ahead of that."

Alicia glanced at the clock. "I hope we have time for lunch. My stomach's growling. Maybe eat at Chabelas."

Fourteen minutes later, Rent noted, "That was quick."

The truck motored past, and the pair followed it thirty miles northward to Calipatria, a small agricultural town north of Brawley. It pulled into a compound similar to the one south of the border—EV charging stations, warehouse/maintenance facility, chain-link fence topped with razor wire, half a dozen similar trucks parked within.

Las Chabelas would have to wait. They grabbed tacos at Birrieria La Patria, then split up. Alicia had a meeting with a potential client not far from their current position. She dropped Rent off at the Lithex field office and drove to her rendezvous.

* * *

"My name stays out of it," the man said.

"No problem," Rent assured him. "I'm just looking for background so I have a better idea of how the process works."

The project manager of the Lithex lithium extraction operation had agreed to speak to Rent under the condition that he and his employer remain anonymous.

He drove Rent from the office in Calipatria to the facility adjacent to the geothermal plant. He explained that the process involved forcing the brine through a "media"—a filter—that separated the minerals from the hot saltwater, from which they extracted the lithium through a series of chemical interactions.

"This process is not only faster than the conventional evaporation process, which can take as much as two years, it's more sustainable environmentally," the man said.

He further noted that until recently, most of the world's lithium ended up in China for refining and was used in the manufacture of batteries of all types, from flashlights and phones to electric vehicles and mass storage. But Congress had recently passed a law mandating that all lithium mined in the United States had to stay in the United States.

"That's why we now have these huge investments in lithium extraction and refinement and battery manufacturing in this country, so we're not reliant on China."

The man then chuckled and leaned closer to Rent in a conspiratorial manner. "You didn't hear this from me, but a big irony is that many of these EV trucks you see around here actually have sodium-ion batteries in them, not lithium."

"Oh?"

"It's cheaper and safer, and, again, more environmentally sustainable, and they're already being made in the good ol' U.S. of A."

"I hear they're not as good as lithium."

"They're getting better. Besides, these trucks are not long haul. Most of them don't go more than a hundred, a hundred fifty miles a day, and as you can see, we have plenty of electricity for recharging."

He went on to explain that the technology would likely be on par with, or even exceed, lithium batteries in a few years. "Not only much cheaper to produce but safer. They don't catch on fire."

"But isn't that counterproductive?"

"How so?"

"You're in the lithium business but employing a competing technology."

The man smiled knowingly and winked. "Our parent company may have its hands in that competing technology as well."

Rent asked about the potentially hazardous byproducts of the lithium extraction process and their disposal. The man said they put it in barrels, which were hauled away by a hazmat contractor to an approved disposal site.

"By any chance an outfit called Incinergy?" the reporter queried.

The man nodded. "Yeah, which is another irony."

Rent waited for the man to elaborate.

"It's owned by that Lustrous outfit."

"And that's a problem?"

"Not so far, but there's something about it that seems a bit odd. They have a facility near here that's boarded up like Fort Knox, as if they're afraid some jihadist is going to blow the place up."

Rent nodded but withheld any mention of his morning's activities.

The man chuckled and shook his head. "What a sorry bunch of wannabes. That Johnson character fancies himself as the second coming of Warren Buffett. What a joke."

Rent frowned. "Aren't they a partner or at least an investor in your lithium operation?"

"Again, you didn't get this from me," the man said, lowering his voice to a conspiratorial whisper as if others were present. "That's what they want everyone to believe, but the short answer is no. As far as I can tell, Coachwhip Lithium Mining and Extraction Consortium, or 'Climax' as they like to call it, is, for all practical purposes, a shell company, and appropriately named."

"Oh?"

"Do you know what a coachwhip is?" the man asked.

"Anything like a buggy whip?" Rent speculated.

The man chuckled. "It's a snake, nonvenomous. Which seems suitable for this application."

"Ah, I get it."

"I don't think they have any assets to speak of, just a website proclaiming all sorts of bullshit. We've warned them, and they've toned it down somewhat, but it still grates. They're trying to capitalize on our good name, making inferences about their relationship with us. They're desperate to do a deal, but so far *nada*. God only knows how many investors they've fleeced."

"What about the geothermal plant?"

"Which geothermal plant would that be?"

"Sultan Energy."

"Same thing. Hocus pocus. Pull back the curtain and there's no there, there. If I didn't know any better, I'd say they're hiding something."

"That explains Perkins," Rent said.

"Who?"

"The CEO of Sultan. Lawyer. Done time in the big house for fraud."

"Looks like you've got your work cut out for you, Mr. Investigative Journalist. Now, I need to get back to work."

"One more question: What do you know about Algodones Solar, their supposed solar farm?"

"That outfit is legit as far as I know, but that's out of my area of expertise."

"What about a guy known as 'BJ'? Who may or may not be Robert Johnson, Mike Johnson's phantom brother."

"As I said, I need to get back to work."

As Rent left the building, he wondered, *Is this guy the whistleblower? His voice seems vaguely familiar.*

* * *

Rent reunited with Alicia, and they compared notes.

"We lucked out," she said with a mile-wide grin. When Rent remained silent, she opened her briefcase, extracted an envelope, and handed it to him.

"Open it," she said.

He opened the envelope and extracted what turned out to be a check. His eyes widened in disbelief. "Eight thousand bucks?"

Alicia nodded, still grinning. "He would have made it out for ten grand but said it would draw too much attention from the financial authorities." She explained that he was a retired farmer who had leased most of his farmland to a solar energy outfit.

"His name is Miguel Mendoza. He's civic-minded and involved in local politics—on the board of Comité Civico del Valle—but suspicious of certain activities going on around here. He doesn't want to involve cops or the Border Patrol because he's certain some of them are on the take."

She went on to say the man had been making observations and documenting what he'd seen, but too many people know who he is; he needs someone who won't arouse suspicion to continue the investigation. She handed Rent a 9x12 manila folder.

"He started a spreadsheet of truck movements and border guards, and he has photos, although they're not great."

"Trafficking?"

"He's not sure what to think; at least not without more evidence, which he wants me to gather. Isn't that incredible?"

"It is," Rent agreed. "But it also seems to be more than just a coincidence."

Alicia nodded. "You're right. He contacted me because he'd read all the stuff you wrote about the welfare fraud and Hannah's death—that's how he got my name—and he's been following your more recent articles on geothermal and lithium. He also likes that I have a Latino name and can *habla* some *Español*."

"Why didn't he just call me?"

"Because he's afraid you'd put his name in one of your articles."

Rent shook his head. "I protect my sources."

"Even so, he's scared, Rent. He's convinced there are some very bad people involved . . ." She pointed a finger at her head, thumb raised, mimicking the profile of a gun. ". . . and pow."

"Did you tell him I'm in town?"

"No, and let's keep it that way for now. How'd your meeting go?"

23

The following evening, Rent attended a music recital at Rachel's school. Afterward, he congratulated her on her performance.

"Are you happy with your playing?"

She shrugged. "It was OK, but I have to play exactly what's on the paper. It's more fun to fiddle, jazz it up a little bit, like we do with *Polly Wolly Doodle*; something you could dance to. But Ms. Reinhold gets mad when I do that."

"Who's that guy?" Rent wondered aloud—although he had already guessed the answer—nodding toward her friend Meghan, who was hugging a man with a handlebar mustache the size of a Texas longhorn.

"That's Meghan's dad. He's weird."

"How so?"

"He makes a lot of stupid jokes, and he wears funny clothes, and he stares at girls' boobs. Not me, because I don't have any boobs yet."

"Rachel," Agnes Powell scolded. "That's no way for a young lady to talk."

"Well, it's true, on both counts," she said and glanced at her father.

Rent gave a slight shake of his head as if to say, *Keep me out of this.* He walked Rachel to the parking lot and said good night to her and her grandparents.

From there, Rent drove to Alicia's house, where he would spend the night. She had left her car at the mechanic's that afternoon and would borrow his truck for a day.

The next morning, they went to his vehicle. He handed her the keys—she would drop him off at the newspaper—then sniffed the air. *Gas?* He sniffed again, then shrugged and got in on the passenger side.

Alicia stepped on the clutch and turned the key. The engine started, then sputtered. She gave it more gas, but it didn't run smoothly. "Maybe yours needs a tune-up too."

Rent shook his head. "I had it in the shop a few months ago. It's been running fine."

"Oh, my god," she exclaimed as she shifted her gaze from the rearview mirror and turned to look directly out the back.

Rent turned as well. "What the—"

Oily smoke billowed up from the rear end of the pickup.

"Get out!" he shouted as he threw open his door and exited the burning vehicle. Alicia followed suit.

Flames had engulfed the underside of the rear end and were spreading along the curb toward the front.

"Call nine-one-one," he coughed out, trying to wave away the billowing smoke. He ran around the front end to the the driver's side, jerked open the door, and grabbed a fire extinguisher from behind the seat. He began spraying along the curb in an effort to stop the spread of the fire, then went to the rear of the vehicle.

"This is like pissing on a bonfire," he muttered.

"Get away from there, Rent," Alicia ordered. "It might blow up."

He joined her on the lawn of her front yard, standing well back from the car. The asphalt had begun to burn, igniting the right rear tire and sending thick, black smoke spiraling skyward. They could feel the heat from the blaze and retreated nearer to the house.

"Well, this sucks," Rent said and began using his phone to take still photos and video of the fire.

"What do you think happened?"

"Fuck if I know, but this is no accident."

"You think it's deliberate."

"It has to be considered. The fire department and cops will investigate. But I'd start with the gas tank."

"What happened to the old trick of sugar in the tank?"

"They obviously wanted to frighten the shit out of us, if not inflict serious bodily harm."

"Or worse."

The sound of sirens grew louder, and a fire engine squealed around a corner, pulling to a stop near the burning truck. The firefighters sprayed the flames with foam, knocking down the blaze in a matter of minutes.

One of the firefighters approached Rent and Alicia, introducing himself as Captain Robert Willhelm. The man gestured toward the smoldering vehicle. "Belong to you?"

Rent nodded. "Mine. And I suspect arson."

Willhelm's brows shot skyward along with the diminishing smoke. "Why do you say that?"

Rent identified himself. "I've been getting threats. Which is not unusual, but they generally are just that."

The captain nodded. "You're the guy that almost got blown to kingdom come at the gold mine in Julian."

Rent nodded in return. *"C'est moi."*

"You have quite a rambunctious fan base, Mr. Beacham."

"You could say that."

"But seriously, if you think this is deliberate, we will investigate."

One of the firefighters called out, "Captain, take a look at this."

"Don't go anywhere," Willhelm said and joined the firefighter, who had kneeled on the ground at the rear of the vehicle.

"I think the fire started here, below the gas tank, or certainly in this vicinity," she said.

Rent had followed so he could listen in. The captain turned to him and asked if he'd been having any problems with the vehicle. Rent replied in the negative. He said he thought he smelled gas, but it didn't seem like anything to be concerned about.

The captain rolled his eyes. "Maybe it's time you took those threats a little more seriously."

A San Diego police car had arrived, and the two cops joined the klatch near the rear of the vehicle. The fire captain explained the situation and the possibility of deliberate sabotage. A patrolman nodded and excused himself.

"I . . . we . . . want to get our gear from behind the seats, if it's not ruined," Rent said.

Captain Willhelm motioned for Rent to follow him to the side of the car and opened the door on the driver's side. He looked around for a moment, then said, "Might be smoke damage, but doesn't look like it got scorched. You got lucky."

"Some luck," Rent muttered.

The captain pulled out a duffel bag and handed it to Rent, then a second bag. "Anything else?"

Alicia had joined them. "My purse," she said. "It should be on the floor in front, on the other side."

"Go ahead," the captain replied.

She walked around the undamaged end of the pickup and retrieved her purse. Rent followed and opened the glove compartment, extracting the vehicle registration and proof of insurance, which he offered to the police officer along with his driver's license.

A police detective arrived and took down an account of the incident from Rent and Alicia. The detective said the truck would be impounded and held as evidence of a potential crime, as well as an investigation by the fire department.

"A bit early for a drink, but how about a fresh cup of coffee?" Rent said to Alicia when the formalities had ended.

"Good idea, and I need to make a few phone calls," she said.

"As do I," Rent seconded.

As Alicia brewed the coffee, Rent called his insurance company to file a claim, then his editor, saying he would be a bit late to the office. He explained what happened.

O'Connor heaved a hefty sigh. "Not again."

"Clark will want in on this," he said.

"She's already working on it, but the cops so far have withheld the specifics about who owned the car."

"Well, now you have it. I need to get a rental car; then I'll be in, pending any further confabs with the cops and fire department."

* * *

Rent arrived at the newsroom just before noon. O'Connor summoned him and Naomi Clark to her office. She looked at Rent, shaking her head.

"I swear, you're gonna be the death of me."

"Not if the bad guys get me first," he quipped.

"Don't be a wiseass. We need to handle this very carefully."

"You mean in terms of who we point a finger at."

"Or who we don't point a finger at," Clark injected.

"Look," Rent said, "we know the Johnsons are behind this, but we can't prove it . . . yet. And there's another aspect to this—someone's been tailing me. But the only thing with any substance is that discredited hack, Connor Furlong, and the Johnsons can deny any association with him, or at the least claim it was an ill-advised joke and either reprimand him or even shitcan his ass."

O'Connor looked at Clark. "Your thoughts?"

"The cops are just saying the usual boilerplate: it's an ongoing investigation and they're pursuing all leads. I asked them, already knowing the answer, if it had any connection to the Wilbury cold case, and the detective looked at me like I belonged in the loony bin."

"So, what's your angle?"

"That a vehicle belonging to a *Herald* employee caught on fire and the cops are treating it as suspicious. That the employee has received anonymous threats, but the source of the threats is unknown. Then give some background on the welfare fraud case last winter and the mine explosion. Anyone with any information should contact the cops."

"What about the fire department?"

"They're not commenting until they conclude their investigation as to how the fire got started."

"OK, let me know if you find out anything else."

As they left their editor's office, Clark said to Rent, "Lunch at Panini? My treat."

"I don't take bribes," he replied.

"As O'Connor said, 'Stop being a wiseass.' I have to talk to you and Velasquez; you know that."

"Yeah, yeah . . . let's go."

They settled at a table on the patio and placed their orders.

"OK, let's unpack this," Clark said.

"Seriously? 'Unpack this'?" Rent chided. "You've been watching too much cable news."

"Up yours. Are you going to tell me how this went down or not?"

"Yeah, sorry. I'm just in a crappy mood, as you might imagine."

Rent told her what led up to the incident, leaving out any mention of the Johnsons and his investigation.

"You're lucky the gas tank didn't explode."

"Gas tanks almost never explode," he said. "I asked the fire captain about it, and he said it's a myth perpetrated by Hollywood FX departments. The gas can burn, but there's no explosion; although if a tire catches on fire, the sudden release of pressurized air could cause a flare-up of the burning fuel, perhaps leading observers to believe the gas tank exploded. In this case, however, first responders put out the fire before . . ."

Clark leaned back in her seat, pretending to fall asleep and snore.

"Now who's being the wiseass?" he said.

"Is that it then?" she queried. "I need something of substance."

"OK, how about this: Yes, the fire frightened me, especially in light of the threats I've been getting. But that's one of the risks of being an investigative journalist, a watchdog who turns up evidence of malfeasance, not only within government but the private sector as well—fighting injustice with the mighty sword of self-righteous indignation."

"You should have stopped at 'private sector,' smarty pants. Now, if you'd be so bold as to give me your girlie friend's number—wait, I probably have it from before." She checked her phone and read the number to Rent, which he confirmed.

"Speaking of, I need to call her," he said.

Alicia answered on the second ring. He told her Naomi Clark wanted to speak to her, to which she agreed, and she told him her car would be ready after four o'clock.

Back at the newsroom, Rent thought about his next move. Someone had made a deliberate attack not only on his life but Alicia's as well. They were fortunate to have escaped with only minor respiratory issues.

He reviewed his notes from their trip to Imperial Valley and began a list of questions for his next round of interviews. He pulled Tom Wilbury's notebook from a locked drawer in his desk and reread some critical pages, marking them with a rainbow of page flags. He needed to make copies of the pages but didn't want to risk being seen by anyone in the newsroom.

I'll swing by Staples on the way to pick up Alicia.

He spotted Clark approaching his desk. He stuffed the notebook into his laptop carrying case, then added the laptop in a more dispassionate manner as she arrived.

"I just heard from the fire department investigator," she said. "His preliminary investigation found that two tiny holes had been drilled in the gas tank, causing it to leak fuel, and wires to one of the tail lights had been rigged to short out and cause a spark when the ignition was turned on and the brakes were applied. He determined that the fire was deliberate and constituted a criminal act and turned it over to the cops."

She paused and stared at Rent for a beat.

"What?" he said.

"They also found something else."

"Are you going to keep me guessing?"

"A GPS tracking device, or at least what appears to be. It got severely damaged in the fire."

"There you have it. They didn't have to tail me. Explains how he found me at the dance."

"Anyway, that's now official," she added. "The cops say it not only constitutes arson but also assault with intent. But no suspects."

Rent stared up at her for a long moment. "I can give them a suspect."

"Who?"

"I'm not at liberty to make a public accusation, so don't get any ideas."

"Bastard."

"You can't use it anyway. You'd have a lawyer on you so fast even your ass would be on fire. Who's the detective handling the case?"

She glared at him for a moment before answering. "I'll get you the name and number."

"It's time to turn up the heat," he said. "They want to light a fire under me, I'll light a fire under them."

* * *

Rent drove to Alicia's to pick her up and take her to the auto repair shop. She stepped out of the house and joined him, carrying a duffel bag. She tossed the bag in the back seat and joined him up front. He cast her a questioning look.

"I'm staying at your place tonight," she said as he pulled away from the curb.

"Ooo-kaaay," he replied, hesitation in his voice.

"Rent, I'm scared. What if they try to burn my house down next?"

"They're after me, not you. You might actually be safer at home."

"Yeah, well, at least you have security at the condo complex and only one way in and out," she contended in rebuttal. "Besides, I want a long soak in that hot tub while sipping a pinot noir. I just want to feel safe. And speaking of feeling safe—"

"Yes?"

"Maybe this fire is a blessing in disguise."

"How's tha— Oh, wait. You're going to tell me I now have to get a *newer, safer* vehicle."

She smirked. "Just sayin'. You could do worse than that rental, the RAV4."

"I'm thinking of a 4Runner, but no rush. I can keep the rental for thirty days. But more important, what about dinner?"

"Changing the subject, are we?" Rent gave her a stink eye. "Since we're going to be on Morena, let's get some Greek food."

"And a bottle of retsina."

She held up her hands and made an X by crossing her forefingers. She then called Zgara Greek Grill and placed their order.

He pulled into a parking space at Morena Automotive; she handed him thirty dollars. "This should cover it."

He tried to refuse it, but she insisted. "I'll see you back at your place."

When Rent got home, he set the table, unpacked the food, opened the wine, then unlocked and opened the front door. As he poured himself a glass of wine, his phone buzzed. He didn't recognize the number, but the prefix seemed familiar, so he answered it.

"This is Detective Sergeant Diana Alvarez, SDPD. I need to speak with you."

"The Diana Alvarez formerly of the sheriff's department?"

"I transferred over."

"Better pension benefits?"

"I'd like you to come down to the station first thing in the morning."

"No can do."

"Then when?"

"You're welcome to come to my place. I'll have the coffee on. And donuts, too." He heard a knock at the door, followed by a hello. "Just a sec."

Rent stepped into the living room and motioned for Alicia to come in, then resumed his conversation with the detective.

"Sorry about that. You were saying?"

"That's not how this works."

"Am I a suspect now? You think I torched my own car?"

"We have to consider all possibilities. It's part of the elimination process."

"Bullshit," he replied. "If you're seriously thinking of going down that path, we're done, and you can talk to my lawyer. You no doubt remember him—A.J. Hawke."

"Look, Rent, I just have some follow-up questions."

"If that's the case, *Diana*, then fire away. And Alicia Velasquez is standing next to me if you need to speak to her as well. I just opened a bottle of wine. Swing on by and we'll have a little reunion."

"You haven't changed."

"I want to get to the bottom of this as much as you do, so let's cut the crap. Besides, I have a possible suspect for you."

"So, you've been withholding information?"

"Would you rather speak to Mr. Hawke?"

She sighed. "Give me your address and I'll see you at nine a.m. sharp."

Alicia helped herself to the wine and put the take-out boxes on the table as Rent concluded the call.

"Fuckin' cops," he muttered.

"Did I hear right? Diana Alvarez?" Rent nodded. "So, she's coming here in the morning?"

"Yeah, you want to stick around? I just might lay Charles Stevens on her, and she's gonna want to know where I got that name."

"Damn . . . more phone calls to make."

"Let's eat before the food gets cold."

She raised her glass. *"Bon appétit."*

"Learning French, too?"

She sighed. *"¡Buen provecho!"*

* * *

After sating their hunger, they put the leftovers in the fridge, poured wine into travel mugs, and changed into their swimsuits. On the way to the complex's pool enclosure, they encountered Ralph, the security guard.

"I heard about the car fire," he said. "Quite a scare."

"Yeah, no kidding," Rent replied. "You remember Alicia?"

The guard nodded. "Welcome to North Rim," he said.

She smiled in acknowledgement.

"Listen," Rent said. "Remember that guy I told you about, lurking by the mailboxes?" Ralph nodded. "He may be the guy who torched my car or at least had something to do with it. And I think he, or an accomplice, has been tailing me. They're not done with this harassment, and it could escalate."

"Can you give me a better description?" the guard asked.

Rent shrugged. "Tall, linebacker build, probably wearing dark clothes and a hoodie."

"Not much to go on."

"Yeah, sorry, but right now it's the best I can do."

"I'll keep an eye out. Enjoy your soak."

They continued on to the vacant hot tub and waded in. Alicia exclaimed how good it felt, even though they were still experiencing the warm days of early autumn.

"So, what's the plan, maestro?" she asked.

"The plan?"

"For the cops. You gonna give 'em Charles Stevens?"

"I thought about it, but that would mean handing over all of the Wilbury stuff, and I don't want to do that. Not yet. I want Johnson to know I have it, and if any more harm comes to me, it will all be handed over to the cops by my lawyer."

"If not Stevens, then who?"

"If I tell you, you will have no deniability."

"I'm in so deep now I'm way beyond claiming any deniability."

Rent shrugged. "Robert Johnson."

"You mean BJ?."

"Phantom brother of Mike Sr."

"And how is he a suspect?"

"That's for the cops to find out. They have way better resources than I or even you have. I'll tell them about the anonymous phone call. And maybe Anthony Perkins."

"Johnson's lawyer?"

"He has a rap sheet," Rent said with a chuckle, "and according to the cop shows on TV, that makes him an automatic suspect."

"You're being a bit underhanded for someone who likes to come off as being holier than thou and self-righteous."

"As the Bible says, 'Fight fire with fire,' or is it 'Eye for an eye'? Whatever. Besides, we don't know that they are not involved in torching my vehicle, nor do we know that they were not involved in Wilbury's murder.

"These things don't happen because some thug went rogue. They were orchestrated by someone, with approval, if not direct orders, from the top brass. Shove that pig's foot a little further into the fire, and that little piggy's gonna start squealing."

She cast him a reproving glance and shook her head. "You and your fiddle-dee-dee jargon."

24

The next morning, Aunt Edith called before Rent had finished his first cup of coffee. She demanded to know all about the fire and this Alicia Velasquez woman. As before, she had seen the story in the newspaper. What were *he* and *his truck* doing at *her house*? Obviously, he'd been there all night.

Rent told her about the threats and what had led up to the fire, then said, "So, what, you're getting prudish all of a sudden?"

"How long have you known this woman?"

"You remember. I met her last winter. She's the private investigator who interviewed Rachel's mother."

"Do I hear wedding bells in the offing?"

"Don't you start. We're taking things slow."

"Not all that slow. And what's a woman doing being a private eye?"

"It's called progress."

Edith sighed. "Yes, nephew, you're right. I'm just an old lady from a bygone era."

When Rent didn't reply, she went on. "Is she Mexican?"

"She's an American, born and raised."

"Sounds Mexican to me. Is she legal?"

"Aunt Edith, what's with you? You haven't gone all red hat on me, have you?"

"Good god, no. Just sayin'."

"It's actually a Spanish name, dating back to the conquistador days, when Spain claimed all of South and Central America and a big chunk of North America. Then Mexico achieved its own independence, which included California, until the U.S. seized it, Arizona, and New Mexico, not to mention Texas.

"If you want to know the truth, Velasquez is just as much, if not more, American as Beacham or Taylor or Edwards or any other name of English or Scottish or Welsh or Anglo-Saxon derivation."

"Humph. Still, I don't know if I'd vote for anyone with a name like that for president."

"Aunt Edith, you are one of the most liberal-minded people I know. Now you sound like a right-wing . . ."

"I have not voted for a Republican since Watergate."

"You voted for Nixon?"

"He said he would end the war in Vietnam. Then he pulls all that bull-pucky."

"Besides, Alicia has no interest in becoming president of the U.S. or Mexico."

Rent heard Alicia descending the stairs. "Listen, I need to go."

". . . maybe if it was a woman . . . like that one in Mexico. Whatshername . . . Shinebloom . . . something like that."

"Claudia Sheinbaum."

Alicia gave Rent a puzzled look as she passed on her way to the kitchen and coffee. Edith continued unabated. "Which sounds German to me. What's with that?"

Rent looked at Alicia, rolling his eyes. "Lots of Germans settled in Mexico in the nineteenth century. That's how Mexico got its accordion music and good beer, from the Germans."

"Or is she Jewish?"

"Geez, Aunt Edith, cut the ethnic snobbery."

Becoming nostalgic, Edith said, "Did you know my mother, your great-grandmother, was a suffragette? She campaigned for the women's right to vote."

"I think you've mentioned it. Showed me a picture of her marching with Susan B. Anthony."

Edith chuckled. "No, no, that was her grandmother. My mother never met Ms. Anthony, as much as she would've liked to. The only time that woman came to Washington State was in the eighteen-seventies, well before my mother was born."

"And it took another fifty years before women got the right to vote. Who knew we'd be delving into history like this."

"Back to Tom Wilbury. We're no closer to solving that mystery, are we?"

Rent reminded her about the man Wilbury had mentioned in his notebook, Stefano Ceccarelli.

"Oh, god, now the Italians and the Mafia are involved?"

"The Mafia are Sicilian."

"Same diff."

"Aunt Edith, it's not his real name. We think his actual name is Charles Stevens, a good ol' WASP name. Does that make you feel any better?"

"Probably a Calvinist."

Rent laughed. "You crack me up. You and your prejudices."

"I don't have a prejudicial bone in my body."

"Whatever. The point is, we think we have identified him, but connecting him with the Johnsons is another matter."

Rent withheld any mention of his encounter with the man suspected of being Stevens showing up at the contra dance.

"I gotta go."

Edith sighed. "All right. Just keep me posted. And give my love to Rachel."

Alicia, hugging a coffee mug, joined Rent at the table. "What was that all about?"

Rent shook his head. "My Aunt Edith. She saw your name in Clark's story about the fire. Wanted to know all about you, wondering if you were legal."

"Maybe she'd like to see my birth certificate. And my parents' and my grandparents'. According to family legend, one of our ancestors signed the Treaty of Hidalgo—under duress, I might add."

* * *

The doorbell rang at precisely nine o'clock. Rent admitted Detective Alvarez; they shook hands, and he motioned toward Alicia, seated at the dining table, coffee mug in hand.

"Good morning, detective," Alicia said.

Alvarez nodded in acknowledgement. Rent offered her coffee. She declined, and he directed her to an armchair. Alicia joined him on the couch.

Alvarez told them what she knew about the incident and asked if they had anything more to add.

"Robert Johnson," Rent said.

Alvarez frowned as she jotted the name in her notebook.

"He's the brother of Mike Johnson Sr., who said he hasn't seen his brother in years."

"So, why him?"

"I got a call a few days ago, and the caller said two words: 'Robert Johnson.' I thought he was telling me his own name, but, no, he—I'm assuming it's a man by the voice; these days you never know—was telling me to look into Robert Johnson. I asked him if the man was related to Mike Johnson, and he said, 'Seek and ye shall find.' Then the line went dead. That's it." Rent shrugged.

"And did you?" the detective asked.

"Like I said, I . . . we . . ." He nodded toward Alicia. ". . . looked into it but came up with hardly anything. Mike Johnson didn't deny he had a brother named Robert, but that was it. No idea where he lived. Of course, he could have been feeding me a load of bull, especially if Robert was doing dirty deeds for him."

Alvarez sighed and stared at Rent with narrowed eyes. "And you could be feeding me a line of bull."

Rent raised his arms in protest. "Hey, I've always been straight with you."

"I'll give you that," she said and shifted her gaze to Alicia. "Anything to add?"

The PI shook her head. "I looked into Robert Johnson for Rent, but like he said, I didn't come up with anything substantial."

"Have *you* received any threats?"

"Fortunately, no."

"So even though the incident took place in front of your house, you don't think you were the intended target?"

"He's the one getting the threats, and it was his vehicle. They probably did it at my place because here Rent keeps it in the garage, and it would be harder to access."

"OK, I . . ." Alvarez began.

"One more thing," Rent said. "Anthony Perkins."

"Who's he?"

"Johnson's business partner and lawyer . . . and brother-in-law."

"And?"

"And he's in your database; he's done time."

Alvarez's brows shot up. "You're saving the best for last?"

"Not really. It's a long shot, but the fact that he's done time—for fraud, not violent crime—gives you some leverage. Might be a little more forthcoming about Robert Johnson or other goings-on within the C-suite. Not only for this case, but the Wilbury murder as well."

"Oh, yeah, like he's going to give us the guy who set fire to your car, who just happens to be the same guy who committed a murder thirty years ago."

"As Archie McNally is fond of saying, 'One never knows, do one?'"

25

Friday morning: Rent's phone buzzed as he plopped into his desk chair in the newsroom. The anonymous caller he had dubbed "Whistleblower." He sighed and swiped the phone, taking the call.

"You talk to Robert Johnson yet?"

"Who are you?"

"A loyal citizen offering you a helping hand. But I speak only on the basis of anonymity."

"I still need to know who you are and whether you're a legitimate source and not some nutcase wasting my time."

"You will have to trust me. I speak with a high degree of authority and authenticity and familiarity with the Johnson business enterprise."

"Vengeful former employee with an ax to grind."

"Have you talked to Robert Johnson yet?"

Rent scoffed and told Whistleblower that he couldn't find any current contact information on the guy, and Mike Johnson said he and his brother were estranged and hadn't spoken in years.

The caller replied with: "Follow the . . ."

"Money," Rent injected.

"No, follow the trucks."

The line went dead.

What the hell? Follow the trucks?

He set the phone on his desk and walked away, headed for the men's restroom. Then it hit him: *Incinergy!* The trucks hauling hazardous waste. He and Alicia had seen the truck heading into the desert in Mexico, and more trucks at the maintenance facility adjacent to the data center. The woman from the civic organization, *whats-her-name*, had mentioned the need for road repairs because of the heavy trucks thundering on the back roads of the county and through their small towns, tearing up the aging pavement and creating dangerous potholes.

I need to get on the road again.

Back at his desk, he texted Alicia Velasquez, wondering if and when she might be going to Imperial Valley again. She called him back moments later, saying she had an appointment later in the week—Miguel Mendoza wanted to meet in person at the Sonny Bono Wildlife Refuge. "He's getting paranoid; thinks his phone might be bugged."

"You still have your driver's license, passport, and Global Entry card handy?"

"Of course," she replied, as if to say, *What a dumb question.*

"How about we get two birds?"

"Two birds?"

"With one trip."

"You want to go with me?"

"Yeah, and we can do some skulking, including across the border. I need to follow the trucks."

"Isn't the cliché 'follow the money'?"

"Yeah, as in follow the trucks and you *are* following the money."

"Would you just tell me what the heck you're talking about instead of babbling riddles?"

"Actually, it involves three birds—your meeting, the trucks, and while you're at your meeting, I can interview Derringer. We'll probably need to spend the night, maybe two."

"Let me think about it. I'm not exactly sitting here twiddling my thumbs, you know. I have an incoming call," she said and disconnected.

Rent stared at his phone. *What's got a bee buzzing in her bonnet?*

* * *

Rent's fingers danced on the keyboard, tapping in time to the tune *Snake River Reel* running through his head. He clicked Save and lowered the screen, preparing to leave the newsroom.

His phone whined with the insistence of a hungry dog. Agnes Powell. He glanced at the clock. *Crap! I'm already late.*

"Agnes, what is it? I'm still picking up Rachel after school, right?"

"As much as I hate to say this, you need to have a talk with your daughter."

"Oh, so now she's *my* daughter, eh? That's rich coming from you."

"You need to speak with her."

"Right now?"

"No, but this weekend."

"About?"

Agnes paused, then sighed. "Boys."

"Rachel has a boyfriend?"

"I don't know what's going on. She's become increasingly secretive, and she gets belligerent when I question her about it. I went through this with her mother. I don't know if I can do it again."

"It's part of growing up. Her hormones have kicked in. She's no longer a little girl."

"I had hoped . . . prayed . . . for it not to happen so soon."

"It's out of her control."

"That's the problem. She's out of control. When I say anything, she hides in her room, probably spending hours doing who knows what on that darned phone when she should be practicing her violin, doing her homework."

"And you think she's doing what, sexting or something?"

"What?"

"Sexting. That's all the rage, or so I hear. Exchanging sexually explicit messages and photos via their phones."

"They've been getting sex education at school. Maybe that's part of it. As I said, you need to talk to her. She won't listen to me, and Frank wants nothing to do with it. He says it's a female matter. He just wants that little five-year-old girl who still adores him."

"OK, I'll have a heart-to-heart and hope it doesn't get too awkward."

Rent disconnected, heaved a heavy sigh of his own, and shook his head, muttering, "I don't have time for this."

"Don't have time for what?" Janis O'Connor inquired.

"Eavesdropping?"

"No, I came by for a status report and just happened to overhear your last comment."

"OK, sorry. That was the grandmother. Rachel, apparently, has discovered boys, and grandma wants me to have a chat with her."

"Hmmm . . . I'd love to be a fly on the wall for that conversation."

"Hey, maybe you—"

"No, no, no, no. Been there, done that. What's going on with the Johnson cartel? If you don't get me an update soon, *we* are going to have a little chat."

"This afternoon. Right now, I've got an appointment at the courthouse. Getting some legal docs."

"They can't email them to you?"

Rent rolled his eyes. "Technologically speaking, they're still in the twentieth century."

"How about ChatGPT? I could look them up for you in a few seconds."

"Yeah . . . no. The odds are good it would make them up."

* * *

Back at the office, Rent stared at his computer screen, reviewing and revising the draft of his latest installment on the Johnson family enterprises. His phone vibrated on the desktop: Rachel.

"Hi, sweetie, what's up?"

"Pick me up at Old Poway Park. Me and Meghan . . . Meghan and I . . . are going to look for frogs for a science project."

"What time?"

"Her mom's coming at four thirty."

"How are you getting to the park?"

"We're taking the bus," she replied, her sarcasm indicating she thought it was a stupid question.

"OK, see you then."

Rent stared at his phone. *And what's got a bee buzzing in her bonnet? Women!*

Rent re-read his story and finished his revisions, sent it to O'Connor, and packed up. At the park, he checked the tracking app on his phone. It indicated Rachel was near the gazebo, apparently in the creek that ran through the park. *Let's just hope it doesn't live up to its name—Rattlesnake Creek.* He spotted her emerging from the streambed.

"Dad, look!" Rachel called out.

Rent joined her and Meghan, and they showed him their captives in a plastic container.

"They're so tiny," Rent said.

"They're tree frogs."

"What are you going to do with them?"

"I'm gonna put 'em back. I took pictures. Meghan's keeping hers, but I think that's mean."

"They're just frogs," Meghan said. "I'm taking them to school on Monday."

"We have to write a report on them. Some frogs are endangered because of loss of habitat," Rachel added.

"That sounds interesting," Rent responded as he glanced around the park. "Where's your mom, Meghan?"

"She's always late."

"Show me where you found the frogs."

Rachel led him closer to the creek and pointed downstream, then descended into the streambed, crouched down, and released her captives.

A car horn interrupted the young naturalist's activities.

"That's her," Meghan said. "*Adios.*"

Rent began walking to his vehicle, Rachel at his side.

"Taco Taco?" he suggested.

"I want to make pasta."

"You're the boss."

She looked up at him and grinned. "You do have shready cheese, right?"

"Will shaky cheese do?"

Rachel narrowed her eyes and grimaced in reprimand.

* * *

On the drive home, Rent turned off the music and glanced at Rachel. She returned his glance, her expression bordering on fearful.

"Your grandmother called me this morning. She's worried about you."

Rachel stared through the windshield.

"She said you've been hiding in your room, spending hours on the phone."

"So? I'm just texting my friends, looking at stuff on Instagram and TikTok. Doing research on indigenous frogs in San Diego. Did you know there are desert frogs?"

"Don't change the channel. She thinks you have a boyfriend."

"He's not my boyfriend."

"So, there is a boy."

"He goes to my school. He thinks I'm cute and wants to meet up."

"You've never met him?"

"Only online. He's shy."

"Then how are you going to meet him?"

"Can we talk about something else? Turn the music back on, please."

"Taylor Swift? I hear she got engaged."

"Audrey Hobert. She sings *Who's the Clown*? She's really funny."

He begrudgingly admitted it sounded "not half-bad." They rode in silence the rest of the way.

At the condo, Rachel grabbed a cold drink from the fridge and poured it into a glass. Rent raised the subject again, questioning her intentions.

"He wants to meet at the park, after school," she said.

"The park we just left?"

She nodded.

"I want to be there. At least in the vicinity."

"No way."

"I just want to be sure it's safe. That he is who he says he is. There are bad people out there, pedophiles pretending to be someone they are not and preying on unsuspecting innocent girls such as yourself."

"Dad, you've been watching too many crime shows on TV. How else would he know so much about what's going on at school, who my friends are? He's just not in any of my classes. I think he's in seventh grade."

"I still want to be there."

"You don't trust me."

"Sweetie, it's not that I don't trust you. I just want to keep you safe. That's my job as your dad."

"I hate you!" Rachel shouted. She sprinted up the stairs to her bedroom and slammed the door, rattling the entire structure.

26

Rent followed Rachel up the stairs and knocked at the bedroom door.

"Go away. Leave me alone!"

Rent sighed and went downstairs. He stared at the framed pencil sketch she had drawn of him playing his fiddle. She had given it to him the previous winter, before they knew they were father and daughter.

He turned on the TV to get the local news headlines and weather forecast. *Will it be too hot to go riding in the morning? Maybe not if we get an early start.*

He went back upstairs and knocked lightly on the door. "Rachel, I'm sorry. I didn't mean to upset you. Will you please come down so we can make dinner? You said you wanted pasta."

The door opened just enough for Rent to see one side of her face. A single eye stared back at him, tears streaking her cheek.

"I love you, sweetie. Come on . . ."

She opened the door and stepped toward him. He wrapped her in his arms, and she followed suit. He kissed the top of her head and held her close.

"I'm sorry I said I hated you," Rachel said, her voice muffled as she spoke into his chest. After a moment, he relaxed his grip and stepped back, and she continued. "But sometimes I get mad at you."

"I know. It's inevitable. It's our chimpanzee genes coming to the fore."

"Are we really descended from chimpanzees?"

"Not directly, but we have common ancestors and share something like ninety-seven percent of our genes." He gestured toward the stairs. "Shall we?"

She nodded, and he led the way to the kitchen.

"What did you have in mind for the pasta?"

"Do you have that curly quinoa pasta from Trader Joe's? I like that."

"I think so. I'll check."

"I found a recipe that uses olives and feta cheese. Do you have kale too?"

He smiled at her. "Yes, chef."

* * *

After dinner, Rent sat on the couch and watched the most recent Derringer for Congress TV commercial on his laptop. *Something's different.* He backed it up and watched it again. *It doesn't seem natural. It's like watching a French movie with the English translation dubbed in. The lips are not quite in sync with the words being spoken.*

He searched the Web and found an earlier commercial. Derringer, dressed in his trademark Wyatt Earp outfit, pointing a pair of derringers at the camera. Rent watched the lips and facial expressions as the man spoke: "I'm aiming for change and a higher quality of life for the good citizens of this district. Together, we're going to recharge this valley, Lithium Valley. Vote Derringer for Congress. I'm Hal Derringer, and I approve this message."

Rent then slowed it down and played it again. *Looks pretty normal here.* He switched to the newer commercial and played it, then slowed it down and played it again.

"Dad, what are you doing?" Rachel asked. "If I'm going to make the honor roll, I have to do my homework."

"Come here, I want you to look at something."

Rachel sighed and left the dining table to join him.

Rent patted a cushion. "Sit here." He rotated the computer so she had a better view of the screen.

"I heard the whole thing . . . several times." She leaned forward, shaking her head. "That's Meghan's dad. I told you he's weird."

"I want you to watch his face and lips closely."

He played the earlier commercial.

"So?"

"Now watch this one." He played the one of Derringer sitting on his Harley, revving the engine, and promising to speed up the sloth-like legislative process in Washington.

"He sounds a little different, and it looks out of sync, like when we're watching Netflix and the audio is slightly delayed. I hate that."

"Do you remember those videos I showed you the other day, the vlogging monkey and George Washington?"

"Yeah, and the one with Jesus. They were funny."

"Uh-huh, and I think something funny is going on in this commercial."

"Play it again," she said. "I see what you mean. Do you think he's an avatar like in those AI videos?"

"It makes me wonder. But how can we tell for sure?"

"Play it again."

Rent played it again, then once more, slowed down.

Rachel nodded. "His lips are definitely out of sync."

He stared at the screen. "Which leads to the obvious next question: Why?" He stood up. "I'm getting some water. You want anything?"

"Ice cream?"

"Is your homework done?"

"It would be if you didn't keep interrupting me."

"You finish up, and then I'll break out the ice cream."

"Don't forget the chocolate sauce."

"Yes, ma'am."

Rent refilled his water bottle and added a few ice cubes, then excused himself to use the bathroom. When he returned, Rachel held up her math worksheet. "All done."

"Do you want me to check your work?"

"It's just ratios and percentages. Easy peasy."

"Did AI give you the answers?"

"No!" she countered, taking offense.

Rent snapped his fingers. "I got it! Steve."

"What are you talking about?"

"Steve, *Esteban*, the librarian, the guy who lives across the alley."

"What about him?"

"He's hard of hearing. Relies on lip reading to understand what people are saying. Everyone wearing masks during the pandemic drove him crazy. Especially doctor visits."

"He can read Mr. Derringer's lips and tell if it's really him or not?"

"Exactly."

"Are you gonna call him?" she asked.

"Text him."

"Oh, of course. Right now?"

"What time is it?"

Rachel checked her phone. "Seven thirty-four."

She then headed for the refrigerator.

* * *

Steve Lopez arrived at the door a few minutes past eight. "This sounds intriguing."

Rent motioned for him to take a seat at the dining table and tapped a key on the sleeping laptop. The screen lit up, displaying the two commercials side by side.

"Play the one on the left."

Lopez did not respond. Rent tapped his shoulder, and the man turned to face Rent, who repeated his words. The man nodded and turned back to the computer, moved the cursor to the middle of the video frame, and clicked. When the thirty-second commercial ended, Lopez faced Rent and grinned.

"He looks like one of those re-enactors who walk around Tombstone pretending to be one of the Earp brothers or Doc Holliday."

"What about his lips?" Rent asked. "Does that seem normal?"

Lopez nodded. "I could understand pretty much all of it. I'd never vote for the guy, that's for sure. He's like those rednecks where I come from."

Rachel tapped his shoulder. "Where do you come from?"

"I grew up on the rez in eastern Arizona."

"Are you an Indian?"

Lopez smiled at her frank query. "Mostly Apache, but one of my ancestors picked up little Spanish blood somewhere along the way, and they adopted some of the Spanish and Mexican culture, trying to fit in. Lot of good that did. I caught measles as a kid. No vaccination. That's how I lost my hearing. What now?"

"Play the other video, the one on the right."

Lopez clicked on the video frame, and his eyes never wavered from the screen. When it ended, he laughed, shaking his head. He turned to Rent and Rachel. "It's nonsense. His lip movements and facial expressions have nothing to do with the words we're hearing."

"I suspected as much," Rent said.

"Is this for real?"

"Oh, yeah. It's airing on TV in the Imperial Valley."

Lopez's face crinkled with amusement. "You gonna do an exposé on this?"

"I'm sure as hell going to start asking questions."

"It looks like an audio loop to me," he said.

Rent frowned. "What do you mean?"

"Every few seconds, the lips repeat the same movements even though the words are different. If I had to put words to it, I'd say he's saying, 'peas and carrots,' like actors do when working on their delivery. Or it could be 'fuck you, asshole.'" He glanced at Rachel. "Oops. Sorry 'bout that."

"That's OK," she said around a spoonful of ice cream. "My dad says it all the time."

Lopez grinned and continued. "But if the people watching are just listening and not paying close attention, it looks real enough to them. Like watching a cartoon."

"Or an avatar?"

Lopez furrowed his brow. "Abattoir?"

Rent shook his head and enunciated more succinctly. "Avatar, like in video games and artificial intelligence. Here, I'll show you." He slid the laptop closer to himself, tapped a few keys, and brought up the vlogging monkey video, then tapped it to play.

Lopez watched with a smile creasing his face. "This is incredible."

"Ain't it though? Watch this." Rent brought up the George Washington video depicting the general at Valley Forge and talking as if he and soldiers were out for a picnic.

"This is crazy shit," Lopez said. "They can rewrite history, and there are plenty of gullible people who will believe it."

"Yeah. It's scary shit is what it is," Rent said.

"Is this it? I gotta early day tomorrow. Driving to Arizona to visit my cousins."

"Yes, thank you for coming over on such short notice."

Lopez stood up. "My pleasure. My wife's going to love this. Or hate it."

"Oh?"

"She does videography, makes videos for businesses. Products and services. This type of thing could put her out of business."

"Let's hope not," Rent said, moving toward the front door. "Thanks again. I do appreciate it."

"Anytime."

27

Rent closed the door behind their departing guest and looked at Rachel. "I need to do an even deeper dive into AI. I'm getting a real funny feeling about this."

Rachel went to the dining table, plopped herself into the chair vacated by their neighbor, brought up the Google home page on the computer, and began typing.

"It's getting close to your bedtime, sweetie."

Rachel examined the results of her search and spoke without looking at her father. "Dad, in case you haven't noticed, it's Friday. If we were at a dance, I'd be up till midnight."

"No, you'd be asleep in a pew."

"Ha, ha. Come look at this."

"As soon as I make some coffee."

A few minutes later, Rent joined his daughter at the computer. "What've you got?"

She pointed at a list of recent news articles:

- HeyGen Releases AI Studio for Talking AI Avatars. What could possibly go wrong?
- See How Easily AI Chatbots Can Be Taught to Spew Disinformation. Notable cases involve audio and video, including artificially generated clips of politicians.
- AI Is Poised to Rewrite History. Literally.
- Mechanize, a San Francisco Start-up Says It Out Loud: It Wants AI to Take Your Job.

- Love Is a Drug. AI Chatbots Are Exploiting That.

Rent stared at the screen, shaking his head, then at his daughter. "I definitely have questions about these commercials. Makes me wonder if even Chuckwalla is behind the curve on this talking avatar technology."

"My social studies teacher said we could use AI and chatbots to do research and help write reports. Meghan and I are making videos for TikTok and YouTube. We made one of a frog talking, like the vlogging monkey."

"What does the frog say?"

"Kiss me, princess . . . rivet, rivet . . . Kiss me, princess . . . rivet, rivet . . . We got over a thousand hits on TikTok."

"But for serious schoolwork, isn't that considered cheating? Or plagiarism?"

"Mr. Billingham said it's not cheating as long as we write the reports in our own words. That AI is no different than looking up stuff in books or a dictionary or encyclopedia or Wikipedia. It's just a lot faster."

"So, are you?"

Rachel didn't answer right away, her eyes searching Rent's face for clues as to whether he disapproved of it or not. She equivocated. "I'm thinking about it. I have to write an essay, do research."

"You *are* using AI."

She blushed. "He said it's OK."

"Because he knows it's inevitable. But who's going to fact-check it for you?"

She shrugged, and he continued. "I read an article by a writer who said he spent hours fact-checking the information he got from AI because he couldn't trust it to be a hundred percent accurate. For example, he said a lawyer filed a motion in court that cited references that did not exist; that AI just made it up. And I heard an NPR news story recently about a list of recommended books by famous authors that was generated by AI, but some of the titles were made up. They were fake."

He looked at Rachel. "Are you crying?"

She wiped a tear from a cheek. "You're saying I can't use AI, but Meghan and my other friends are. They use ChatGPT all the time. It's fun. It's like talking to a real person."

"Oh, sweetie . . . no. That's not what I'm saying."

"That's what it sounds like."

"I'm just saying you have to be careful because sometimes it makes stuff up; it hallucinates. You can't always trust Wikipedia either. The citations have to be examined and evaluated for legitimacy to filter out crackpot conspiracy theories and flat-out disinformation."

She reached for a Kleenex to dry her eyes. "We want to join Girls Who Code." Rent creased his brow as she added, "It's a club where . . ."

"That sounds great. Tell you what," he continued, "you do your research, and I'll help you fact-check it. OK?" She sniffed and nodded. "Now, I think you should get ready for bed and brush your teeth. And don't forget to floss."

"Don't you want to know what I'm writing the essay on?"

"Yeah, sorry. I should have asked. Is it about the frogs?"

She smiled. "No. Halloween and Día de los Muertos—the Day of the Dead. The frogs are for science; the Halloween one is for English."

"I like that. And timely, too. It's only a few weeks away."

"I'm doing it as a graphic essay."

Rent squinted, questioning. "Graphic essay?"

"Uh-huh. Sort of like a graphic novel, but way shorter."

"That's a new one on me, but you can certainly draw," he said, turning to admire the framed sketch she had made of him playing his fiddle.

"I look forward to seeing what you find out and how the two holidays are related—or not. Now, off you go. We need an early start to beat the heat if we're going for a ride."

* * *

Back at Rent's condo following their morning ride, Rachel began her research on Halloween and Día de los Muertos in earnest.

Rent suggested she do a regular search first and see what she finds, then use AI to see how they match up and if the AI hallucinates.

"I'll do it too. I'm curious. And we can compare our results. But you have to do the writing all on your own."

They each worked separately for an hour, then took a break to have a snack and beverage.

"So, what did you find out?" Rent asked.

She looked at him in disbelief. "What is this, a pop quiz?"

"Not at all. I'm just curious what stands out in your mind. What did you learn that you didn't know and that you would have fun showing your friends how smart you are?"

Her face brightened. "OK. Well . . . did you know that Halloween started in Ireland with the Celts, and then the Irish came to America and brought it with them?" She pronounced the "C" in Celts as an "S."

"So, you're saying the Boston Celtics came from Halloween? They do play like a bunch of clowns sometimes."

Rachel gave him a faux slap. "No-o-o. Stop making fun of me or I'll stop telling you about Halloween."

"All right, sorry. Please continue. But one thing: in Ireland they say the "C" like a 'K' as in cat, so it sounds like 'Kelts.' I play some Celtic tunes on the fiddle."

She glowered at him, her arms akimbo. "Are you going to let me finish?"

"You have the floor. It's all yours."

"So . . . Halloween came from the Celtics—with a 'K' sound—and their celebration of Samhain, which started thousands of years ago, way before Jesus." She spelled out "Samhain" and said it was pronounced as "sow-en."

"They built bonfires at night and wore masks and costumes so witches and evil spirits of the dead couldn't recognize them. And the first jack-o'-lantern was made by a man named Stingy Jack, but it wasn't made from a pumpkin."

Rent tilted his head and shot her a wide-eyed look of amazement, a poor imitation of a jack-o'-lantern. "You don't say."

Rachel giggled and said, "I do say. It was carved out of a huge turnip. But after Halloween came to America, they started carving pumpkins instead because they were easier to carve and there were more of them."

"I did not know that. What about trick-or-treating? Where did that come from?"

"I have to do more research, but I read one thing that said it started in Canada by boys pulling pranks on adults."

"Now that's something I never would have done," Rent said with a wink.

"You were probably the worst one."

"Now, now . . . I don't know where you got that idea."

She reprimanded him with narrowed eyes.

"But, hey, you're doing great," he said. "Anything else?"

"Like what?"

"Like why is it celebrated on October thirty-first? Why not September twenty-first, the autumnal equinox? Or in December, like Christmas?"

"Samhain was a celebration of the end of harvest season, when the days got shorter. It was their New Year's."

"Oh, I see."

"Then Christianity came to Ireland, and the priests said it was pagan, so they made a new holy day, All Saints' Day, on November first, and that's how Halloween got its name, from All Hallow's Eve, because for the Celts, the new day actually began at sunset, not at midnight. So, here's the real secret—"

She paused for effect.

"Yeeesss?"

"Samhain is actually the same day as All Saints' Day; it just starts at sunset, and . . ." She paused again. "Some people in Ireland still call it Samhain, not Halloween."

"Wow, you are so smart. You must have gotten that from your father; I mean your mother. What about Día de los Muertos?"

"I only just started that, but it's totally different. It comes from the Aztecs in Mexico."

"So, it's just a coincidence that they are celebrated at the same time?"

"No. When the priests came to Mexico, they did the same thing as with Samhain. They made a new holy day, All Souls Day, on November second, turning the natives' holiday that they celebrated in the summer into the two-day Christian holiday, but the people still do a lot of the same stuff they did before. They honor their dead relatives. There's lots of skulls and skeletons, so it kinda looks like Halloween, but it's not."

"Wow. I didn't know that either. You're off to a good start, sweetie. I can't wait to see your essay and the great pictures you'll draw for it."

"I'm going to draw a Celtic calendar. It's round, like a circle—totally different from the calendar we have."

"So, how did they know to celebrate Samhain on October thirty-first?"

"I have to do more research on that, too."

"I found some information that will help you with that."

"OK, but can we do something else now?"

28

Monday morning, Rent made his way to the break room, where he encountered Greg Papadopoulos, aka "Greg the Greek Geek," and asked him about artificial intelligence companies in San Diego.

"There are dozens of them," he said, "some with a very narrow focus, like defense systems, aviation, automotive, customer support, et cetera." One company, he added, specialized in housekeeping using robotics.

"You mean like Roomba?"

"Yes, but much more sophisticated. For cleaning commercial properties, hotels, office buildings. That sort of thing."

Papadopoulos went on to say that other AI companies were more generalized. "They claim to offer . . ."—he waggled air quotes—"'transparent, ethical, transformative technology' and 'bespoke generative AI applications,' 'integrated seamlessly into enterprise systems.'"

"Bespoke? Surely AI could come up with something a bit less pretentious—even laughable—than that. One might conclude they're an English tailor or cobbler."

The man shrugged. "AI with an Oxbridge accent. They all spout the usual empty buzzwords and hyperbole you'd expect from marketing departments in the corporate sphere. AI just regurgitates whatever BS it's been fed, or it makes stuff up. Superficial generalizations that sound good initially but, upon further examination, lack any practical or pragmatic 'solutions,' as they like to call it."

"You say that as if it's a bad thing."

They both laughed, and Papadopoulos continued. "The issue with AI, as I see it, is that these tech evangelists believe it's a magic wand, so it becomes a 'solution' in search of a problem. Thus, AI outfits are sprouting like mushrooms after a rainstorm and having cash thrown at them as if it were Monopoly money. A bit like the tech bubble in the nineties when the Internet and World Wide Web took off. I suspect a lot of them will be weeded out when the bubble bursts."

Papadopoulos paused for a beat, then continued. "An industry analyst I spoke with said, 'There is no AI revolution. It's a cash bonfire. The financial model is upside down.'"

"How so?"

"It doesn't have economies of scale," Papadopoulos explained. "The AI firms gloss it over, but unlike traditional software, where more users cost less to serve and the per-unit cost decreases, AI gets more expensive due to the high cost of computing. According to him, the bubble will burst; many tulips will wither and die."

Rent pondered his colleague's assessment for a moment, then asked the question at the forefront of his mind: "You know anything about Chuckwalla Enterprises, some kind of AI outfit under the aegis of Lustrous Consulting, the Johnson family's ever-expanding 'enterprise'?" Rent inquired, waggling air quotes of his own.

His colleague frowned. "Chuckwalla? Isn't that some kind of desert reptile, like an iguana?"

"Yeah. The data center is located in the desert, in Mexicali."

Papadopoulos's eyes widened. "South of the border?" Rent nodded, and Papadopoulos continued. "Never heard of it. Does it have anything to do with the story you're working on?"

"That's what I'm trying to figure out. The Johnsons have their fingers in so many pies, it leaves my head spinning."

"Maybe that's the point. Distraction. Like a magician and sleight of hand."

"Or like a politician. You may be onto something there."

"I can get you a list of prominent San Diego AI companies, but as I said, there are dozens of them, and they're into every aspect of business. Are you looking for anything in particular?"

"Marketing, PR, political campaigns."

Papadopoulos snorted. "Politics and AI. Now there's a minefield waiting to explode. I'll see what I can find."

* * *

Rent hunched over his laptop, checking his text messages. One from Alicia:

Before we leave, scan vehicles.

He left the newsroom and drove to her house. She stepped out holding an electronic device that, at first glance, looked like an electric toothbrush. She led him to her Honda CR-V, turned on the device, and pointed it under the frame as she crept the length of the car. As she reached the rear end, the device began beeping.

She handed it to Rent, along with a pair of latex gloves, and told him to lie on his back and see what he could find. He followed her instructions, moving the device back and forth until he had homed in on a specific location.

"I don't see anything."

"You have to feel around for it. It won't bite you."

"Got it," he said, and he scooted out from under the car.

She held open an evidence bag. He dropped the tracking device in the bag, and she switched it off.

"Now do yours."

It took him only a few minutes to find an identical device fastened to the undercarriage of the rented RAV4.

"Devious bastards. These are like the one the cops found on my pickup."

She nodded. "Fifteen bucks online. I have several. I'll get these to Alvarez. Maybe they can lift some prints."

"That scanner of yours is pretty slick too."

"Fifty bucks on online."

"We should put these things on some of the Incinergy trucks," Rent said.

"Yeah, if we could ever get close to them."

* * *

That evening, once the traffic jam on I-8 east had cleared out, Rent and Alicia headed east for the two-hour drive to Imperial Valley, Alicia at the wheel. On the way, they reviewed their plans for the next two days. Up before dawn to "follow the trucks." Interviews in the afternoon. Stakeouts after dark. Repeat.

Rent took up a monologue on AI, as if delivering a crash-course lecture on the state of the industry and reciting its potential pitfalls. "There's so much BS being tossed around, *artificial* becomes the operative word," Rent said.

"If you say so," Alicia replied, having remained silent throughout his rant.

He glanced at her, brows furrowed. *What's eating her?*

They descended the treacherous chicane that led them out of the boulder-strewn mountainous terrain onto the flat expanse of the Anza-Borrego Desert. Rent chuckled and said, "Chicanery. Now there's an appropriate description of it."

"Rent, will you please stop."

He stared at her for a moment. "Do you want me to drive?"

"No, I want you to STFU—shut the fuck up. Enough of this AI crap."

"Geez, I thought you were interested in this stuff. It's practically taking over our lives."

"Apparently, it has taken over your life already," she retorted and sped up to 85, weaving in and out of slower-moving cars and trucks.

"Whoa, that was close," he muttered.

More minutes passed until she eased off the accelerator and levered the turn signal. The car began to slow, and she braked as she took the exit ramp into the Sunbeam Rest Area.

"I need to use the bathroom," she said and parked.

Rent got out and stretched his legs. Chatting grackles flitted from palm to palm in the warm twilight; a black-necked stilt foraged in the small pond adjacent to the structure.

Alicia returned to the car and sat in the driver's seat. Rent joined her. When she made no effort to start the car, he asked, "Are we going? Or spending the night here?"

"In a minute, but first there's something I need to say."

She stared through the windshield for a moment before turning to face him. She swallowed, then began.

"I'm feeling used and unappreciated. All too often, the time we spend together is related to your job—"

"Alicia, I—"

"Let me finish."

"OK."

"Yes, we spend a lot of time with one another, and I do like being with you. Mostly. But maybe it's too much time."

"Are you saying you want to break up?"

"No! Not at all. It's just that so much of the time we spend together is about your job or your daughter and not just me, your girlfriend, your lover.

"I want to feel special too. I get a phone call or text, and I'm hoping to hear or see a 'Hi, how are you? I miss you.' Maybe an eggplant emoji. But more often than not it's you wanting something, a name or phone number looked up, or do I want to go to a soccer game, or a contra dance, or a music recital involving Rachel.

"Don't get me wrong. I like Rachel, and I know how much she means to you, but I also need to feel loved and have you to myself once in a while."

Rent exhaled a long sigh. "OK, I'll try to do better. I do want you in my life, and I didn't realize . . ." His voice drifted off as he reached out to touch her thigh.

She swatted his hand away. "Not now. We need to get moving if we're going to get an early start.

"Vámonos. Estoy cansado."

* * *

Alicia lay on her side, curled up at the edge of the mattress, her back to Rent, who lay on his back, staring at the ceiling. He rolled over, his back to her, and willed himself to sleep. It did not come. He felt her stir as she rolled over onto her back.

"I'm sorry," she whispered. Rent remained silent. "I'm sorry I got short with you. I didn't mean to sound harsh. But I had to say something; get it off my chest."

Rent felt her fingertips on his shoulder, and he grasped them with his own. They felt so tiny, delicate, fragile. They lay there, unmoving, for a long moment until he rolled into her and stretched an arm across her abdomen. She twisted her head and kissed him lightly on the cheek. He slid his hand under her pajamas top, moving it slowly toward her breasts, but she stopped him.

"Not tonight," she said as she raised up on one elbow, briefly touched her lips to his, then rolled away and pulled the top sheet taut over her shoulder.

"Maybe we could have an actual date," she said in a low voice, as if speaking to herself. Rent could barely make out her words as she continued. "Go to Las Chabelas, have some tequila shots and beer, dance to *my* music for a change."

29

The following day, Rent and Alicia followed Incinergy trucks to the waste disposal site in Mexico and back to the border. Alicia pulled to the side of the road and stopped just short of the SENTRI lane leading across the border from Mexico into the United States.

A seemingly endless parade of trucks crossed into and out of Mexico. Most of them were box trailers, and they could only guess what the cargo consisted of. Many of them crossing into the U.S. were directed into secondary inspection and opened up for greater scrutiny by U.S. customs officials. Drug-sniffing dogs patrolled the compound.

The Incinergy trucks seemed to breeze through with only a cursory stop at the primary inspection point. Alicia used a stopwatch to time them and recorded the figures on a spreadsheet.

"I'm impressed," Rent said.

She glanced his way. "In what way?"

"You are so organized. So precise."

"It's all part of the job. Much more boring than Jim Rockford would have you believe."

"That's probably a good thing."

"It beats getting the crap knocked out of you all the time." She glanced at the rearview mirror. "Uh-oh. We've got company."

A Mexican police car had pulled behind them, and two uniformed officers emerged from the car. One approached the driver's door while the other took a position on the opposite side. Alicia rolled down the window.

"¿Hablas Español?" the officer asked.

"Pocito," she replied.

The man spoke in Spanish, and she got the gist of it: She had parked illegally and would be fined, and he wanted to see identification, proof of ownership, and insurance. She and Rent produced their passports, and Rent pulled the registration and insurance documents from the glove compartment. The officer took them to his car.

"You think Mendoza will notice this item on your expense report?" Rent said in an effort to lighten the moment.

"Right now, I'm more concerned about having my car towed."

"Another Incinergy truck just pulled into the FAST lane, this one with a dump trailer."

"Keep an eye on it, and maybe we can be waiting for it on the other side."

The officer returned and handed the documents through the window. *"Doscientos dólares,"* he said.

"Two hundred dollars," Alicia translated.

Rent's face contorted. "For a parking ticket?"

The officer spoke again, and Alicia translated as best she could. "I think he wants us to follow him to the police station."

"Fuck me," Rent muttered.

Alicia leaned her head out the window. *"¿Dólares aquí?"* she asked, preferring to pay him on the spot, and the man nodded his assent. She turned to Rent. "How much cash do you have?"

Rent reached for his wallet. "A hundred maybe? You don't suppose he'd take a credit card."

"Fat chance," she said and turned her eyes back to the police officer. She countered with, *"¿Uno cien dólares?"*—$100—and reached for her purse.

The officer shook his head. *"Ciento setenta y cinco."*

"These numbers are getting a bit complicated for me," she said as she fished out her wallet from her purse. "I think he's now asking for a hundred seventy-five."

She examined her wallet and turned back to the police officer. *"Ciento cincuenta,"* she offered and translated for Rent. "Hundred fifty."

The man nodded and held out his hand. Alicia pulled some bills from her wallet.

"Fucking extortion," Rent muttered and handed her five twenties.

Alicia showed the bills to the officer, and he nodded again, his face expressionless. He accepted the money and said, *"¿Todo es bueno?"*

"Sí, todo es bueno," she replied.

"Vaya con dios."

Alicia sighed heavily. "Let's get the hell out of here."

"Wow, you handled that well," Rent said.

"Thanks to my friend Ellis. She told me about her encounter with a cop in Tijuana on her way home from Camp Salvador. She negotiated the guy down from four hundred to two hundred."

* * *

Back on the U.S. side, they parked at Maggio Road and climbed atop a hillock, where they had a better view of the border crossing.

Rent peered through the spotting scope. "Here comes that Incinergy truck. He barely slowed down at the inspection point."

Alicia had brought along folding chairs and umbrellas for their stakeout. "It's getting hot. We're not gonna last long."

"There must be a better way of doing this."

She said she would go over it with Miguel Mendoza at their meeting and see what he says. They stayed there for another twenty minutes. As they began folding the umbrellas and chairs, a white SUV with a green stripe pulled up, and two uniformed agents got out: Border Patrol.

"Whatcha lookin' at?" one of the officers inquired.

"Birds," Alicia said. "Heard a report of a rare trogon spotted here. It would be a lifer."

"Uh-huh. Not waiting to transport illegals then?"

"No, sir," Alicia said. "Minding our own business."

"Then how about minding it somewhere else?"

"Last I heard, this was still a free country," Rent said.

"If you're an American citizen, it is," the man replied, then focused his eyes on Alicia. "Otherwise, I need to see your documentation."

"And if we don't, what're you gonna do, ship us off to El Salvador or Sudan?"

Alicia jabbed an elbow into Rent's ribs.

The officer flicked his brows at Alicia before shifting his gaze to Rent. "Don't press your luck."

Alicia intervened. "No problem, officer. I have my passport in the car." She retrieved her passport, along with Rent's, and handed them to the man. He examined them both, lingering on Alicia's, then handed them back.

"As I said, I suggest you do your so-called bird watching a little further away from the border. I'd hate for there to be a misunderstanding."

Rent opened his mouth, starting to speak, and Alicia jabbed him again. "We were just leaving," she said, and turned to Rent. "Grab the scope." She pocketed the passports and gathered up the chairs and umbrellas.

Once in the car and headed north, she questioned, "Why do you always have to be such a wiseass? They could have detained us for God knows how long just out of spite."

Rent shrugged. "If we don't stand up for our rights, soon we have no rights."

"There's a time and place for that. This is not the time nor the place," she retorted. "¡Vamos!"

They spotted the truck as it neared Calipatria and followed it to the same facility as before.

"Maybe we ought to stake out this place tonight. See who's coming and going," Rent said.

"Good idea," Alicia replied, "but right now we have meetings to get to."

30

Rent entered the candidate's campaign headquarters, introduced himself to the twenty-something blonde receptionist, and she escorted him to the candidate's private office. Rent gave Hal Derringer a quick once-over as he took a seat across the desk from the congressional candidate. A framed photograph of him, his wife, and daughter perched on the credenza behind him.

That black hair looks like a Rudy Giuliani dye job, and what's with that mustache? Does this guy own a mirror?

Rent began with a general question about Derringer's key issues as a conservative candidate facing the popular liberal incumbent, Diego Rivera. Derringer pointed out that he won the primary by nearly twenty points. He cited immigration, water rights, green energy, the Second Amendment, and reducing restrictions on the "highly and unjustly regulated" mining of lithium as his chief planks as a member of the House of Representatives.

"So, immigration is your top priority?" Rent asked.

"It's the current administration's top priority, and it's a huge issue for California, so, yes, I intend to support the president's agenda in that regard. We have to take control of the border and deport these illegals that are committing crimes and terrorizing our law-abiding citizens."

Rent rolled his eyes. "Is this your warmup for the Fox News interview?"

"It never hurts to drive home your talking points."

"These aren't my talking points."

"Grammar Nazi, are you? You know what I mean."

"And the Imperial County sheriff has endorsed these talking points?"

"We've asked for his endorsement, yes, and he's been cooperative in identifying and rounding up these lawbreakers."

"That's not what I hear," Rent fired back. "It's my understanding that the sheriff's office has joined a growing number of law enforcement agencies that are limiting their participation in the federal program unless it comes with a warrant from a judge."

"As I said, the sheriff is being cooperative in these efforts to combat crime and illegal immigration."

"You are aware that being undocumented is not a criminal offense; it's a civil offense."

"That may be, but I'm talking about those who are committing violent crimes—rape, murder, drugs. I want to see that the president's arrest and deportation quotas are being met."

"So, you believe that the quotas are a coherent immigration policy and not an arbitrary political calculation that has proven to be impractical, if not unlawful, and leading to the arrest and detention of law-abiding American citizens, while court ruling after court ruling demand that habeas corpus and due process be adhered to as defined in the U.S. Constitution."

"There are some issues to be addressed, but something has to be done about the millions of people living in this great country illegally."

"What about the undocumented who live in your district, in this very town, who constitute a significant part of agricultural labor, pay taxes, pay into Social Security even though they're not eligible to claim it when, and if, they retire. What's Big Agra have to say about this policy? And why aren't the people hiring these undocumented workers being arrested?"

"Many of the undocumented workers have fake papers, so it's not always immediately clear that they are, in fact, illegal. The employers are unknowingly hiring illegals. In many cases, they are victims, not perpetrators."

Rent scoffed. "Many of these businesses advertise in papers south of the border, promising jobs if they cross the border any way they can."

Derringer ignored Rent's assertion. "Besides . . ." The man leaned forward and lowered his voice to evince a conspiratorial tone. ". . . the administration has instructed ICE to turn a blind eye on businesses in the agricultural, hospitality, and meatpacking industries."

"Lobbyists threatening to withhold big beautiful campaign donations, are they?"

When the candidate did not immediately respond, Rent continued. "As for criminality, the FBI has shown that undocumented immigrants have low criminal rates, and demonizing them only makes them less cooperative with law enforcement when it comes to solving actual criminal cases."

"As I said, this administration is addressing important issues facing our country that the liberals and progressives of previous administrations have failed to do. He has a mandate and he's taking that very seriously. He'd be able to accomplish more if it weren't for those activist judges rewriting the Constitution. At least we've got some of their gun-rights restrictions overturned."

Rent lifted a hand, indicating he got the man's point. "OK, enough about that," Rent said. "Let's talk about the sudden flood of AI technology into our society, its impact on the labor market, and a call for greater regulation. Some folks are saying that this will be the greatest issue facing our country, and the world, going forward."

"Aren't you going to ask me about Lithium Valley?"

"OK. What are you going to do to get lithium production moving forward?"

"I'm glad you asked that," he answered and spouted the same happy talk Rent had heard before, about how lithium extraction would improve the lives of everyone living in Lithium Valley.

"That's great in theory, but what's the hang-up?"

"Liberals and so-called progressives and their never-ending lawsuits and regulations. I'm going to introduce legislation to turn that around."

"Are you going to introduce legislation regarding AI as well?"

"Back to AI, are we?" Derringer said he applauded AI as an important tool for business, bringing billions of dollars of investment into that sector of our economy—the fastest-growing segment of high tech in the nation, if not the world.

Rent nodded. "Yet, isn't it also threatening massive layoffs and unemployment? Some AI companies are even bragging about it. Robots now reign in manufacturing, and next in line are low-level white-collar jobs."

"AI is creating many new, higher-paying jobs," Derringer replied. "I imagine even you, if you lose your job, could be upskilled."

Rent forced a pained smile. "Upskilled. Uh-huh. But, due to increased efficiency and robotics, won't fewer jobs be created than those lost?"

The man shrugged and leaned back in his chair, arms crossed. "That remains to be seen."

Rent glanced at his notes and said, "One AI guru says he believes AI would eventually create—and I quote—'radical abundance' and wealth that could be redistributed to laid-off workers."

"Do you have a question?" Derringer asked.

"I'm leading up to that. What's your opinion on the notion of a 'universal basic income' as this guy and several other AI entrepreneurs have suggested? That AI will generate so much wealth that folks left out of the labor market will receive monthly stipends from the government that will—and again I quote—'allow them to maintain a high living standard'? That sounds a bit naïve to me."

"It's one of several aspects of AI that's open for discussion."

"Seriously? Could . . . would you support that as a conservative member of Congress? A Congress that has a significant number of members who want to put a job requirement on Medicaid, do away with SNAP, and eliminate Social Security? How is a 'universal basic income' not that dreaded and derided doctrine known as 'socialism'? And where does the money being distributed come from if not from exponentially higher taxes on those making the big bucks?"

"As I said, it's open for discussion. Is there anything else?" Derringer responded as he glanced at his watch. "I have an important meeting to . . ."

"What about increased regulation of AI? A number of people, even within the AI community, say it needs greater regulation to combat a flood of AI-generated deepfakes fueling fraud, harmful impersonation, and sexual abuse, not to mention legal and financial scams?"

When Derringer did not respond immediately, Rent continued. "Meanwhile, the current administration chucked out the previous administration's AI executive order and removed federal AI guidelines from official websites. In addition, others, in particular the billionaire CEOs of some of the largest and most powerful companies—Musk, Bezos, Zuckerman, et al.—adamantly oppose increased AI regulation and are lobbying Congress for a ten-year moratorium on any such regulation, saying 'onerous regulations' need to be rolled back, not increased."

"I would support that legislation," Derringer responded. "Greater regulation will hinder innovation and slow the adoption of this cutting-edge technology—a technology changing so rapidly that the regulations can't keep up and would quickly become out of date, if not irrelevant, and work at cross purposes. There are also First Amendment and free-speech issues to be addressed."

"But what about abuse? The use of generative AI, and now agentic AI, to make it easier and more efficient to commit fraud, the wide dissemination of not only misinformation but disinformation and deepfakes?

"We've already seen disturbing examples of this. Elon Musk has sued the state of California to block its election deepfakes law. In addition, he and others opened the floodgates for propaganda to spread unchecked during the previous election cycle."

Rent's phone vibrated in a pants pocket. *Crap. I forgot to switch to airplane mode.* He pulled it out and glanced at the screen. Message from Alicia. He looked at Derringer. "Sorry, please continue."

Derringer leaned forward as if to emphasize his point. "As usual, the *media* . . ." He said "media" in a tone of derision while contorting his face. ". . . blows this way out of proportion, crying Chicken Little. And you can quote me on that. From what I've seen, the so-called deepfakes don't amount to anything more than amusement for the masses on TikTok and YouTube. Some are actually pretty funny. My daughter has shown them to me."

"Would you include your own commercials in that category?"

"You've seen them, have you?"

"They're hard to miss."

"I'm having fun with them, but when it comes to the underlying message, I'm dead serious."

When Rent did not reply, the candidate took a deep breath and continued. "There will always be bad actors out there trying to game the system, but I don't see a need for more onerous regulations tying the hands of our burgeoning entrepreneurs unless significant problems emerge. We'll cross that bridge when we come to it."

"So, you see no need to be preemptive. Cut it off at the pass, so to speak?"

"History has taught us that leads to overreach."

"History, eh? What about AI in political campaigns? I think you would agree that AI is a cost-effective tool to produce promotional material and commercials for broadcast media, radio, TV, podcasts, and so on. Is that why Lustrous built a data center in Mexico and launched its own AI venture, in part to support your political campaign?"

"I'm glad you asked that," Derringer replied. "The data center has a much greater purpose than supporting my campaign. Even now, Chuckwalla has many clients using its powerful data-processing capability as well as its proprietary platform, AIsha. It's already improving efficiencies in our other operations, including JMJ . . ."

"The design and construction of ADUs and affordable housing and cramming as many units as possible into small spaces," Rent injected. "Or so Mikey, your father-in-law, told me."

"Exactly . . . creating efficiencies and maximizing gain. Ditto for the other operations, including the solar farms, geothermal power, lithium mining, hazardous waste disposal . . ."

"Has AI improved the design of your incinerator technology, or does it still emit highly poisonous dioxins into the atmosphere? Another area where the current administration has rolled back regulations."

"You'll have to talk to BJ about—" He cut himself short. "That's preposterous. Where the hell do you get off making unfounded allegations?"

"Your grandfather-in-law said that thirty years ago, and look where that got him."

"It got him where he is today, a highly successful businessman. But you'll have to talk to him about that."

"Oh, don't worry, I will. And who's BJ?"

"Will that be all?"

"One more question: What does AIsha do, exactly?" Rent asked.

Derringer spouted the usual clichés of improving enterprise efficiencies, scaling without increasing headcount, development of bespoke apps tailored to a client's unique needs. He ended his spiel by saying Rent would have to talk to Chuckwalla CEO Ramesh Kumar for specific details, provided it didn't violate any confidentiality agreements with his clients.

"I've tried, but so far he has not responded."

"He's a busy man."

"Does Chuckwalla and its AIsha platform produce videos? Videos with sound?"

"I suppose it has that capability. Again, you need to speak to Ramesh."

"Thank you for your time, Mr. Derringer. I do appreciate it, and good luck with your campaign."

The receptionist, who looked as if everything about her consisted of a deepfake—from her perky blonde ponytail to her Grand Canyon-esque cleavage and obvious Botox to the fanciful pedicure— reappeared almost ghostlike. She shot a knowing glance at Derringer, then escorted Rent from the building with an artificial "Have a nice day."

* * *

Rent spotted Alicia parked at the curb and joined her.

"How'd it go?" she asked as she pulled away.

"Typical politician. BS on steroids," he replied. "*¿Y tú?*"

"*Un poco de lo mismo.*"

"Oh, yeah?"

"Waste of time," she translated. "He didn't make any sense. I think he's having an affair with an employee, his missus got suspicious, and now he's trying to turn his *señorita* into a scapegoat. *¡Imbécil engañoso!*"

"So, no glass slipper on a satin pillow for her."

"Hardly."

Rent jerked a thumb over his shoulder. "I wouldn't be surprised if a little hanky-panky isn't going on back there as well," he said, adding, "I don't know about you, but I'm hungry enough to eat a chuckwalla."

Alicia crunched her face. *"Lo siento, señor. La verdad, tengo una más apetecible por chuckwalla."*

Rent chuckled, not able to translate precisely, but he understood the bit about "no appetite for chuckwalla."

"Figuratively speaking," he replied.

She returned to Brawley's main drag and pulled up in front of a Subway sandwich shop. Rent looked at her askance.

She smirked and said, "I have a coupon."

* * *

Rent and Alicia found Miguel Mendoza seated in the shade at a table at the Sonny Bono National Wildlife Refuge. He told them how he had used a stake-bed truck to follow the Incinergy trucks across the border and get the IDs of agents waving them through.

"There are two CBP agents for sure, possibly more, but I'm afraid they're getting suspicious," he said.

He handed them a sheaf of papers. "These records document the dates and times I observed this, along with the names of the agents."

He had done the same for the Mexican side as well. "But I don't know how much good that will do."

Mendoza also informed them that CBP agents, along with other law enforcement types, hung out at a bar in El Centro. "You ought to check it out."

* * *

They returned to the motel to cool off, shower, and get some rest before their stakeout at the maintenance facility after dark.

Alicia stretched out on the king-size bed. "Nap time," she said.

Rent joined her. "That would be nice, but I have trouble sleeping during the day."

She rolled into him and laid an arm across his bare torso. "I have cure for that."

After they woke, they ate their Subway leftovers, then tended to their paperwork. Alicia organized the information they had gathered, while Rent worked on a draft of his next piece on Lustrous, Lithium Valley, and the Derringer campaign.

As twilight began to set in, they drove to the bar in El Centro that Mendoza had told them about. They noted a few expensive vehicles in the parking lot and logged the makes and models, along with the license plate numbers, including a red Maserati.

"These guys must get paid big bucks," Alicia said.

"Let's go inside and check it out," Rent replied. "I could handle a burger and fries."

"No booze," she cautioned.

They stepped through the doorway and let their eyes adjust to the dim light, then found an empty table. As they looked over the menu, a man in uniform stopped and loomed over them.

"Well, well, if it isn't Rent-a-Bum, the infamous yellow journalist, and Little Miss Pee-eye," the man said.

Rent recognized him as one of the agents they had encountered near the border that morning.

The man continued, "I don't want to have to say it again: Time for you to move on, far away from the border."

"Or what?" Rent asked.

The room went silent, other than Robert Plant belting out a lyric from *Stairway to Heaven*.

The man shrugged, then grinned as he surveyed the room before looking straight into Rent's eyes. *"Hasta la vista, bay-bee."*

The room echoed with a forest of laughter.

31

Idiots!" Rent muttered as they drove away from the bar.

"To whom are you referring?" Alicia asked, a tone of annoyance clouding her query.

"Us. You and me."

"Speak for yourself."

"We should be in disguise. You know, if you can't beat 'em, join 'em."

She stared at him, her brow corrugated.

"I was in Food4Less the other day, and standing just inside the door is this dude dressed like an ICE agent. Total camo, heavy boots, unmarked vest, black mask, and stocking cap. The only thing missing was an AR-15. I couldn't believe it. Scary as all hell. Even so, I had to stop myself from laughing out loud, thinking, *Is this guy for real? This is a grocery store.*

"When I checked out, I asked the clerk about him. She scoffed, saying he was store security, and whispered, 'We call him Mr. Scarecrow.'"

"So you want us to become scarecrows?"

"Yeah. These private militia types already patrol the border. We could just pretend to be part of that. Give us some cover."

"Uh-huh. Driving a Honda CR-V."

"So we rent a honkin' Dodge Ram pickup and get outfitted at Walmart. You can expense it to Mendoza. Meanwhile, let's check out the Incinergy field office."

* * *

They drove slowly past the Incinergy maintenance facility in Calipatria. The place looked deserted. Alicia suggested they get some coffee and a bite to eat and come back. An hour later, they returned.

"Looks awful quiet to me," Rent said.

"I'll park down the road, and we can walk back," she replied.

"Pretend we're looking for owls?"

She scoffed. "Lovers out for a nighttime stroll."

"Carrying a telephoto lens?"

She parked the car, and they sauntered back, acting nonchalant. Still no action, so they kept on for several hundred yards, then retraced their steps and sat on a lone hay bale.

After twenty minutes, Rent grew impatient and stood up saying he needed to water a bush. As he returned, Alicia whispered to him. "Over here."

He joined her, and she told him a pickup had pulled up to the compound entrance, but she didn't recognize the two men who got out.

"They look Mexican. They're standing by the gate, smoking. Thanks to the security light, I got photos."

The pair crept back to their lookout spot. A few minutes later, a red Maserati arrived, the gate opened, and the car went through, followed by the pickup. The vehicles parked next the building and two men got out of each vehicle.

The men greeted the each other perfunctorily. One of the guys from the Maserati unlocked the office door, and they all went inside, but not before Alicia whirred off more photos.

"That car looks like the one we saw at the bar in El Centro."

She photographed it and enlarged it on the camera's screen to read the license plate. "I think it's the same car."

"Gotta be one of the bigwigs," Rent said.

A few minutes later, a large door on the side of the warehouse rattled open. One of the first arrivals emerged, got in the pickup, drove it into the warehouse, and the door rolled down.

"This is the handoff," Rent said.

Fifteen minutes later, the door opened again; the truck rolled out and stopped. The bed of the truck had been filled with bales of straw.

"Wanna bet what's hidden under that straw?" Rent muttered.

The three other men came out, shook hands and said a few words, although neither Rent nor Alicia could make out what they said.

One of the men got into the truck and it drove off. The other two went back inside, closed the warehouse door, then emerged from and locked the office door. They got into the Maserati and eased out of the compound, then waited until the gate had closed before driving off.

"I hope these photos turn out OK," Alicia said. "I'll print them on the Epson Picturemate in the motel room."

* * *

The next morning, they returned to the border in the rented Dodge Ram and began surveillance in earnest, equipped with snacks and a Styrofoam chest containing iced beverages and fresh fruit. Border Patrol officers didn't exactly welcome them, but they didn't intervene, either.

"I just hope we don't run into the guy from the bar," Rent said. "Or we might be on the stairway to heaven."

* * *

They spent the day crisscrossing the border, following the trucks and their occupants, at times getting waves and thumbs-up from passersby, while others gave them the finger and cursed them. They noted shift changes, officers leaving work while others arrived, one driving an Escalade SUV.

On the U.S. side, an Incinergy truck pulled into a truck stop, even though it did not require conventional diesel fuel. The driver used the restroom and returned to the truck with a bag of snacks and cold drinks.

Rent waited for the man in the expansive shadow cast by the big rig. The driver, startled at Rent's sudden appearance, seemed fearful and glanced around as if expecting others coming to apprehend him. Rent removed his mask and told him not to worry; he just had a question for him.

Rent showed him a picture of one of the men they had photographed at the maintenance facility. The man's eyes flitted about like an oriole fearful of being picked off by a Cooper's hawk.

"Bee Jay. *El Jefe,*" the driver said.

Rent then showed him another photo. The man's eyes bugged out, and he reached for the door handle, saying, "No, no . . ."

Rent stepped between him and the idling truck. "You recognize this man. Who is he? *¿Quien es?*"

"He bad man. *Muy malo.*"

"What's his name? *¿Como se llama?*"

"*Señor Chooker-illi.*"

Rent asked him what he was hauling.

The man shook his head. Rent ordered him to open the trailer, which had a distinctive "53" painted near the front end, signifying an oversized 53-footer. The driver swung open one of the doors to reveal it contained no cargo.

"Where are you going? *¿A dónde vas?*"

"Superfund."

"*Muchas gracias,*" Rent said and stepped away.

The driver wasted no time climbing into the truck and driving off as Rent rejoined Alicia.

"*¡Excelente!*" he said and told her what he had learned about the two men in the photos—BJ and Stevens—and that the man, apparently, hauled toxic waste from the superfund site near El Centro.

"We'll know for sure soon enough," she said and held up a tracking device.

"On his truck?"

"*Sí, señor.*"

Rent gave her a thumbs-up. "But we need to be careful how we handle this. The photo of Stevens scared the crap out of him. I don't want him to be collateral damage."

"But Stevens is the one guy that ties all of this together, right? And BJ—Robert Johnson—is probably in deep as well."

"Yeah, but every time I ask about him, they change the subject."

As dusk fell and the temperature dropped to a more pleasant degree, they returned to the bar in El Centro that CBP agents and like-minded law enforcement types frequented. They wandered through the parking lot, noting the newer and more expensive vehicles, nodding with an air of familiarity to any patrons arriving or leaving. Some of them greeted the pair with, "Thank you for your service."

Rent chuckled at the irony. "Shall we go inside and stir things up?"

"Are you crazy?"

"Just a little joke."

"It's not funny."

They had returned to the Dodge Ram and opened their respective doors when the familiar red Maserati entered the parking lot and backed into a space nearby. Rent left the door ajar and sauntered toward the car as two men emerged, both wearing identical smoke-blue Southern pullover shirts bearing the Lustrous logo.

"Hey, Chuckarelli, long time no see," Rent called out, still dressed in his militia attire except for having traded his fleece beanie for a red cap.

Stevens's head twisted toward Rent as if yanked by a lanyard. "Who the fuck are you?"

Rent stopped at the front of the car. "Sorry about the mask, but we can't be too careful these days. Wouldn't want to be doxxed and swatted now, would we? I thought you were a friend of my dad's. I guess I'm mistaken."

Stevens's predator gaze chilled Rent to the point of generating a slight tremble in his hands and arms. Rent shifted his focus to the man the truck driver had identified as Robert Johnson. He had stepped around the rear end of the car to stand beside Stevens.

Rent touched the brim of his hat to acknowledge the man. "BJ," he said.

Startled at hearing his moniker stated aloud, his cougar-like eyes narrowed. "Do I know you?"

"Maybe another time. We were just leaving," Rent answered and stepped backward, retreating but not turning his back on the two men until he had established some distance between them and himself. They continued to glare at him, their faces as hard as if chiseled in granite.

Rent turned away and rejoined Alicia at the pickup. When he got into the truck, he noted the camera and telephoto lens in her lap.

"Got 'em," she said.

"Good. Now, let's get the hell out of here."

"Don't we want to follow that Maserati?"

"We could be here all night."

"Nah, I doubt they hang out with the drones for long."

Rent pulled over and parked. Alicia's prediction proved to be accurate. Twenty minutes later, the Maserati emerged from the parking lot, and they trailed it from a discreet distance.

"Looks like they're headed to Brawley," he said. "Same as us."

They followed the car to a residential section of the town.

"This is the same neighborhood as Derringer," Rent muttered.

When the car turned into a driveway, Rent stopped and doused his headlights. They watched as BJ and Stevens got out and entered the house, then eased by, noting the address.

"Nice enough place, but nothing special," Alicia said.

"Keeping a low profile," Rent offered.

"With a red Maserati?"

Rent shrugged. "Keeping up with the Derringers."

As they drove away, he said, "When I first saw BJ up close, I thought I was looking at his brother, Mike Johnson. Same Nordic face and ice-blue eyes."

"Maybe they're not just brothers," she replied. "Maybe they're twins."

"That could explain a lot of things."

* * *

They dined at Las Chabelas, the first decent meal they'd had in days. Rent ordered fish and shrimp tacos with rice and beans, and a bottle of Modelo Negra beer. Alicia went for the Chabelas Salad and the Spanish beer Estrella Damm.

She tipped the glass to her lips and swallowed a mouthful. "Damn good!"

After eating, they went into the bar. Alicia ordered tequila shots and began dance moves while standing at the bar.

"Come on, dance with me," she urged.

"I'm a musician, not a dancer."

She batted her eyes. "Yes, but it takes two to tango, if you catch my drift."

* * *

They slept well past daybreak. Rent awoke with a groan.

"Way too much fun last night."

"No, just what I . . . we . . . needed," Alicia countered.

They got coffee and breakfast from the motel lobby and returned to their room. Rent updated the draft of his story, while Alicia tracked down the owners of the more expensive vehicles parked at the bar in El Centro. She also looked up property records for those individuals.

"You've got to be kidding me," she said.

"What is it?" Rent asked.

She pointed to a record for one of the CBP agents they had seen driving the Escalade.

Rent leaned over to read the text on the screen, then straightened. "He also owns a racehorse? What the . . ."

"And he also owns a boat moored in San Diego."

"How can he afford that on a CBP salary? Or, if he's paid that well, I'll make that my career move when I get laid off from the newspaper."

The Maserati, it turned out, was registered to Incinergy, and the house they had followed it to was owned by Lustrous.

"No wonder we couldn't find Robert Johnson. He doesn't have anything in his name," Rent said. "Maybe he doesn't even exist."

A Mercedes-Benz G-wagon she found registered to none other than Charles Q. Stevens of Yuma, Arizona.

"That does it for now," she said, closing her laptop.

"Yeah, me too," Rent said.

They packed up, checked out, and returned the rental truck. On their way home, they stopped at Sunbeam Lake County Park and met with Mendoza to share what they had learned.

"*¡Dios mío!*" he exclaimed. "You are amazing, Alicia."

She blushed. "I do the best I can. And this guy helped out a little, too."

"This is just what we need to bring these *cabrones* down," he replied. "Sorry for my coarse language."

"I've heard worse," she said, casting her gaze toward Rent.

"What do we do now? Go to the cops?"

"Soon, but not quite yet," Rent answered. "We need to figure out a way to catch them red-handed. Lay a trap for them."

Mendoza rubbed his hands together. "Just like in the movies."

Rent nodded. "Yeah, something like that."

* * *

"A-B-C?" Alicia inquired, holding up a bottle of pinot noir. "This calls for a little celebration."

"Perfect," Rent replied. "I'll do the honors." He opened a drawer and withdrew a corkscrew.

She huffed a derisive laugh and handed him the bottle. "It's a screw cap from Trader Joe's, silly."

They had returned from Imperial Valley and picked up burgers and fries from In-N-Out—Rent had an unused gift card from Christmas. As they approached Alicia's driveway, she noticed a U-Haul truck parked near a neighbor's house on the opposite side of the street.

"Must be getting a new neighbor," she said, turning into the driveway and parking.

Hard thumping on the door and loud shouts shattered their brief moment of sojourn before Rent could unscrew the cap.

"Now what?" he exclaimed as he left the kitchen and strode toward the front door, Alicia trailing in his wake.

He heard a muffled "Police! Open up!" and more pounding on the door.

"What the fuck?" Rent muttered as he opened the door, confronted by a group of masked individuals dressed in military garb, sunglasses, and brandishing weapons of war. One of them had a door buster already being thrust forward. The agent tried to stop its progress, but the heavy battering ram had too much momentum and struck Rent in the abdomen. He curled over and collapsed on the floor, moaning.

Two others stepped through the doorway. Their uniforms did not display any identification other than a generic "POLICE" inscribed on the back of their armored vests. They kicked Rent aside to confront Alicia Velasquez. "You're comin' with us."

"¡Joder!" she uttered. "Under what authority? Where're your badges? A warrant?"

"We don't need no stinkin' badges," one said, eliciting guttural laughs from his companions. "Now turn around."

When she refused to comply, the other grabbed her shoulders, twisted her in a half turn, pulled her hands behind her back and fastened flex cuffs on her wrists. When Rent tried to rise and intervene, a third agent shoved him backward. Rent lost his balance and fell on his ass, the momentum snapping his head back and striking the arm of a chair.

He struggled to his feet as they pushed Alicia through the doorway and onto the front porch. She tripped on the threshold and nearly fell. "Where are you taking her?" he shouted and attempted to follow.

An agent stopped him, lifting his automatic rifle and thrusting it crosswise into Rent's chest.

"Don't worry, white boy," the man said. "Not interested in you. Only this brown-skin gal."

32

Rent watched the unidentified agents force Alicia into a black, unmarked Suburban and drive off. The remaining agents climbed into the U-Haul and followed.

"'Brown-skin gal' my ass, you motherfuckers," he shouted as an image of the renowned Texas fiddler Eck Robertson flashed through his mind.

He slammed and locked the door in an act of futile defiance, then winced as he touched the lump forming on the back of his head. He leaned against the door and placed his hands over his face, exhaling a regretful sigh as he pondered the horror he had just witnessed.

He swiped his phone screen and selected "A.J. Hawke" from his list of Favorites.

"Who'd you piss off this time?" the attorney asked.

"ICE," he said. "They abducted Alicia."

"The private investigator?"

"One and the same."

"Well, that sucks. Did they say why?"

"Hell no. A half dozen masked thugs in fatigues just cuffed her and dragged her off. One of the assholes even had the audacity to quote the 'no stinkin' badges' line from the Bogart movie."

"Oh, my. How eloquent," Hawke snarked.

Rent gave the lawyer a brief summary of the investigation he and Alicia had embarked upon and recounted the earlier confrontation with the CBP agents in Calexico.

"It's harassment, plain and simple; terrorist tactics. Reminiscent of the habeas corpus case you won a few months back."

"I'll put Matt on it," Hawke said, then chuckled. "He bills at a lower rate. As if you could even afford that."

"Smart ass," Rent muttered as the line went dead. While waiting to hear back from Hawke, he pulled Alicia's identification from her purse: passport, Real ID driver's license, and Global Entry card. After a few minutes of scouring her desk drawers and adjacent file cabinet, he found her birth certificate, along with divorce papers. He felt a twinge of guilt for rifling through her personal affairs, but what choice did he have?

Gotta get this resolved before she's shipped off to a hellhole in some shithole country.

He then snapped pictures of each item and texted the photos to Hawke. He grabbed a beer from the fridge and slumped in a chair with a heavy sigh. *What the fuck have I gotten her into?*

He glanced at the phone screen, still displaying his photo gallery. *What's this?* He tapped the image, and it began moving—a video of Alicia being taken by the ICE agents. He had no memory of taking it.

* * *

Rent woke up in his own bed, his brain thick with fog as dense as a June Gloom marine layer. He barely remembered driving home from Alicia's house. He showered while the coffee brewed.

His phone vibrated when he picked it up, indicating a missed call or a new text message. A glance at the screen told him both were in evidence: O'Connor wondering why he wasn't at work and a text from A.J. Hawke's paralegal, Matt Van Dryden, saying he needed Alicia's actual identification. Which meant a dreaded trip downtown. He called O'Connor, explained the situation, and said he'd be at the newsroom as soon as he completed his errand.

At the lawyer's office, Hawke explained the status of Alicia's case. ICE had all but admitted she shouldn't have been arrested but came up with a flimsy excuse, saying they acted on a tip from an authoritative source. However, they refused to identify the informant.

"I called in a few favors and got some strings pulled through the FBI to expedite this," Hawke said. "I also filed a motion in federal court, demanding her immediate release and, barring that, appearing in court before a judge, forcing ICE to show cause—for which they have zero evidence. That's why we need the ID, in case it comes to that."

While en route, Rachel called. He cut her off, telling her Alicia had been taken by ICE and he would call her back.

He entered the newsroom, and O'Connor hustled him into her office, along with Naomi Clark.

"Holy shit, Rent. This is so not right," Clark said. "I've made some calls, but no one will talk to me."

"Rent, what can you tell us?" O'Connor asked.

He eyed her for a moment and took a deep breath before responding. "Hawke's working on it and seems hopeful, but right now who knows what the hell those jackboots are gonna do? And it's all my fault," he added, his emotion-laden voice cracking like thawing river ice.

"Don't be so hard on yourself," the editor said. "Someone's got an ax to grind. Getting desperate."

"Yeah," Clark added. "Apparently, setting your car on fire wasn't enough."

"It's got to be more than just looking into the Lustrous business entities. Even if they've exaggerated their stake in the geothermal and lithium operations, that may be unethical but not illegal."

"Unless they're defrauding investors," O'Connor tossed in, raising the ante.

"It has to be more. Something that could bring down the entire house of cards and possibly implicate one or more of them in Wilbury's murder."

O'Connor stared at Rent like a concerned parent. He shifted his gaze to Clark.

"One more thing." He held up his phone. "I have video."

"What?"

"I'll text it to you right now. You can put it on the web with your story."

Rent went to his desk to reassess his next moves. His phone chimed. Incoming text message: Agent 99.

> **Ready to throw in the towel and focus on the positive for a change?**

Fuck off, Mcfluff.

He rested his elbows on his desktop, head in hands.

"Rough night?"

Rent straightened up. "Hey, Dan. You could say that." He then related to his colleague the latest development.

"That's a bit close to home. Anything I can do?"

"Short of a jailbreak?"

Dan Rowland chuckled. "Just let me know."

Rent nodded and stared at his laptop, debating whether to open it or not. *I need more coffee.*

Back at his desk, he checked his messages. Producers from the local TV and radio stations had called, wanting interviews.

He sighed, opened his laptop, and brought up his to-do list. He needed to make follow-up calls to a number of people but had no desire to do so. Not while Alicia was still in custody.

He slammed a fist on his desktop with enough force to bounce his phone and computer.

This not knowing is killing me.

His phoned chimed, announcing an incoming call. He didn't recognize the number, but the area code suggested it could be Imperial Valley. He took the call and identified himself.

"Mr. Beacham, this is Miguel Mendoza. Sorry to bother you, but I'm concerned about Alicia Velasquez. She was supposed to call me this morning. There have been some new developments."

Rent told him about her abduction by ICE.

"Retribution. It has to be."

"I agree. But for now, all we can do is wait and hope for the best."

"I really need to talk to someone and don't know who else to call. I can't trust anyone."

"Miguel, right now I am totally frazzled, so telling me anything at this moment would be a waste of time. All I can say is document whatever it is, and Alicia . . . or I . . . will get back to you as quickly as we can."

"I understand. *Mucho éxito.*"

Rent disconnected and set the phone on his desk, then opened his laptop. Might as well at least *try* to do something productive. He opened an existing file to get oriented and typed: Lustrous . . . geothermal . . . lithium . . . hazardous waste . . . data center south of the border . . .

Then it came back to him. *Oh, shit. City council and the ADU ordinance.*

Dan Rowland returned. "There's a media mob outside, so if you're thinking of leaving anytime soon, I wouldn't recommend it. Your video has already gone viral."

"Fuck me," Rent muttered. "I can't just sit here doing nothing."

"Meet me around back."

Rent exited through the service entrance and got into Rowland's car. They drove around the building and past the media mob. Rent waved as they passed. "Where're we headed?"

"Been to Athena Café lately?" When Rent didn't reply, Rowland continued. "The Greek place in Pacific Beach."

Rent shook his head.

"Good. We can hide out there; get some lunch."

Afterward, as they drove back, they spotted a group of protesters who were waving signs and shouting.

"Pull over," Rent said and rolled down his window. "What's going on?"

One of the protesters stepped up to the car. "We're against this huge fucking so-called ADU project slated to destroy our neighborhood!"

Rent identified himself, produced his phone, and began recording. "Who's the developer?"

"JMJ, who do you think? The greedy bastards!" the woman answered. Her tanned and sun-wrinkled face spoke of the many hours she'd spent in the popular beach area. "If we don't stop them, they'll cram too many people into too small of a space, create even more traffic congestion, and wipe out street parking. It will ruin the quality of life we enjoy in this laid-back community."

She stepped back, held up her sign, and resumed shouting. "Hey . . . you . . . no ADU! Hey . . . you . . . no ADU!"

Rent and Rowland got out of the car and spoke with a few others who expressed similar sentiments, and they found the lawyer who had filed the lawsuit representing the protesters.

"These are not humble granny flats like the city intended," the attorney said. "They are sprawling, three-story, investor-backed apartment structures masquerading as ADUs."

* * *

By the time the two journalists returned to the newsroom, the media crowd had dissipated. Rent returned to his desk and followed the city council proceeding online. The council members would be voting on whether to place additional restrictions on ADUs, limiting the number of units that could be built on a single lot.

Mikey Johnson spoke, spouting the usual arguments for increased density and affordable housing, arguing that the restrictions not only conflicted with state law; they might even violate state law. He all but threatened to file a lawsuit of his own.

"Yada, yada, yada," Rent muttered as he pecked away at the keyboard. *At best, this provides the Johnsons with a brainless distraction from the other shit they're involved in.*

During a break, he got more coffee. He'd barely slept the night before, his mind conjuring up images of Alicia—shackled, shaved head, shorn of her long black locks—sitting on a bare concrete floor amid dozens of other detainees.

The meeting ended with the council narrowly voting in favor of the restrictions. He got statements from council members, pro and con, and made his final call to Mikey Johnson.

"You just can't leave us alone, can you?" the JMJ CEO said. "Always critical; never see our side of things. Our project complies with all statutory regulations regarding the construction of ADUs, which are critical to resolving the housing crisis in America's Finest City," the man said. "We will fight this action and the lawsuit to the full extent of the law."

"Oh, I see your side of things—exploiting an unintended loophole in the law in order to maximize your profit while the impact on the community at large be damned."

"You better watch your back, Beacham."

"May I quote you on that?"

* * *

The following day, even though it was Saturday, Rent tried to get some work done at home, but he couldn't concentrate, fretting about Alicia.

His phone chimed. Rachel. He sighed and took the call. She wanted to know if Alicia had been released. He updated her and said he needed to stay off the phone.

"But I need to talk to you about something. It's really, really important."

"Can't it wait till later?"

"Da-ad . . ."

His phone dinged, announcing an incoming call: Hawke. "Gotta go." He ended the call and accepted the new one. "Please tell me she's been released."

"Not yet, but in a few hours," Hawke said.

"Thank goodness. And thank you."

"They knew she was a U.S. citizen. For whatever reason, they're just using terror tactics to frighten her . . . and you. But it's bad optics for the White House, so they expedited her release.

"Meanwhile, maybe you should think about switching to another beat that's not so dangerous, such as gardening or fashion—there's a laugh—or maybe sports. The Padres are contenders this year."

"Borrrr-inggggg. Millionaire adolescents playing games that only run up the price of beer, and franchise owners who celebrate paying a guy twenty-five mil to do what—whack a ball over a fence—while opposing a minimum wage hike to a mere twenty-five bucks an hour for the poor folks who clean up all the shit left in the stadium at the end of the game."

"I'm just sayin', tread carefully, my friend. Beware of whose toes you step on."

"Like that Mexican drug lord who put a price tag on *your* head?"

"Touché."

* * *

Rent paced the small living room, the waiting interminable. The clock had never ticked so slowly. His phone, which he held at his side in a death grip, chimed. He lifted it and eagle-eyed the screen. Not Hawke. He sighed and took the call.

"Aunt Edith, I hate to give you the bum's rush, but I have to stay off the phone."

"I saw the news. That's inexcusable!"

"I know. She's going to be released any minute now. That's why I have to stay off the phone."

"Call me as soon as she's home safe."

Rent ended the call. "Fuck it." He grabbed a scribbled note that had the address of the detention facility. "I'll wait there."

As he drove south toward the border, Rachel called.

"Crap! I forgot," he muttered and answered, apologizing for not calling her back. "It's been really crazy these last two days, so make it quick."

"My life's crazy too," Rachel retorted. Her voice broke, and she began crying.

"Oh, sweetie . . ." Rent croaked as his eyes began to water.

"I'm afraid I'll never see her again."

"She's being released. I'm on my way to pick her up now. Gotta go."

No sooner had he ended that call than Agnes Powell rang.

"You need to talk to that daughter—"

Rent interrupted her. "I just spoke to her. She's upset about Alicia."

"There is that, but that's not why I'm calling."

"Boys again?"

"Worse."

"Are you going to enlighten me?"

"That chat thing they're all doing these days."

"A chatbot? Artificial intelligence?"

"Yes. She spends—"

"Fine. I'll talk to her. But I'm almost to the detention center. I'm picking up Alicia. Surely, you've heard what happened to her."

"Yes, that's too bad. But something has to be done about this immigration mess. You should go to church more often. Meet a nice girl."

"You mean meet a nice *white* girl, not some gal with a perpetual tan. Goodbye, Agnes."

* * *

Rent picked up Alicia outside the detention center at Otay Mesa. As he drove away, she leaned back in her seat, heaving a hefty sigh.

"That was living hell. I'd rather have been rolling around in a pigsty."

Rent drove her home. As they entered the house, she said, "I'm going to take a long, hot shower. Join me?"

"How could I refuse?"

In the bedroom, Rent peeled off his T-shirt and Alicia exclaimed, "Ohmygod!" She leaned over to examine the dinner-plate-size bruise on his midsection. She lifted a finger as if to touch it.

"Don't you dare," he said.

She straightened up and leaned toward him to give him a hug, careful not to put any pressure on his wound. "I'm so sorry."

"It's not your fault. Just more retribution from those assholes. No doubt the Johnson boys are behind this."

She stepped back and examined her wrists, which sported purplish bands. "I'm not in much better shape. But if we cave, they go scot-free."

"I'm sorry I got you into this mess."

"I volunteered."

"Even so, I should go it alone from here on out."

Alicia glared at him, her face a mask of ferocity. "No. *We* are going to get those *hijos de puta!*"

33

Rent finally got his interview with Ramesh Kumar, CEO of Chuckwalla Enterprises, so he could wrap up his latest piece for the newspaper.

He opened with a softball question about the name of the company. Kumar said they chose "chuckwalla" because it represents a creature that survives, if not thrives, in the arid desert climate, defying the odds—a metaphor for the underdog AI outfit going up against the likes of Google, Microsoft, Meta, OpenAI, et al.

The executive sang the praises of the company's proprietary AI app, AIsha, employing boilerplate superlatives for the value of AI and the future of global economies.

"The best thing about it is that it's so simple to use," he said. "Short learning curve. Even my sixty-eight-year-old grandmother got the hang of it right out of the box, so to speak. She loves talking to AIsha through the chatbot feature; it's her new BFF.

"It's also helping Gran to organize and plan her retirement, creating monthly and annual budgets that include travel she was afraid she couldn't afford. She's going to India next month.

"She's even making short videos of her cat to wow her friends on Facebook and Instagram."

When Rent asked about collaborations and contracts, Kumar declined to provide any specifics, other than to say they had licensed OpenAI's latest release, GPT-5.

"I hope it's better than GPT-4o," Rent said.

"Why do you say that?"

Rent told him about his attempt to identify an old song and how the chatbot not only got it completely wrong, it made stuff up. "It flunked the test. Or, as you AI gurus euphemize it, it hallucinated —not once, but three times."

Kumar shrugged it off. "That's why we upgraded. It's still being perfected."

"So, what's next for Chuckwalla, 'clankers'?"

Clankers being a satirical term for AI robots.

Kumar tried to suppress a smile. "We are looking into robotics, yes, but nothing specific at this time."

Rent asked about government regulation—guardrails governing AI technology. Kumar said leashes would be better than guardrails.

The CEO quoted a respected law professor who wrote that "AI is too heterogeneous and dynamic to operate within fixed lanes," i.e., guardrails. Whereas "leashes are flexible and adaptable" and would "permit AI tools to explore new domains without regulatory barriers getting in the way."

"You don't think that, combined with the ten-year moratorium, opens the door to abuse?"

Kumar scoffed. "AI is a tool, like a hammer, saw, or screwdriver, any of which can be used as a weapon, but is their use being regulated? No."

"That's a false equivalency; hardly a fair comparison. A five-year-old might fall for it, but I like to think my readers are a bit more sophisticated than that. I don't know of any 'smart' hammers employing generative AI or agentic AI to pound a nail."

Kumar smiled. "Maybe a 'smart' hammer would never miss and bend a nail before it's been pounded all the way in. Besides, does anyone even use a hammer these days, other than five-year-olds? Pros use nail guns."

"You're evading my question. You know very well AI is being used to create realistic videos that portray falsehoods and fake news, and uninformed people believe it's real.

"It has no morality," Rent added. "It's purposely designed by actual intelligent beings to optimize engagement, to flatter its users to keep them hooked. But it's not intelligent at all, is it? It's just a highly sophisticated data retrieval process that responds to prompts."

Kumar scoffed as Rent continued.

"Eliezer Yudkowsky, a decision theorist, told *The New York Times* that these generative AI chatbots are just giant masses of inscrutable numbers, and the companies producing them don't know why they behave—or should I say misbehave—the way they do."

Kumar shrugged. "As I said, we're still working on it, but we're almost there."

"But isn't this problematic, even dangerous, in a variety of ways? Just this morning I saw a report about how cybercriminals are using AI to impersonate CEOs and senior executives through deepfake voice and video.

"And what about the upcoming election? I've already seen multiple AI commercials for a local candidate as well as other political ads mischaracterizing opposing candidates with outright falsehoods."

"We have defamation laws to cover that. Besides, politicians lie all the time."

"And AI just provides a more effective tool for that? Not to mention that this particular candidate is married to the granddaughter of your boss, Mike Johnson Sr."

Kumar glared at Rent for a moment before answering. "Look, Mr. Beacham, I don't know what bug crawled up your ass, but Chuckwalla is an ethical company, and we urge our clients to employ our technology ethically. But ultimately, we have no control over how they utilize it. We do live in a country that permits free speech and freedom of expression."

"For now," Rent countered.

"Will that be all?"

"One last question. Does AI pose an existential threat to the human race as the Rationalists and others fear?"

The man laughed out loud and said, "Have a nice day, Mr. Beacham."

* * *

The following day, Rent entered the newsroom and headed for his desk. As he passed Janis O'Connor's office, she crooked a finger, signaling him to join her.

"Good morning, boss, what can I do you for?" he said as he entered.

"We are not amused," she responded. "I'm already getting calls about your Chuckwalla story, pro and con."

Rent shrugged and took a seat. "You expect nothing less."

"This is about more, not less," she replied. "More as in a deluge, with your pal Mike Johnson leading the charge. He tossed out accusations like 'fake news' and you being a 'pawn of the deep state.' He wants his letter to the editor to be published prominently as a rebuttal to the 'scurrilous portrayal'—his words—of the technology in general and the impugning of his company in particular."

Rent rolled his eyes. "Did he threaten to set my car on fire again, or report Alicia to ICE?"

"Nearly. What really stuck in his craw was the sidebar on the Zizian cult and the deaths associated with it."

"But no complaint about the people who died in autonomous car crashes, or the teen suicides associated with the use of AI chatbots, or deepfake videos that conspiracy theorists accept as living proof. I suppose that's just 'collateral damage' to him."

"I'm going to run it."

Rent shrugged again. "So, he's not disputing facts, just the way I framed it."

"More or less."

"Well, if it stirs up controversy, thus selling more newspapers, isn't that ultimately a good thing?" He grinned. "Maybe I even deserve a raise."

"Don't push your luck. You're just fortunate to have a job. How's Alicia doing?"

"Traumatized for sure, but she's a fighter and insists we continue the investigation—after another day or two of recovery. She said she needs a complete disinfection, mentally as well as physically, after spending the better part of two days in that hellhole."

"What's next?"

"We're talking to a guy in the valley who has some leads for us to follow up on regarding the trucks used by Incinergy. He's thinking they may be hauling more than just hazardous waste. By the way, he contacted Alicia first. Got her name from the series I did on welfare fraud."

"I'm impressed."

"I keep getting calls from a guy who insists I look into Robert Johnson and to, I quote, 'follow the trucks.' He may be a whistle-blower, but so far, no specifics."

O'Connor nodded, checked her watch, then looked at Rent. "Well?"

"Well what?"

"What are you waiting for?"

* * *

Back at his desk, Rent checked his email. *She's wasting no time getting back in action.*

Alicia had sent him photos from their surveillance activities from the previous week. Photos of BJ Johnson, Charles Stevens, and their associates at various locations, including the Incinergy facilities in the U.S. and Mexico, as well as the bar in El Centro. The batch also included images of Incinergy trucks at the border and at the waste disposal site in Mexico. He replied:

Fuckin' lovely!

Rent scrolled through all the images, then began jotting down the file numbers of a select few.

* * *

Janis O'Connor waved Rent into her office. Clark and Rowland were looking over their editor's shoulder at a computer screen. They both glanced at him, their faces grim.

Rent joined them and watched a short video, horror, followed by rage, contorting his face.

Those motherfuckers. Maybe I should rephrase the question: Does AI pose an existential threat to Rent Beacham?

The video depicted him in a bar reminiscent of The Harp talking to a colleague and saying, "Fake news? You bet. I make shit up every day and the dumb-fucks who read our newspaper swallow it hook, line, and sinker."

O'Connor played it again.

"Enough," he said.

"It's gone viral on TikTok and YouTube. Posted by someone going by the pseudonym 'Byanose.'"

"Gotta be Furlong behind this."

"Our lawyers have already gotten it taken down, but the damage has been done," O'Connor said. "We'll publish a disclaimer on the front page, and the editorial board is working on a piece for the op-ed page, decrying the potential for widespread abuse of AI and calling for sensible regulation."

Rent strode back to his desk.

Fake news? I'll give you some not-so-fake news.

He attached the chosen images to an email message to Mike Johnson Sr. with a CC to Anthony Perkins and a BCC to O'Connor. In the message box, he typed: "For your consideration . . ." Then he clicked the Send button.

These will definitely stir things up a bit.

His phone buzzed.

That was quick.

He glanced at the screen. Not Johnson. Rachel.

"Hey, sweetie. You all right?"

"I got an E!"

Rent held the phone away from his ear for a moment before responding.

"Hello? Dad, are you there?"

"You don't have to shout. I can hear you just fine. Now, what's this about an E?"

"My teacher, Mr. Billingham, said I used AI to write my report on Halloween. Or you wrote it for me. But it's not true!"

"I'm confused. I thought he allowed you to use AI."

"He did, but he's saying I used it to do everything, to write it and to draw the graphic images and everything. But I didn't. I only used it for research, like he said. But now he won't listen to me. It's not fair."

Her voice broke and she began crying.

"Do you want me to talk to him?"

"Would you? Please, please?"

"Of course. What do your grandparents say?"

"Grandpa believes me, but Grandma doesn't."

"I'll call the school and arrange a meeting. Meanwhile, send me a copy of your final version—the one you handed in. Take deep breaths and try to calm down. I'll get this sorted out."

"Thank you, thank you. I love you."

Rent ended the call. *Just what I need . . .*

* * *

The newspaper's editorial, which ran in community newspapers as well as the *San Diego Herald*, fell on deaf ears, apparently. A new deepfake political ad, paid for by a conservative political action committee, portrayed Derringer's opponent admitting in a private conversation that the Democrats had rigged his election by enlisting undocumented farm workers to cast ballots, then laughing about it.

Rent had been joined in his living room by Alicia and his hearing-challenged neighbor, Steve Lopez.

Another ad depicted Derringer aboard his Harley, soaring over the Colorado River and Grand Canyon a la Evel Knievel. In mid-flight, the Harley morphs into a white-winged stallion, and Derringer assumes a likeness of Wyatt Earp, guns drawn, landing on Independence Avenue in Washington, DC, ready to do battle with the "woke forces of darkness" as he gallops up the steps of the U.S. Capitol.

Rent scoffed. "He's riding Pegasus? Looks more like something out of *Blazing Saddles*."

"Yeah, but I'll bet his base is eating it up," Alicia replied.

Rent turned to Lopez. "What do you think?"

The man shrugged. "The audio is still not quite in sync, but it's better than before. Ironically, only those of us who are hard of hearing would notice it."

Alicia prepared to leave as Lopez departed.

Rent frowned. "You're not leaving?"

"I need a good night's sleep. Long day tomorrow."

"You don't get a good night's sleep here?"

She gave him a furtive glance and grin. "Only when I actually sleep."

Rent went to bed and tried to snooze but couldn't get the deepfakes out of his head. He got up and went to his computer, typing: Does AI pose an existential threat to the human race?

He queried three different chatbots—duck.ai, ChatGPT-5, and Google Gemini. They all gave similar responses, although ChatGPT-5 provided the most thorough response.

They all agreed: There is no current existential threat to the human race from AI, particularly in an apocalyptic sense. They and a number of "experts" suggested that the greatest threat may be more subtle in that reliance on AI to perform routine tasks could undermine people's capacity for good judgment and critical thinking, which could lead to catastrophic outcomes.

Meanwhile, one of the greatest *immediate* threats of AI is "misuse of the technology, exploiting the ability of AI to generate realistic-looking text and images to create and spread misinformation."

Exactly.

34

Rent had not settled into his chair in the newsroom before his first call of the morning lit up his phone. He sighed in resignation and swiped the screen to take the call.

"Beacham," he said, already knowing the identity of the caller—and the reason for the call.

"We're ready to serve the papers unless you want to rethink your decision to publish any of those photos."

"Gee, and I thought you folks were all for free speech and freedom of the press."

"If you publish even one of them, you and your publisher will regret it. Notwithstanding that they are obviously fakes."

"Oh, I'm sorry. I guess I didn't make myself clear. We have no intention of publishing any of those images. At least not at this time."

"Then what's your point?"

"My point is, I want an exclusive interview with the Johnsons and hear them explain to me why they have not done anything illegal and are not doing anything illegal now, or—"

"As if."

"Or I turn all of the images—and the data we have collected relevant to Incinergy and its border crossings—over to the FBI."

Anthony Perkins did not respond immediately. Rent could hear the man's rapid, shallow breathing, as if he was out of breath.

"Mr. Perkins?"

"As I said . . . you will . . . regret this . . . you son of a bitch."

The line went dead. Rent sat back in his chair for a moment.

Shit!

He got up and crossed the newsroom to knock on O'Connor's door. She waved him in. He took a chair and told her about the call from Perkins.

"You have no intention of turning that stuff over to the FBI," she said.

Rent shook his head. "Not unless the Feds force my hand. But they're not happy about my peeking into the Johnsons' activities. An agent called me last week and told me to back off, that I'm blowing open their own ongoing investigation."

"You're obviously on the right track."

"So, how do we handle this?"

"Well, you've called Johnson's bluff. The question is, which cards do you play?"

"It's showdown time."

"Showdown?"

"Yeah. Like in poker. Show your cards. Lay them down on the table. Showdown."

She rolled her eyes. "As I said, which cards do you play and still keep us from being sued? What do we know for certain?"

"Incinergy," he responded. "It's the Lustrous subsidiary that hauls truckloads of stuff across the border, both directions. Hazardous waste to a site in Mexico, and, in some cases, they return with sand that goes to a cement maker.

"High-quality clean sand is becoming harder to obtain. At least that's what I'm told. It's a critical component of concrete that the construction industry cannot live without. They can't use sand from ocean beaches because of the high salinity; it's corrosive."

"Enough of the lecture. What's the problem?" O'Connor asked, playing the devil's advocate.

"The *problem* is that no one inspects these vehicles, not the Mexicans when the trucks cross into Mexicali, and especially not the CBP when trucks come back through Calexico. They just get waved through by border agents who drive expensive cars, live in very nice houses, and in one case an agent even owns a racehorse. All on a CBP's lowly salary."

"Which suggests smuggling."

"Ace-high straight."

"Any evidence beyond that?"

"The late-night meetings at Incinergy facilities on both sides of the border. We have photos and audio. BJ and his sidekick, Stevens, and a couple of guys that speak English with a thick accent. The hazmat disposal site in Mexico appears to be owned by a company associated with a drug lord's legal business entities."

"Which suggests drugs, fentanyl. No surprise there. That comes out of Mexico. But what are they taking into Mexico?"

Rent paused a beat before answering. "Alicia and I have asked ourselves the same question. Which leads to the underlying question: What would a Mexican drug cartel want from the U.S. that it can't get at home?"

"Guns . . . and ammo."

Rent flicked his eyebrows. "Royal flush. The trucks, not always but often, go in for maintenance in a warehouse or repair shop, whatever you want to call it, before crossing the border. Who knows what's going on behind those closed doors? Robert Johnson, aka 'BJ,' Mike Johnson's brother—and maybe his twin brother—appears to be in charge, although his name does not appear anywhere. Not on the Lustrous website, nor on any legal documents that we could find. The car he drives—a Maserati, no less—is owned by Incinergy, and the house he lives in is owned by Lustrous. Ditto for his partner in crime, Charles Stevens, aka 'Chuckarelli,' who appears to be in charge of security at the various entities operated by Lustrous."

"He's the guy you suspect killed Wilbury?"

"Or if he didn't do it, he had a hand in it. I suspect Robert Johnson may have been involved as well."

"I understand the motive for killing Wilbury, to shut him up. But why risk getting involved in smuggling?"

"All I can figure is that Lustrous is underwater financially. They're all in with lithium, the white gold rush in Lithium Valley, but a combination of lawsuits, politics, and technological hurdles has held up production. Their investors are getting anxious because Lustrous has nothing to show for it other than happy talk.

"Meanwhile, they got into AI—chasing their other pot of gold at the end of the proverbial rainbow—but that's going to take time before it pays off, if ever. An AI guru, no less, has predicted that this is a bubble about to burst. There have been a number of notable failures already.

"Hazmat may be good business but not lucrative enough, and their ADU jackpot has run up against increased regulation and lawsuits, stalling construction or having to reduce the size of pending projects."

O'Connor nodded, her patience wearing thin. "So . . ."

"They're stretched too thin and—mixing the gambling metaphors a bit—betting on the come while the dice keep turning up craps. Or should I say, aces and eights?"

"But you can't prove any of that."

"Not yet. Not unless the whistleblower gives me something more substantial than just 'follow the trucks.' But the Feds would love to have the stuff we've gathered on the border agents and the clandestine trysts at the Incinergy maintenance facilities."

"What about the Wilbury stuff?" O'Connor asked. "That's rock solid."

"It's also thirty years old."

"There's no statute of limitations on murder."

"True, but regarding the dead man's notebook, the cops might argue I'm withholding evidence, although they have shown no interest in anything we've given them up to this point. I'm keeping that up my sleeve for the time being. However, we could stir the pot a little more."

"In what way?"

"We put pressure on the cops and district attorney," he answered. "Why aren't they doing anything to solve the Wilbury case? Clark gave them copies of the falsified reports, for both the boatyard and the incinerator. Why aren't they interviewing the Johnsons and any employees who were working for them back then, including Stevens, and demanding financial documents linking them to Wilbury and his sudden move to Washington?"

"Clark has tried that, and they say it's not a priority and they're understaffed—and the Feds, apparently, told them to sit on it for now."

"Let me think on it," he replied.

"Well, don't take too long thinking; I don't need to remind you we have blank pages to fill seven days a week."

Rent returned to his desk and reviewed yet again everything he had on the Wilbury case. It included the man's journal entries confessing to falsifying the environmental data and trying to extort more money from Mike Johnson, as well as his upcoming meeting with the so-called investor and the last entry he ever made: *The shit is about to hit the fan.*

* * *

Two uninterrupted hours passed. Rent thanked his lucky stars for shining so brightly. His phone brought him back to Earth.

Agnes. What the hell does she want?

He answered with a recriminating sigh. She leapfrogged any conventional greeting.

"Is Rachel with you? Because if she is, there's going to be hell to pay."

"No," he replied. "In fact, I haven't heard from her since dropping her off at your place on Sunday. What's going on?"

"Rachel hasn't come home from school. I called Meghan's mom, but she said Meghan told her that Rachel got a ride with someone else."

"Have you talked to the school?"

"Not yet. I called you first in case you were the one who picked her up, even though that violated the custodial restrictions."

"Agnes, no. I wouldn't do that. Call the school and find out what they know, if anything, then call me back."

35

As soon as Agnes disconnected, Rent opened the tracker app on his phone. The location had not changed for more than an hour: Old Poway Park. Rent checked in with his editor.

"You are aware that we have a newspaper to publish," she said.

"Rachel left school, and no one knows where she is. I need to find her."

"Call the cops."

"They're just gonna say wait and see if she turns up in the next few hours."

O'Connor sighed. "Just go. You're not going to do me any good at this point anyway."

As Rent raced to Poway, Agnes Powell called back, saying Rachel had not shown up for orchestra practice after school.

Rent parked near the barbecue restaurant and checked the tracker app again. It still had the phone in the park.

Rachel had opposed having the tracker app placed on her phone, but Rent promised not to "spy" on her. He did not use it often, but he found that the blinking light on his own phone served as a comforting beacon of sorts, a reassuring lighthouse guiding him into port and reconnecting him with his beloved daughter.

He jogged past the eatery toward the fountain, scanning the area in hopes of seeing Rachel.

Nothing.

He showed Rachel's picture to people walking by, but no one remembered seeing her.

He went to the gazebo and circled it, then pressed a button in the app to alert the phone, hoping to hear a response. *Nothing.*

He continued on to the bridge over the creek that ran through the park and surveyed the area. Birds chirping and calling, along with the traffic noise and other people talking and shouting, made it hard to hear. He sent the alert again and cupped his ears.

A flash of light from a reflection of sunlight caught his eye, and he leaned over the rail of the bridge.

There!

A cell phone lying in the streambed, dangerously close to the water's edge. If it had not been the hottest, driest time of year, and the creek not much more than a trickle, the device would have been underwater.

He scrambled over the rocks into the streambed and grabbed the phone. He immediately recognized it as Rachel's, thanks to the glitter, rhinestones, and stickers on its protective lavender case.

He stepped into the shade behind the gazebo and tapped in the four-digit PIN. *Nothing.*

"That little . . ." he muttered, looking skyward, as if asking the gods for guidance.

He and Rachel had agreed on her mother's birthday—0824—as the phone's access code, and he promised to only use it in case of an emergency. She had seemed skeptical but agreed after a brief episode of pouting.

I wonder how long it took before she changed the code?

He tried her birthday—1813. *No good.*

His own birthday. *Nothing.*

Then the melody of a fiddle tune ran through his mind, along with the words to the accompanying song: *In 1814, we took a little trip . . . the Eighth of January.*

Change the sequence to day, month, year: 8 January 2013.

He punched the numbers 8113. The home screen materialized in an instant. *That little imp!*

He opened the Messages app to see if her texting offered any clues. The most recent texts, only a few hours old, appeared to be from schoolmates, but as he scrolled through them, an unfamiliar name appeared, obviously a pseudonym: **ixystz**.

Interesting. He tried to sound it out: *ix-yst-ʒ . . . exists? Or I exist? Shit, what does it matter?*

He read the most recent exchanges. Sure enough, she had arranged to meet this person at the park, on the rocky riprap lining the streambed behind the gazebo, where she had found the frogs.

That little sneak!

He glanced around, looking for anything that might indicate she had been there, then returned to the creek and walked downstream until he reached the next bridge over the creek. *Nothing.*

What had he hoped for? A shoe? Her backpack?

He climbed out of the streambed, sweating in the sweltering late summer heat.

I need water. But I gotta find Rachel.

He returned to the area between the gazebo and the fountain, again showing passersby his wallet photo of Rachel astride her pony and asking if they had seen her. They all shook their heads, apologized, and wished him good luck. One offered him a small bottle of water, which he accepted gratefully.

He sought the shade of the gazebo, opened the bottle, and gulped down half of its contents. He leaned against the rail.

I have to call the cops. But I better make sure she's actually missing.

He called Agnes Powell to find out if she had any news.

"No. I'm about to lose my mind. That darned kid, just like her moth—"

Her voice cracked, and she began sobbing. Her husband, Frank, came on the line.

"All we know is that she left school early, possibly using a forged excuse. The school is worthless; doesn't know a goddamn thing. None of her friends seem to know where she is. We even called the doctor, just in case, but she had nothing scheduled for Rachel and hasn't seen her since her last visit."

"I found her phone."

"What?"

"I'm at Old Poway Park, and I found her phone, but she's not here, and no one I've talked to has seen her. Have you called the cops?" Rent asked.

"No, have you?"

"I was about to, but I wanted to check in with you and the school first, in case she's shown up somewhere."

"We were waiting to hear from you."

"OK, I'll check in with the school one more time, and if she's not there, I'll call the cops."

"We're her legal guardians; shouldn't we do it?"

"And I'm her dad. Besides, Agnes is so distraught, and I'm just a few blocks from the sheriff's station."

"Fine, have it your way. Just find that girl."

The line went dead. Rent called the school and got the same report. He looked at the keypad on his phone, wondering if he should call 911, drive to the station, or call one of his contacts within the San Diego Sheriff's Department. A deep voice interrupted him.

"Sir? Sir? Maybe I can help you."

Rent turned to find a large man dressed in a tattered T-shirt and jeans, straggly hair hanging to his shoulders and a full beard drooping onto his chest.

Homeless. Shit.

Rent displayed a forced smile. "How's that?"

"I'm Clint," the man said. "I was sittin' over there." He gestured toward a bench under a portico on the building housing the restaurant and restrooms. "I overheard you talkin' to folks and showin' them a picture."

"What of it?"

"If you show me the picture, maybe I can help you."

Rent eyed the man for a long moment.

The man insisted. "You're looking for a young girl, right?" Rent nodded. "I think I saw her."

Rent placed his hands on the railing and leaned closer to the man, who was standing on the lawn outside the gazebo.

"Where?"

The man nodded toward the bridge on the opposite side of the structure.

Rent gestured for the man to join him. "Come on up here and get out of the hot sun."

The man climbed the steps to the gazebo and stopped a few feet away from Rent, who again extracted his wallet from a rear pocket of his slacks. He showed Clint the photo of Rachel.

The man nodded. "I'm perty sure that's the girl I saw."

"Show me."

Clint, who had a nearly six-inch height advantage over Rent, turned and strode to the opposite side of the gazebo. He stopped and pointed toward a large shrub near the end of the bridge that arched over the creek. "Right there. She was standing there, looking around and then at her phone, like she was waitin' for someone."

"What was she wearing?"

The man described her school uniform and said she had a backpack and was carrying something, like an instrument case, maybe a violin or something like that.

"Then what?"

"What do you mean?"

"What . . . the . . . fuck . . . happened?"

Clint narrowed his eyes and glared at Rent. "You don't have to get all shirty about it. I'm just tryin' t'be helpful."

"I'm sorry, but I'm her father, and she's gone missing. She was waiting to meet a boy—at least I think it's a boy."

"I didn't see no boy."

"What, exactly, did you see?"

"Well, I wasn't payin' that much attention. I see them kids all the time comin' through here, all times of day, and night, too."

Rent's brow furrowed. "At night?"

Clint nodded. "I live here." He motioned toward the bench again. "I'm security." When Rent seemed skeptical, the man added, "On a informal basis. I reported a bunch of hooligans late one night makin' a lotta noise, turning over trash cans. And one night I reported a fire that someone started t'other side of the creek. That could've been a disaster."

"So, you didn't see a boy about her age join her. Anyone else?"

"Like I said, I wasn't payin' all that much attention, but at some point, I saw a man standin' there, talkin' to her."

"A man, not a boy."

Clint nodded.

"What time was this?"

The man held out his hands and extended his arms. No wristwatch.

Rent sighed. "What'd he look like?"

"Big guy. Big as me. Had on nice clothes. Not a suit or white shirt and tie, but like he was going to a pool party or some such."

"A polo shirt."

"Yeah, something like that."

"Respectable looking. Nothing to get concerned about."

"You might say that. I see all types come through here. Daryl, for example. He's one scary dude. Always yammering. Saying a bunch o' nonsense about love." Clint pointed a finger at his head and whirled it in circles. "He's loony tunes. But it weren't him."

"And?"

"What?"

"You saw Rachel talking to this big guy in nice clothes. Then what?"

"Is that her name? Rachel? In the Bible, Rachel was . . ."

Rent rolled his eyes in frustration. "What the hell happened?"

"Nothing."

"What do you mean, nothing?"

"Last I saw, they walked off together. They went across the bridge and towards t'other side o' the park. That's it. I needed to use the bathroom, so—"

"She went willingly?"

Clint shrugged. "I guess so. I just figured it was her dad or someone she knew."

A feeling of dread coursed through Rent's body. He still held his wallet in his hand. He extracted two twenty-dollar bills and handed them to Clint before returning the wallet to its pocket. "Thanks for your help. Treat yourself to some barbecue."

The man accepted the money and offered a slight bow of his head. "You are entirely welcome, sir. Good luck in finding your daughter.

36

Rent stepped away from Clint and swiped open his phone screen, a thumb hovering over the number nine.

What're the cops gonna do? It's only been a couple of hours.

He scrolled through his contacts, touched the screen, then tapped the phone icon. It rang four times before being answered. He thought he would be directed into the voicemail void.

"To what do I owe this honor? Or dare I even ask?" a voice answered.

"Rachel is missing."

"What?" replied Sgt. Diana Alvarez.

"I wouldn't be bothering you if it wasn't important."

"You do remember I'm in homicide, right?"

"I don't know who else to call. Washington would give me the bum's rush."

"Tell me what's going on."

Rent explained the situation as briefly as he could, reminding her of the prior threats, the swatting incident, and the car fire involving Alicia Velasquez.

"Déjà vu all over again," she said in reference to the death of Rachel's mother the previous winter.

"Let's hope not."

"So, you're convinced she's not just missing, but she's been abducted."

"Exactly."

Alvarez sighed. "Shit. And at this point, nothing much to go on."

"No, other than what Clint told me."

"Ah, yes, Mr. Clint."

"So, he's known to you."

She chuckled. "He likes to think of himself as a one-man security detail in the park. That justifies him making that bench his home."

"He claims he's done some good."

"Like the fire."

"He mentioned it."

"It's quite possible he also started that fire just so he could be the hero. The sheriff tolerates him to a degree as long as he doesn't cause any trouble. But enough about Clint."

"As I said, I think the guy he saw could be the same guy that's been following me and threatened me after the dance. I'm pretty sure his name is Charles Stevens, aka Stefano Ceccarelli, and probably a few other aliases."

"Where are you right now?"

He told her.

"The Poway Sheriff's Station is just a few blocks away. Go there and file a report. They can initiate an Amber Alert and send a forensic team to the park. They'll want her phone. You and the grandparents need to be available to be interviewed."

"I'll go to their place when I'm done at the station."

"Good luck."

"I'm going to need it. Thanks for your help."

"*De nada.*"

Rent ended the call and drove to the sheriff's station, where he filed his report, noting that when last seen, Rachel was wearing a white blouse, red-and-blue plaid skirt, lavender backpack, and carrying a violin case.

He exited the station and sat in his vehicle. He had to make a number of calls, beginning with the grandparents. He gave them an update and said he'd be at their place shortly. He offered to stop at Taco Taco for takeout and wrote down their orders in his reporter's notebook. As he finished, he received an incoming call.

"I gotta go. See you in a few."

He sighed and answered.

"When were you going to inform us of this breaking news?" Janis O'Connor asked. "I've got Clark here, and we're on speaker."

"You're on my list but not my priority. I knew you'd get the alert from the sheriff soon enough."

"My feelings are hurt," Clark replied.

"What do you want? I have a few more calls to make."

"What the hell do you think we want? A first-hand account."

"Then you need to talk to Clint. I wasn't there."

"Who's Clint?"

"The homeless guy who saw it go down."

"Homeless?"

"How about 'unhoused'?"

"That's not what I meant," Clark replied. "You're serious? A homeless guy is the key witness?"

"He's not just any homeless guy. He's got a stellar reputation. Even the cops speak highly of him."

"You're shittin' me."

"I'm not. Seriously, you should talk to him."

"You got his number?"

"He doesn't even own a watch."

"So, I gotta drive out there in rush-hour traffic and try to find this guy wandering around the park?"

"He lives on a bench at the back of the restaurant, off the kitchen."

O'Connor intervened. "That's enough, you two. Rent, I want you to take some personal days until this gets sorted out. Let's just hope Rachel's OK and she's returned safely."

"Yeah, let's hope so."

"Don't do anything rash or stupid," she said.

"And don't get your ass blown to kingdom come again," Clark added.

"Goodbye. I'll call back when I get these other calls out of the way."

"We do have a deadline," O'Connor reminded him.

"Poor choice of words, don't you think?" he replied and ended the call. He leaned back in the seat, set his phone on the passenger seat, and closed his eyes, breathing slowly.

Fuck me!

Slamming car doors startled Rent back to the moment. Two sheriff's deputies had gotten into their patrol vehicle and were buckling up. The vehicle jerked forward, and its tires squealed as the officers left the parking lot in a rush.

He checked the clock on the dashboard: 4:38 p.m. He picked up the phone and called Alicia.

"I was just about to call you. What the hell has happened? Are you OK?"

"I'm OK. I wish I could say the same for Rachel. What have you heard?"

She told him how she had been alerted by her breaking news scroll. "Where are you?"

"I'm at the sheriff's station in Poway. I'm done here and about to head over to the Powells'. I fear it's going to be a long night."

"Are you staying there? Or do you want to come here? I don't think it's safe for you to go home."

"I'm not staying there. Agnes is a total wreck, and it would drive me over the edge. But I don't know that I'd be any safer at your place."

"You've got to stay calm. We can talk about it, maybe come up with a plan."

"A plan for what?"

"To track this guy down and rescue Rachel," she said.

"Isn't that what the cops are supposed to do?" Rent snapped back.

"Which cops?"

"What do you mean?"

"Just because she was abducted in Poway doesn't mean she's still in Poway. Think about it. Where is the primary location for the Johnson business operations?"

"These days, Imperial Valley."

"Exactly. And don't forget Mexico."

"How would they get her across the border?"

"The same way they get all their shit across the border. One of their big trucks and a sprinkle of *mordida* to grease the wheels."

"Yeah, you're right, as usual. I'll call you later."

He drove to Taco Taco, home of the famous 99-cent fish taco. While he waited for the order, he called Aunt Edith and told her what had happened.

"It's all my fault," she said. "I should never have told you about that dead body."

"It's not your fault. If it's anyone's fault, it's mine. I'm the one poking the stick into the hornet's nest."

"Have they demanded a ransom or made any demands on you?"

"Not yet, but I imagine they will."

"Don't do anything stupid. You barely got out alive the last time."

"You think I'm not aware of that? The food's arrived. I gotta go."

He picked up the bag of food and stepped out into the vast parking lot, which served the Poway office of the Department of Motor Vehicles, a Walmart Supercenter, and several other business establishments. He glanced around, not sure of what he expected other than a sea of countless cars, all baking in the late afternoon heat.

* * *

The Powells greeted Rent with grim faces. Agnes's swollen eyes flared red. They ushered him into the dining room, where the table had been set.

He laid out the cartons of food, then went to the bathroom to wash up, splashing cold water on his face. His hands trembled as he lifted a towel off the rack. He sucked in several deep breaths before returning to the dining room.

"Something to drink?" asked Frank Powell. "Beer, wine, something a bit stronger?"

"Just water for me," Rent answered. "I need to keep my wits about me."

Frank nodded and filled a glass with iced water from a pitcher, handing it to Rent. Agnes had already opened a carton and spooned an enchilada onto her plate. Rent took his seat and retrieved two tacos, one fish, the other shrimp. Frank joined them, placing his items on a plate with deliberation and precision.

Rent had taken only two bites when his phone signaled an incoming text message. He withdrew it from a back pocket and glanced at the screen. It displayed "Lewis," Rent's despised nickname for Naomi Clark. Frank and Agnes shot him anxious looks.

"Work," he said. "I gotta deal with this. I'll step out back, if you don't mind."

The grandparents nodded in unison. Rent went to the patio behind the house, sought a bit of shade, and called her back.

"Speak to me," Clark said in greeting.

"What do you want to know? Did you talk to Clint?"

"Almost there. I want to know what the cops aren't telling me."

"I don't know any more than they do. My daughter is missing and most likely abducted by a very bad man."

"Ha, ha. Let's cut through the crap. This has everything to do with a dead body on San Juan Island and your investigation into Lustrous Consulting Group and its various corrupt business practices."

"You looking to get sued?"

"Not particularly, but I'm on the right track, correct?"

"Speculation. No way you can tie the two at this point. Besides, that's my story."

"You've gotten threats."

"Who said?"

"The cops. It's in their presser."

"Anonymous. All you're getting from me is that I'm angry and horrified that anyone would kidnap an innocent twelve-year-old girl as a form of retribution against me, if that's what's underlying this outrageous and unlawful act. The persons behind this abduction are cowards, too afraid to confront me directly."

"Oh, my. Filled with bravado, are we?"

"Unless things change, I'm meeting with the sheriff's flack in the morning to videotape a public appeal for information anyone may have, if she hasn't been found by then."

"Have you received any communication from the abductor? A ransom demand or some sort of deal?"

"I can't comment on that."

"Can't or won't?"

"Both."

"Call me if there are any developments. And, Rent, I seriously do feel sorry for you and Rachel and hope this gets resolved quickly and without any harm coming to her."

"I appreciate that."

He disconnected and returned to his dinner.

"Do you want me to zap your food in the microwave?" Frank asked.

Rent shook his head. "I'm not really hungry anyway."

Agnes stared at him. "Who was that who called, your little PI *chiquita?*"

"No. One of my work colleagues. But so what if it was?"

"You gonna marry her, pop out a brood of half-breed fruit pickers? I'm not sure I like Rachel being around that Jezebel."

"What the fuck are you going on about?"

"Don't use that kind of language in my house!"

"Don't you use that kind of language about my friend. She happens to adore Rachel, and Rachel adores her. As for marriage, that's not even open for discussion. We're just taking things slowly, see how it works out. We enjoy each other's company, and that's enough for now. And since I don't appear to be welcome here, I'll be going. If I hear anything, I'll let you know."

Frank got up. "I'll show you out."

Rent stood and began packing up his food.

"This is all *your* fault," Agnes said, jabbing a finger in his direction. "Just like Hannah's death was *your* fault. You can't just mind your own darn business. You gotta go sticking your big snotty nose in everyone else's business. I hope there's a special place in Hell for you."

Rent stared at her in disbelief. "You know, I almost feel sorry for you."

He put the food cartons in a plastic bag and carried it with him as he followed Frank to the front door. The man opened the door and stepped outside.

"Rent, I'm sorry about that. Agnes didn't mean it. This mess has hit her really hard. She's afraid she's going to lose her granddaughter in addition to having lost her daughter."

"I get that, but she doesn't have to take it out on Alicia."

"I know. I'll have a word with her when she calms down a bit."

"Good luck with that."

* * *

Even before he reached Alicia's house, phone calls and text messages began pouring in from local and national news organizations. He wanted to turn off his phone, but he couldn't for fear of missing a call from Rachel's abductors, plural; there had to be multiple people involved.

He joined Alicia in the living room, where she had the TV on, monitoring local news, and a bottle of red wine on the coffee table.

"I'll get you a glass."

"Just give me a sip of yours. I need to keep a clear head."

She handed him her glass, and he took more of a gulp than sip before returning it.

"You're sure?"

He nodded, leaned back against the cushion, and took a deep breath, then sat up straight and slapped his forehead.

Shit!

"What?"

"The luggage tracker, the air tag. This thing has me so rattled I'm not thinking clearly. Definitely no more wine."

Alicia stared at him, her brow furrowed like a fallow alfalfa field. "What are you talking about?"

He explained how he had convinced Rachel to hide an air tag in her backpack so she could locate it if she mislaid it or it got stolen. He would be doing the same with his laptop computer.

She had resisted at first, arguing that it just gave him another way to spy on her, just like the tracker on her phone. He promised he would not sync her air tag to his phone. "Only you will be able to track it," he had assured her.

"Do I hear a 'but' coming?" Alicia wondered. Rent gave her a tight smile. "You did sync it to your phone."

He nodded.

"So, you do spy on her."

"Not exactly. I just test it periodically to make sure it's still working, that the battery hasn't died."

"Then you'd better do it again, as in this instant."

Rent picked up his phone and opened the app. The whirling dots danced a circle on the screen as if it were a Maypole, attempting to locate the device. A map popped into view.

"Holy shit."

He showed the screen to Alicia.

"*¡Madre de Dios!*"

"They didn't waste any time getting her out of the county."

"At least it's not out of the country. Yet."

The blinking icon placed the backpack in Westmoreland, a small town in Imperial County, northwest of El Centro.

Rent stood up. "Let's go."

Alicia grabbed his hand and pulled him down onto the couch. "Not so fast, cowboy."

"What do you mean?"

"For starters, think. Don't just go off half-assed and get yourself shot."

Rent sighed in resignation. "I can't just sit here and do nothing."

"You're not doing nothing. You're going to call the cops and give them the GPS coordinates."

"Yeah, and the stormtroopers barge in and *she* gets shot."

"Besides, just because her backpack is there doesn't mean she's there. For all you know, they tossed it to the roadside and some kid picked it up on the way home from school."

"I want to be there."

"It's two hours away."

"So, I wait to make the call."

"*¡Estúpido!*"

At that moment, Rent's phone vibrated. Startled, he almost dropped it. He didn't recognize the area code. He swiped the Answer icon and took the call. "Beacham."

"Listen carefully." The voice sounded muffled and as if the speaker strained to achieve a low gruff.

"I'm listening," Rent replied and activated the voice recorder on the phone.

A different voice responded. "Dad? Is that you?" Rent emitted a primordial gasp. "Please, Dad, say it's you."

"Yeah, it's me."

"You have to do what they say or they'll kill me and then kill you."

Gruff Voice came back on the line. "You better listen to yer kid if you ever want to see her alive again."

"What is it you want?" Rent asked, believing he already knew the answer.

"You stop playing Mr. Snoopy."

"That's it?"

"And you're gonna sign over that gold mine in Chariot Canyon."

"What?"

Rachel shouted in the background, "No, not our gold mine!"

"You heard me. I know all about you and what you did. And now friends of mine are doing hard time because of you. It's what I call justice."

"You motherfucker!"

"I'll be in touch."

The line went dead. Rent immediately called the number back but got no answer.

He looked at Alicia, whose face had blanched.

"Cocksucking assholes," he muttered and stood up. "I'm hittin' the road."

"Not without me, you're not."

37

Rent went to his rental SUV, got in, and started the engine, then began tapping his fingers on the steering wheel.

Come on, Alicia. No time to waste.

She stepped out of the house and approached the driver's side of the vehicle. Rent pressed the switch to lower the window in the door. "What're you doin'?"

"Rent, don't be foolish. Think. What's your plan?"

"To rescue Rachel."

"Uh-huh. You're going to rush over there, waltz right in, grab the girl, and walk out, and we all live happily ever after."

Rent sighed and turned his head, staring through the windshield.

"We have to think this through—not to mention calling the cops. That's their job."

Rent shifted his eyes to the dashboard. "Shit."

"What now?"

"I'm low on gas."

"Let's take my car. All my surveillance gear is loaded, and I filled up the tank this morning for tomorrow's stakeout, which might turn into tonight's stakeout."

"I'm still driving."

"No. You're in no condition to be driving, especially in that traffic mess heading into East County."

"I need to grab things at my place."

"I'll meet you there. And you better be there, *muchacho*, or you will have hell to pay."

Second time today I've heard that.

Rent nodded, put the vehicle in gear, and pulled onto the road. He glanced in the rearview mirror—Alicia, arms akimbo, shaking her head.

At home, Rent got his pistol and ammunition and placed them in a duffel bag, along with a dark-blue jacket and a matching stocking cap with face mask, and gloves. He also grabbed his laptop, binoculars, and a sherpa blanket, although the overnight temperature in Imperial Valley was unlikely to dip below the mid-70s.

He changed from his casual business attire to a T-shirt and jeans and put on his Merrell hiking boots. *Who knows what may transpire?* At the bottom of the stairs, he put on a straw lifeguard's hat and picked up a gallon of water.

A car screeched to a halt in the alley. Alicia. She tapped the horn as he emerged from the garage. He tossed his duffel bag onto the back seat and set the water on the floor, then joined Alicia up front.

"Shit, I forgot the remote."

He got out and ran into the garage, grabbed the remote from his vehicle, and rejoined her as the garage door descended.

She had backed up the alley, so she put the car in Drive before Rent had the door closed.

"You do have your *telephono, sí?*"

He extracted the device from a back pocket of his jeans. "Right here."

"And the deed to the gold mine?"

"As if."

Alicia chuckled. "*Vámonos!*" A warning beep grew insistent. "Fasten your seatbelt."

As he did so, she eased the car down the alley and around the complex's circular driveway, cursing the speed bumps, then pressing the accelerator harder as they climbed the hill to Linda Vista Road. She turned left at the light.

"Where're you goin'?"

"You'll see. Just relax."

She turned left at Via de Las Cumbres, then again at the bottom of the hill, heading east on Friars Road. Instead of getting on the freeway, she continued on. As they crossed over the 163, they could see the southbound traffic below at a standstill; ditto for I-8 east.

"I think we can bypass much of this gridlock by staying on Friars, then take Mission Gorge to Santee and get on the freeway there."

Rent shrugged. "If we're lucky." His phone buzzed. He glanced at the caller ID—a TV reporter—and sent it to voicemail. A moment later, the phone buzzed again. He had no choice but to take the call.

"*Sí, el jefe.*"

"Are you trying to be cute?" asked Janis O'Connor.

"I have no new news to report."

"You haven't heard from the kidnappers? No ransom demand?" Naomi Clark in the background.

"Not a peep."

"Strange. Let us know when you do," O'Connor said. "I'll hold it as long as possible."

"I will, assuming I do get a call."

"Make sure you do. Anything from the cops?"

"No, and I don't expect to. I'll give them another call in case the perps called her phone."

"Hang in there," she said and ended the call.

"Lying to your boss, eh?" Alicia said. Rent shrugged. "Will you?" she pressed.

"Will I what?"

"Call the cops."

"Eventually. But first, let's get over there and assess the situation."

"Now you're making sense."

They rode in silence as they worked their way through the traffic signals, able to pick up speed as they went over the hump adjacent to Mission Gorge, past Cowles Mountain, and down the grade into Santee. There, Alicia turned on the 52 east and the connector to 67 south until it intersected with 8 east. The traffic was moving below the speed limit as it left El Cajon but at a reasonable speed. Once up the steep grade and past Alpine, Alicia nudged the speedometer up to eighty.

"Now we're cookin'," Rent said and felt some of the tension leave his body. "We should have made some coffee."

"I brought the thermos," she said. "We can fill it at the casino. I need to use the restroom anyway."

After leaving the casino, Alicia kept up her quick pace, keeping an eye out for the highway patrol. She let the "Zonies"—travelers from Arizona—lead the way, some of them pushing ninety.

They crossed the mountains and transited the serpentine route down the east side to the desert and past Ocotillo. A half an hour later, she turned off the freeway at Forester Road and headed north to Westmoreland as the sun began to dip behind the peaks to the west. They traveled at a good clip on the two-lane arterial, passing vast fields of lettuce, alfalfa, and other crops. At one point, Rent thought he saw a burrowing owl perched behind a mound of earth at the edge of an irrigation ditch.

"Call the Brawley Inn and reserve a room, preferably at the back, first floor."

Rent looked up the motel on his phone and made the reservation.

"What's your app say?" Alicia asked.

Rent checked the air-tag tracker. "Still showing in Westmoreland."

"Maybe they've settled in for the night. We're almost there."

"Time to call the cops?"

"Not yet," she said. "Let's locate the place first. I don't know how accurate those things are. No point in sending them to the wrong house, or wherever they're keeping her."

They pulled up to the stoplight at the center of town. "Which way?"

"Go straight."

Alicia eased the car through the intersection, then pulled over to let a stake-bed truck go past. Rent looked at his phone, then pointed. "Straight ahead two blocks and to the left."

She put the car in gear and rolled back onto the roadway, proceeding to a stop sign ringed with blinking red lights.

"Go left here. I think it will be on the right side of the road."

She did as instructed and idled slowly forward. In the dim light, they could still make out weather-worn houses that had seen better days. Dismal old cars and appliances sat in a few of the yards, palms and cottonwoods towering over them.

"Almost there," Rent announced, then ordered her to stop. "If this thing is even close, it's that last house on the right."

The house sat back from the road on a large lot, adjacent to a field littered with the drying stalks of a plant Rent could not identify. A large flock of gulls descended, squawking, onto the field.

The main section of the house in question looked forlorn, but it had a number of obvious additions, including a large garage on the left side that looked almost new. A short breezeway connected it to the house and no doubt provided a pleasant bit of shade on a hot afternoon. Somewhere, a dog barked.

"Lights are on, but no vehicles in the driveway," Rent observed.

"Get the address from the mailbox."

Rent jotted it down in his reporter's notebook. Alicia then drove past the house and continued on for several hundred yards before turning around. She came to a stop on the other side of the road, next to another field, it, too, occupied by a flock of gulls.

She retrieved her binoculars and camera from the backseat. "I'm going to do some birdwatching," she said and exited the car.

Rent started to open his door.

"Stop," she ordered, "and stay where you are."

"I'm going to rescue my daughter."

"Like hell you are. You could get yourself killed, and your daughter, too. Is that what you want? Let me check things out first. Meanwhile, call the cops."

Rent sighed, then made the call to the sheriff's station in Poway. He asked for the deputy he had given his report to, but she had left for the day. Her replacement said he had been briefed on the case and would contact his counterparts in the Imperial County Sheriff's Office.

Rent stared out the window, pounding his thighs with his fists. *I can't just sit here.*

Alicia had crossed the road and had her back turned as she scanned the field, trying to look like a birder, letting her field of view shift briefly toward the house, then back to the gulls. She took some photos as well, including of the house.

Rent slipped out of the car, opened the back door, and retrieved his binoculars. He stayed on the opposite side of the road as he crept forward, also mimicking a birder. He found a deep shadow beyond a tall cottonwood and stopped, fairly certain he could not be seen in the dwindling twilight. He could discern movement in the house and hear voices through the open windows, possibly from the inhabitants or a TV. He could not make out what they were saying. He heard a phone ring and being answered, but again could not hear the conversation clearly.

Footsteps startled him, and he whirled around.

"I thought you were going to stay in the car."

"And I thought of barging through that front door."

At that moment, the gulls rose almost as one as the large garage door rumbled open. Headlights from a vehicle inside the garage nearly blinded him and Alicia. The vehicle's engine roared to life and lurched forward, heading toward the road.

Alicia stepped behind the cottonwood and pulled Rent with her. The vehicle, a large, late-model, extended-cab pickup, didn't even slow down as it reached the road and veered left, its headlights panning the cottonwood. Alicia brought up her camera and whirred more than a dozen photos of the truck as it turned onto the road and away from where they stood.

"I saw her," Rent said.

38

"Come on, let's follow," Alicia commanded and ran to the car. "I'm sure of it," Rent continued, trailing in her wake. "I'm sure I saw her face pressed against the rear window. She must have seen us."

"Which means the driver probably did too," Alicia said as she got into the car.

"Yeah, but he wouldn't know who we are," Rent replied as he deposited himself in the passenger seat. "He'd probably think we're neighbors out for an evening stroll."

"Keep an eye on that truck," she ordered as she started the car and began pursuit, leaving the headlights off. "If that is her, they will be suspicious of anyone they see."

"Brake lights, left-turn signal on."

"Headed north. Could be going anywhere."

"Better than south to the border."

When they reached the intersection, she turned into the northbound lane of Forester Road. They soon exited the residential area and returned to the vast spread of agricultural fields.

"Get my camera and look at the photos; maybe I got a shot of the truck's license plate." When they passed an intersecting road, she turned on the headlights. "I'll try to close in on it, but not so quickly as to arouse suspicion."

After two and a half miles, the road made a sharp right, then a sharp left, becoming Gentry Road. Another vehicle pulled onto the road in front of them, drove for about a mile, then turned off. That had given Alicia the opportunity to close to within a hundred yards of the truck, where she held steady at that distance.

"Any idea where they might be headed?" Rent queried.

"Could be Calipatria, Niland, Slab City. Beyond that and you're into the Coachella Valley and then Palm Springs."

"If the Johnsons are behind this, they're probably going to keep her in this area. Whoa, what's this?"

The red and blue lights of a law enforcement or emergency services vehicle lit up the sky ahead of them.

"It's headed this way," Alicia said.

The vehicle reached them less than a minute later and whizzed past at high speed.

"Sheriff's car," Rent said as he turned in his seat. "I bet I know where they're headed."

"Just keep your eyes on the truck in front of us."

The large pickup turned right onto Eddins Road. Rent checked the air tag app again. "It's moved," he said. "She must have it on her. Looks like he's headed into Calipatria."

She pressed harder on the accelerator to close in on the truck, which slowed as it left the agricultural area and entered the town proper.

They followed the truck as Eddins Road became West Main Street, to an intersection in the middle of town. Other vehicles, including a large semi, crisscrossed the intersection.

"Damn, I think I lost him."

"Go straight through the intersection, then turn left when I tell you to . . . the next street."

Alicia turned left onto North Railroad Avenue, which paralleled the railroad dissecting the small town. She doused the headlights again and continued on the frontage road. Large stacks of hay lined the right side; to the left sat small, one-story houses until the residential area ended and they entered an industrial zone on the northern edge of town.

The truck veered left into a dirt lot and disappeared behind a one-story building that appeared to be a combination office and warehouse. Alicia slowed but continued on and pulled onto the right shoulder of the road, where she jerked to a stop. She took the car out of gear and her foot off the brake pedal.

"Get out," she ordered. "Quick! And close the door quietly."

Rent opened his mouth to question her intentions.

"Just do it and hide behind the hay and keep an eye out for that truck in case it leaves."

"Where are you going?"

"Just do it for chrissakes."

Rent obeyed, and Alicia pulled away with only a dim light emitting from the vehicle's dashboard. He eyed the building across the street. The office had lights on, but the warehouse section remained dark.

A few minutes later, a woman's voice startled him. "Anything?"

"The window blinds make it difficult to see inside, but I can see movement."

"We'll have to get closer."

"Where's the car?"

"Near the end of the road, in a deep shadow cast by a haystack. Here," she said, and handed him his stocking cap. She then pulled one over her head and face. He could barely make out her features in the low ambient light of the town.

"Yikes. You're scaring me."

"You look pretty scary yourself. Let's go."

They crossed the road and crept close to the building, flattening themselves against the exterior wall of the warehouse. They then edged closer to the office, where they could hear muffled voices.

Rent's phone vibrated in a back pants pocket.

"Fuck!"

"Shhh."

He glanced at the screen. "I think it's the cops."

"Go to the other end."

Rent moved as silently as he could to the opposite end of the building and answered the call with a whisper.

"We entered the house," a voice said, "but there was just some old lady who knew nothing about a girl being kidnapped. We also checked with the neighbors. *Nada.* Now we're wondering if you sent us on a wild goose chase."

"No, I did not. Did you find anything at the house that maybe got left there?"

"Like what?"

"Like a lavender backpack or violin? She had them with her when last seen."

"Let me check."

While waiting for a response, Rent peeked around a corner of the building. The big truck they had tailed sat parked by the office door. The deputy came back on the line.

"We found 'em. The old lady said they belonged to her granddaughter."

"Did you look inside for some sort of ID? Rachel's name is embroidered on the inside, and she should have some schoolwork with her name on it, and the sheet music inside the violin case probably has her name or her teacher's name on it."

The man sighed. "Let me check."

Rent moved back into the deep shadow of the building while he waited.

The male voice returned. "They're sending someone back in. I'll call you back. Are you at home now?"

"Um, not exactly."

"Well, keep your phone handy in case we need you to come into the station."

"Will do," he replied.

Rent went to the opposite corner and peered around it. He could just make out Alicia crouched below a window. His phone vibrated again.

"What'd you find out?"

"You were right. The backpack appears to belong to a Rachel Powell. Is that your daughter?"

"Yes."

"It doesn't mean for certain she was here."

"But you have the items and you're questioning the woman, right?"

"I'm sorry. I can't comment on that."

"I'm her father. I have a right to know."

"Sir, it's an ongoing investigation. We'll keep you informed on a need-to-know basis."

"That's a two-way street, deputy."

"Sir, if you are withholding any information or in any way obstructing this investigation . . ."

Rent ended the call.

Alicia joined him. "What are the cops saying? Anything?"

"They found her backpack and violin at the house, but they're not telling me anything beyond that. What did you find out?"

"Rachel's in there, with at least three men."

"You saw her?"

"No, but I heard her. I think she recognized the guy from the dance, and she asked him if he murdered Tom Wilbury."

"What?"

"Yeah, brazen as all get out."

"What did he say?"

"One of the other guys wanted to know what she was talking about. But I couldn't make out what they said after that because the AC unit kicked in."

As if on cue, Rent's phone vibrated again. He glanced at the screen. "I think it's him."

"Answer it."

Rent accepted the call. "Listen, motherfucker . . ."

"No, you listen. If you somehow put the cops on my tail, you'll never see her alive again."

"How could I put the cops on you? I don't know *who* the fuck you are or *where* the fuck you are."

"Well, someone sure as hell must know. We're going to do this deal tonight or it's over."

"I can't."

"You don't have a choice."

"I don't have the deed to the gold mine at my house. It's in a safe deposit box, and I can't get to it until the bank opens tomorrow."

"Then here's what you're gonna do. You're gonna get that deed the minute the bank opens tomorrow morning and you're gonna drive to that gold mine and sign it over to me. If you don't, guess where that little cunt is gonna end up."

"You will regret this, motherfucker," Rent retorted, then realized the guy had already ended the call.

Rent looked at Alicia. "I'm going in."

"No. If you bust through that door, he's gonna kill you, then Rachel."

"What do you suggest?"

"I already called the Imperial County Sheriff's Office and told them there's a hostage situation here. I gave them the GPS coordinates and suggested they approach silently; otherwise, the kidnappers might take off if they suspect anything. Although, they may have trouble escaping."

"Why's that?"

"You might say I took the wind out of their sails."

Rent eyed her for a moment. "Even so, there's time before the cops get here. We can't trust them not to blow it. I'm going to get my gun. We can get him in a crossfire."

"Rent, you barely know how to shoot that thing, let alone shoot a live human being."

"Why do you have to be so fucking rational?"

"It keeps me above the sod, for one."

"I want to see Rachel. Does she look OK?"

"I couldn't see her. I only heard her speak."

Rent sighed. "This waiting is killing me."

"They'll be here soon. We should probably wait in the car. We don't want to be mistaken for the perps."

"I feel as if I'm abandoning her."

"You're saving her life is what you're doing."

Alicia turned to sneak back to her car. Rent didn't move, as if unwilling to follow.

At that moment, a chorus of protests came from outside the building.

"*Algún chupapollas me ha cortado los neumáticos,*" one man shouted.

"*El mío también,*" said another.

"*Voy a matar a ese hijo de puta.*"

The voice sounded closer.

"Run," Alicia ordered, sprinting toward her car.

39

Rent took two steps, then veered right toward the office window, which hung partially open, leaving a small gap between it and the sill. He peered in but could not see anyone.

"Rachel," he called out in a loud whisper.

"Dad?"

"Over here. At the window."

Seconds later, her face appeared. Rent tried raising the window sash more, but it jammed, leaving only a narrow opening.

"Come on, you can squeeze through."

Rachel hesitated, then placed her hands on the windowsill and poked her head through the opening. Rent got his hands under her arms and pulled her toward him.

"I'm stuck," she said.

"Push with your feet."

"I am."

A man appeared in the doorway on the opposite side of the room, his eyes blazing. A hand went behind his back as if reaching for something.

Rent jerked Rachel toward him, and she became unstuck. He fell backward, hitting the ground hard with Rachel lying on top of him. The window glass exploded as the sound of a gunshot pierced the air. Rent felt the sting of shattered glass on his face as he rolled to his left, taking Rachel with him.

She smelled of sweat, and he breathed it in deeply. It reminded him of sitting on his dad's lap as a youngster, his father just home from work, wearing a threadbare white T-shirt odiferous of sweat. Being held closely not only made the smelly shirt tolerable, it had become synonymous with love.

He got to his knees and scrambled out of the lighted area, tugging Rachel with him. He could see the silhouette of the gunman shadowed on the ground; then it shrank and disappeared.

"He's going out the other side. Come on."

He sprinted toward the road and the stacks of hay, Rachel on his heels. They hid behind a haystack, catching their breath.

"I'm so scared," Rachel said and began sobbing.

"It's almost over, sweetie," he said and held her close. He then released her and peered around a corner of the haystack.

The gunman came around the side of the building and walked to the shattered window, peering at the ground; then he looked in their general direction. "I know you're out there. I will find you."

At that moment, red and blue flashing lights lit up the night sky. Seconds later, two sheriff's patrol vehicles came speeding up the road, then turned into the dirt lot, their headlights shining on the building where Rachel had been held. The gunman fired at one of the cars, shattering the windshield, then disappeared around the end of the building. The deputies scrambled out of their vehicles, guns drawn, two following the footsteps of the gunman, the other pair going around the opposite end of the building.

Rent and Rachel found Alicia's car and got in, Rent in front and Rachel in the backseat.

"That was close," Rent said.

Alicia shook her head. "You're a cat with nine lives."

"Let's get out of here," Rent said.

"Yeah, I want to go home," Rachel seconded.

Alicia began to speak as several gunshots rang out. They all instinctively ducked, then waited, barely breathing.

"As I was about to say, we sit tight and wait for the cops to find us, or we call 'em and tell them where we are."

She and Rent removed their ski masks.

"I need to pee," Rachel said.

"Step outside and squat," Alicia said. "That's what I do."

"Ewww," Rachel replied.

"Your choice," Alicia responded and stared out the open window.

Rachel sighed, opened the door, and got out, the interior light momentarily illuminating the inside of the vehicle.

"You are one tough cookie," Rent said to Alicia.

She turned to face him. "And you are an idiot. But I'm glad you're both OK." She then grimaced.

"What?"

"You're bleeding. Your face. It has a bunch of tiny cuts."

"He shot out the window. It'd probably be worse if I didn't have that hat on."

"I have a first aid kit in back."

She started to open the door when a voice ordered, "Stay where you are, hands where I can see them."

A bright flashlight lit up the car. Alicia raised her hands on either side of her face, as did Rent.

"There are three of us," Alicia said. "There's a young girl beside the car relieving herself. I doubt she would want to be in your spotlight."

"I'm done," Rachel called out as she stood up, straightening her skirt. "Can I get back in the car?"

"Go ahead, but keep your hands where I can see them," the deputy said.

Rachel got into the car and mimicked the posture of the two adults. They looked like a trio of scarecrows from the adjacent field.

The deputy stepped closer. "Who are you and what are you doing here?"

Rent started to reply, but Alicia touched his arm. "Shush." She then addressed the deputy. "I'm Alicia Velasquez, the one who made the nine-one-one call advising you of the hostage situation. The girl in back is the former hostage. She escaped only moments before you arrived. This man beside me is her father."

"Let's see your ID. All of you."

"It's in my purse, in the backseat," she said.

The deputy shined his light through the back window. "The green bag?"

"That's it."

"You, the girl," he said. "Hand me the purse."

The deputy opened the rear door, and Rachel handed him the purse. He stepped back from the car and shined his flashlight inside. Satisfied, he handed it to Alicia. She withdrew a leather wallet and handed it to the cop. He opened it and held it in the light of his flashlight.

"Humph. PI, eh?"

"Yours truly," she replied.

"How about you?" the deputy said, looking at Rent.

Rent handed him his driver's license and, unable to restrain himself, his press pass. The deputy examined both. A slight smile creased his face as he shook his head. "So, we got a private investigator and an investigative journalist."

"And the investigative journalist's daughter who was abducted this afternoon in San Diego County," Alicia stated. "Oh, and by the way, I'm also a former cop. I assume you have the perps in custody."

"The alleged perps," he said.

"Can I go home now?" Rachel inquired from the back seat.

The deputy laughed. "Not a snowball's chance. My sergeant will be over here in a few minutes. Don't go anywhere."

The sound of a siren filled the air, and flashing lights again lit up the night sky as an ambulance arrived.

"Someone get shot?" Alicia asked.

The deputy nodded.

"Not one of yours."

The deputy shook his head.

"The guy gonna make it?"

The deputy shrugged. "As I said, don't go anywhere. I'm gonna go get my sarge."

Rent leaned back in his seat. "Might as well get comfortable. We're gonna be here a while."

40

Rent awoke to the smell and sound of coffee brewing. *I must be dreaming after a nightmare of a night.* He elbowed into a half-sitting position in the bed and assessed his surroundings: generic motel room, two queen-sized beds. He could hear the shower running; Rachel lay snuggled under the covers in the other bed, snoring softly.

Rent spotted his jeans lying next to the bed and put them on. *Where's my shirt?*

The coffee machine completed its cycle, and Rent helped himself. The shower stopped showering and, moments later, Alicia emerged, wrapped in a towel, with another towel forming a caftan on her head.

"Pour me a cup?" she asked as she gathered items of clothing and headed back to the bathroom. She accepted the coffee on the way and disappeared into the steamy room.

Rent sipped his coffee and went to the window. He pulled the heavy blackout drapes back but left the gauzy ones in place. Full daylight lit up the parking lot, and palm fronds fluttered in the morning breeze. Crows cawed and flitted from one tree to the next, rarely flying in a straight line. Pigeons and Brewer's blackbirds foraged on the pavement.

"Welcome to Brawley," he muttered and turned back to face the room. His phone buzzed on the nightstand. "Crap," he muttered and answered. "Hello, Lewis. What got you up at this ungodly hour?"

"You know damn well why I'm calling. And stop calling me Lewis."

"Yeah, sorry 'bout that, but I am in an extremely foul mood at the moment."

"Tell me about it. I say that literally as well as figuratively."

"I can't. I haven't even had the thumb screws put on me yet."

"This story is front-page news. I want the exclusive. What the hell happened?"

"What do you know?"

"That Rachel was abducted, then rescued, and three as-yet-to-be-identified men are in custody, one of whom got shot by a cop but is expected to live."

"That pretty well sums it up."

"Fuck you."

"Sorry, but as I said, I'm in a foul mood and have to report to the sheriff's office, along with Rachel and Alicia, and I'm about to endure hours of grilling by doubting detectives."

"Alicia is with you?"

"She's one of the heroes of the hour, along with Rachel herself."

"Lay it on me."

"I'm about to get in the shower, then get some breakfast before entering the torture chamber."

"I do have a deadline."

"There's that ugly word again. Besides, it's still early."

Clark sighed. "Why do you have to be such a fucking asshole?"

"Just part of my good nature, I guess. Tell you what, I'll call you after I get to the sheriff's and have a better idea of where things stand. They won't be happy about me talking to you."

"Tough shit. I have a job to do as well."

"I'll call, promise."

"You better."

The call ended, and Rent tossed the phone on the bed. Rachel stirred and rubbed her eyes, then glanced toward the door, her head still on the pillow. "Dad?"

"Over here, sweetie, by the window."

She turned and smiled. "I dreamt that you got shot."

"Well, I did, sort of."

She focused on his face. "Oh, my gosh. Does it hurt?"

"Only when I don't stay absolutely still."

"I'm hungry. I never got any dinner except those snacks from the machine."

"They serve breakfast here. Get dressed. We can walk over."

She sat up, lifted the covers, and looked down. "I don't have any pajama bottoms."

"And you're wearing my T-shirt."

She giggled. "It's now my nightgown. Where's Alicia?"

The bathroom door opened, and Alicia stepped out. "Who's next?"

"Me," Rachel said. "Dad, turn around and don't look."

He did as instructed, and she scurried to the bathroom. Alicia joined Rent and smiled.

"My bare-chested hero. You could be a cover model for a romance novel. You might have to trim that beard, though," she added as she rubbed his chin and gave him a peck on the cheek.

"Yeah, right," he muttered and sipped more of his coffee. "When I get my shirt back, I want to get something to eat. I'm starving."

"Let's go to Walmart and get her some clean clothes—and you another shirt. We can get a good breakfast at Las Chabelas on the way to El Centro. We need to be at the sheriff's station by ten."

"What about you? Don't you need some clean clothes?"

She nodded at a small suitcase. "I always keep a spare set in the car. As you are so fond of saying, 'One never knows, do one?'"

"Aren't you the girl scout."

"Not always," she said with a grin, then pinched his butt.

* * *

They entered the sheriff's station, and Rent checked his phone: 9:58 a.m. Detective Sergeant Romero Hernandez introduced himself and said they would begin by interviewing Rachel. As her father, Rent would accompany her. Alicia would be interviewed separately, followed by Rent individually.

Hernandez led Rachel and Rent to Interview Room 2. A female detective joined them and introduced herself as Felicity Garrido. They all took seats at a small table, Rent and Rachel on one side, the detectives opposite them.

Rachel grabbed Rent's hand under the table, and he gave it a reassuring squeeze. Hernandez started to explain to Rachel how the interview would go.

Rent's phone vibrated in his pocket.

"Turn that damn thing off," the detective ordered.

Rent did, then said, "She knows the drill. She's been in the hot seat before."

Hernandez shifted his gaze from Rent to his daughter and nodded. "That's right. You were involved in the incident at that gold mine."

Rachel nodded and wiped at a tear descending her cheek.

"I'll get you a tissue," Garrido said. She rose from her chair and left the room.

Hernandez looked back at Rent. "And you nearly got your ass blown off when that mine exploded." Rent shrugged. "You just can't seem to stay out of trouble, can you?" the detective added.

"Am I in trouble?" Rent asked.

The man stared at him for a moment before responding. "That remains to be seen."

Garrido returned and offered a tissue to Rachel, then rejoined her colleague at the table.

"Rachel, how old are you?" Hernandez asked.

"Twelve. I'll be thirteen in January; the eighth of January. My dad—"

Hernandez raised a hand. "Just answer the questions as directly as you can."

Rachel looked at her father, tight-lipped, and Rent patted her arm.

"You're not in trouble," the detective said. "We just need you to tell us what happened so we can prosecute the men who did this to you. Do you understand?"

She nodded, looking at the detective as if to say, *I might be twelve, but I'm not stupid.* "I know. I had to do this when my mom—"

She choked up and began sobbing. Rent put an arm around her. "I'm sorry you have to go through this again, sweetie."

She sniffed and reached for another tissue to wipe her nose and dry her eyes. "I'll be OK."

Hernandez asked her to start at the beginning. She explained, with furtive glances at Rent, how she had met this boy online. "He said he was a student at my school, and we set up a meeting at the park. But then this man showed up. I think he's the same man who was at the dance."

Hernandez frowned. "Dance?"

Rent started to speak, but the detective waved him off. "I need to hear it from her."

Rachel explained how Rent played the fiddle for contra dances, and she had gone with him. "I even got to play my birthday song, the *Eighth of January*," she added with a smile.

"And?" the detective said.

"And this scary-looking man was there, and he said something to my dad afterward when we were getting into the car."

"What did he say?"

"I was on the other side of the car, putting in my violin, so I didn't hear what he said."

The detective looked at Rent with raised brows.

"He threatened to harm Rachel if I didn't stop my investigation."

"Investigation?"

"I'm looking into the activities of a business enterprise that may be tied to a three-decades-old murder in Washington State—a business that has operations here in Imperial County."

"Oh?"

"A consulting firm that has subsidiary operations in the area."

"Let me guess—geothermal and lithium," Hernandez said.

Rent nodded in response.

"The Johnson family," the detective continued. "Big fish in this small pond, and now they're dipping their wicks into local politics. You think they have something to do with the abduction?"

Rent shrugged. The detective sighed, leaned back in his chair, and crossed his arms over his chest.

"And that led to the shootout at the OK Corral in Calipatria last night," the detective concluded.

"If you say so," Rent replied.

Hernandez glanced at Garrido, shaking his head, then turned back to Rent for a moment, finally settling his intense gaze on Rachel. "Let's get on with this. Please continue, Miss Powell."

At that moment, someone knocked at the door, then stuck a head in. "Sarge, we need you for a sec."

Hernandez excused himself and left the room. An awkward silence ensued until Rent spoke. "So, deputy—"

"Detective."

"Sorry, detective. Do you get to ask any questions?"

"We'll see. Mainly, I'm here as part of my training and as a witness, and because I'm female." She nodded toward Rachel.

"Just curious," Rent said.

The door opened, and Hernandez entered the interview room. He rolled his eyes at Garrido as he retook his seat. He looked across the table at Rachel. "Please continue."

Rachel said the scary man told her he was the boy's father, that his son was very shy and wanted to meet her in a less public place. "I refused and called the man a pervert. I tried to get away from him, but he grabbed my arm so hard that it hurt. I started to dial nine-one-one, and he tried to take my phone, and it flew out of my hand and into the creek. He had a knife and said he would slit my throat and I would bleed like a stuck pig if I didn't shut up and go with him. I thought he would kill me if I didn't."

"So, you went with him peaceably, as if he was a teacher, or a friend, or even your father?"

Rachel nodded. "I was so scared I was afraid I'd like pee my pants, except I had on a skirt."

Hernandez stifled a chuckle. "And then what?"

"He took me to a big truck—it was black—and he put me in the back seat and told me to lay down and be quiet, or else. Then he drove away. I was afraid to look out the window, so I don't know where he took me. He drove for a long time, and I really needed to pee, but he wouldn't stop. He took me to a house, and he left me there. It must have been in the desert because it was really hot. He made me call my dad and tell him he had to stop snooping and he had to sign over our gold mine. Otherwise, he would kill me. And there was this old lady, and she made me some tacos. They were really good. I had a book in my backpack, so I read for a while, then I heard the truck come back. That's when I had the idea."

"The idea?"

"My dad put a tracker app on my phone so he could spy on me—"

"To keep you safe," Rent injected.

Hernandez daggered Rent and shook his head slowly, then nodded at Rachel.

"But I lost my phone, so I knew that wouldn't be any good. But I also had an air tag in my backpack, so I could find it in case I lost it or someone stole it."

She paused and looked at Rent. "My dad wasn't supposed to track me with that, but I figured he would anyway. At least I hoped so. So, I took it out of my backpack and put it in my undies—I had on a skirt, and it didn't have any pockets—just in case they took my backpack away from me."

Garrido smiled and shot a sidelong glance at Hernandez. He chuckled and said, "Clever girl."

"Anyway, a different man came to get me. It was nighttime by then, like really dark, and he took me to that place where my dad rescued me. I knew he would because when we left the house where the old lady was, I looked out the window and I saw two people standing across the street, and I shouted, but I didn't think they could see me, so I put my face right on the glass. I was sure it was my dad."

"Did the man driving the truck say anything?"

"He told me to shut up. He tried to slap me, but I was too far away, and he almost drove off the road."

"Then what?"

She explained how they stopped at a building in a strange town, and he took her inside. The man who kidnapped her was there, along with another man she had never seen before.

"So there were three men."

Rachel nodded.

"Please say 'yes' for the recording."

"Yes, there were three men, and I was really scared. I didn't know what they would do to me."

"Did they do anything to you?"

"You mean did they touch me or try to rape me?"

"Well . . . uh . . . yeah."

"No. They just made me sit in a corner."

"Did they talk? Did you overhear any conversation?"

She related how the men discussed what to do next because an Amber Alert had been issued, and they didn't want to get caught with her. One of them said they could throw her in an irrigation ditch and no one would ever find her.

"Then the main guy—one of them called him Chuckarelli—said no, that he had tried that once before and now it's come back to bite him in the ass."

Rent reacted. "He said those exact words?"

Hernandez glared at him. "I ask the questions," he said, nodding at Rachel.

"Uh-huh. Those exact words: 'It's come back to bite me in the ass.' I remember it because I thought it was so funny. Then he said they have to keep me alive and trade me for the gold mine, and as long as me and my dad—my dad and I—kept our mouth shut, we would be safe."

"And you believed him?"

"That's when I asked him if he killed Tom Wilbury."

41

"Who the hell is Tom Wilbury?" the detective asked.

Rent answered, "The dead guy in Washington I told you about earlier."

"Holy sh—" The detective caught himself. "Sorry, but this story is getting weirder and weirder by the second."

Rent continued, "As I said to begin with, I believe this abduction is part of an effort not only to cover up a three-decades-old murder but ongoing criminal activities by that self-same party."

"And that self-same party is who? The Johnsons, perhaps?"

"I can't comment on that."

Hernandez's eyebrows shot skyward. "Can't? Or won't?"

Rent shook his head. "Revealing a name or names at this time would jeopardize my investigation."

The detective snorted. "Your investigation."

"Yes, my investigation, because law enforcement and the justice system dropped the ball on this years ago."

"Oh, my, getting a bit cocky, are we? After your big exposé on welfare fraud, I suppose."

Rent shrugged. "If the truth hurts . . . I'm sure your arrestees could shed some light on this matter—unless they plead the Fifth."

Hernandez glared at him.

"Look, detective, I have my suspicions, but right now I don't have enough to connect all the dots. If I start divulging names prematurely, my ass, and my newspaper, will be slapped with a defamation lawsuit

—again—and these guys will get away with whatever they're doing —again."

Rent paused for a breath, then continued, "I obviously have touched a nerve, but so far all I get are denials and anonymous threats, one of which has played out with the kidnapping of my daughter. I think you'll find that those three thugs are the hired help out to make a little dough on the side, not the brains of the outfit."

Hernandez sighed. "OK, let's get this over with."

He nodded at Rachel to continue. She told him that saying the name Tom Wilbury made the Chuckzilla guy really mad, and the other two wanted to know what she was talking about.

"He called me the 'C' word and told me to shut the 'F' up and told the other guys to forget about it. Then Chuckzilla made a phone call, but I couldn't hear what he said, and the other two went outside to smoke or something, and then one started shouting that his tires had been slashed and Chuckzilla ran outside too and then my dad came to the window and pulled me out, and we got shot at but he missed and we escaped and hid behind the haystack until the cops showed up. There were gunshots and shouting and me and my dad . . . my dad and I . . . got in the car with Alicia and waited until that cop came and started asking us a bunch of questions. The End. That's my story and I'm sticking to it."

Rachel leaned back in her chair and crossed her arms with an emphatic flourish.

Hernandez couldn't help but chuckle over her impertinence. "OK, I think that's enough for now."

Garrido turned off the recorder and looked questioningly at her colleague. He told Rachel she could wait in the reception area and told Rent he would be questioned next, after a bathroom break.

"Wait," Rachel said. All eyes turned on her. "What about my backpack and violin? I need them."

"They're evidence," Hernandez said.

"Of what?" Rent inquired. "If you actually need the backpack, it can be replaced, but she needs its contents for school, and what good is the violin to you?"

Hernandez mulled it over for a beat. "I'll see what I can do." He turned to Rachel. "But now that you mention it, where's the tracking device you hid on yourself?"

"I have it in my gear bag," Rent said.

"I will need that."

"Do you know what those things cost?"

"Not my department. It's material to the case."

They all filed out of the room; Rent escorted Rachel to reception, where they found Alicia seated. She stood and shot a questioning look at Rent, then Rachel, who grinned and said, "I told them everything."

"You did great, sweetie," Rent said as he draped an arm over her shoulders. "I don't think I'll be too much longer, and we can hit the road." He shifted his gaze to Alicia. "How'd it go?"

She shook her head. "Those two goons could barely get beyond the fact that I'm a PI and accused me of withholding evidence and obstruction, and threatened to have my license pulled."

"And?"

"I said go ahead. Meanwhile, I'm calling my lawyer."

Rent chuckled. "They must have loved that."

"Oh, yeah. They left the room for several minutes, then returned."

"That must have been why Hernandez left the room during Rachel's interview."

"Could be. Anyway, they cooled it. I told them how I got involved and what transpired from my perspective. What now? Are we free to go?"

Rent shook his head. "Afraid not. They still need to interrogate me."

"Oh, great. We'll be here all day, if not the night."

"Nah, Hernandez has Rachel's testimony, and yours, so he knows more than I do. I'll corroborate some of the things Rachel said."

"They're not happy about us not calling them sooner and telling them about the trackers," Alicia said.

"Tough shit," Rent responded. "If they want to make a mountain out of it, they can deal with the one and only A.J. Hawke. My guess is the DA will dismiss it since he has the three guys in custody. He's got bigger fish to fry. Now, I need to get the air tag out of the car."

Rent retrieved the tracking device and returned to the station. Hernandez was there, handing over to Rachel the contents of her backpack and the violin. "Sorry about the backpack, but it may be critical to the case, tying the kidnappers to the abduction."

He then held out his hand, palm up, toward Rent. Rent placed the air tag in the man's hand.

"And your phone."

"What?"

"We need the tracker data."

"How long will that take?"

Hernandez shrugged.

"You don't actually need my phone," Rent said. "You have the tracking device. Just install the app on one of your phones and sync it with the device. I'll give you the access code."

The detective eyed Rent for a moment. "I can see why you have a reputation for being a pain in the ass."

"According to whom?"

"Al Washington for one."

"Oh, yeah, there's a credible source."

"And I'm keeping the phone. It's evidence."

"But I need it. It has all my contact information on it."

"Sorry, but them's the rules."

"Oh, for fuck's sake," Rent muttered. "Come on, let's get this over with before lunch."

Fifty-three minutes later, Rent returned to the reception area. Rachel ran to greet him.

"Can we go now?" she pleaded.

"Yes, we can go. Grab your stuff."

Alicia stood and gave him a questioning look.

"Everything's fine," he said. "We may have to come back, but if those clowns plead out, we're done."

"Hallelujah. *!Gracias a Dios!*"

42

On the drive back to San Diego, Rent borrowed Alicia's phone to access his data in the "cloud." He had more than a dozen text and voicemail messages. He ignored them and called Naomi Clark; she wanted to interview him and Rachel.

"No, not Rachel. I have to protect her from the news media spotlight."

Clark persisted. "Why was she abducted? Does this have anything to do with Tom Wilbury's death and/or your investigation into the Johnson family's businesses? Or both?"

Rent said he couldn't comment but would in due time. "For now, it's in the hands of the cops. You need to speak with them."

"You're a dirty bastard. But rumor has it that you pulled her to safety and almost got shot in the ass again."

"No truth to the latter, but, yes, I will confirm that I pulled Rachel out of the window, and we ran to safety."

Rachel, eavesdropping, spouted off. "He's my hero. He rescued me from the bad guys, just like I knew he would."

"I'm quoting her on that," Clark said. "Later, gator."

They stopped at Descanso to see the horses and ate dinner at the Descanso Junction before taking Rachel to her grandparents' house. During the remainder of the drive, Rent commented on how lucky the timing turned out to be, that he and Rachel didn't get shot.

"That guy wouldn't've had a chance to get off another shot."

"What do you mean?"

"You think I was just sittin' on my ass in the car with my fingers crossed?"

"You . . ."

"I had a bead on him and was about to shatter his sternum if the cops didn't arrive when they did."

Rent stared at her for a moment. "Holy moly. Don't mess with Velasquez."

"And don't you forget it."

"By the way, how did you manage to slash the tires on those trucks?"

"Who says I did?"

"You did. You said you took the wind out of their sails."

"Did I? I don't recall, your honor."

"Don't be coy."

"Off the record?"

"Sure. Between you and me and the gate post."

"I have a combat knife and know how to use it."

"Yeah, but that takes a lot of strength. Tires are tough."

"Are you saying I'm a ninety-pound weakling?"

"What? No. I don't think I could do it."

"Valve stems are vulnerable."

"Ah, yes. Either way, it was *Flat on the Frog*."

"'Flat on the Frog'?"

"Fiddle tune I play."

She shook her head. "Is there anything you don't have a fiddle tune for?"

* * *

The following morning, back in the newsroom, Rent used his desk phone to call Detective Hernandez. He requested details on the identities and status of the three kidnappers. The detective refused, citing the time-worn excuse: "It's an ongoing investigation."

"Look," Rent countered, "we can either work together on this, or you can flail around and get nowhere. Yeah, you'll get the small fry and call it a result, put two or three bad guys behind bars, but you won't get the puppet master who's pulling the strings. You get him, and you get promoted to lieutenant."

Hernandez remained adamant, and Rent ended the call.

He left and got a replacement cell phone from his provider. The first call he received came from a number he didn't recognize but, on a hunch, answered it anyway.

"Hello, Mr. Beacham, this is Felicity Garrido, the detective from the Imperial County Sheriff's Office."

"Surprise, surprise."

"What do you mean?"

"I spoke with your sergeant a while ago, and he gave me the bum's rush."

"Yeah, he mentioned it," she said. "That's why I'm calling. But I'm not at the station. I'm calling from my private phone, not the department issue."

"Being secretive, are we?"

"Sort of."

"He won't be happy with you."

"I'm well aware of that, but I'm getting suspicious of his motives. Romeo drives a nice car and has an expensive bass boat he cruises up and down the river on . . ."

"Romeo?"

"His nickname. He fancies himself as a ladies' man. My point is, I don't see how he can afford it on his salary."

"Have you asked him?"

"God no. Are you kidding?"

"But you think he might be on the take."

"I don't know, but something seems fishy, if you'll pardon the pun."

"So, why are you calling me?" Rent wanted to know.

"This is between us, no one else," she said.

"OK."

"We're getting nowhere in this investigation, and Romeo doesn't seem to give a damn, like he considers the case closed as far as our investigation is concerned. Charles Stevens, the Chuckarelli guy, and his two *compadres* aren't saying anything. They've lawyered up. Stevens is still in custody because he shot at law enforcement. One of the other guys was offered bail, but he refused it. I think he's afraid ICE will be waiting for him if he walks out the door. The third is still in the hospital. The DA is building a case against them, but so much of it is circumstantial."

"Rachel ID'd Charles Stevens as her abductor," Rent said.

"Yeah, but he denies it," Garrido replied. "He's saying she's confused due to the trauma of it all, and because of her age she's susceptible to being coached by us so we can close the case."

"What about the text messages and that phone number?"

"Burner phone. No longer in service. But what's with that username, *ixystz*?"

"Yeah, it's a bit odd. I think it's tech-slang for 'I exist.' Or it's an AI hallucination. How does he explain Rachel's presence at that place in Calipatria?"

"He claims she was a runaway and broke in, probably looking for petty cash or anything of value. That he's just an innocent bystander who got swept up in the Amber Alert."

"Oh, for fuck's sake."

"Yeah, exactly."

"And the old lady who made the tacos?"

"She claims to have early onset and thought the girl was one of her grandchildren."

"They've circled the wagons."

"That's about the size of it."

"So, where does this leave us?" Rent wanted to know.

"I was hoping you could tell me," Garrido answered.

"Just between the two of us, right?"

"On my honor."

"How do I know I can trust you?"

"I'm told I have a nice smile."

"So did the Sirens of Greek mythology."

"It was their singing, not their smiles, that lured the ships ashore."

"Whatever. I'm just sayin'."

"I understand your skepticism," she said, "but all I can say is you have to trust me. There's a lot more going on than meets the eye, if you'll pardon the cliché. That's why I've told you as much as I have. I shouldn't even be talking to you. I've told you too much already."

Rent pondered her comment for a moment before responding. "You're going to keep me up to speed on your end and any progress in the kidnapping case."

"I will, but it's a two-way street," she fired back.

"We have to meet in person. I'm not doing this over the phone."

"Are you familiar with Jacumba?"

"Sure. The hot springs. Sits on the border by the big, beautiful wall."

"Tomorrow? It's my day off. There's a park. Big snake sculpture at the entrance. Eight a.m."

"That means I have to set my alarm."

"And no funny business."

"Wouldn't think of it. Well, I might think of it—you do have that nice smile—but I'll be bringing my sidekick along."

"Alicia, the PI?"

"*Exactamente.*"

"And here I thought you were her sidekick."

"Aren't you the comedienne."

"Buenos tardes, Señor Beach-ham."

Rent chuckled and returned to documenting the events of the past two days. He called Mike Johnson and left a message, not expecting to hear from the man any time soon. He called Rachel, who said she's now the most popular girl in sixth grade. Everyone wants to know all about her abduction.

* * *

The following morning, Rent rose before dawn and made the 70-mile trek to Jacumba, where he met Detective Felicity Garrido at the park. He had invited Alicia, but she declined, needing to play catch-up with her other investigations.

Garrido had dressed casually in a T-shirt, shorts, and sandals, and had let her hair down, easily passing for a tourist. Rent insisted that she be checked for a wire, although he didn't know how he would accomplish that without Alicia.

Garrido glanced around and, seeing no one else in the park, pulled off her T-shirt, exposing a sports bra, then twirled like a ballet dancer doing a pirouette. "Satisfied?" she asked. "Or do you want me to drop trou as well?"

Rent blushed and shook his head. Garrido smirked and put the shirt back on, saying, "Now my turn."

Rent's face turned crimson. "Be my guest," he said, "but you're the one who wanted this meeting, not me. I'm not investigating the sheriff's department—at least not yet."

Garrido gestured toward a picnic table in the shade of a tree, the morning air still relatively cool. They sat down, Rent on one side, Garrido opposite. A pair of Harris's hawks flew in and perched in a bare tree near the baseball field. *An omen?* Rent wondered.

"I told you yesterday everything I know at this point in time. What have you got to trade?" she asked.

Rent replied that he believed the kidnapping was directly related to his investigation into the Tom Wilbury murder, as well as the Lustrous Consulting Group and its hazmat outfit, along with its operations in geothermal electricity production and lithium mining.

"Which all boils down to the Johnson family," Garrido said. "That really complicates things."

"How so?"

"They're the new kids on the block in Imperial Valley—glad-handing, throwing their weight around, tossing out money like candy at a Fourth of July parade."

She went on to describe how Mike Johnson, along with his son and granddaughter, was supporting conservative candidates for elective offices, bragging about the power of free enterprise and how lithium—white gold—was going to improve the economy and raise the standard of living for the local populace. And for the icing on the cake, the grandson-in-law had tossed his hat in the ring for the congressional seat.

"There's a lot of smoke coming out from behind those mirrors, if you ask me," she said. "Not to mention a lot of their trucks transiting through the valley and to the border."

"The border?" Rent acted as if this came as news to him.

She nodded. "Some of the trucks cross over into Mexico. And don't forget their AI data center on the outskirts of Mexicali."

"The trucks are going to a data center in Mexico?" Rent tried to sound skeptical.

"I don't know. But they're hauling something across the border."

"Toxic waste, under the banner of Incinergy, one of the subsidiaries?" Rent suggested.

Garrido shrugged. "Maybe it's entirely innocent. But why build their data center in Mexicali if they're so interested in improving the economy on this side of the border?"

"Cheap land, cheap labor?" Rent wondered aloud.

"Tell me about Tom Wilbury," Garrido said.

Rent laid out the background story: the boatyard scandal in the mid-nineties, suspicious EIR, faulty incinerator, lawsuit, Wilbury moving to the San Juan Islands in Washington, then disappearing, only to reappear nearly three decades later as a corpse and initiating a cold-case homicide investigation.

"So, you think the Johnsons have something to do with his murder," she responded, a statement, not a question.

"That's what started this whole thing, yeah. Wilbury was under contract as an environmental consultant. It can't be coincidence; his journal backs it up. I start asking pointed questions, and suddenly I'm getting anonymous threats, which led to me being swatted, to me and Alicia nearly getting burned alive, Alicia's abduction by ICE, then to Rachel's abduction. And here we are today. Are they all connected? That's what I'm trying to find out. Johnson has a history of playing fast and loose with the law and regulations, and he's amassed a fortune over the years through property development and, most recently, ADUs, along with his expansion into these other enterprises. It ought to raise a few eyebrows, if nothing else."

"Wow. I can barely get my head around all of this."

"Yeah, as the saying goes, it's complicated," Rent said. "I think Stevens, or whatever the hell his name is, holds the key to it."

Garrido cast a questioning gaze at Rent, who continued.

"I'm pretty sure he was involved in Wilbury's murder, operating under an alias as Stefano Ceccarelli, aka Chuckarelli, and we know he's involved in Rachel's kidnapping. Those are the first dots I've managed to connect."

"And he's had ties to the Johnson family for all these years?" Garrido asked.

Rent nodded. "It seems so, as a 'security consultant.' But it's those dots we have yet to definitively connect. Without his direct testimony, or maybe one of his hirelings, we can't pin it on any of the Johnsons —not senior or junior—nor any of their associates. They have deniability to go along with their well-manicured respectability. We need direct evidence, not circumstantial."

"Maybe I can figure out a way to turn up the heat. Get one of the kidnappers to cut a deal."

"What about your Romeo?"

"He's not *my* Romeo!"

"Sorry. Just kidding."

Garrido acknowledged that he could be a problem. But if she could come up with more evidence or compelling testimony and get it in front of the DA . . . "The canaries might start singing."

43

Back in the newsroom, Rent called Mike Johnson again and left yet another message.

Do I have to go to Montana to confront this guy? Time to go nuclear.

He pulled out the three-ring binder he had begun assembling, which included the incriminating material documenting the falsified boatyard EIR, the malfunctioning incinerator, Perkins's fraud and prison, Tom Wilbury's move and subsequent disappearance, and Wilbury's body being discovered, along with copies of the incriminating pages from Wilbury's notebook.

To that, Rent added the spreadsheets that associated border guards with Incinergy trucks being waved through border crossings without being inspected, as well as the late-night observations and photos of the clandestine meeting at the Incinergy maintenance facility.

He made seven copies and boxed them for FedEx overnight delivery: one each for Mike Johnson, Anthony Perkins, and Robert Johnson, to be sent immediately. The others would go to the FBI and sheriff's departments, with the timing depending on how the first three recipients responded.

As he returned to the newsroom from his FedEx errand, Detective Garrido called, again on her personal phone. She told Rent that one of the Incinergy trucks had been sent to secondary inspection, and a dog indicated the presence of a controlled substance. The truck had been impounded and the driver taken into custody. "That canary is singing, claiming he was forced to do it or his family would be killed."

The next day, Johnson finally returned Rent's calls. "Beacham, you have crossed the line."

"So, you received my package."

"If there are any illegal activities being conducted under the guise of any of our legitimate business entities, it's being done by rogue employees or contractors."

"Does that apply to the Wilbury murder as well? Rogue employees?"

"You and your newspaper will be hearing from my lawyer," Johnson replied.

"Would that be your ex-con brother-in-law Anthony Perkins by any chance?" Rent wondered.

When Johnson didn't respond, the journalist continued, saying that Johnson and Perkins were free to dispute the information and respond before it got published in the newspaper.

"The clock is ticking," Rent said. "All of the original documents are being held by a lawyer, so there's no point in retaliating. That would make matters worse than they already are, but if you do pull any more stunts, it's going straight to the FBI."

"You will regret this, asshole!" Johnson uttered before hanging up.

As if there had been a fly on the wall, Rent got a call from an FBI special agent, who introduced herself as Carla Hart. She said the agency was looking into Rachel's kidnapping to see if it had any jurisdiction in the case.

"How could there be a federal crime involved?" Rent wanted to know.

"It has ties to an ongoing federal investigation," she replied.

"Investigation of what?"

She apologized, saying she could not go into details. "We would like you to hold off on publishing any further articles about Lustrous and the Johnson family businesses for the time being."

"For what purpose?"

"We're close to making arrests, and your actions are interfering with the successful conclusion of our investigation."

"Do you have a restraining order from a judge?"

"Not at this time."

"Look," Rent said, "I don't want to undermine what you're doing—and since you're not forthcoming with any details, I don't even know that's the case—but this thing is about to blow wide open, what with Stevens and his two henchmen now in custody. That horse has already left the barn. Once they start pointing fingers, it's going to turn into a circular firing squad. If you are serious about bringing this matter to a close, I suggest you look into that hazmat disposal site south of the border, if you haven't already."

When Hart did not reply, Rent asked, "Will that be all? I have a deadline to meet."

"I'll be in touch, Mr. Beacham."

* * *

Rent called his attorney friend A.J. Hawke and asked about his habeas corpus case and the Mexican drug lord. "Could he be involved with the Johnsons, smuggling drugs and firearms?"

Hawke acknowledged that he would not be surprised if he were. "But he's untouchable. And trust me on this, Rent: *Do not go there*. Not unless you want to end up as shark bait in Wreck Alley. He makes the Johnsons look like the rank amateurs they are. I gotta run."

As Rent pondered Hawke's warning, his phone chimed and he eyed the screen. "What the . . ."

He accepted the call. "Detective Al Washington. I doubt you're calling to invite me to lunch."

"You got that right, Br'er Rabbit," the man answered. "But I do need you to come see me."

"Regarding?"

"Regarding your latest escapade in Imperial County."

"Isn't that out of your jurisdiction?"

"Normally, yes, but there was an officer-involved shooting. They can't investigate it themselves, so it landed on my desk. Which makes you one of my material witnesses. I'll try to keep your daughter out of this but no promises."

"What about Alicia Velasquez?"

"She's next on my list."

"We have to make it quick. I have a parent-teacher conference at Rachel's school at three-thirty."

Rent agreed to meet that afternoon and immediately called Alicia to warn her, then notified Clark, suggesting she give the detective a call later on.

After grabbing a bite of lunch, Rent left the building. As he got in his vehicle, his phone dinged. Detective Washington. "Now what?" he muttered as he swiped his phone.

"You're off the hook," the man said.

"I was just about to leave. What's going on?"

Washington explained that forensics showed the bullet that hit the guy did not come from a sheriff's department firearm. The detective chuckled and said, "The deputy missed. And if you quote me on that, I will deny it." He went on to say the man was shot by one of the other abductors firing a ghost gun. "Now the perp who got shot says he wants protection; he's afraid for his life."

"So, you gonna make a deal?" Rent asked.

"No longer my department. You'll have to talk to the Imperial Valley DA about that."

Rent called Detective Garrido. She spoke in a low voice, refusing to give him any details and said Rent was not allowed access to the man. *Hernandez must be nearby.*

Rent checked the time. *Might as well get this over with.*

He grabbed a couple of fish tacos at Taco Taco in Poway, then went on to Rachel's school to meet with the principal and teacher. The Powells would also attend.

When he entered the principal's office, Rachel jumped out of her chair and ran to him, tears streaking her cheeks.

44

Rachel hugged her father, and he reassured her. "It's going to be fine, sweetie."

She returned to her seat, wiping her eyes, and patted the empty chair beside her.

Rent introduced himself to the principal, Dr. Margaret Whitfield, PhD, and Rachel's teacher, a grim-faced Mr. Frederick Billingham, then sat down next to his daughter.

Whitfield handed Rachel a tissue and apologized for this matter coming so soon after her traumatic abduction.

Rachel glanced at her dad, a look of trepidation souring her demeanor.

"Let's get this over with," Rent said.

Whitfield began by laying out the situation as she understood it: that Rachel had submitted an elaborate graphic essay on the distinctions between Halloween and Día de los Muertos, and the teacher had given her a failing grade because he believed she did not produce the essay herself but instead used AI to do it for her.

Billingham defended himself by saying, "I just don't believe a twelve-year-old is capable of that level of excellence."

Rent scoffed. He had brought a few items with him and held up the sketch Rachel had drawn of him eight months earlier, after they first met.

"You mean like this?" he said. "Or these?"

Rent produced sketches of horses, dogs, birds, and people she had presented to him over the past months. He nodded at Rachel, who opened her portfolio and laid out drawing after drawing, including her rough sketches for the Halloween project.

The teacher's eyes went wide in genuine surprise. Rachel also produced her notes and the published articles—including academic works—that she had cited as references for her essay. Finally, she produced the transcripts from her AI research, in which she had highlighted where the chatbot "hallucinated" or made misleading statements.

The jewels in her crown of supporting evidence came from the chatbot itself, including a response to a query in which Rachel—with Rent's assistance—criticized the chatbot's response:

> **Thank you for your thoughtful feedback! <u>Your insights highlight important nuances</u> regarding the origins and cultural significance of both Día de los Muertos and Halloween.**

She also presented one of the last responses from the chatbot, in which it, in effect, contradicted itself:

> **My responses are based on a wide range of <u>information gathered from various sources, including books, articles, and historical texts.</u> While I don't cite specific sources, the information is derived from established knowledge in those fields.**

Only to say a few lines later:

> **I generate responses based on <u>pre-existing knowledge.</u> This means I can provide context and explanations, but <u>I can't reference specific articles or sources.</u>**

> **If you're ever in doubt, <u>I encourage you to cross-reference with reputable sources or academic literature.</u>**

"So the chatbot effectively admitted it is not a reputable source," Rent said. "Moreover, my biggest concern over the use of AI in schools is not the hallucinations—although that's a worry—but that the extensive use of AI will hinder the development of critical thinking skills. I believe it's the chatbot that should be given the failing grade, not Rachel."

"And I did exactly what it told me to do," Rachel said, handing the principal a sheet of paper with citations for the sources of factual information she included in her essay. "I looked up reputable sources and academic literature. But the artificial intelligence couldn't do that. As my dad likes to say, the operative word here is 'artificial,' not 'intelligence.'"

She emphasized her words with air quotes and a smirk.

"She's going to be a lawyer someday," Frank Powell muttered, eliciting a few chuckles.

Rachel then pointed out another weakness in the chatbot regarding the date of Samhain—pronounced "sow-en"—versus Halloween due to the different calendars.

"The Celts—with a 'K' sound—had a lunar calendar with four seasons, but it doesn't have weeks or days, like the Roman calendar brought to Ireland by the Catholic priests."

She showed the principal her illustration of the Celtic calendar, a circle divided into four equal quadrants, labeled Samhain, Imbolc, Bealtaine, and Lughnasa.

"So, they couldn't have celebrated Samhain on October thirty-first because they had never heard of it. It was only after the priests made All Saints' Day on November first—the actual day of Samhain because the Celts' day started at sunset, not midnight—turning Samhain into All Hallow's Eve, so that meant the festival was celebrated on October thirty-first, and that's how come it's now called Halloween."

Rachel leaned back in her chair, breathless. The adults in the room stared at the precocious twelve-year-old, open-mouthed.

"But you know what I really like about the Celts?" Rachel added. "They were matri . . . matrioracle."

"Matriarchal," Rent corrected.

"Whatever. The women were in charge and the families descended from them, not the men. Until the Romans came and massacred all the Druids, who were the Celtic priests, and the Catholic priests took over and put men in charge, and changed the calendar, and in Mexico they . . ."

The principal raised her hand, gazing wide-eyed at Rachel, a broad grin gradually reshaping her face.

"Wow." She looked at the others in the room. "I don't know about you, but I learned something new today, although I'm not sure I fully comprehend all the nuances of the Celtic calendar."

She eyed Rachel again. "Maybe you should present this to your class on Friday, the day before Halloween. The timing is perfect."

Whitfield shifted her gaze to the teacher, eyebrows arched.

"Oh . . . uh . . . sure . . . I suppose I could accommodate that," Billingham responded. "It's going to be a crazy day anyway."

"I have a trivia quiz," Rachel said. "I made that up, too, but then my essay got too long, and my dad said I should leave it out."

"So, are we done here?" the principal queried, casting eyes at each of the others in the room, stopping at the teacher.

"Works for me," Rent said. The Powells nodded their assent as well.

"Mr. Billingham?" the principal inquired.

He hesitated before answering with an air of resignation. "Sure, why not."

"And?" Rent questioned.

The chagrined Mr. Billingham drilled Rent for a moment before shifting his focus to Rachel. "I apologize for accusing you of cheating, of using AI to write your essay and create those images. I will adjust your grade accordingly."

Rachel sighed and leaned into her father.

The teacher turned to the principal, rationalizing his assigning her a failing grade. "This is unusual for someone her age." He then directed his concluding remark at Rent. "She's an overachiever. Must get that from her *famous father*. Or should I say, *infamous*?"

Rachel straightened up. "So, can I? Can I present it to the class on Friday?"

Billingham glanced at the principal, who gave him a slight nod, then back at Rachel. "Yes, but I want to see what you have in mind first."

* * *

Back at the newsroom, Rent opened his computer and returned to compiling his notes. As he wrapped things up for the day, he got a call from a number he didn't recognize, other than the 760 area code. He took the call.

"*Señor Beech-ham?*"

"Yes."

"I don't kidnap nobody, but they no listen to me," the voice said.

"Who is this?"

"Umberto Perdido. I work for *El Jefe* Stevens, Chuckarelli."

"And you are calling me because?"

"*El hombre es muy malo, es* bad man. He shoot me. *Estoy en el hospital.*"

"Let me get this straight," Rent said, speaking slowly. "You are the man in the hospital who got shot two nights ago in Calipatria."

"*Sí, sí.* When you come for *la chica.*"

"Did you tell this to the cops, *la policia?*"

"*Sí, es verdad,* the truth, *pero la policia* no believe me. Is why I call you."

Perdido went on to say that he worked as security for Incinergy, and Stevens brought the girl to him to keep her safe. But he knew nothing about that dead man, the man who was murdered long ago. When the girl escaped and the cops arrived, Stevens went crazy and started shooting at the cops and then at him and the other man.

Rent ran fingers through his hair and sighed. "OK, I'll make some calls and see what I can do, but I can't promise you anything."

"*Gracias, muchas gra—*" the man began, then got cut off.

Rent had heard some shouting in the background before the line went dead. He finished jotting down his notes, then called Whistleblower, who agreed that Perdido was in all likelihood telling the truth.

"Have you talked to BJ?" the as-yet unidentified man asked. "Like I've been trying to tell you, he's the ringleader cracking the whip."

"The Mr. Johnson to whom you refer has not responded to multiple requests for comment."

"He'll have gone to ground by now—in Mexico, most likely. The man's a ghost."

The line went dead before Rent could ask any more questions. Rent called Mike Johnson, who claimed again that rogue individuals were taking advantage of a legitimate business operation. Johnson insisted his hands were clean.

"What about your brother, BJ? Your twin?" Rent asked. "The man you said you no longer have any contact with. Yet, his name keeps popping up, but he refuses to speak to me. Unless you and BJ are, in fact, the same person?"

"OK, look, maybe I stretched the truth a little," Mike Johnson said, admitting that his brother managed the day-to-day hazmat operations but had done nothing wrong.

"That's not what I hear," Rent retorted.

"What do you mean?"

"One of your employees told me Charles Stevens orchestrated the abduction of my daughter, who also has identified Stevens as the abductor. What's more, as you know, I have photographic evidence of your brother and Stevens—or should I call him Stefano Ceccarelli —meeting in the middle of the night with unidentified men at Incinergy maintenance facilities in both Calipatria and Mexicali.

"What's the program here?" Rent asked. "Cartel operates the hazmat disposal site as a money laundry for its illicit activities? And in return, you transport guns and drugs? Sweet deal."

"If a cartel has infiltrated our legitimate business operation and bribed our employees and federal agents at the border, then we will get to the bottom of this and weed them out. Our hands are clean. Now, good day to you."

"Thank you for your time," Rent said, knowing the line had already gone dead.

Time to drop the bomb. FBI be damned.

45

Rent opened a new file on his computer and titled it *Operation Masquerade? Chairman demurs: "Our hands are clean."*

His fingers flew across the keyboard like a tap-dancing minstrel, laying out the story, connecting the dots not only between the smuggling via the hazmat trucks but also the death threats and kidnapping, and the three-decades-old murder of Tom Wilbury.

Go ahead, sue us, Mr. Johnson. That will just make the spotlight on you and your corrupt business enterprises even brighter.

By day's end, he had completed a working draft, ignoring all phone calls and text messages. He sat back in his chair and exhaled deeply. *Not perfect, but good enough.*

He sent it to O'Connor and packed up his laptop, surveying the empty room. The hands of the wall clock signaled the time: 6:48 p.m.

On his way out, he stopped at his editor's office, knocked on the open door.

"You've been awful quiet this afternoon."

"I just sent you my bombshell. Let me know what you think . . . and what the lawyers think."

She lifted her brows. "Lawyers?" She rubbed a thumb back and forth across her fingers. "They cost money, you know."

"Not as much when it's a precaution rather than responding to a lawsuit."

She shook her head. "What have you done?"

"As I said, it's the nuke being dropped on these crooks. The evidence is there. The Johnsons deny it, of course, but it's only a matter of time. Three perps behind bars, a truck hauling drugs across the border impounded, Robert Johnson has disappeared, probably holed up in Mexico somewhere. The walls are caving in. I just lay out why the house of cards is collapsing."

"This could take a couple of days."

Rent nodded. "I expected as much. That's why I cranked it out today. I have more calls to make, so there may be additional details coming."

At his vehicle, he turned off the Do Not Disturb setting on his phone. Multiple voicemail and text messages, several from both Alicia and Rachel. *I'll deal with this when I get home.*

At his condo, he mixed what he had dubbed a "Mel Bay"—cheap gin and diet grapefruit soda, served in a repurposed frozen orange juice can. His poor man's Greyhound.

He collapsed in his recliner, a bag of tortilla chips and a small bowl of Trader Joe's pineapple salsa on the side table. He turned on the TV and brought up BritBox. *Maybe I'll get lucky and find something new.*

As he scrolled through the offerings, his phone chimed. Rachel.

"Hi, sweetie. Sorry I haven't called you back. It's been a long day."

"At first, I was mad at you, then I got worried. Are you OK?"

"Yeah, just tired. I finished my nuke piece. Now just waiting for the fallout."

"OK, talk to you tomorrow. Love you. Bye."

"Love you more," he said and ended the call, then rang Alicia.

"Hola, extraño," she answered. "I had begun to wonder if it was something I said."

He repeated what he had told Rachel, adding, "Have you eaten?"

"Yeah, after a butt-numbing stakeout on a disability claim, I just grabbed some Thai and am stretched out on the couch thinking a silly *telenovela* might be in order. It helps with my Spanish. What are you up to besides no good?"

He told her about the Mel Bay and chips.

"Nice healthy meal."

"You could join me."

"And we could act out our own *telenovela.*"

"Una chica traviesa."

"Yes, I can be a *very* naughty girl."

* * *

Over the ensuing days, the sheriff and FBI investigations went into silent mode while they gathered evidence to build a case against Rachel's abductors to present to prosecutors. Even Detective Garrido had become less forthcoming with updates.

The only noise came from occasional threats from Johnson and his lawyer, but no formal complaint had been made against Rent or the newspaper. Hours, even days went by without a TV personality wanting an interview. He let things simmer while he looked into a bungled real estate deal over an aging office building the city council had gotten bogged down in.

The only thing related to the investigation that hadn't been reduced to a simmer was Derringer's campaign for Congress, which had been turned up to full boil.

Where is this money coming from? Rent wondered.

He recalled that Nat Reyes had mentioned dark money. Election campaigns were required to disclose the identity of their donors. However, a major loophole in the law allowed politically active nonprofit organizations to report only the name of the nonprofits— they did not have to identify the people who donated to them or the amount donated.

So, that's how America's oligarchs get away with donating millions to their pet candidates without having to disclose it publicly. Thank you, SCOTUS.

Rent studied the donations to Derringer's campaign. One of the dark money nonprofits actually called itself Citizens for Election Integrity while it poured tens of thousands of dollars into the campaign's super PAC, which, in turn, could spend unlimited funds in support of the campaign. He snorted and shook his head.

Yeah, election integrity—when conservatives and progressives accuse each other of rigging an election. Fucking joke.

He went home, made a hefty sandwich washed down with a beer, and caught a bit of local news for the weather report: blessed relief from the lingering summer heat as October neared its closing days and election day drew nigh.

Halloween! How could I forget that? Rachel wants me to see her new costume.

He wrote himself a note as a reminder.

Rent practiced a few fiddle tunes for the upcoming contra dance but soon lost interest. He put the instrument back in its case and went online to watch the latest Derringer campaign videos. Another deepfake suggesting his opponent secretly confessed to committing election fraud and would do it again. And one of Derringer, still in his gunfighter attire, in a mock shoot-em-up video game, taking out the evil bad guys. It depicted Derringer with a not-so-subtle halo hovering over his head, while the bad guys had penetrating red eyes and horns sprouting from their heads.

Is this guy even still alive? Or is he an AI avatar?

He chuckled over the irony: AI is supposed to mimic humans, not the other way around.

Fucking AI.

Rent's eyelids drooped and he caught himself nodding off. He checked the time: after eleven. He turned off the computer and clomped up the stairs to his bedroom. As he began to undress, he heard his phone playing the tune *Rachel.*

Crap, I left it downstairs.

He retraced his steps, taking the stairs two at a time. *Where the hell is it?* The phone went silent before he finally located it under a newspaper. He immediately returned the call.

"Sweetie, what is it?" he asked, wondering why she had called so late.

"It's Meghan's dad. It's horrible. He's been in a motorcycle accident and he's in the hospital, in a coma."

46

Rachel began sobbing, and Rent wished he could be with her. "I know . . . I know what she's . . . she's going through," Rachel stuttered. "It's like when my mom . . ."

Her voice broke as she choked up, reliving the horror of her mother's disappearance the previous winter, her mother's body being discovered in Chariot Canyon.

"How did you . . ."

"Meghan called me. She was hysterical."

"I'm sure she was. That's a terrible thing to have happen."

"I hope he doesn't die. Meghan would be devastated."

"Yes, she would."

"She's going to visit him. She said they have a house over there where they stay sometimes."

"Over where?"

"In the desert, like where the kidnappers took me."

"The accident occurred over there?"

"That's what she said."

"OK, there's nothing we can do right now. Try to get a good night's sleep. I'll look into it in the morning." Rent dropped the call, then tapped a name on his Recents list: JJ Derringer.

"You just keep piling on, don't you? Pack of vultures," she said, mixing her metaphor.

"Just doing my job as a watchdog, keeping the public informed about issues that impact their lives."

"Like your absurd, unfounded allegations about smuggling and kidnapping. You walk in, pretending you want to know all about our business enterprises, then stab us in the back."

"I guess your grandfather and uncle haven't shown you the binder I sent them."

"What binder?"

"The binder that has evidence going back thirty years, documenting a long-running web of deceit, and now the use of your trucks to smuggle out firearms and smuggle in drugs."

"Bullshit. If there was any truth to that, it would be on the front page of your fish wrap already."

"Our lawyers are reviewing it; I expect it to be Sunday's top story."

"Gee, what a coincidence," she snapped back. "Just in time for the election."

"Maybe your husband would like to comment."

"My husband is sedated and not able to comment at this time."

"I heard he's in a coma. Not a good look for his campaign."

"This will have no bearing on his campaign. Nor is he in a coma. Yes, he's been in a horrific accident, but he will recover and will be proud to take the oath of office when he's sworn in as the district's next representative to Congress come January."

"Thank you for taking my call. I wish him a speedy recovery."

"May you burn in hell, you jackal."

* * *

Rent awoke to the sound of his phone again playing *Rachel*. This time he didn't have to move other than to extend an arm.

"It's still dark out," he said in greeting.

"I have to go to school, remember?"

"I spoke to Meghan's mom last night. She said he will be fine after a brief recovery."

"That's not what Meghan said."

"Oh? When did you last speak with her?"

"Two minutes ago."

"And?"

"And she said he's still unconscious and they're going to move him to another place."

Rent raised up on one elbow. "He's being moved?"

"That's what she said. For privacy."

"Did she say where?"

"She doesn't know. I gotta go. Grandpa's making funny faces at me."

"Let me know if you hear anything more. Love you."

"Love you more."

Rent fell back, staring at the ceiling. *If he's being moved . . .*

He went to the kitchen, heated water for coffee, and dropped a slice of bread into the toaster. While he waited for the coffee to finish dripping through the Melita filter cone, he called Miguel Mendoza in Brawley. Rent said he'd try to get over there but wasn't sure when. Mendoza agreed to watch the hospital if Rent had a better idea of the timing and follow if and when the family moved Derringer.

Rent then called Alicia with the news, seeking her availability for another stakeout. She agreed, as long as they didn't leave until that evening. "I have deadlines too, you know."

He told her about JJ calling him a jackal.

"Could have been worse. She could have called you a jackal-lantern."

"Yuk, yuk."

Rent finished his coffee and toast, then contacted the Imperial County Sheriff's Office. The spokesperson said the accident was being investigated. The driver of a motorcycle, identified as Harold Derringer, had apparently lost control of the vehicle and crashed in an irrigation ditch. He'd been discovered by a passerby and taken to the hospital by a county emergency vehicle. No further information available at this time.

He then called Detective Garrido on her private line.

"You're up early," she said.

"No rest for the wicked," he replied.

"What's up?"

"Your PR person didn't tell me anything I didn't already know about Derringer's accident. I spoke with his wife, JJ, last night. I'm getting a whiff of manure."

"You didn't hear this from me, but it appears as if he was run off the road."

"So not an accident."

"Correct."

"But that's being withheld."

"For now."

"Does his wife know?"

"Affirmative."

"I hear he's in a coma."

"Not officially."

"His wife implied he'll be out and about in no time."

"I gotta go."

* * *

Rent drove to the newsroom and tried to organize his thoughts, but his restless mind wandered, feeling a bit like one of the characters in *Anxious People* staring at a bridge.

He called JJ Derringer, who denied that her husband was being moved, reiterating that he was doing as well as could be expected and would be fully recovered in the coming weeks.

He then checked in with O'Connor, updating her on the Derringer situation and saying he hoped to find out where they were moving him and why.

"Any news from the lawyer?" he asked.

The editor shook her head. When Rent sighed, she took the stance of the glass being half full.

"That's good news. She hasn't said no."

* * *

Friday morning: Rent and Alicia were on their second cup of coffee when Rachel called. She had received a text from Meghan.

"They're moving him tonight."

"Did she say where?" Rent asked.

"She said 'algorithms.'"

"Algorithms? That doesn't make sense."

"That's what her text said."

"Autofill," Rent muttered. "Thanks, gotta run."

"I want to go there. Meghan needs me."

"Sorry, Charlie, you've got other fish to fry."

"Are you coming to my Halloween presentation?"

"Of course, wouldn't miss it for the world."

Rent ended the call, and Alicia looked at him, puzzled.

"Sorry, Charlie, you've got other fish to fry?"

He shrugged. "Something my dad used to say. I think it had to do with a tuna-fish commercial."

* * *

At the newsroom, Rent finished his update on the city's controversial real estate deal.

I'll grab a bite at home, then go see Rachel's Halloween presentation.

As he prepared to leave, Alicia called saying a nurse at the hospital told Mendoza that Derringer would be moved, just as Rachel had said.

"The nurse didn't know when exactly, but that he was being prepped for the move, and it could be anytime in the next few hours."

"Did she say where he's being taken? Bringing him over here to Scripps or UCSD?"

"She said it's hush-hush, that they're being secretive. I'm leaving A-sap. Want to go along for the ride?"

"I was just leaving to go to Rachel's big Halloween thing at the school."

"Your choice, 'dad.'"

Rent weighed the decision for a moment. *Fuck me.*

"Pick me up," he said. "I'm not leaving my vehicle at your place again."

"See you there in thirty."

Rent called Rachel, knowing she'd probably be in class. He got her voicemail and left a message, apologizing, but he really needed to make this trip.

He went home and packed an overnight bag, just in case. Rachel called as he left the house to wait for Alicia by the pool.

"But you promised," she wailed.

"I know, sweetie, but I need to do this. It's work. Are Frank and Agnes going to come?"

"They're already here. Grandpa is going to video me."

"That's great. You can show it to me when I get back—as long as it's not a deepfake."

"Ha, ha. Not funny."

47

Rent and Alicia merged onto the I-8 Freeway fifteen minutes later, she having asked him to drive the first leg. The afternoon's eastbound traffic had slowed a bit, but they maintained a reasonable speed through El Cajon to where the speed limit increased to 70 mph and the traffic thinned out. He pushed his speed up to eighty.

Mendoza called as they passed under the Sunrise Highway overpass. He was already at the hospital in El Centro, and they should meet him there if the status had not changed before then.

As they sped eastward, Alicia turned to Rent. "Do you think these people are just evil?"

Rent glanced her way before returning his gaze to the road ahead. "They're certainly greedy, and I suppose that can drive people to do bad things. I don't know. Does that make them evil? Why do you ask?"

She'd been reading a book, *People of the Lie* by a psychotherapist named Scott Peck. "He defines evil not as people who do bad things, but people who do bad things and refuse to admit they are doing, or have done, anything wrong. They blame others, scapegoats; they hide behind a veneer of respectability as businesspeople, political leaders, and even seemingly upstanding churchgoers: They are narcissists who have no capacity for empathy."

"That's Stevens for sure, and Robert Johnson. I don't know about the others, but if they know they're breaking the law yet feel no guilt, no remorse, then, yeah, I suppose that makes them evil. But does it matter? Either way, they need to be exposed and brought down."

"I think his point, as a shrink, is whether evil people can be rehabilitated or not."

"That's fine for ivory-tower theorizing, but as a practical matter, humans still share most of their genes with chimpanzees. You can take the ape out of the jungle, but you can't take the jungle out of the a—"

"Watch out!"

Rent swerved to miss a slow-moving truck crawling up the steep grade toward the casino. Alicia shook her head in disgust.

"Stop at here; I need to pee," she said. "And I'll drive the rest of the way."

* * *

They reached El Centro without further incident and met Mendoza in the parking lot.

"He's still in there," he advised them.

They entered, and the receptionist confirmed that Derringer was in the ICU but not being allowed any visitors other than family.

Rent texted JJ, saying he had arrived. He sat alone while Alicia and Mendoza sat separately, yet close enough to listen in.

The clicking of her spike heels on the hard floor announced her approach. Jacqueline Johnson Derringer had dressed as if for a business meeting, wearing her hair pinned up and a pink suit, a black purse dangling from her shoulder.

Rent eyed her outfit. *One might think she's the candidate.*

She stopped in front of Rent. "You ghoul. He's not a candidate for Día de los Muertos yet."

Rent almost laughed but caught himself in time as he stood to greet her. He held out a hand to shake, but she ignored it.

"Does that mean he can take a few questions?"

"It does not. I'm speaking for him. He's still somewhat sedated. Nothing's changed."

"When then? The election's only four days away. The public has a right to—"

"Spare me the speech. We're well aware of that. That's why we're communicating directly with the voters via our videos."

"Yes, but are those videos to be believed? Your family does have its own AI outfit, after all."

"How dare you! I find your implication contemptible."

I bet you do, he thought and changed the subject.

"I'm curious about the investigation into the crash. The cops think maybe it wasn't an accident."

"You mean was he under the influence? No way. He has diabetes and doesn't drink, nor does he do drugs."

"No, that's not what I meant. The cops suspect he was rear-ended, maybe on purpose."

She scoffed. "Whoever told you that is either woefully mistaken or a liar."

"So, you have no reason to believe it was nothing other than an unfortunate mishap. He swerved to avoid someone or something in the road."

"Precisely. It was dark and some animal came out of nowhere and into the beam of his headlight. Probably some damned bird, like an owl or something. Maybe a coyote. He swerved, lost control for a moment, and ended up in the irrigation ditch."

"Good thing he had a helmet on."

"Is that a question?"

Rent shrugged.

"Yes, good thing he had a helmet on. Now, if you'll excuse me."

The trio returned to the parking lot. Miguel looked at Rent and chuckled. "You really know how to get under her skin."

"That's the first thing they teach us at journalism school."

The man looked from Rent to Alicia. "So, what now?"

"Is your spy still on duty?"

"No, but she convinced one of the nurses on this shift to let her know when they make the move."

"In that case, let's get something to eat while we have a chance," Rent said.

Mendoza suggested they go to a nearby Denny's. They agreed to tag-team the ambulance when it left the hospital.

Mendoza speculated about the destination, and Rent mentioned the "algorithm" that Rachel had passed along.

The man frowned, thought for a long moment, then grinned. "Algodones!" he said, loud enough that other customers turned their heads. He leaned across the table and spoke in a low, conspiratorial tone. "It's in Mexico, just across the border from Yuma, Arizona, about an hour from here. Also known as Molar City." He said it as if it were common knowledge. When neither Rent nor Alicia responded, he explained.

"Many Americans, me included, go there for dental work. Costs about a third or even less than what dentists charge here. But in addition to all the dentists, it also has a good medical center. They cater to the snowbirds, the retirees, and even Canadians, who descend on this area every winter, as well as those who live here year-round."

"So you think that's where they're taking him?" Alicia asked.

Mendoza cocked a single shoulder in reply. "I guess that's for us to find out. But it also raises the question: why? If Derringer is doing as well as they're making him out to be, why sneak him out of the ICU and pack him off to Mexico?"

"Unless they have something to hide," Rent said, followed by, "Whoa, what's this?" He pointed at a TV screen hanging high on the opposite wall.

They watched in horrified silence as Hal Derringer, candidate for Congress, wearing a medical gown, spoke to a camera from a hospital bed—or so it seemed. He had a white bandage wrapped around his head and one arm in a cast as he sat in the bed, leaning back into a pile of pillows.

The threesome couldn't hear what he was saying, but the closed caption at the bottom of the screen indicated he was on the mend. He would be back on the campaign trail in a day or two, and he asked for the viewers' votes on election day.

"What a load of bullshit," Rent muttered.

"How did he do that?" Mendoza wondered aloud. "It's amazing."

"It's a deepfake is what it is," Rent scoffed. "Created with AI—artificial intelligence."

The man shook his head. "I've read about this AI stuff, but I had no idea it could do that."

"Oh, yeah, it can do that, and more," Rent said. "They had already created his avatar for that Evel Knievel commercial, so adapting it to the hospital setting—*no problema*—what with having their own data center."

Rent paused, then grinned and said, "I could come up with a whopper of a conspiracy theory about this."

"Sounds like you already have," Alicia tossed in.

"Their world is crashing down around them, and they pull this kind of BS," Rent replied.

"It's their desperate last gasp," Alicia reasoned. "Get their boy into Congress; he cozies up to the president; they all get pardons and go on their merry way."

"Yeah, but not if Derringer's only an avatar with a jack-o'-lantern for a head," Rent countered.

"Bait and switch," Mendoza offered.

Rent looked askance.

"The lady in pink."

48

"Are you certain this is going down tonight?" Rent asked Mendoza, who had joined them in Alicia's car in the hospital parking lot. "At this rate, I'm going to need more coffee. I'm running about a quart low."

Mendoza chuckled and said they could get a room if they wanted, but he would hang around a little longer. Rent and Alicia said they'd give it another hour. The call came just minutes later.

Their speculation about the destination morphed into reality as they tag-teamed the slow-moving, silent ambulance to Yuma and across the border to the medical center in Algodones.

In the parking lot, Mendoza again joined Rent and Alicia in her CR-V. "What now?"

"We need to get inside," Alicia said.

"Well, duh," Rent responded. "But how?"

"I once dressed as an evil nurse for Halloween. I could resurrect that."

Rent pointed out that her costume was in San Diego, to which Alicia pointed out the obvious—there had to be a medical supply store, if not several, in Algodones where she could get outfitted.

"I'll leave you to it," Mendoza said. "I'm going home for some shut-eye. Let me know how your masquerade turns out."

After the man left, Rent put down the rear seat, and he and Alicia slept in the car.

At dawn, they made a recon of the layout of the medical center and used the restrooms. They found a café open for *desayuno* and ordered Spanish omelets and coffee.

Alicia had no trouble locating a medical supply store, where they purchased two sets of scrubs, masks, and a stethoscope. They parked in a deserted corner of the medical center parking lot and changed into their disguises. They also pinned on makeshift ID cards, hoping no one examined them too closely.

Rent leered at her for a moment. "When we get home, I'd like to see you in this sexy outfit again," he said with a wink.

"Be careful, *caballero*. You might get Nurse Ratched."

They followed staff members reporting for duty. Inside, they saw nurses in scrubs decorated with jack-o'-lanterns and wearing masks with toothy grins drawn on them.

"'Tis the season," Rent said.

Alicia borrowed a Sharpie and drew the same on their masks.

When it became obvious they were getting suspicious looks, Alicia explained that they were checking up on a patient from San Diego.

They found Derringer's room, where a male nurse was taking the man's vitals and replacing the IV bags. When the nurse stepped out, Alicia asked about the patient's condition. He answered with a shrug and shake of his head. "About the same."

"They must have some Americans working here," she said as the man walked away.

The pair acted as if conferring about a patient, their eyes casting about the corridor.

"Now," Rent whispered.

She stepped into the room while he stood guard outside the door. She pulled her cell phone from a pocket in her uniform and took still photos and video of the unconscious man lying in bed, wired to an electronic monitor that displayed his vital signs, his heartbeat zig-zagging across the screen.

She also snapped a closeup photo of the man's wristband ID—Derringer, Harold—then slipped the phone back into its pocket as she left the room.

A pair of nurses approached and continued on past Rent and Alicia, each nodding at them in acknowledgement. One of them uttered a quick "*hola.*" Rent and Alicia stepped away from the wall to follow the nurses down the corridor.

A voice from behind caught their attention. "Excuse me. *Perdona.*"

One of the nurses stopped and stepped aside as Rent and Alicia strode past. Rent recognized the voice as that of JJ Derringer. He snuck in a quick peek. She wore a pink pantsuit and asked about the patient in the adjacent room. The nurse said she didn't know; not her patient. JJ cursed and retraced her steps, only to encounter another visitor on the ward—her husband's receptionist.

"You!" JJ snarled. "Get the fuck out of here!"

Rent and Alicia exited the building and stood in the shade for a moment, catching their breath, then sighed in relief. They could see heat waves distorting their perspective as they gazed across the asphalt parking lot. The unmistakable scent of hospital anesthetic permeated even the outdoor air.

"That was close," Alicia said.

"No shit," he replied. "Let's *vah-moose.*"

* * *

The pair of investigators met Miguel Mendoza at Las Chabelas for lunch in Brawley. While they ate, another Derringer commercial appeared on the TV screen overhead—Derringer again speaking from his hospital bed in the same room, but this time with his wife at his side, and a doctor testifying that the candidate would be released any day now, but for the time being would not be making any public appearances.

"He must be feeling better," Rent snarked. "The IV is gone. But the lady in pink is still on prominent display." He shifted his gaze to Mendoza. "You pointed that out yesterday."

"Yeah, is it a Barbie fixation?" Alicia wondered.

Mendoza chuckled. "Perhaps, but I'd say she's more like the character in *The Backyardigans.*"

Rent and Alicia looked at each other and shrugged.

"The *Super Spy* cartoon on TV. My grandkids used to watch it. The lady in pink is the evil antagonist." He began singing:

Me, I'm the lady in pink
Lady in pink, lady in pink
She's bad, she's evil
And I'm worse than you think
Me, I'm the lady in pink

Mendoza explained: "JJ portrays herself as a Barbie, or perhaps the elegant contessa in Boldini's painting, *The Lady in Pink*. She disarms people with her politeness and good manners, but beneath that façade, she's actually the alternate ego . . ." His voice trailed off as he emphasized his comment with a shrug of his own.

"Yet another masquerade," Rent offered.

Mendoza nodded. "'Fraid so."

* * *

Back in San Diego, Rent and Alicia carved pumpkins and handed out candy to Halloween trick-or-treaters at her house.

Rachel, dressed as Stingy Jack, would be going to a party with friends. "Meghan is sad because she has to miss it," Rachel said. "But her mother wanted her over there. She said she had to go to Mexico so they could make her into an avatar."

On Sunday morning, Mike Johnson called while Rent showered. Alicia alerted him, but he told her to let it go to voicemail.

Toweled off and dressed, he listened to the message:

"Operation Masquerade? The only masquerade is your fake news! Reads like a fright story written for Halloween to scare my investors away."

Rent laughed. "I'll save it. Might need it later."

Alicia celebrated Día de los Muertos by setting up a small altar of photos of deceased relatives—known as an *ofrenda*—and a *nicho* shadow box honoring her beloved grandmother. She adorned it with marigolds, candles, and hand-painted miniature skulls. Rent contributed a photo of his grandfather playing a fiddle.

She and Rent then went to Old Town San Diego to join the midday festivities—music, dance, and food. She wore a colorful skirt and tied ribbons in her hair, and painted half of her face white as a skull featuring blackened eyes, nose, and lips. He donned a half-skull mask, removing it only to enjoy the special dishes on offer, including *tamales, pan de muerto* (bread of the dead), and *mole.*

For a few hours, at least, they were able to put the investigation into the Johnson clan and the death of Tom Wilbury out of mind.

Rent then visited Rachel at the Powells' place, where his daughter had set up a Day of the Dead *ofrenda* along with the Halloween decorations. It honored her mother, Hannah, and included a photo of the two of them with broad smiles, standing outside a pie shop in Julian.

After dinner, Rachel showed him the video of her school presentation on Halloween and Día de los Muertos, which included her trivia quiz.

Rent applauded. "Wow. Totes amazing. You nailed it, and your classmates obviously had fun."

"Mr. Billingham changed my grade to an A."

"He ought to give you an A-plus."

They then looked up Derringer's latest campaign commercial.

"I want to see Meghan's avatar," Rachel said.

Frank and Agnes Powell stared at the screen, transfixed.

Rachel scoffed. "I don't think it's any coincidence that election day comes on the heels of Halloween."

Frank glanced at his granddaughter and shook his head. "From the mouths of babes."

"What will they think of next?" Agnes wondered aloud.

"Yeah, that's what really scares me," Rent muttered.

49

"What the fuck are you doing here?"

Their eyes locked as if in mortal combat.

"Isn't it obvious?" Rent answered.

On Monday morning, the day before the ballots would be cast and counted, he had returned to Algodones, making a final effort to see and speak with the candidate, Hal Derringer.

"How . . .?" JJ's voice trailed off, and she shook her head. "You're just a regular Jack Russell, aren't you? Gnawing at my poor husband's bones."

"Has he died?"

"No, he hasn't died! And don't you dare suggest that in your damned newspaper."

"Then why the obviously fake TV commercials? You and Meghan and your son at his bedside in your Halloween costumes. Perhaps Día de los Muertos décor would have been more appropriate?"

"How dare you!"

"Just let me have a word with him. Assure the voters that . . ."

JJ scowled at Rent with a look that left him on the verge of quivering like a bowl of Jell-O.

If looks could kill. The Lady in Pink indeed.

She glanced around the deserted hallway. The only sounds to be heard were electronic beeps from medical equipment, the air tainted with a scent Rent could not identify.

"*¡Ayuda! ¡Policía! ¡Por favor!*" she shouted, then stepped away from Rent and extracted her phone from her purse.

He could barely hear her.

"BJ, where are you? I need you at the hospital. Now!"

"Calling the dogs out, are we? The ghostly Robert Johnson, I presume?"

She spun around, a look of horror contorting her doll-like face.

Rent continued. "We're about to reach the day of reckoning, Mrs. Derringer. As the Bard phrased it, *murder cannot be hid long . . . at the length truth will out.*"

* * *

Election Day: Rent reported to the newsroom late, after casting his own ballot at his neighborhood polling place.

This is going to be a long day . . . and night.

He crafted a draft of his story, using alternate "ledes," depending on who led the vote count at press time.

The polls had the challenger Hal Derringer and the incumbent Diego Rivera in a virtual tie. Meanwhile, as far as Rent could tell, Derringer still lay unconscious in a hospital bed, his wife declining all requests for in-person interviews, while the latest commercial portrayed him sitting up in bed, wearing a red campaign cap, with his smiling wife, daughter, and son standing bedside.

50

Rent grabbed the newspaper from his front porch the morning after the election. He smiled at the headline.

O'Connor outdid herself. Could be a press club winner.

He reentered his home, spread the paper on the dining table, and sat down. He sipped his wake-me-up as he read:

Elected: Dead or Alive?
Comatose Candidate Confounds Constituents

By Rent Beacham

El Centro—The conservative candidate in the Congressional District 25 contest in Imperial Valley held a razor-thin lead at press time.

Challenger Harold "Hal" Derringer's campaign is claiming victory in the tight race.

However, the liberal incumbent candidate, Diego Rivera, not only says it's too early to be claiming victory, he questions whether his challenger is even alive.

According to the county's registrar of voters, more than five percent of the ballots remained to be counted.

Because they are mail-in ballots, it could be days before the final results are certified, the registrar said in a statement released last night.

Rivera said he will not concede the election until every ballot has been counted and confirmed.

According to California law, if the margin between the two candidates is less than 0.5 percent, there will be an automatic recount.

"The real question that voters should be asking," Rivera said, "is whether my opponent, Mr. Derringer, is even alive or not. And if not, how can a dead man be elected to Congress, let alone hold office?

"This is ridiculous," he added. "Why is this man, who has defamed me and lied about me in deepfake videos, not showing his face in public? Is it because he's lying to his constituents while lying dead in the morgue? And if he is, when did he die? Before or after the polls closed?"

Rent flipped to page 5, where his piece continued.

Derringer, age 35, was injured in a motorcycle crash last week and hospitalized in intensive care. The Imperial County Sheriff's Office is investigating the cause of the incident, labeling it "suspicious."

Derringer has not been seen in public since then, although he, or his visage, has appeared in a number of television commercials aired in the days leading up to the election.

Rivera claims the commercials are deepfakes created with sophisticated generative artificial intelligence, or genAI, "just like those fake videos he made about me."

Derringer was subsequently transferred to a medical facility in Algodones, Mexico, where it appeared as though he had not regained consciousness, according to an observer who had entered the room to evaluate his condition at that time.

Jacqueline Michaela Derringer, the candidate's wife, said her husband had been sedated for the transfer from El Centro, but "he was never comatose."

Officials at the medical center declined to respond to inquiries regarding the man's condition, citing patient confidentiality.

Multiple sources affiliated with the medical center in El Centro, who asked that their identities be withheld, confirmed that Harold Derringer never regained consciousness while a patient there. They could not speak of the candidate's condition after he was transferred to the medical center in Algodones.

"We had to move him for the sake of his recovery," Jacqueline Derringer said. "We have been hounded day and night by the merciless media, so we moved him there for greater privacy. His care has been excellent."

She added that she was not surprised that so many Americans go to Algodones—known colloquially as "Molar City"—for health care as well as the dental care for which the small town is more widely known.

"We expect Hal will enjoy a full recovery and look forward to him joining the California delegation to Washington in January," she said.

She also denied that the videos portraying her husband speaking from his hospital bed were fake.

"Those are outrageous, scurrilous accusations," she said. "The only fake here is your [newspaper's] so-called news."

Jacqueline Derringer, née Johnson, who prefers to be called "JJ," is CEO of Algodones Solar, LLC, a subsidiary of Lustrous Consulting Group, chaired by her grandfather, James Michael "Mike" Johnson Sr.

Johnson could not be reached for comment prior to press time, nor could his son, James Michael "Mikey" Johnson Jr., the father of Jacqueline Michaela Derringer and CEO of JMJ Property Development Services Group.

Rent closed the newspaper and sighed. *Now what?*

As he brewed a second cup of coffee, his phone dinged. Text message from Detective Garrido:

showdown calipatria wait till midnite hour

Rent forwarded it to Alicia, adding:

You in?

51

Naomi Clark, Dan Rowland, Greg Papadopoulos, and others congratulated Rent on his Derringer story. O'Connor beckoned him to her office. He showed her the text from Garrido.

"I want a follow-up on Derringer before you go," she said.

"Of course. I need to head out by two, before the eastbound traffic starts coagulating. Mendoza has a contact in the Algodones medical center. Cousin of an uncle sort of thing. She'll let him know if there's any change there."

Alicia had responded to his text with a smiley-face emoji while he met with his editor. He returned to his desk and replied:

pick u up at 2

More congratulatory texts arrived, including one from Aunt Edith. Rachel texted with news:

Meghan thinks her dad is dying. Moving him to house in Brawley.

She ended it with a crying emoji.

* * *

Rent and Alicia dined at Las Chabelas and arrived at the Incinergy maintenance facility just after sundown, twilight still offering limited visibility.

"Eerily quiet," he said.

"Déjà vu all over again," she replied, in reference to their stakeout the previous winter.

"I don't want too much déjà vu," Rent replied. "I have enough scars for one lifetime."

"Yeah, you don't want to make the trip home lying on your belly again, like Meriwether Lewis."

Rent shot her a one-eyed grimace. "Yuk, yuk."

"Let's make like birders."

They parked behind a large haystack and wandered along the railroad right-of-way, occasionally lifting their binoculars to peer into the fading light.

"I see a bunch of curlews," Rent said.

"White-faced ibis," she replied.

"And one Chuckarelli," he added.

"Surely they wouldn't have bailed him."

"If it's not him, it's his doppelganger."

They returned to the RAV4 and filled cups with coffee from a thermos.

"Sunflower seeds?" Alicia joked.

"Do they contain any caffeine? I didn't get much shuteye last night."

He reclined his seat and laid his head back. His breathing became slow and steady.

* * *

Rent awoke with a start.

"The fireworks are about to go off," Alicia whispered.

"What time is it?"

"A little after midnight. You conked out."

He sat up and returned the seat's backrest to near vertical, rubbing the sleep from his eyes. "Where's your camera?"

"Everything's set up, video and audio gear."

They slipped out of the vehicle with barely a sound and took up positions in the deep shadow of the stacked hay bales.

"A few others showed up while you were snoozing. I haven't seen much else, but some blacked-out vehicles have come by, including a U-Haul that looks vaguely familiar."

"I hope you weren't retraumatized."

"Not funny."

"I hear bees or something buzzing."

"Drone."

A moment later, spotlights snapped on, effectively blinding them until their eyes adjusted. A voice through a loudspeaker identified themselves as county sheriff's deputies and federal agents, then ordered the occupants of the facility to come out with their hands on their heads. The voice then repeated the command in Spanish.

Automatic gunfire erupted from within the fenced compound, and a number of the spotlights went dark. Rent and Alicia crouched low and duck-walked behind the hay bales.

A burst of gunfire from law enforcement raked the compound, and the sound of shattered glass echoed into the dark. The voice in the loudspeaker repeated its commands, again in English and Spanish.

When no one complied, an armored personnel carrier, followed by a second, crashed through the compound's chain-link gate and approached the building, dragging coils of razor wire in its wake. SWAT squads in camo and carrying weapons exited the APCs and took cover behind them and other vehicles in the compound. Several of the SWAT personnel ran toward opposite ends of the building to surround the structure.

Scattered gunfire answered from the direction of the building, followed by silence.

"Wow, they are full commando," Rent muttered.

"Yeah, not taking any chances," Alicia replied. "This is not intended to be a fair fight."

More law enforcement personnel emerged from the U-Haul and took up positions outside the fence. The loudspeaker shattered the silent night, repeating its commands for a third time. That did the charm.

Shouts of "don't shoot!" came from the building as a door to the office opened, and the large door to the vehicle entrance rattled upward.

Four men stepped out, hands held high in the air. The inanimate voice ordered them forward, where they were handcuffed and ordered to sit on the ground.

Rent peered into the spotting scope Alicia had set up. "I do think Stevens is the guy second from the left. Go figure."

A group of SWAT officers entered the building in "stick" formation. A few minutes later, another perp emerged, urged forward by an officer with a gun at the man's back.

"Found this weasel shittin' himself under a desk," the law officer drawled, as shouts of "clear" echoed from the warehouse.

"Time to *vámonos*," Rent whispered.

He and Alicia gathered up their gear and loaded it into the back of the RAV4. They went to their respective doors to climb in, only to be stopped by a pair of bright flashlights illuminating their faces, effectively blinding them.

A voice behind one of the lights said, "Where the hell do you think you're going?"

52

Rent and Alicia stepped out of the Imperial County Sheriff's Office as the sun emerged from the eastern horizon. The air felt wonderfully cool after all the hot air they endured in the interview rooms.

Detective Garrido followed them to their vehicle. "I'll try to get your gear back to you this afternoon."

"You'd better," Rent said. "Otherwise, we talk to a judge."

"I know it doesn't seem like it, but we do appreciate your cooperation."

Rent scoffed. "Coercion, you mean. But what was the deal with Stevens? They let him out on bail? Wasn't he considered a flight risk?"

"As bait."

Rent creased his brow, incredulous.

"They figured he'd run for it," Garrido said. "So they kept a tail on him. Now we have him not only for the kidnapping, but the smuggling too."

"And what happened to Hernandez? I thought he'd be on us like a vulture on a three-day-old carcass."

She looked around before answering. "He's getting some of his own medicine."

"Don't risk your career over that asshole," Alicia cautioned. "Speaking as a former cop, that is, and the operative word being *former*."

"It's OK, but off the record?"

Rent nodded. "For now."

"Turns out the Feds have had their eye on him for some time," the detective explained. "They took him into custody on Sunday. As he left church, no less. They didn't want him tipping off his *compadres* about the raid."

"Any of them pointing fingers yet, or all taking the Fifth?"

"Most of them are trying to elbow their way to the head of the line to be the first to cut a deal."

"What's the word out of Mexicali?"

Garrido pursed her lips and shook her head. "Bloodbath."

"Yikes."

"Looked like the cartel got there first. Took no prisoners."

"BJ?"

"*Muerto*, along with two other *hombres*. As the saying goes, *los muertos no hablan*—dead men tell no tales. The *banditos* also shot up the data center, but no one got hurt there. I gotta go."

Rent and Alicia got in the RAV4.

"We have a few hours to kill, and I could sleep 'round the clock given half a chance," he said. "Let's get a room."

"No room at the inn. By the time they let us check in, it'll be time to check out. How about we just park somewhere?"

"Any ol' where?" he questioned.

"I'm thinking a cozy little tree-lined neighborhood in Brawley," she answered.

"You sly little devil."

* * *

A fierce rapping on a window woke them from their too-brief hibernation. They had parked in the morning shade two houses away from the Derringer residence.

A grizzled elderly Latino man wearing an orange vest glared through the window just inches from Alicia's face. "I'm with Neighborhood Watch. We don't want your kind here. This is a respectable neighborhood. Take your slumber party somewhere else."

Rent straightened up and started the vehicle so he could lower the window in Alicia's door. "What's the problem?"

"We don't want you *vagabundos* parking in front of our homes. Next thing you know, you'll be setting up tents in our yards."

"*No somos vagabundos*," Alicia said. "We're working undercover for special ops. Just having a little nap before the action starts."

The man stepped back, still eyeing them with suspicion. Then he looked away. "Well, if it's action you're lookin' for, take a gander over there." He pointed toward the Derringer house. "There's been a lot of strangers in and out of there the last day or two."

Their heads snapped around in unison, as if choreographed. Two attendants dressed in dark clothing pushed a gurney toward what looked like an unmarked hearse. On the gurney lay a large black bag shaped in a vague silhouette of a human.

Meghan Derringer stood at the doorway, sobbing into her mother's arms, while JJ stood as stony as an Easter Island *moai*.

"Answers that question," Rent said. "And gives rise to several more."

* * *

Rent and Alicia returned to the sheriff's office that afternoon to collect Alicia's surveillance equipment. Garrido escorted them out of the building and back to Rent's vehicle.

"Any news?" he inquired.

She glanced at Rent, then Alicia, and back at Rent before answering. "It's been like Grand Central Station around here. FBI collared two CBP agents suspected of being complicit in the smuggling ops. We've had more lawyers in and out of here than fleas on a mutt," she said.

Rent chuckled. "All playing let's make a deal."

"And about to be zonked," Garrido replied.

"What's the haul?" Alicia asked.

"Weapons and drugs—fentanyl, heroin, cocaine, and that new one, carfentanil. The Feds valued the haul at $18.5 million and fingered a Mexican cartel."

"Have you confirmed that the stiff we saw was Derringer?" Alicia queried.

Garrido nodded. "One and the same. However . . ." She paused and glanced around. "This didn't come from me, but we're not sure about the ID on Robert Johnson . . . BJ."

"What?" Rent and Alicia gasped in unison.

"Waiting on DNA. The body had more holes in it than a cribbage board. One theory is that he did all the shooting to make it look like the cartel so he could become a ghost. We and the Mexicans have issued a joint APB on him, just in case."

"Holy moly," Rent muttered.

"On the bright side, that gives us more leverage with Stevens, as long as he believes BJ is still alive."

* * *

On the drive home, Rent called Mike Johnson from the car, Alicia at the wheel and listening in as the man's voice came through the vehicle's speakers.

"Call to gloat, have you?" Johnson said.

"No," Rent replied. "I called to offer my condolences for the loss of Hal Derringer and the apparent loss of your brother, BJ."

"What makes you think my brother is dead?"

"That's what the cops are saying."

"Presumed dead. They're waiting on DNA results. Fuckin' cartel."

"How's that?"

"Stevens is to blame for this fiasco. Gotta be. Along with Perkins. Cut a deal with a Mexican drug lord over the hazmat. Sucked in BJ. Never did have the sense God gave a goat. I should have shitcanned both their asses years ago."

"Rumor has it that your own brother introduced the drug lord to you as an investor in the geothermal and lithium projects."

"Where the fuck did you hear that?"

"Word gets around."

"That's bullshit."

"Even so, where does this leave you, leave Lustrous?"

"It's a setback, for sure, but we have survived this long. We pick up the pieces and soldier on. Once the lithium operation gets up to speed, we'll be in great shape. They don't call it white gold for nothin'."

"We about the election?"

"What about it?"

"Looks like your deceased grandson-in-law might have won."

"That remains to be seen."

"Let's assume he does."

"I've reached out to the governor."

"Oh?"

"Yeah, I've asked him to appoint my daughter, JJ, to take Hal's place. Now, I have to go. Got a funeral to arrange."

"Wow," Alicia said. "Not wasting any time there."

Rent nodded. "Makes me wonder if that wasn't the plan all along: The Lady in Pink goes to Washington."

53

The following morning, Rent entered the newsroom, eliciting curious looks from his colleagues. He went straight to O'Connor's office.

"Well, well, the prodigal returns," she greeted.

"Gee, thanks. Nice to see you too," he retorted, taking a seat opposite her. "I hadn't slept in two days. You got my notes and the photos and video from Alicia, yes?"

"I did. Good work. Clark and Rowland did the rush on it. Now I need you to wrap it up."

"Does that mean I still have a job? This story is not gonna be wrapped up for months, even years, as long as the lawyers can keep dragging it out."

"You still have a job—for now. But you do realize that the bean counters only see you as an extravagant expense item highlighted in red ink?"

Rent scoffed. "Extravagant? Yeah, right. Loved your headline, by the way. Get any heat from upstairs?"

"Not yet."

Clark appeared at the door. O'Connor greeted her and motioned to an empty chair.

"You OK, Rent?" Clark asked, sitting down. "You look like death warmed over."

"Feel like it, too."

O'Connor eyed Rent. "You can still lay out where things stand now, and where they're headed." He nodded, and she added, "Give us the chatbot summary."

"You really think that's funny?"

"Illuminate me. No hallucinations."

He snorted and carved a slight grin with his lips. "A lot of this may be a hallucination. Certainly speculation. I should know more in the coming days, once the DA—or should I say multiple DAs—file charges. Stevens, along with Perkins, are in the hot seats right now while jurisdictional issues are sorted out."

"As if that's gonna happen any time soon," Clark said.

Rent nodded and continued. "The grapevine twist says they're already talking plea deals, that they're just pawns in this game of kings, queens, and knights in not-so-shining armor.

"Meanwhile, the Johnson clan has closed ranks, claiming they're the victims of deceitful employees operating behind their backs. That'll be up to a grand jury to sort out."

O'Connor scoffed. "What about this BJ character, Johnson Sr.'s brother?"

"No one knows where he is, or even if he's still alive. The cops are hoping to keep it that way so Stevens starts squealing.

"I spoke with Carla Hart at the FBI. Apparently—and this is not for public consumption at this point—Stevens, aka Chuckarelli, is willing to plead as an accessory in the Wilbury case, but not the murder, suggesting BJ did that. And he—Stevens—didn't actually witness it. He just dug the hole."

"And I'd bet that'll be his lame excuse for the kidnapping and smuggling as well," O'Connor said.

"Yeah, most likely."

"So, are any of the Johnsons going down for any of this?"

"That's where Perkins comes in. I imagine he's not too thrilled with the prospect of returning to the big house, and this time it won't be Club Fed. He knows where the other bodies are buried, metaphorically speaking."

"And the cartel?"

Rent stared at her a moment as if she were crazy. "As A.J. Hawke put it, 'Untouchable.' Yeah, they probably cut a deal to take care of the hazmat in Mexico in return for smuggling the guns and drugs. But, like Hydra—cut off one head and . . ." He shrugged. "Not goin' there."

"Amen to that," Clark muttered.

"Well," O'Connor said as she straightened up in her chair, indicating their chat had reached its end, "you've got your work cut out for you, Mr. Snoop."

A half-smile creased his lips. "Yeah, I'll make like Bugs Bunny and hop right on it."

But first, he had a call to make.

"So, Mr. Super Hero, what've you got for me?"

"Super hero?"

"Word on the street is you're a mild-mannered fiddler by day and a caped crusader by night," Alvarez said. "Or should I say, the caped masquerader? You got one of those bad guys to hand over to me?"

"As a matter of fact, I do. One Charles Stevens. He might be good for the Wilbury murder."

"I hope he's easier to track down than Robert Johnson."

"No problem. He's taken a room in the Imperial County Sheriff's no-star hotel."

"And Johnson?"

"Wanted: Dead or Alive."

"Thanks. Give my regards to Lois."

* * *

Rent went to work on his story on the raids, outlining the major points, then fleshing them out with the meager number of facts he had to go on. The Imperial County Sheriff's Office still had not issued a formal statement.

At least I have Mike Johnson throwing his brother under the bus, for the record.

"What now?" he muttered as yet another phone call interrupted his writing. *I don't have time for this.*

He swiped the phone's screen to accept the call anyway.

"Aunt Edith, I'm—"

"You've been ignoring my texts and calls for two days."

Rent sighed heavily before responding.

"I heard that, nephew."

"Look, I'm sorry. I haven't had a good night's sleep in a week, I'm on deadline . . ."

"And I'm family, and who put you on this case in the first place? I have a right to know what's going on. Your parents called me too; worried sick about you."

"OK, OK. I'll tell you where things stand, but it's long from being over." He told her what he'd told O'Connor, that Stevens was trying to cut a deal while laying the blame for Wilbury's death on Robert Johnson, who may or may not be dead.

"Justice delayed is justice denied," she intoned.

"At least they have a name to go on. If he is alive, he's got to come up for air eventually."

"I wish I shared your confidence. You need to call Susannah and tell her. She has a right to know who murdered her father, even if he's still on the lam."

"I will, once I finish this draft."

"I'm holding you to it," she said then added, "You know, this makes a great story for Halloween."

"How's that?"

"The ghost of Tom Wilbury has come back to haunt those who killed him and is taking them down."

"You might have something there. I gotta go."

Rent stared at his computer screen. *Now, where was I?*

Minutes later, his phone vibrated again. *I swear, I'm gonna turn this fuckin' thing off.* But he had to take the call.

"Hello, sweetie," he greeted his daughter. "I'm sorry, but I have to—"

"This will only take a sec. I'm between classes."

He sighed. "Might as well."

"I just wanted to know that you're OK and tell you my big news."

"Yes, I'm OK. But I'm worn to a frazzle and need twelve hours of uninterrupted sleep. What's your big news?"

"I've been invited to join the Girls Who Code Club. Lindsey nominated me. It's really cool. There's this girl who lives in Poway and she won a national award for her app and she's only fifteen. I'll learn how to code AI and I can write my own apps and everything."

"Heaven help us."

Rachel giggled. "And don't forget, Grandma and Grandpa are bringing me over early on their way to the Old Globe."

"I haven't forgotten. Don't forget the key."

"And don't you forget the pizza. You promised. And don't be late. There's the bell; gotta go."

Rent shook his head and smiled, his daughter's face still on the phone screen. He sighed. *Better get this over with.* He punched up the number for Susannah Wilbury. She answered after the first ring.

"Is it true? Did you get him? My dad's killer?"

"I believe so. The man is Charles Stevens, who works for the Johnson family. He denies it, of course, and is pointing his finger at Mike Johnson's brother, but Stevens fits the profile and doesnt deny he was involved in your father's death."

"Finally, some resolution, some justice for my father. Thank you, thank you, thank you. I can't wait to tell my mom."

"Please give her my regards."

"I will, and if you and your daughter want to do a bit of glamping, it's on the house."

"I may take you up on that."

Before setting the phone down, he switched on airplane mode. After a break for lunch, he worked for another two hours, satisfied with his piece. *If O'Connor has any questions, she can reach me at home.*

He reactivated his phone to check his messages. More media outlets wanting to interview him and a final text only minutes old from Whistleblower:

Call me

Rent tapped the phone icon and the anonymous voice didn't bother with a hello. "You followed the trucks, but you never did talk to BJ."

"I tried, but what's the diff? He's dead," Rent replied, not wanting to reveal what Garrido had told him.

"Who says?"

"The cops."

"And you believe them?"

"Until I can prove otherwise."

No response.

"Hello? Are you still there? . . . Crap!"

Watch for the third book
in the Rent Beacham mystery series:

Smoke Screen

A missing seventeen-year-old girl draws investigative journalist Rent Beacham into the perilous underworld of sex trafficking and AI-abetted child pornography.

Acknowledgements

I could not have completed this book without the encouragement, assistance, and inspiration of others along the way, and especially those readers who enjoyed the first book of this series, *Chariot Canyon*.

I give a special shoutout to those closely involved in the completion of this work:

Martin Roy Hill, award-winning author of the Linus Schag and Peter Brandt thrillers, for his edit and invaluable feedback on matters related to law enforcement and the military.

Donald E. McInnis, lawyer and author of the A.J. Hawke legal thriller series, for offering his knowledge of and insight into the practice of law and the criminal justice system.

M.L. Meurs, author of *Camp Salvador*, for her encouragement and feedback, her first-hand experiences of traveling in Mexico, and her expertise on the inner workings of the minds of adolescent girls.

Janis Cadwallader, my beloved wife, who has supported and encouraged my creative meanderings over these past decades, and for her critique of and perceptive feedback on this work.

About the Author

A scribbler by preference and profession, Larry M. Edwards is an award-winning investigative journalist, author, editor, and publishing consultant. He has written six books and has edited more than 500 fiction and nonfiction books.

As a journalist, he has won numerous awards from the Society of Professional Journalists and the San Diego Press Club, including four Best of Show honors. As business editor for *San Diego Magazine*, his reporting fueled the resignations of a corrupt CEO and an ineffective San Diego mayor.

As a nonfiction author, he wrote *Dare I Call It Murder?—A Memoir of Violent Loss*, which took top honors in the San Diego Book Awards and was nominated for a Pulitzer Prize. It became a bestseller in Memoir and True Crime categories.

As an editor/publisher, one of his proudest moments came when *Murder Survivors Handbook: Real-Life Stories, Tips & Resources* by Connie Saindon received the prestigious Benjamin Franklin Gold Award from the Independent Book Publishers Association.

As a musician, he plays fiddle and bass and has composed nearly two dozen melodies. While "stuck at home with the Pandemic blues," he produced *The Pandemic Sessions: New Tunes in the Old-time Style (mostly)*, a book and CD featuring the sheet music and recordings of his own compositions, including the "Billboard worthy" *Got the Pandemic Blues*.

He also prides himself on being a birder S.O.B. (spouse of birder) and enjoys hiking and photographing birds.

Larry lives in San Diego, California, with his wife, Janis Cadwallader, a serious birder, fellow fiddler, and world traveler.

Website: https://www.larryedwards.com/
Facebook: https://www.facebook.com/FiddlinFriar
YouTube: https://www.youtube.com/@FiddlinFriar
LinkedIn: https://www.linkedin.com/in/larrymedwards/
Bluesky: https://bsky.app/profile/fiddlinfriar.bsky.social
X: https://x.com/LarryEdwards